Bubbles
ABLAZE

Also by Sarah Strohmeyer

Bubbles Unbound

Bubbles in Trouble

Bubbles

ABLAZE

SARAH STROHMEYER

DUTTON

DUTTON
Published by Penguin Group (USA) Inc.
375 Hudson Street, New York, New York 10014, U.S.A.
Penguin Books Ltd, Registered Offices: 80 Strand, London WC2R 0RL, England
Penguin Books Australia Ltd, 250 Camberwell Road, Camberwell, Victoria 3124, Australia
Penguin Books Canada Ltd, 10 Alcorn Avenue, Toronto, Ontario, Canada M4V 3B2
Penguin Books (N.Z.) Ltd, Cnr Rosedale and Airborne Roads, Albany, Auckland 1310,
New Zealand

Published by Dutton, a member of Penguin Group (USA) Inc.

First Printing, July, 2003
10 9 8 7 6 5 4 3 2 1

The treatments contained in this book are to be followed exactly as written. The publisher and author are not responsible for your specific health or allergy needs that may require medical supervision. The publisher and author are not responsible for any adverse reactions to the treatments contained in this book.

LIBRARY OF CONGRESS CATALOGING-IN-PUBLICATION DATA:

Strohmeyer, Sarah.
  Bubbles ablaze / by Sarah Strohmeyer.
    p. cm.
  ISBN 0-525-94738-8 (alk. paper)
  1. Yablonsky, Bubbles (Fictitious character)—Fiction. 2. Coal mines and mining—
Fiction. 3. Women journalists—Fiction. 4. Beauty operators—Fiction. 5.
Pennsylvania—Fiction. I. Title.
  PS3569.T6972B823 2003
813'.54—dc21   2002154664

Printed in the United States of America
Set in Janson Text
Designed by Daniel Lagin

PUBLISHER'S NOTE
This is a work of fiction. Names, characters, places, and incidents either are the product of the author's imagination or are used fictitiously, and any resemblance to actual persons, living or dead, business establishments, events, or locales is entirely coincidental.

This book is printed on acid-free paper. ∞

For Elaine and Wendy,
for sending me to the Patch

And for Dad

ACKNOWLEDGMENTS

As the Great Depression loomed, the grandfather I never knew, a Lithuanian and a coal miner in Kingston, Pennsylvania, lost his job when the mines closed. Unlike many of his neighbors, who returned to the hills and dug their own holes, he hanged himself and left his impoverished family to plow its own fate.

This might not sound like the proper acknowledgment for a humorous mystery involving a deceptively ditzy hairdresser, yet it is. Because out of those hills and those hard times come some of the craziest characters I've ever met. For those stories I thank Rachel Sweterlitsch and her daughter, Lisa, who introduced me to the fictional Koolballs and their kin.

Elaine Urban, owner of Elaine's Hair World in Bethlehem, Pennsylvania, and Wendy McCole, originally from Shenandoah (pronounced "Shen-doh"), Pennsylvania, first proposed that coal country might be an interesting place for Bubbles to investigate a murder (or two). Visits to the smoldering town of Centralia cinched it. Thanks to the miners at the Pioneer Coal Tunnel in Ashland who took the time to tell their tales and to those at the Museum of Anthracite Mining.

Thanks also to Kim Martin for envisioning the Teen Safety Car. It is a brilliant concept that could save young lives. Ann Marie Gonsalves reminded me that Bubbles needed to do the grunt work. Barbara Peters cautioned me against "dumbing down," as did my husband, Charles, who provided invaluable editing and support. Alexandra Merriman contributed helpful teenage fashion sense. No Bubbles book could be written without my editor, Ellen Edwards; my agent, Heather Schroder at ICM; the Naughty Girls of Middlesex and the wonderful, varied Bubblesheads.

Finally, a thank-you to my father, John Strohmeyer, son of a coal miner, who had enough perseverance to overcome an awful childhood. Like the well-seasoned newspaper editor he is, he steered me to the obvious nut graph that I'd missed.

Bubbles

ABLAZE

Chapter 1

Looking back, I guess my first mistake was to assume that a rookie reporter could pursue both a hot story and a hot sex life. I mean, what was I thinking? One glance at a crusty old city editor and the truth is obvious: The only time sex coexists with journalism is in a newspaper's police log. And even then, it's usually followed by the word "crime."

My case, unfortunately, was no exception.

The evening began with me between red satin sheets in the Passion Peak Resort—one of those fancy and romantic Pocono Mountain lovers' hotels that I'd dreamed of staying in since I was a little girl.

Hunky Associated Press photographer Steve Stiletto was late, as per usual. As an international photojournalist more accustomed to dodging bullets than punching clocks, he considered punctuality an option. Even when the option was making love to a thirty-something, living Polish-Lithuanian Barbie named Bubbles who hadn't had sex in five months, twenty days and four hours. And, yes, I was counting.

This time he had an acceptable excuse. The President was hitting the hustings for Pennsylvania Republicans, and Stiletto was to shoot him at every stop. As soon as Air Force One left for Washington, Stiletto vowed to develop his film, send it off to the AP office in New York and meet me at the Passion Peak for our first night of sexual intimacy.

In the meantime, I made sure everything was perfect. I had arranged and rearranged the cinnamon-scented candles around the champagne-glass style Jacuzzi and practiced seductively unrolling my stockings from their black lace garters . . . until one got a run when it snagged on my acrylic nail. Finally, after lying on the circular bed and staring at my reflection in the overhead mirror for so long that I started seriously considering liposuction, I dialed the front desk.

"Has a Steve Stiletto left a message for me by any chance?"

"No Stiletto," said the clerk. "Salvo."

"Mr. Salvo?" Uh-oh. Mr. Salvo was my boss at the Lehigh *News-Times*. "And you didn't put him through to my room?"

"In case you're unawares, this is a honeymoon hotel. We got an automatic do-not-disturb policy. I told him to fax over the message and I'd get it to you ASAP."

"Bet he took that well."

"Let's just say I never knew ASAP referred to unmentionable body parts." There was the rustling of paper. "I got it right here. On company letterhead, no less."

A fax on *News-Times* stationery meant trouble and I was right. The one-page letter contained an urgent message, along with detailed directions to an abandoned coal mine called simply Number Nine in the nearby town of Slagville, where a Lehigh businessman had reportedly been found fatally shot in the chest earlier in the evening. It promised to be a media circus.

Because I was in the area, Mr. Salvo concluded, I could beat the pack of other Lehigh Valley reporters and get an exclusive for tomorrow's paper—that is, if I hustled. A police press conference was tentatively scheduled for eleven thirty P.M.—one half hour before the final edition deadline.

The stamp on the fax said 9:15.

The time on the heart-shaped bedside clock was 11 P.M.

Mr. Salvo was going to have my bleached blonde head on a plate.

I shoved my gartered gams into a pair of black spandex pants, wiggled into an apricot-colored turtleneck and scribbled a note for Stiletto that I intended to sound sexy, but which came off instead as a desperate plea for him to stay awake until I returned. I dropped it off with the front desk clerk and hopped in the Camaro.

The murder scene would be crawling with reporters by now, I thought, as I goosed it down Route 15. Like most Pennsylvania highways it was as smooth as a brick patio. *Bumpity bump, bump, bump.* I veered off an exit to a deserted, winding road. Occasionally, my headlights illuminated large coal breakers that loomed on the hillsides, towering and rusted.

It was October and dead leaves blew in whirls across my hood. I used my windshield wipers to swish them away, keeping an eye out for the turnoff to the Number Nine mine. My last hope was that I would make the press conference so at least I'd have some bit of information, anything, to call into the newsroom by midnight. If I completely failed, Mr. Salvo would suspect that I'd blown off the assignment for a roll in the hay with Stiletto and I'd never get another opportunity like this again.

Mr. Salvo rarely assigned me breaking news stories as it was. Those were reserved for the newsroom stars, the elite Columbia journalism school graduates or the seasoned veteran reporters. As a full-time hairdresser with a GED and eight years of Two Guys Community College under my belt, what I usually got were the dregs—strawberry festivals and county fairs.

For months I'd been begging Mr. Salvo to throw me a bone, to give me a chance at hard news. And here he had given in and what had I done? Dropped the ball. Why? Because of sex. Sex. Sex. Sex. It has cursed me all my life. Got me knocked up in high school and shotgun wedded to my now ex, Dan the Man. I should Superglue my legs together.

Who was I kidding? Not even Superglue could hold up against a Mel Gibson dead ringer like Stiletto. His long, slow kisses could melt steel. And, oh, the possibilities of what he looked like under those well-worn Levis of his, well . . .

I was so deep in my naked Stiletto fantasy that I nearly missed the turnoff to the mine's access road, which was unpaved, rocky and rough. A couple of times the Camaro scraped bottom, and the engine whined pitifully as my poor, two-toned car crept up the vertical hill. I had to stand on the gas pedal to get to the top.

As it turned out, I needn't have bothered.

Not only was I late for the press conference, I had missed it entirely. The clearing around the mine entrance was deserted. No cops or news vans in sight. I'd have expected yellow police tape marking the murder scene or a patrolman to shoo away curiosity seekers. But there were only black and bare trees.

That's when I really got worried. Perhaps I had misread Mr. Salvo's directions. Maybe the press conference was underway right now, except it was back at the police station or at another location.

I flicked on the map light. It blinked twice. Not a good sign as my battery was on its last legs. My watch indicated it was a little after eleven-thirty, so I wasn't that late. I scanned Mr. Salvo's note for clues and found none except the sending fax number. All the *News-Times* exchanges began with 457. This one was 238. And the area code was local to this part of Pennsylvania—570, not Lehigh's 610.

Mr. Salvo hadn't sent this fax at all.

A mournful howl echoed from the hills and I suddenly felt very alone and small.

Moments like these I needed a cell phone. I don't have one because they scare me. Not because of brain cancer or distracted driving. But because, with my pathetic technical skills, I'm afraid I'll accidentally leave one on and be stuck with a thousand-dollar bill and yet another collection agency after my overcharged tail.

I opened the glove compartment and pulled out my yellow flashlight from ShopRite. Then I gathered my purse, including my reporter's notebook, and exited the car to do a quick inspection before heading back to the Passion Peak. To cover all my bases, so to speak.

A chilly breeze blew across the mountain and I folded my arms tightly to keep warm. Too bad I hadn't thought to bring a coat since my 98 percent spandex turtleneck provided all the insulation of Kleenex. I ventured a few yards, my heels crunching on the gravelly surface as I surveyed the area. The place smelled of rotting leaves and faint traces of wood smoke while the flashlight revealed no signs of a press conference having been held minutes ago. There was only an empty coal car perched at the mine entrance. A slag heap. A few molding wood beams.

And a late model gold Lexus with the license plate STINKYK4.

STINKYK4! I stopped in my tracks.

Couldn't be. Why, that rat. That fink! There was only one Stinky K in my life and he lived right here in Slagville. His real name was Carl Koolball and he was a consummate, pencil-necked geek. Stinky annoyed everyone with his practical jokes. He was always slipping whoopee cushions onto coworkers' seats or unscrewing the salt shaker caps in his company's cafeteria— that is, when he wasn't engrossed in his job as a cartographer for a mining company.

Unfortunately, he was also the husband of my absolute favorite cousin, Roxanne, who, besides introducing me to the exciting world of neighborhood hairdressing, snuck me into my first Journey concert when I was fifteen.

Leave it to Stinky Koolball to play a prank on me. Mama must have let it slip to Roxanne about my stay at the Passion Peak and he took it from there. But how did he get hold of *News-Times* letterhead?

The Lexus was vacant and locked. That could only mean Stinky was somewhere in the woods spying on me, having a laugh at my expense.

"I hope you're happy, Stinky Koolball!" I hollered. "You completely ruined my night."

I cocked an ear. No response. I tried a different approach. "Come on, Stinky, puhleeese. This isn't funny anymore."

Still nothing. Fine. I spun on my heels and headed back to the Camaro. What a waste of time. I got into the car and turned the key in the ignition. Maybe, if I hurried, Stiletto would be still be at the Passion Peak, relaxing on the circular bed, a glass of champagne on the nightstand. Then again, maybe he figured I'd chickened out and split.

Geesh, I wished this car would start. The ignition beeped once, whirred and then died. *Click. Click.* Nothing more. I turned the key again, although this time I couldn't even conjure a *whir* or a *beep.* The car was dead. Not even a spark. What luck.

I slumped in the front seat and let out one sigh short of a sob. The Fates were against me. It was as though some cosmic force—in this case my cousin's husband—didn't want me to get together with Stiletto, didn't want my life to take a positive upswing with a man who might actually love me forever. A man who sent a tingle of sexual electricity to my lilac fingertips every time he smiled with that generous mouth.

The wind intensified, whipping my car mercilessly. No heat. No light. No radio. No way to communicate to the outside world. I'd just have to wait for Stinky to return to his Lexus so he could give me a jump.

I didn't wait long. For somewhere in the distance, over by the coal car I estimated, echoed the sizzling crack of a gunshot.

My heart stopped. Deer season come early? I thought optimistically. A coal cracker jacker?

But then there was another shot. And this one came straight from the mouth of the mine.

Like a thunderclap, the gravity of the situation hit me. Here I was, a single mother alone in the woods, possibly the victim of cruel mischief, miles from any home or business, with a dead battery and a nutcase shooting guns off in a mine.

I considered my predicament. I could sit here, cowering in my Camaro, or I could find Stinky and get him to stop scaring me and start jumping my battery.

"Stinky!" I shouted again, getting out of the Camaro and marching over to the mine. I leaned against the rotting wood beam and poked my head into the dark abyss. "Stinky Koolball, come out of there. Come out or you'll have to answer to LuLu Yablonsky." Great, evoking my mother's wrath like I was back in grade school.

"Ohhhh. Ugghh. Ohhh."

There was that moaning sound again. And it was coming from right behind me.

I froze for a minute, unsure of what to do. Carefully, slowly, I directed the flashlight beam into the coal car and gasped at what it revealed. A man's body, legs at odd positions, a white oxford shirt torn and stained with brown patches. Face bloodied.

It couldn't be. It was.

Stiletto.

Chapter 2

In the hours that followed it was a question I would mull over and over. Were we pushed or did the car just start down the mine shaft on its own? As I was more concerned with taking care of Stiletto at the moment, I hadn't really been paying attention.

"Stiletto," I cried, climbing into the dirty coal car and pouncing on his body. "Steve. Say something." I quickly unbuttoned his shirt to help him breathe.

Even in this pummeled state, Stiletto resorted to his standard cocky self. "Jesus, Bubbles," he murmured. "Now's not exactly the time."

"Sorry." I shifted my weight off his abs and picked up the flashlight, examining him for major injuries. I couldn't see any obvious damage. Just blood. Had Stinky gone completely *loco*? Whoopee cushions and squirting corsages were one thing, but clocking my boyfriend unconscious was another. What kind of joke was this, anyway?

"What are you doing here?" I asked. "Why aren't you with the President?"

"It was supposed to be a surprise." Stiletto winced. "I switched shifts with Cardozo so I could be with you."

I slapped my cheek. "You are sooo sweet. To give up the President for me."

"President's not nearly as good a kisser." He cracked a half-hearted smile. "Anyway, while I was driving up here, Salvo e-mailed me on my cell phone. Something about a murder and a press conference. Asked me to shoot it since I'd be in the area. I figured it wouldn't take more than a half hour. Wow, was I wrong." Stiletto pulled himself up and rubbed the back of his head. "I really got clobbered. Feel."

I gently touched the spot. Even beneath Stiletto's longish, wavy brown hair, the lump was the size of a grapefruit. I didn't want him to worry, so I said, "It's not so bad," although I was thinking, Oh, boy. This guy should be in the hospital.

"It's bad. The creep hit me hard." Stiletto sat up further to stretch his legs. "What time is it?"

I glanced at my watch. "Eleven forty-five. When did you get here?"

He wiped his bloodied nose on his sleeve. "Around nine. Press conference was supposed to be at nine-thirty. When I pulled up and saw no one around, I called Salvo from my Jeep."

Jeep? Hmmm. I didn't remember seeing any Jeep. I thought it best not to mention that, though, considering Stiletto's incomprehensible affection for the drafty, rusted vehicle. In his injured state there was no telling what he'd do if someone had stolen his Jeep.

"What are you doing here?" he asked. "How come *you're* not at the hotel?"

"Mr. Salvo sent me a fax to the Passion Peak saying a Lehigh businessman had been found shot dead in this mine. Except my message said the press conference was at eleven-thirty."

"Yeah, well the whole thing is bogus. We've been set up." Stiletto pounded on his legs to get the circulation going. "Salvo said he didn't know what I was talking about, hadn't e-mailed me on the cell phone, hadn't heard about a murder. Next thing I knew a fist crossed my nose, I got hit on the back of the head, lights out and then you were here."

I sat back on my heels and considered this.

"So you didn't hear the gunshots?" I said.

"Gunshots?"

"Two of them. From the mine. Minutes ago."

"That can't be good." Stiletto squinted in confusion. "Is it my imagination or have we started moving?"

It appeared as though we had. The coal car was creaking with increasing speed down the rails and into the murky mine shaft. A flash of panic shot through my veins. I definitely did not want to go into an empty mine in the middle of the night.

"We've got to stop it," I yelled, searching for a brake lever.

"We've got to get out of here," Stiletto said. He took my hand, but it was too late. We had tipped over a steep decline and were hurtling downward with rapid momentum.

I found the lever and tried to push it forward with no luck. The car just kept speeding faster. A hard object flew past us, grazing my forehead. I shut my eyes and prayed for the best.

"Ahhhh!" I heard myself scream as we descended into the dark abyss. Water sprayed my face and wet my hair.

Stiletto yanked the lever from my hand and pushed it forward with all his might. There was a loud screech, the acrid odor of rusted metal heating up and then the car slowed, which was a good thing as we had arrived at what seemed to be more than a puddle. It was like an underground lake. Water splashed up, around and into the car.

We stopped.

"Whew!" I leaned back against Stiletto's heaving chest. The cavern was pitch black, cold and reeked of dampness—a lot like my basement before I bought the Kenmore dehumidifier. Moisture dripped onto my hair and shoulders, sending shivers over my body with each drop. I put my hand out and touched a wall of rock about an inch from the car's side; that's how narrow the tunnel was.

"You okay, Bubbles?" Stiletto asked softly. "This is getting to be quite a night. Not exactly the romantic evening we had planned, is it?"

I thought of where we were supposed to be—in a sensual entwining amidst warm red satin and cinnamon candlelight. I hoped I'd blown out those candles because we were trapped at the bottom of a clammy and frigid mine with no way to get out. It would be quite awhile until we returned to the Passion Peak.

"I'll be a lot better when I can see." My fingers groped around the car floor. "Where's that flashlight?"

"I think it fell out on the ride down. I'll use my camera." There was the whine of a flash charging.

"You've been hit over the head, stuffed in a coal car and you still have a camera?"

"It's a gimmicky Japanese job another AP photographer bought me when he was in Thailand. I had it in my back pocket. Here."

For a little Japanese job it emitted a huge burst of light. What it illuminated caused me to gasp in astonishment.

"Ohmigod. Do it again."

"You saw it too, huh?"

This time Stiletto leaned over me and, nearly tipping the car forward, activated the flash a second time. A blanket of white light revealed the track, which, indeed, was partially submerged. The passageway ahead was an empty black hole.

Except for the body slumped against the far right wall.

My first reaction was, poor Roxanne. Stinky had played his last practical joke.

"Do you think he was the one who got shot?"

But Stiletto didn't answer. Despite his injuries, he was out of the car and stomping through the water. "Let's see now. Here we go." He picked me up and I flung my arm around his neck, careful not to touch his bruised cranium.

Although he was working hard to sound calm, Stiletto was on high internal alert. The sinews in his neck stood out like steel rods, and his heart thumped faster than a racehorse's. He took about ten paces and then let me down gently onto fairly dry ground.

It was still so dark that I couldn't even make out shapes. Stiletto moved around and then said, "Aha!"

A beam of light shot out. Stiletto was wearing a headlamp.

"I don't even want to know where you got that."

"From him," he said, pointing to the lump against the wall. "It was on his head. Though why it wasn't lit is a damned good question."

I knelt down. The man appeared to be in his mid-fifties. His hair was black and plastered neatly to the side into a hair-sprayed helmet. He was wearing a pink Izod polo shirt, an Eddie Bauer green down vest, spiffy khaki Dockers and a pair of brown Rockport Professional Walkers. His only adornments were a Rolex rip-off watch, a thick gold chain around his neck and a salesman's smile despite a six-inch bloody hole blown into the middle of his chest.

"I'm guessing he was the target of the gunshots you heard." Stiletto was putting his tiny Japanese job to work, shooting like a madman.

It was not Stinky. For one thing, no pocket protector. "Is he dead?"

Stiletto paused from shooting and looked at me like I was an idiot. "You could drive a truck through that hole. Of course he's dead."

I studied the corpse while Stiletto continued clicking away. For some reason this man's face was familiar. Familiar in the way movie stars and TV actors are. As though you know them when you really don't.

Stiletto stooped down to get a tasteful profile shot. Newspapers are generally reluctant to plaster bloody corpses on page one, unless the corpses belong to impoverished foreign rebels and refugees. Inside the newsroom, however, up-close murder scene photos are hot property. We journalists aren't much more than voyeurs and gossips when you get right down to it.

"I guess this whole evening wasn't a hoax after all," Stiletto said.

I nodded in agreement. "The fax said there'd been a businessman shot dead in a coal mine and what do you know. . . By the way," I looked up at him, "what *do* you know?"

"Don't tell me you don't recognize him," Stiletto said.

"Haven't you been keeping up with the news like Tony Salvo keeps nagging you?"

I bit my lip. Truth was, although I was supposed to read the *News-Times* cover to cover, including, ugh, sports and stock quotes, usually I couldn't get past the comics, marriage announcements and coupons. The rest was too boring. It was obvious from Stiletto's response, though, that our Mr. Body had been some big shot. But who?

I never had a chance to ask because at that moment there was an abrupt flash of yellow and white light that reflected off the tunnel's walls. For a nanosecond I cheerfully hallucinated that the police had heard reports of the gunfire and had come to our rescue. I didn't have a chance to discount that as ridiculous because my attention turned to what sounded like a tremendous explosion followed by an odd rumbling and rolling sound. Stiletto took two strides and grabbed my hand.

"What was that?" I asked.

"I don't know, but we better run."

Next thing, we were scrambling down the tunnel, away from the coal car and the body. Little stones were slipping into my sandals and digging painfully into my toes, but I didn't dare stop to remove them. We sloshed through puddles and came up against rocks that forced us to turn left or right. Stiletto's headlamp cast eerie shadows against the wood beams supporting the black rock walls.

I was getting short of breath and I couldn't take it anymore. Stiletto was dragging me, but to where? We were stuck in a tunnel. There was no way out. Or was there?

As we passed what Stiletto's headlamp showed to be a deep crevice, I dug my heels in and tugged at him.

"C'mon, Bubbles," he urged. "What're you—"

Breathless, I pointed to the crevice. Stiletto nodded and I stepped in, crouching as far as I could against the wall while the rumble roared louder. Stiletto shielded me with his body and we both closed our eyes. I tried to pray, but all I could think about was my teenage daughter Jane and whether or not she was going to go along with her boyfriend G's asinine plan to pick grapes in France after graduation from Liberty High School.

And then it hit us.

We waited until the rumbling stopped and the falling rocks settled down. Both of us coughed with violent urgency, vainly trying to clear our lungs. Still, we were alive and that was enough for me.

"You still with me, Bubbles?" Stiletto pulled me to him tighter.

I nodded into his chest. "I'm breathing."

"You know," he began, after a particularly nasty hacking fit, "it may sound dramatic, but I think someone is trying to kill us."

"Kill us? Get out of here."

"I'd love to." He flashed me a smart-ass smile. "Seriously, look at the facts. First we get called to a deserted coal mine on a hoax, I'm knocked unconscious and thrown in a coal car. Then the car activates and hurls us into this pit where we find a dead body and there's an explosion."

I tried to unstick a few lashes that had gotten plastered together with mascara and dust.

"What I've been trying to figure out," he continued, "is who. I mean, off the top of my head I can name five people who'd want to do me in, from Slobodan Milosevic to a couple of wise guys from the Bronx. None of them would think of calling me to Pennsylvania coal country and none of them would want to harm you."

He pulled me tighter. "Bubbles. Someone wanted us to die . . . together."

I ran over my list of enemies, which, unlike Stiletto's, failed to include the dictator of a small European country. Aside from the occasional client whose eyebrows I had overwaxed, there was my ex-husband, Dan the Man, his wife, Wendy, and some people I had ticked off by misspelling their names in newspaper articles.

That brought me full circle to Stinky and that didn't make much sense. Stinky and I had hit the dance floor a few times at his wedding to Roxanne and shared cleanup duty during holiday dinners. Unless he was seriously ticked that I had washed fewer plates than he had, I couldn't conceive of why he'd want to blow me up. Plus, how could he have known about Stiletto?

"I can't believe Stinky would try to kill us," I said. "We danced the Hokey Pokey. Twice."

Stiletto held me at arm's length. "Stinky? Who the hell is Stinky?"

I filled in the details about my cousin's husband and finding his locked Lexus at the coal mine.

"Lexus, eh. He must be doing pretty well if he's driving a Lexus," Stiletto said. "That is, if you're into sedans. Maybe he's joined the coal country Cosa Nostra and been dealing coke. That would explain the explosion and the fancy car."

Being from Lehigh, a steel town on the Jersey border, I knew the coke he was talking about, and it wasn't the kind people snort up their noses. That was Stiletto's idea of a clever pun.

"We can talk about this later," I said. "Let's find a way out."

There was barely enough room to move. Stiletto's headlight was still operating, so we could see that we had been blocked in by the explosion. Stiletto started clearing rocks away on his side and I started to look for a passageway.

"Stinky's a map geek," I said, running my hands along the crevice wall. "He spends his days charting underground tunnels for miners. He might enjoy playing practical pranks, but he's incapable of hurting someone intentionally, much less hooking up with organized crime."

"That's what Angela Gambino said."

Cool air flitted over my fingertips. "Who's she?"

"The cousin of John Gotti's wife. And you know who he was."

I was almost positive John Gotti ran a pizza parlor in Allentown, but I didn't say so. Instead I said, "I think I found a way out. Fresh air."

Stiletto inhaled a few times. "You're right. I can smell it."

I extended my three-inch nails along the rock wall behind me. Sure enough, the crevice didn't end. It just turned. Tightly. Very tightly.

"What're you doing?" Stiletto asked as I leaned down and unstrapped my slingbacks. I didn't want to risk ruining a nineteen ninety-nine pair of faux alligators from Payless. They were brand new.

"I'm gonna try and fit through here," I said, squeezing into the passageway, my feet delicately feeling their way along cold, sharp rocks.

Stiletto took off his headlamp and handed it to me. "Take this. I'll stay here."

"Why don't we go together?"

"Too dangerous. Two people climbing out of the mine are more likely than one to cause falling rock and possibly a cave-in. That would be the end of both of us. When you're out, you can call in a rescue team from my cell phone that's probably still in the Jeep."

I swallowed the lump in my throat. Dear brave, stoic Stiletto. Always making me his top priority. I slipped my arms around his neck and kissed him on the cheek, the light accidentally bonking him in the forehead.

"Ow," he said.

"You're the best, Stiletto."

"Yeah, yeah, yeah. Now get going." He gave me a gentle pat on the rear as I wiggled into the passageway.

"Coal mines are filled with passageways, you know," I said instructively as I inched along the corridor that couldn't have been more than a foot wide.

"They are? What for?"

"Because this is anthracite." I sucked in my stomach and squirmed past a jutting rock. The conversation kept my mind off what dreaded slope or wall might be around the corner. Or worse—the possibility of long-legged, fast-running centipedes. My archenemies.

"Usually you can't strip anthracite," I continued. "You find a vein and mine it from the bottom up. Like sucking out the crème in a HoHo."

"How do you know so much about mining?"

"Fourth-grade field trips. Used to scare the living daylights out of me when they put us in the coal cars and sent us plunging into the pits. Thirty eight-year-old kids screaming their heads off. Better than Dorney Park. If the teachers couldn't kill us that way, then they made us tour the fiery blast furnaces down at steel. I'd like to meet the genius who thought it was a good idea to . . . ahhh!"

I had taken one step and nearly plunged a good ten feet.

"You okay?" Stiletto called.

I was more than okay. I was ecstatic. The narrow passageway opened onto a larger, vertical one that extended through many levels of the hill. Both ways. Down and up. There was a whoosh of fresh air and my headlamp revealed a rusted iron ladder that appeared to have been constructed ages ago and hardly used since. It might as well have been an elevator, I was so happy to see it.

Anthracite miners were like groundhogs, I thought, swinging onto the ladder. They dug so many tunnels over tunnels, they forgot about them.

"I'm fine," I called back, my bare feet carefully gripping the ice cold metal rungs. "There's a ladder to the top."

"Be careful, Bubbles. Whoever wanted to kill us might still be hanging around. Drive the Jeep to town as fast as you can. Keys are in the ignition. Drive fast and don't look back."

But I didn't have to drive into town. Waiting for me when I emerged from the mine were fire trucks, two cop cars and one ambulance. Everything I could have wanted—except sure footing.

For when I took that last step out of the mine, I had made the crucial error of stepping on a keystone, dislodging it and sending an avalanche of rocks, slag and dirt into the hole below. Stiletto would be hard pressed to get out now. That is, if he wanted to get out alive.

Just as well since his beloved Jeep appeared to have been blown to bits.

Chapter 3

Slagville Chief of Police Jack Donohue, a grandfatherly man with fluffy white hair and a doughy face, was either innocently blunt or diabolically cruel. I pegged him as one of those small-town police chiefs who would do well as the *jefe* of a Colombian drug cartel.

"Nah, the odds are your fellow there is cooked," Donohue said, sitting on the ambulance cot across from me. "After hanging around old collieries as many years as I have, I got a sixth sense about these things. When I was working security in the Kingston mine, why we'd lose a man a month back in the day."

I tried to take a sip of the coffee he had handed me in a Styrofoam cup, but my hand shook so violently the bitter brew just splashed off my lips. It had already been over two hours since I'd emerged from the hole and been ushered into this brightly lit ambulance where Donohue awaited, police forms, tablet and pen in hand. I'd been here so long that the chief had run out of questions to ask and still rescuers had not been able to reach Stiletto.

"Any number of things could have done him in. Concussion. Lack of oxygen. Flooding even." Donohue held out his mammoth hands and ticked off these deadly ends one by one. "Now if the black gas got him, that's carbon monoxide poisoning, and, oh boy, you'll have yourself a handful there, missy. First it feels like the flu. Headache. A buzzing in the ears. Nausea. Next thing's death or permanent disability. Personally, I'd rather be dead than a vegetable."

I blinked and pictured Stiletto as a carrot.

"Yup. You'll be spoon-feeding him pudding at the nursing home if that's the case."

"How old is this mine?" I asked in a feeble attempt to change the subject.

"Opened about 1901 and operated until the Depression hit. It started up again after World War Two." Donohue unscrewed a thermos and poured himself another cup. "McMullen's only operating two mines now. They're barely taking out two-hundred-thousand tons of coal a year. Peanuts. And from what I hear he's cutting back."

"Who's McMullen?"

"You don't know who Hugh McMullen is?" Donohue guzzled his coffee. "McMullen is the fourth generation owner of McMullen Coal Inc., which is what owns the Number Nine mine below us. He's on his way up from Pittsburgh as we speak."

I nodded as though interested, trying my darnedest to keep from imagining Stiletto wearing a bib and drooling cream of wheat.

"What about my Camaro?"

"It's been towed down to the Texaco. You had more than a weak battery there, hon. I'm thinking alternator."

Alternator! That fell into the category of nightmare repair. And me here with three-hundred bucks in my savings account—my incredible windfall from the nineties economic boom.

"Okay. We've taken a ten-minute break." Donohue checked his watch. "Time for more questions."

It was difficult to believe there could be more questions. Donohue had already asked me my mother's maiden name, the last time I voted and where my daughter went to school. That was after he grilled me about the apparently bogus fax I'd received, the body in the mine and the explosion.

"Back to your car," he said, flipping open to a new page on the legal tablet. "Where'd you buy it?"

I thought back. "One of my clients at the House of Beauty had a son-in-law who lost his license in a DUI. Had to sell it cheap. What does that matter?"

"You'd be surprised." Donohue looked up from the tablet and scrutinized me. "How do you feel about legalized gambling coming to Pennsylvania?"

I was about to object again, but Donohue said, "Just answer the question."

"I don't know," I shrugged. "It's already one state away in Jersey. Why do we need it here?"

"Uh-huh." Donohue made a check mark. "But no personal religious objection? You ain't one of them fundamentalist Christians or nothing."

"I'm Roman Catholic. We've been gambling every Wednesday evening for centuries."

Donohue grinned. "Got that right."

"But I still don't see—"

"Are you now, or have you ever been, the victim of blackmail?"

I brought my hand to my chest. "I'm a hairdresser in a two-sink salon in Lehigh. A divorced mother of a teenage daughter and I'm usually in bed, alone, by ten. Who'd want to blackmail me?"

"Stinky Koolball, that's who."

Stiletto's fate slipped my mind.

"Stinky Koolball a blackmailer? You've got to be kidding."

"What, you're shocked? A half hour ago you provided a sworn statement in which you posited that Stinky Koolball had sent you the fax that nearly got you killed. And, lo and behold, the number on the fax was traced to an establishment, one Mr. Koolball has been known to frequent."

Stinky's Lexus was gone when the cops arrived, Donohue had told me. I showed them the fax and they had traced the number to a pay phone outside a Slagville bar called the Hole. I didn't know how you sent faxes from pay phones, but Donohue assured me it could be done.

"Yeah, but Stinky wouldn't try to hurt me," I said. "Play a joke that got out of hand, maybe. But whack Stiletto? Explode his Jeep? Blackmail? That's not the Stinky I know."

"Then you don't know Stinky. He's a changed man." Donohue leaned forward conspiratorially. "He got laid off last month as head cartographer for McMullen Coal and started acting postal. Calling up people, making threats. Guess you might say he went *loco mentis*."

"He hopped a train?"

Donohue blinked. "Means crazy as a rabid coon. It's Latin."

"Really?"

"All I know is he's one dangerous S.O.B. Roxanne kicked him out after the blackmail. Since then he's been laying low, hiding from authorities. Until you came to town and just happened to stumble upon his car at the Number Nine mine late at night."

There was the implication that my arrival was not so innocent. "I didn't want to get involved," I said. "I was doing my job."

Donohue tossed the cup in a wastepaper basket. "Gonna have to arrest you anyway." He unhitched a pair of cuffs from his belt. "Trespassing. Theft of private property. Noise in the nighttime. And, depending on what forensics determines when we find that body, conspiracy to commit murder."

"Oh, please." I put my coffee on the floor and crossed my arms, hiding my wrists. "The only gun I've ever held blows hair. And I never saw that dead man before in my life."

"That's not just some dead man," said Donohue. "If it's who I'm betting it is, the local rag's gonna regret they didn't send no one out tonight. Hold out your wrists so I don't have to get physical."

There was an excellent chance Donohue would have cuffed me then and there had not an anxious fireman shown up at the door of the ambulance.

"You better come quick, Chief," he said, taking off his helmet and wiping a brow. "It's bad."

I sprang into position. "You find Stiletto?"

The fireman frowned in sympathy. "I'm sorry, miss."

Donohue plunked his hard hat on and hustled out of the ambulance. "You wait here," he said, pointing a stern finger in my direction. "I don't want to add fleeing an arresting officer to your list of charges."

And they were gone. I sat down on the cot and gazed forlornly at my once well conditioned hands, which, scratched, bloodied and swollen, mirrored what I was feeling inside. I'm sorry, miss. What did that mean? I'm sorry miss, I don't have time to talk? Or I'm sorry miss, your boyfriend is toast?

How could I have left Stiletto down there? I should have dismissed that ladies and children first stuff and insisted that he follow me. I considered Donohue's list of hazards. What had killed him? A falling boulder? Rising water? Bad air?

My cheeks felt wet and I realized I was crying. Self-pity and exhaustion combined for a total meltdown. I threw myself on the cot, the sheets damp under my face. Scenes of Stiletto flashed in my mind like a montage of sappy Hallmark greeting cards filled with blurry photos. Stiletto precariously perched on a beam at the Philip J. Fahy Bridge in Lehigh, giving me the thumbs up. Laughing as we sat in his Jeep, top down. Wrestling a hired assassin to the ground. Making out with me on the hood of my Camaro in a downpour. Helping me break into the home of a brownie-baking neo-Nazi. Gallantly carrying me in his arms under a moonlit sky.

Our plans. All our plans for the future were . . . ruined! And we *never even had sex!* What a waste. Well, that's the last time I ever make a personal chastity vow. Curse you, Oprah!

There was a "thump" on the metal ambulance floor and then a voice boomed, "What the hell happened to my goddam Jeep?"

My head popped up.

"Stiletto?" I turned.

Sure enough, there he was, his chest naked and covered in sweat and grit, his biceps bulging. His nose swollen and bloodied. Those mischievous blue eyes flashed under the ambulance's fluorescent lights. He'd never looked so Mel. Better even than in *Braveheart.* Would someone please get this man a kilt!

"You're alive," I said, wiping my eyes and hoping they weren't underlined by streaks of black mascara. "But the rescue workers—"

"Would've taken forever to reach me. I couldn't wait around like a helpless baby, for Christ's sake. Here, I got your shoes." He tossed me my slingbacks and opened a bottle of water from the ambulance's supply, consuming it in one manly swig, his Adam's apple bobbing up and down.

"I'm gonna kill that Stinky friend of yours." Stiletto wiped his mouth with a broad forearm. "He put the explosives in my Jeep. My Jeep! I took that Jeep cross-country. I loved that Jeep."

"I doubt Stinky blew it up. Like I keep telling everyone, he's not that kind of guy. Anyway, forget Stinky. What about us? We survived!"

Stiletto snapped out of it and grinned warmly. "You're right. We survived. For now."

With two long strides, Stiletto approached me on the cot and planted a purposeful kiss on my lips. "You were fantastic back there, Bubbles," he whispered. "So brave. I can't wait to get you alone at the Passion Peak when this is over. We'll find our would-be killer and then we'll go away together. Someplace secluded and safe where no editor can reach us." He leaned down and kissed me again.

I felt slightly woozy. Stiletto's kisses, even furtive ones, were intoxicating—as was the idea of life without editors. "At least we ended up in bed together." I patted the cot.

He nuzzled my neck. "My only regret was not having made love to you, Bubbles. That's what I was thinking when I was stuck in the mine."

That's what he was thinking when he was stuck in the mine? I would have been thinking, Oh, my God. Oh, my God. I'm gonna die!

"How did you get out?" I said.

Stiletto's lips traced the curves of my neck. "I climbed."

Like, duh.

"Cleared the rock that had fallen behind us and found a fairly open passageway. The rescue workers had enough lights down there to illuminate Manhattan." Then he sat up, as though he'd had a breakthrough. "Speaking of Manhattan, I gotta call the AP office in New York if I want to make the late-edition deadline."

"The AP? Why not the *News-Times?* This could be my Big Break."

Stiletto searched the ambulance for a phone, checking the dashboard, behind the cot, the medicine cabinet. "I'd like to help you out with that, Bubbles, but you know I only freelance for the *News-Times* when the AP doesn't want the story. I'm a staff photographer for the AP. I have to contact them first. It's in my contract. And I'm positive they'll want this."

I thought of the photos he had taken of the body in the mine. Those photos were really good and my newspaper story would be nothing without them. What to do? What to do?

I might love Stiletto. I might want to rip off his clothes and make wild monkey love to him right on the ambulance floor. But for now he was working for the AP, the dark side, and I was desperate to get hold of those pix.

"Oh, don't tell me the AP national desk cares about a mine explosion in itty-bitty Slagville, PA?" I cooed.

"They do when Bud Price is dead in the middle of it. I thought it was him."

"Bud Price?" Who the heck was Bud Price?

"You got it. I overheard the rescue workers talking. Price drove up to Slagville tonight to check out the Number Nine mine. Guess the Fords weren't hot off the lot today. Aha! A phone." He had opened a wall cabinet and found a cell phone. "The disturbing irony is your fake fax was right. Price was a prominent Lehigh businessman. Emphasis on the *was*."

I stared at Stiletto dialing the phone. "You don't mean Price of Price Family Ford in Lehigh?" I could hear the blaring ads now: Price Family Ford. Where the Price is *always* nice. "Since when does the AP care about a salesman who screams on cable TV?"

Stiletto put the phone to his ear. "Since said salesman won legislative approval to bring casino gambling to Slagville. It's been nothing but controversy since. My guess is some religious fanatic got it into his sick head that Price was responsible for the downfall of Slagville society and took matters into his own hands. Then this sicko, whoever he is, decided to settle some score with us."

That would explain Donohue's questions about legalized gambling and whether I had religious opposition to it. It did not explain, however, why Stiletto and I, of all people, had been the so-called sicko's subsequent targets.

"How do you know about stuff like this?"

"Because I read the newspapers, Bubbles." The phone wasn't working. Stiletto glared at it with contempt. "Price's Family Casino has been headline news for weeks."

Shoot. I knew there had to be a reason why Mr. Salvo told me I had to read the newspaper. And here I thought he was just trying to boost circulation.

"You can hang up anytime," said a no-nonsense voice behind us.

Stiletto grimaced. "Shit," he said, tossing the phone onto the cot.

Chief Donohue's portly frame stepped into the ambulance. "Gosh. It's so nice to be around folks who are up on their current events," he said, strolling over and slapping a cuff on Stiletto's wrist and its mate on mine. "So rare that we're treated to intelligent conversation about local enterprise."

The metal of the cuffs transmitted the heat rising in Stiletto's body. "I don't know who the hell you think you are—" he began.

"Stiletto," I cautioned, "think of Clint. Swearing at cops only makes their day."

Donohue patted Stiletto all over, a eureka look coming over his face as he reached in Stiletto's pocket. "My, my, my, what's this?" he asked, holding up a plastic canister of film. "Taking some vacation shots?"

"Property of the Associated Press," Stiletto said. "Confiscate that and you're facing a First Amendment lawsuit that'll bankrupt you out of doughnuts for eternity."

"Sweet talk won't get you nowhere."

Donohue shook out a baggie and dropped in the film. "In the meantime, this is evidence. I don't have much truck with journalists . . . unless they're hairdressers."

He turned and winked at me. "Nice hairdressers like Bubbles don't cause trouble, do you?"

I blinked innocently. "No, sir."

Out of the corner of my eye, I could see Stiletto flashing me an incredulous look.

"Yes, you've been very cooperative, I must say, Bubbles." Donohue turned to lead us out of the ambulance. "Don't you worry your pretty head about a thing. I'll have you processed and out of my jail in a jiffy."

Stiletto raised an inquisitive eyebrow in my direction.

I arched a defiant (not to mention perfectly plucked) eyebrow in response.

Stiletto and I had been the only two journalists at the scene of what promised to be a blockbuster of a news story. But for the first time in our relationship, we were on opposites sides. He with the Associated Press. Me with the *News-Times*.

We both wanted the same things—to find our apparent murderer and win the scoop of the year. And we both wanted to hop each other's bones. The question was whether we could have it all.

"The gauntlet," I said to Stiletto, "has been run."

Stiletto's lips twitched in amusement. "I believe, my dear, you mean thrown."

Chapter 4

I was left with no choice but to make my one phone call to the most deceitful person I knew. He who had no compunction about lying, browbeating and whining to get his way. Dan the Man. My ex-husband and, not surprisingly, a darned good criminal defense lawyer. (For more explanation, see above.)

"It's three a.m.," he barked when I placed my call from the Slagville Police Department. "What have you done now?"

I explained what I had not done, but for what I had been erroneously charged. I waited for the inevitable: his protests that he was too busy and that Slagville was too far away. When the inevitable came, I reminded him about the dirty little secret I'd discovered—that he had fraudulently filled out Pennsylvania Student Assistance Corporation loan applications to pay for my community college education.

"What's that chief's name again?" he asked.

As I provided the particulars, I could overhear Wendy demanding to know what I wanted at that hour of the night. Wendy is Dan's second wife, chicken-bone thin and just as dry. Her only attractive quality was a fortune she stood to inherit from her father's cheeseball empire. After Dan met her, he had his name legally changed to Chip and gave up knockwurst and the World Wrestling Federation for the Episcopal Church and golf at the country club. As though that was all it took to shed his German working-class heritage.

"Jane wants to talk to you," Dan said when I was finished. "She got in around one this morning and I read her the riot act. I'm telling you, the kid's out of control."

While I was out of town, Jane was supposed to check in at Dan's by midnight—sans G the slack-jawed boyfriend. This was one area where Dan and I agreed. No G. Lots of parents worried about their kids messing around with dope. In our case G *was* the dope.

"Let me talk to her."

The Slagville patrolman sitting at the desk where the phone was located put aside his *Field and Stream* and pointed to his watch. "One minute," he said.

I nodded.

"Mom! I can't believe you got trapped in a coal mine explosion. How boss is that?"

Only a teenager would describe near death as boss. "Pretty boss. Listen, Jane, you gotta call Mr. Salvo for me at the paper. Make sure to ask him about the fax he supposedly sent to the Passion Peak and let him know what happened. Dad will tell you all about it."

"What about Stiletto? Isn't he there with you?"

"Yes, but . . ."

The patrolman was winding his arm for me to wrap it up.

I pressed my mouth against the receiver. "We're kind of competing for the same story."

The patrolman leaned forward.

"I'll explain later. Leave a message for me at my cousin Roxanne's. Mama has the number."

Jane was no fool. "Gotcha. You're going undercover, aren't you?"

"Ten-four. Are you giving your father a hard time?"

"Yes."

"Good. Keep it up."

Dan must have threatened to bring the full wrath of the American Civil Liberties Union upon Donohue for holding two journalists investigating a story, because Stiletto and I were released early the next morning, a Thursday, as soon as the sun rose over the ash-strewn, stripped hills of Slagville.

Not only were we let go, we weren't charged with any crimes, Stiletto got his film back and we were provided with cups of sugar-laden Dunkin' Donuts coffee and directions to the Texaco gas station three blocks away so that I could pick up my car.

Stiletto and I stepped onto the sidewalk outside the Slagville P.D., blinking under the bright blue sky and breathing in the fresh autumn air. It was one of those old-fashioned crisp fall mornings where for once the world seemed in order. The children were in school. Parents were at work. Bills were paid and houses were clean. Productivity was all around us and it was comforting to be alive.

Not comforting enough, though. It's funny how surviving a murder attempt can change your perspective on life. Yesterday, I had blithely gone shopping, packed my bags for the Passion Peak and driven to a lovers' retreat, humming Aerosmith all the way. Little did I know that I was being watched the entire time, that somewhere out there an evil maniac had been implementing a deadly plan to make that day my last on earth.

The concept was too bizarre and scary for my rather peaceful mind to grasp. I decided that, until there was more evidence, I would stick to my theory that Stinky had set us up. My mission, therefore, was to find my cousin's crazy husband and make him spill the beans.

"Something's not right," Stiletto said, glancing around the wide tree-lined streets of Slagville. "It's off."

"Maybe you're just feeling the aftereffects of last night. How's your head, by the way?" I reached over and touched the back of his head. The grapefruit had been reduced to an orange, although his nose remained swollen.

"Still hurts." He gently removed my hand. "It's not my head. I mean something's out of place in this town."

We turned onto Main Street, which ran straight up and straight down a steep hill and was lined with row homes of varying colors—brick red, spring green, baby blue and peeling white. Because they were built on a slope, each rooftop leveled off at its neighbor's second-story window.

The screen door of every home was covered with cardboard scarecrows, witches, and ghouls. Some front windows were ornately decorated with plastic moving pumpkins or ghosts that moaned as we passed. As in the south side of Lehigh, people here did not mess around when it came to Halloween.

Men were on stepladders cleaning out gutters, or on their knees painting trim and recaulking brick. Women were inside frying onions and apples, sending mouthwatering smells from their open kitchen windows. We approached a set of padded matrons in aprons and hair nets who had paused from sweeping the spotless sidewalks to gossip. As we passed they went mum and gaped openly at Stiletto. One woman started giggling so hard her friend poked her with a broom to make her simmer down.

"Women go gaga for Steve Stiletto," I said, as we entered the Texaco parking lot. "What's out of place?"

"Take this, for example," he said, nodding at the red-winged horse that flew above the Texaco sign. "It's like 1963. I bet most of these people never heard of the Internet. Or computers for that matter."

Indeed, at that moment a fresh-scrubbed attendant in a white jumpsuit stepped sprightly from the gas station. "Just adding up the morning's receipts in my ledger book," he apologized, wiping ink off his fingertips. "What can I do you for?"

I asked for the Camaro back and did not get the fairy tale response of, "Oh, sure, it's over here. That'll be ten bucks for a spark plug."

"Sorry," he said, shaking his head. "We had to order a new alternator from Detroit. We don't stock parts for that model year."

"They don't stock parts past 1935," Stiletto whispered, as the clerk checked to see what time I could pick up the car.

"Tomorrow by noon at the earliest," the clerk said. "Anything else?"

Stiletto requested a rental with four-wheel drive, standard shift and no top.

The attendant pointed to a beige-toned Crown Victoria LX with cruise control, automatic transmission, power windows and power steering. "It's the only one we got. You can rent stick-shift cars in Wilkes-Barre, but," he shrugged, "how you gonna get there without no wheels?"

Logical.

Stiletto pulled me aside as the attendant, whistling a Frank Sinatra tune, skipped to the office so he could take an imprint of my Visa. Since Stiletto's wallet had perished in the explosion, he had been forced to rely on the graces of my plastic.

"I can't drive this," he said.

"Why can't you drive it?" I ran my finger along the chrome. "It's deluxe!"

"It's an old lady's car. It's got . . . automatic transmission."

I cupped my hands to the windows and peered inside. Over-stuffed beige leather seats. Cushy arm rests. Seemed mighty darn nice to me. A welcome change from that cruddy Jeep with its worn-out shocks.

"Look," I said, pointing. "It's got tilt-a-wheel."

"Oh, brother."

"Here you go, sir." The attendant handed Stiletto a set of keys and me my Visa. "She's all gassed up and ready to roll. Enjoy!"

Stiletto managed to smear a polite smile on his face and open the door, though he cursed vehemently as the luxury car *ding-ding-dinged* to warn him that the seat belts weren't on. As I walked around the front I saw a rather large AARP sticker promi-nently displayed on the bumper next to AAA, the auto club. I didn't have the heart to tell him.

"That's okay, you can drop me off at Roxanne's," I said, in an attempt to ditch him so I could get Roxanne alone. "That way you won't be bored by our girl talk. You know, babies and hot guys and stuff." If that didn't send him screaming in the other di-rection, what would?

But Stiletto only replied absently, "Uh-huh."

Roxanne's salon, the Main Mane, took up one half of Roxanne's house, a large vinyl-sided building at the end of Main Street (of course). As we got closer, I worried that perhaps my request to be dropped off hadn't registered with Stiletto, especially when he reminded me that we could stay at Roxanne's for only a few minutes.

"How come?" I asked, now praying that the backup plan I had put into motion would work.

"I've got to meet the AP reporter assigned to the story. Luckily, she's already in the area, visiting family. She grew up in Slagville."

"She?"

"Nice kid. Esmeralda Green."

What a name. "Sounds like a witch."

"Some witch. She's a former model, though you probably won't recognize her face."

"Why not?"

"She used to model underwear."

The muscle under my right eye twinged. Stiletto grinned.

"It's how she put herself through Yale, in fact."

It twitched again. "You're making this up."

Stiletto pulled in front of the Main Mane and parked behind Roxanne's brand new gold Ford Explorer with its 62XS vanity plate. Stiletto killed the engine before stroking my cheek. "Don't worry, Bubbles. No one else compares to you. You're one in a million."

"I'm not worried," I said as flashing blue lights appeared in the rearview. "Not now."

"What's this?" Stiletto said, rolling down the window. Chief Donohue leaned in. The Texaco attendant was by his side and my eye twitching miraculously ceased.

"Going for a little joyride?" Donohue asked.

"I'm sorry, Miss Yablonsky," the attendant squeaked, "but I had to place a call to the Visa company. Seems your card is over the limit."

I shut my eyes and waited for the aftershocks. In this situation Dan would have put his fist through the roof and the lecture would have been more rapid fire than an auctioneer's. How could you have not paid that bill, blah, blah, blah.

"Bubbles, I'm surprised at you," Stiletto said in a calm voice.

I cocked open one eye. He was resting his arm along the door and there was an approving smirk on his face. "I've run across *National Enquirer* reporters with more ethics. Guess you don't pull any punches, do you?"

"Excuse me?" I said.

"Were you that desperate to make sure I didn't talk to Stinky's wife? First you try to put me off with threats of girl talk and then this." Stiletto shook his head slowly. "My, my. What other tricks do you have up your fluorescent orange sleeve?"

"It's not orange," I said. "It's apricot."

"If you wouldn't mind returning the car, Mr. Stiletto," Donohue said, "I'll provide an escort back."

"Of course not, Chief," Stiletto said, starting it up again.

I opened my side. "All's well that ends well," I said brightly. "Why don't I wait for you here?"

"What a brilliant idea. Why didn't I think of that?" Stiletto said. "Although, since it's your credit card, shouldn't you be the one to drive back while I interview Roxanne?"

Whoops.

"Not me, babe," I said, stepping out. "You know I can't drive automatic. I only know how to drive stick."

Chapter 5

Something was missing in the Main Mane and it wasn't pink organdy curtains, mint-green walls, rust-colored shag carpeting, plastic plants and a low table littered with tattered magazines. It was customers. Thursday morning and the place was dead empty. In the hairdressing world, this meant Roxanne was at the edge of bankruptcy, if she hadn't fallen over already.

"Bubbles, how are you, hon?" Roxanne stepped out of the supply room and clicked over to me in her purple high heels, clasping me so hard to her bosom that puffs of Lily of the Valley powder rose from her chest. "Chief Donohue telephoned me this morning and told me the whole story."

I wiggled free of her perfumed grasp and sucked in fresh air before I passed out. As a kid, I had been in awe of my older cousin Roxanne's flair with cosmetics. She'd been the one to teach me that white shadow across the bottom of my lids made my eyes wider and that the key to plucking eyebrows was to carefully trim them first. She was still doing that white lid thing, although at age forty it merely accented her wrinkles instead of making her look like a go-go girl, and she hadn't cottoned on to the concept of "light fragrance."

"Did Donohue mention that someone tried to kill me?"

"He did, but I didn't believe it. I mean, who would want to kill you, Bubbles, especially by blowing you up? It's so violent."

"Don't take offense, but my personal opinion is it was one of Stinky's practical jokes that got out of hand. I was hoping maybe you'd heard from him so we could clear this mess up. I'd like to find out if I've offended him or ticked him off in such a way that he needed to get back at me."

At the mention of Stinky's name, Roxanne's face melted. "I haven't heard 'boo' from the Stinkster. After Donohue told me that you spotted the Lexus there, I worried Stinky blew up, too." Tears sprung from the corners of her eyes. "He hasn't even called me to say he's okay."

"I'm sure he's okay," I said, although I doubted that highly. I put my arm around her and squeezed her shoulder. "Stinky's fine."

"You don't know. Stinky hasn't been fine for some time." She turned away and wiped her cheeks with the backs of her hands. I couldn't help but notice a pair of glittery amethyst earrings and matching necklace. Stiletto was right. No matter how weirded out Stinky might be these days, he was doing very well—at least financially.

"Gotta keep positive," she said, sniffling. "Say, where's that well-hung hunk of yours, Stiletto?"

"Stiletto's having a problem with the rented Crown Victoria." I nodded in a what-can-you-do way. "I'm sure he'll be around." Oh, yes. He'd be around.

"A Crown Victoria. My, my." Roxanne fanned herself at the thought. "Nice to have boku bucks. Is it true that he's a millionaire?"

It was true but not a fact Stiletto was proud of. In Stiletto's mind the wealth he had inherited from Henry Metzger, his heartless stepfather, was dirty money. Out of nostalgia he maintained the family mansion back in Saucon Valley, an exclusive suburb for steel executives near Lehigh, but he had set aside the rest for charity and still kept his apartment in New York. We didn't talk about his portfolio much.

"He lives mostly on his AP salary," I said. "Anyway, what's this about—"

"I hear he's got a set of shoulders on him that could build Rome," Roxanne interrupted, her eyes gleaming.

"More like Easton."

"That'll do," she said. "And to think of you stuck with that chastity vow. Girl, I'd have thrown myself on that man without so much as a howdy-do."

I would have thrown myself on him if it hadn't been for that bogus fax sent by your crazy husband, I thought ruefully.

"So what do you mean by Stinky hasn't been fine for some time?" I asked.

I expected Roxanne to tell me what a rat her blackmailing psycho husband had been. Instead she said, "I did an awful thing, cousin. Just awful." She brushed back a strand of copper hair. "Coffee, sugar?"

Was that an offer of coffee or coffee with sugar? "Thanks," I said, perching myself on a padded stool by the makeup counter.

"You know that he quit his six-figure job at McMullen Coal, right?" Roxanne poured the coffee.

"Six-figure job? What are they mining over there, gold?"

"That was a recent salary hike. Stinky was making one-sixth that before." She dumped two spoonfuls of sugar in each cup. Gag. "Early this year, McMullen Coal moved Stinky off maps and over to special projects where he got tons more money and even two new cars. We were in heaven for about six months and then . . . I probably shouldn't talk about it."

"Then Stinky got fired for going wacko. Donohue told me."

"That's a bunch of bull, if you pardon my French." She held out her pinky. "Pinky promise to keep this quiet, just between you and me. Because I definitely do not want this to get out around town."

I dreaded promises. As soon as you make them, you want to break them. "Pinky promise," I reluctantly agreed, hooking my pinky in hers.

"Stinky discovered that after he left the cartography division of McMullen Coal, the maps of the Number Nine mine had been tampered with. They hadn't been updated since the mine reopened briefly earlier this year."

I dropped her pinky. "Is that a big deal?"

"If they didn't update the maps intentionally, it is. It could mean McMullen was trying to rob coal." Roxanne stirred the coffee slowly. "Stinky told his supervisors at McMullen that fudging maps could get miners killed and he demanded they correct them. He even threatened to tell the state if they didn't. But despite all the promises from the supervisors that the maps would be updated, last month Stinky checked the records and found out that no maps had been changed. Then he went into the Number Nine mine and found out that more coal was gone."

My internal alarmed beeped so loudly Roxanne could've heard it. News story. News story. *Ding. Ding. Ding.* I glanced at my pinky. Drat that pinky.

"So he quit. And then things got really nuts." She poured a half a carton of Lehigh Valley Dairy milk in our coffee. "The day Stinky left his job, he came home from the hardware store with a bag of locks. Put new deadbolts on all the doors and windows."

"Why?"

"Beats me." She slid me my cup of coffee. "He spent those first few days doing nothing but writing letters to the state and following me around the house ranting and raving about spheric trigonometry and the CMIS and interlobate moraine."

"I buzz cut an interlobate moraine once," I said. "For a tip, he gave me advice."

"I think interlobate moraine is some kind of dense rock, Bubbles," Roxanne suggested.

"So was he."

I thought that was pretty funny, but Roxanne didn't crack a smile. "I was so eager to get him out of the house and out of my hair that I let him go with his buddy up to the Hole, a bar on the north side of town."

Roxanne sipped her coffee and I recalled what Donohue had said about the fax coming from a pay phone outside the Hole. Score one for my theory that our intended killer was really the Stinkster.

"Next thing I know," she continued, "Stinky stopped complaining about McMullen Coal and was spending every night at the Hole and every day in the basement, hammering and sawing and drilling. Wouldn't let me come down to see what he was up to. And then they stopped calling."

"Who?"

"My clients, of course." Roxanne said this as though I hadn't been following along. "Ten women whose hair I've been cutting for two decades suddenly don't show. They were such regulars I mentally referred to them by their time slots. You know how that is. Tuesday at one. Friday at four. That kind of thing."

Regulars that regular don't simply quit a salon without some drama. Two women in a spat might stop coming so they won't run into each other. One woman might leave because she had a fight with a stylist, but ten? No way. Not without rumors of legionnaires in the air conditioner or bubonic plague on the toilet seat. A prized Friday at two would be hard-pressed to no-show should a nuclear war be imminent.

"What happened?"

"Stinky and his practical jokes is what happened." Roxanne rolled her eyes. "Get this. The first client I telephoned, Thursday at ten, said Stinky had left a message on her answering machine saying that if she didn't pay him fifty dollars, he'd tell her husband, Joe, that she was really a size sixteen, not a ten like Joe thought, and that she had no intention of going on a diet like he wanted. Cookie?" She handed me a half-eaten box of Shop Rite oatmeal raisin frosted.

I thought about the size sixteen. "No thanks."

"To each her own." Roxanne bit into an iced oatmeal and continued. "Wednesday at six-thirty said Stinky vowed to show up at a PTA meeting and announce that her kids had lice and couldn't get rid of them 'cause she cared more for her job than her family. And Saturday at eight said Stinky knew all about her pregnancy scare and how miraculous it was since Mr. Saturday at eight had undergone a vasectomy years before."

"Oops."

Roxanne played with her pink leatherette cigarette case while I stared at the sugar-laden coffee. Then it dawned on me. The worst that can ever befall a hairdresser had happened to my cousin. She'd been bugged.

"He'd been eavesdropping on the salon," I blurted. "Stinky was listening from the basement."

"Ain't that a pisser?" Roxanne said, slipping into Pennsylvania vernacular. "What a sense of humor that clown has."

"Did you ask him if he'd been eavesdropping?"

"See now, there's the worst part. I got so mad at him that I broke my promise and went down to the basement. You wouldn't believe what I found. Wires. Tubes. All these canisters and—this is the strangest part—blow-dryers."

"Blow-dryers?"

"I counted twenty of them, though others were in pieces."

"Did you ask him what he was doing with all those blow-dryers?"

Roxanne shook her head. "Didn't have a chance. I was too mad. When Stinky came home from the Hole, I was waiting with that stuff in a pile and his bags packed at my feet. Then I read him the riot act. Cuz, I really went to town."

She started tearing up again. "I told him it was bad enough, the years of fake dog doo and the nut jars with springing snakes. I didn't like his little pranks. Still, I had tolerated them. But this, listening in on clients and then pretending to blackmail them, this was too much. It wasn't just tasteless and cruel, it stood to ruin my business."

"You were right, Roxanne," I said, handing her a tissue from a box on the counter. Your business has been ruined, I caught myself from adding.

"I wasn't right. I was wrong. I lost my husband and now I'm alone. I was stupid." She dabbed her eyes. "How could I have been so stupid?"

I rubbed circles on her back. "Roxanne, I do something stupid every day."

"Yeah, but you can't help it," she said. "You're Bubbles. You bleached your eyebrows in junior high school and ended up in the emergency room."

I dropped my hand. Perfectly innocent mistake. How was I to know Clorox could make you blind? Wasn't bleach, bleach? "So what was his response?"

"He was stunned." Roxanne blew her nose. "He was so . . . crushed. Stinky took his bags and left. He said, 'I should have left a long time ago.' That was the last I heard from him. Until Donohue called me this morning and said you'd seen his Lexus at the Number Nine mine."

I twirled the glass ashtray, thinking of Stinky. Then a bell rang in what some people consider a very large space between my ears. "Hold on. What buddy did he meet at the Hole?"

"Bud."

"Okay." Let's try it again. "What bud?"

"That was his name, Bud. He was a car salesman, I think."

A mouthful of supersweet coffee log-jammed in my throat. With great effort I swallowed it and said, "Bud Price?"

Roxanne's eyes opened wide. "You know him?"

Even though I was a tad sketchy on Bud myself, I related what Stiletto had told me and Roxanne snapped her fingers. She slid off the stool and skipped over to the magazines on the coffee table, pulling out a copy of yesterday's *Slagville Sentinel* newspaper. She opened it to a feature on Bud Price and a picture of him standing at the entrance of a mine, a roulette wheel in his hand. He was dressed in the same pink Izod shirt I'd seen on the corpse.

I gasped. "That's him! That's the man I saw shot dead last night."

"Gosh. It never occurred to me that they were one and the same." Roxanne stared at the newspaper. "Guess I should start reading the paper instead of buying it just for the customers. Mostly I skip to the coupons and 'Dear Abby.'"

Must be genetic.

The headline read: "Price Sure Casino Is Safe."

Outside came the sound of someone having great difficulty climbing the steps.

"My walk-in." Roxanne handed me the newspaper. "The first in a month. She called this morning." My cousin ran to the door like a school kid at a birthday party. "Mrs. Wychesko. Come in!"

Mrs. Wychesko, a heavy jowled woman in a ratty raccoon coat and gray plastic rain scarf, entered wheezing. "Those steps, Roxy, they'll be the death of me," she said, removing her rain scarf and folding it into a little fan. Roxanne introduced us and we nodded and smiled at each other, but I wasn't eager to stick around.

I had important research to do.

Ten minutes later I was in Roxanne's white enamel tub with the green-blue ring around the drain, enjoying a deep, detoxifying bath and reading about Bud Price's plans to further family togetherness through craps.

The article was an update of Bud Price's fight to bring casino gambling to one of the most destitute regions of Pennsylvania. It had been that destitution, Price's excellent salesmanship and even testimony from a few has-been celebrities that prompted the legislature to issue a waiver permitting "limited" gambling on two hundred acres on Slagville's border that Price had purchased from McMullen Coal the year before.

However, Price needed more than the legislature's approval. He needed state building permits—an unfathomable prospect considering his casino was sited for the Dead Zone.

The Dead Zone was a buffer of land between McMullen Coal's active mines and the neighboring town of Limbo, which sat on top of an underground mine fire. The fire had started one Memorial Day forty years ago when a lit cigarette ignited trash and then a band of anthracite. The blaze had been so devastating that the federal government had paid each Limbo resident forty grand to move out.

In turn, the government barred McMullen Coal from digging under the two-hundred-acre buffer area—which later took on the name the Dead Zone—for fear that new shafts would open pathways to the fire, bringing in dangerous oxygen and causing explosions. That land had been a white elephant for McMullen's company—until Price offered to buy it last year, along with the mining rights, for twenty-five-thousand dollars.

Price had retained numerous experts who testified before state officials that it was impossible for the fire to spread under the Dead Zone, provided there was no underground mining. Opposing environmentalists argued that the fire could turn at any time, new shafts or not, and they painted the picture of a casino full of grandmas at slot machines collapsing into a giant sinkhole faster than the *Titanic* sank into the North Atlantic.

But their valid concerns fell on deaf ears in a region where unemployment hovered at twenty percent. Folks in Slagville wanted a casino that would bring in hotels, restaurants, an amusement park and jobs, jobs, jobs, and they pledged to descend on Harrisburg in busloads until they got it.

The permit proposal was under advisement. State planners were expected to issue a ruling by November—after elections, the article noted.

I studied a photo of Bud relaxing poolside at his estate in the nouveau riche Lehigh suburb of East Hills with wife, Chrissy, who was wearing a teeny-weeny black bikini. Despite her mass of ash blond hair, Chrissy was too old to be a Chrissy anymore. She was at least a Chris, if not a Christine. Her skin was sun-dried cowhide and stretched nearly as tight in a face-lift that was as painful to observe as it must have been to undergo.

The paragraph on Chrissy could have passed for a singles ad. She liked gardening, horses and had recently become involved in the Lehigh Women's League as well as the historical society. In addition to being an avid golfer, Chrissy was a demon on the tennis court and spent every Christmas skiing in Aspen with her daughter, Sasha.

I put down the magazine and soaped up my legs while I pondered the enticing revelation that Stinky and Bud Price were drinking buddies. I considered Stinky's locked and vacant Lexus. Maybe they arrived at the Number Nine mine together the night before. But why? And why trick Stiletto and me into showing up, too, just to try to blow us up? If Stinky had wanted me to be present, all he had to do was call me up and ask. He didn't have to forge a letter from Mr. Salvo.

Now Price was dead and Stinky was missing. And Stiletto and I had barely escaped with our lives.

I had just finished rinsing my hair when the door slammed downstairs and the distinctive low and mellow tones of Stiletto emanated through the heating ducts. Yipes!

I leaped out of the bathtub, dried off and wrapped my hair and body in Roxanne's hot pink towels. Then I hopped down the stairs.

Stiletto was leaning close to Roxanne, who had the photo album open from which she was removing pictures of Stinky. I heard her remark, "That's when Stinky met Bud Price. Now, I don't know if you know who he is—"

"Roxanne!" I shouted, clasping the pink towel with one hand and waving the other.

Stiletto took in my skimpy covering. "Another distraction, Bubbles?"

"You two know each other?" Roxanne asked, tick-tocking a finger between the two of us.

I landed at the bottom of the stairs. "Roxanne, this is Stiletto."

"The Stiletto? Like the knife?" She batted her false eyelashes.

Stiletto flashed me a victorious grin. Finally, finally someone had bought that, "Stiletto like the knife" line of his. "My, I've heard all about you from Aunt LuLu," she gushed. "Didn't I see a profile of you on *60 Minutes*?"

"Only CNN," Stiletto replied with false humility. "It was more a feature on land mines."

"You risked your life showing how innocent children played around those hidden underground explosives every day." Roxanne clasped her hands together. "You were so brave to—"

"Okay, okay," I said, moving between them. "Break it up. Roxanne, don't you have a client to tend to?" I pushed Stiletto toward the door. "And don't you know this is a girls-only salon, Steve?"

"Don't make him go," whined Mrs. Wychesko from the chair as Roxy returned to finish rolling up her hair. "He's so cute. He could be our mascot."

Stiletto tucked the pictures in his back pocket. "I've got to leave, anyway. I have to shoot the owner of McMullen Coal."

"Oh, please don't!" Roxanne squealed. "Hasn't there been enough violence already?"

Stiletto stared at her like she was loopy and I explained that Stiletto meant shoot photos, not bullets. "You talking about Hugh McMullen?" I asked, seething inside with envy.

"Very good, Bubbles. Don't tell me you've actually been reading the newspapers?"

I resisted an urge to tweak his sore nose. "How did you get an interview with McMullen?"

"He drove into the gas station while I was returning the car. How's that for kismet? If your Visa card hadn't been as worthless as the plastic it was printed on, the AP wouldn't have gotten an exclusive."

"Exclusive?"

"Esmeralda Greene snagged that, actually. She picked me up at the Texaco and worked her charm on McMullen, got him to say Price shouldn't have been trespassing in his mine. Nice guy."

Drats, I thought, my hands balling into fists.

He checked his watch. "She's probably finishing up with him now. I better get back there."

Stiletto gave my bare shoulder a paternal pat. "You'll find after working in this business as long as I have, Bubbles, that some of the best scoops come from just being in the right place at the right time. It's not your fault that you didn't get the McMullen interview first. There are other stories in your future."

It was all I could do to keep from tearing my hair out. In fact,

I was so furious that I barely heard the *pfft* and Stiletto yell, "Jesus H!"

He winced and slapped the back of his neck. "What the . . . ?"

Before anyone could answer, he had collapsed onto the floor, face first.

Roxy's Homemade Detoxifying Bubble Bath

Jojoba oil is a natural detoxifying agent that can be found in co-ops or health food stores. This bath is nice because it's both bubbly and softens skin. Next time someone makes a crack about you lying about in the bath reading mysteries, note that this is vital to your health and if they want you to live longer they should let you be. So there.

5 ounces of liquid body soap
1 tablespoon of jojoba oil
2 vitamin E capsules, split open
1 drop of vanilla

Mix ingredients in a bowl and return to an old shampoo bottle. (Don't forget to mark clearly.) Dump ½ cup under running warm—not hot—bathwater. Relax and enjoy.

Chapter **6**

"**B**ull's-eye!" Genevieve proclaimed, bringing down her pea-shooter. "Should've gotten me one of these years ago. Handy little buggers."

Genevieve, my mother's sidekick in their Lehigh pierogi shop and a certified conspiracy nut, stood in the doorway admiring a thin brown straw clutched in her massive mitt. Her Pittsburgh Steelers linebacker frame was supersized by a bright yellow- and purple-flowered dress and white knee-highs slipping down her tree trunk legs.

"What did you do that for?" I demanded.

"Saved your life, didn't I?" Genevieve said. "Strange man at the door. You half naked. Shoot first, skip the questions. That's my motto."

"That's not a strange man. It's Stiletto." I turned his head so Genevieve could see.

Genevieve peered down at him, unconvinced. "Well, his Jeep wasn't parked out front." As though that provided justification.

"That's because his Jeep blew up," I said. "Look what you've done. And he fell on his nose, too. He was punched in that nose last night. It's still swollen."

"Nice going, toots. Serves the scum right." Mama appeared, looking ridiculous as usual. Ever since she'd fallen for a hard-living race car driver who'd loved her and left her at the penitentiary gates, Mama had adopted a "bad girl" attitude—which took some imagination since Mama's bad girlhood was a good fifty years behind her.

Today her wider-than-it-is-tall frame sported faux leather

pants, Kmart mini boots and a scoop-neck tee that strained painfully over her sagging breasts. Spandex abuse. Head to toe she was in black, except for her lips, which were a smudged crimson. Gone was the grandmotherly coral of yesteryear.

"Hey," Mama furrowed her wrinkled brow. "I've seen him someplace before."

"That's because it's Stiletto," I said, getting exasperated. "Genevieve shot Stiletto."

"Don't get huffy, Bubbles," Mama said. "She was just trying to protect you. Kids these days. No sense of gratitude."

"Amen," said Genevieve.

Stiletto groaned. I removed a tiny quill from his neck and pinched it between my fingers.

"What is this?" I stood, handing Genevieve the quill.

"Tranquilizing dart," Genevieve said. "Only, I used up all the free samples they handed out at End Times Survival Camp so I had to improvise. This one's dipped in Sominex. Tripled the dose just to be safe."

Roxanne and Mrs. Wychesko, apron still around her neck, approached.

"What a shame," Mrs. Wychesko said, cocking her head. "I liked him much better alive."

"He is still alive," I said. "Isn't he?"

"Let's see." Mama brought back her foot to kick him.

"Stop that." I pushed her aside. "Have you no respect?"

"I've never witnessed anything like that in my life," Mrs. Wychesko said. "It was all slow-mo."

Roxanne was none too pleased. "You can't leave him here for all the world to see. It's not good marketing to have customers lying in the doorway, shot in the neck. Business is bad enough."

Genevieve leaned down, shoved her size-twenty-two arms under his shoulders and dragged Stiletto across the orange shag rug to the couch in Roxanne's parlor. With a grunt she picked him up and threw him on the cushions, tossing a black and multicolored crocheted afghan on him as an afterthought. If Stiletto ever spoke to me again, I'd be amazed.

Mama took me aside. "Listen, I didn't raise up an ingrate. When Jane told us this morning that someone had tried to kill you, Genny ripped off her apron and rushed right up here to be your one woman personal security entourage. The least she deserves is a simple thank you."

She might be dressed like a slut, but she was still my mother. I did as I was told when Genevieve returned.

"Thank you, Genevieve," I droned, "for shooting my boyfriend with Sominex."

Genevieve blushed. "Aw, that's okay, Bubbles. It was a pleasure."

I slapped my head. It was no use.

Mama looked around the salon. "Hell's bells, it's great to be back in my hometown. Nothing like visiting the old stomping grounds of one's youth to feel invigorated again. Biggest mistake I ever made was leaving Slagville for Lehigh. Yessiree. 'Course it's hard to stick around when there ain't no work."

"How come you're here, anyway?" I asked Mama. And how soon will you be leaving, I wanted to add. "Don't tell me you're part of my security entourage, too."

"She's looking for the Nana diary," Genevieve cut in.

"The Nana diary?"

Mama's kohl-lined eyes narrowed with suspicion. "At my last visit up here someone swiped Nana Yablonsky's diary, the one that contains all our best pierogi recipes."

"What if it gets in the hands of Mrs. T?" Genevieve asked, crossing herself at the mention of the doyenne of the flash-frozen potato ravioli. "She's right in Pottsville. She could make a killing on your grandmother's secrets."

I doubted Mrs. T was willing to risk her empire on Nana Yablonsky's gut-wrenching venison and vinegar specialties.

"Point is, we gotta find out who stole the Nana diary and get it back." Mama pointed to my towel. "What were you doing? Taking a bath while Stiletto was hot on the investigation?"

"I was dirty. It was gross in that mine."

She stood on tiptoe and cupped my chin. "You listen to me, sweetie pie. If you want to find the filth that tried to kill you and your man, then you got to get some dirt on your pretty polished nails."

"I'm gonna call Mr. Salvo," I said, removing her hand from my chin and strolling over to the telephone. He wasn't in the newsroom this early, so I left a message on his voice mail about last night and how to reach me at Roxanne's.

Then I called my salon boss and best friend, Sandy, at my other place of employment, the House of Beauty, on Lehigh's south side. It made me homesick to hear the blow-dryers and happy chatter in the background.

"I wondered when you were going to call. This place has been frantic with gossip," Sandy shouted into the phone. "Is it true someone's out to kill you?"

"I don't know. That's why I thought I'd stick around in Slagville to find out. Also my alternator's busted."

"Take all the time you want. Tiffany will fill in. Honestly, Mrs. Coleman will be relieved."

"I thought Mrs. Coleman dreaded Tiffany."

Sandy stopped blow drying. "Yeah. But Tiffany doesn't have a price on her head. Mrs. Coleman was worried she'd be blown away if you were doing her hair and the hitman showed up."

Mrs. Coleman watched too much HBO.

"By the way, Martin wonders if the explosion could have been spontaneous combustion. Sometimes he comes across that in the bakery. Bread has too much yeast and boom!"

Thank you, Sandy's wacky baker husband. "It was a mine, Sandy, not a doughnut."

When I hung up, Mama was right behind me, hands on fake-leather hips.

"Now I suggest you find something decent to wear and hurry up or we'll be late."

"Where are we going?"

"To Madame Vilnia's."

"Good idea," Roxanne said, rolling the last curler into Mrs. Wychesko's hair. "She knows everyone and everything in town. If the person who lured you up to the Number Nine mine last night is from Slagville, Vilnia will know who it is. Wear the black knit hanging in my closet, Bubbles. My funeral dress. Madame Vilnia likes women to be modest. No pants. That goes for you, too, Aunt LuLu."

"I ain't changing for nobody," Mama said.

I protested that visiting local hags was not a way to research newspaper articles, but Mama and Roxanne would have none of it.

"What you should be worried about," Roxanne advised as I climbed the stairs, "is where you're going to get a live chicken at this last minute's notice."

Having been unsuccessful in rounding up a breathing bird, Mama and I had been forced to stop off at the A&P to purchase our gift for Vilnia. I lobbied for an African violet or scented candles, but Mama was adamant. It was poultry or bust.

"I hope this works." Mama pouted at the four-pound Perdue Oven Stuffer Roaster on her lap. "Usually Vilnia likes them alive. Back in the old country the wise women got only living chickens as payment for their services. Vilnia's gonna be insulted when she sees someone else snapped the neck first."

My stomach turned. Between Roxanne's oversugared coffee, Chief Donohue's doughnuts and chicken decapitation, I was ready to puke.

I swung Genevieve's boat of a Rambler into the patch, an outcropping of run-down row homes on the outskirts of Slagville that had been built once upon a time by the mining company for its laborers and their families. The homes were painted every color of the rainbow, as if to counteract the dark and dusty life of the pitch black mines. Compact, well-tended gardens in the back yards brimmed with autumn pumpkins, carrots, spinach and broccoli.

Mama grabbed the roaster and we climbed the stairs. We rang the doorbell and waited in the cool air. The patch was in a hollow, damp and cold. I pinched the plunging cleavage of Roxanne's "modest" black dress, which clung to my every nook, curve and cranny. If this is what Roxanne wore to funerals, what was her New Year's Eve getup? Pasties?

The door opened and a doddering man in gray pants and a white T-shirt answered. He removed a set of old-fashioned headphones, the kind from the public library, and ushered us in without a word. We entered a dimly lit living room lined by wood-paneled walls and numerous family photos. A gigantic La-Z Boy faced a wide-screen television. A game show played on what I thought was mute until I realized that it was attached to Mr. Vilnia's headphones.

He pushed on the swinging door into a white kitchen where a woman sat at a table cutting carrots. There were various pots boiling furiously on the stove and the oven light was on, revealing a bubbling apple crisp. The room was a steam bath of cooking carrot, cabbage and apple.

"Visitors," he announced.

"Well, don't just stand there," the tiny woman barked. "Let them in."

"Yes, dear," he mumbled, waving the way for Mama and me to enter. Then he turned like a zombie and returned to the game show.

Clutching the carrot knife, Madame Vilnia stood, so short she and Mama were eye to eye. She was rounder than my mother (if that were possible) and older. She wore a gray tweed dress, bifocals and large plastic pearls at her flabby neck. Her lips were a bright shade of carnation, unlike my mother's bloodred ones—of which Vilnia clearly disapproved.

"Long time, no see," Vilnia said. "I heard you were back in town."

Mama raised her nose and sniffed. "Do I smell Zupa Kartoflana with mint?"

"So what if you do?" Vilnia circled Mama slowly, taking in the hot-dame biker package. "Seeing you, I remember that there's a reason why women shouldn't wear slacks. Your legs look like knockwurst. Only one woman could pull it off and she's dead."

"Jackie O," Mama said, getting misty eyed. "Come to think of it. . . ."

Oh, no. I wasn't going down that road again. I yanked the Oven Stuffer Roaster out of Mama's hands and thrust it toward Vilnia. "For you."

"Not another chicken." Vilnia's shoulders drooped. "Can't you come up with anything else? There's a Bed Bath & Beyond in Wilkes-Barre, you know. You two ever hear of napkin rings?"

"I knew we should have brought candles," I said.

"It cost eight-fifty, that chicken," Mama said. "In the old country a professional gossip would've been proud to get Perdue."

"Old country, mold country." Vilnia opened the Frigidaire and tossed in the gift. It joined a half dozen frozen roasters. "This is America in the twenty-first century. Palm pilots. No-fog showers. Refrigerators in drawers. Get with it."

Mama poked her in the chest, right under the pearls. "No one tells me to get with it, sister."

"This is your sister?" I asked. "I didn't know you had a sister, Mama."

The women quit their bickering. "Let me venture," Vilnia said. "This is Bubbles."

"I told you Vilnia was good," Mama said, dropping her finger. "She knows everything."

"Including who killed Bud Price? And where Stinky is?" I asked. "And if he was the one who tried to kill me and Stiletto? And if he sent me the bogus fax?"

"Kid comes with tall orders," Vilnia said to Mama.

"I blame TV. You got cake?"

"What do you think?"

We sat as Vilnia put out coffee cups and unwrapped an Entenmann's cinnamon crumble cake.

"Here's the skinny," Mama said as Vilnia served us each a slice. "Bubbles got a fax from her editor ordering her to cover a press conference at the Number Nine mine, where a businessman has been found stabbed."

"Shot," I corrected.

"Don't talk with your mouth full, Bubbles." Mama handed me a napkin. "Anyway, turns out her editor didn't send the fax. No one knows who did. Though Bubbles did end up finding a businessman dead in the mine last night. Bud Price."

Vilnia crossed herself. "May he rest in peace."

"What we want to know is who sent her the fax. According to the sending telephone number, it had to have been someone from this area, with access to *News-Times* stationery, who also would have known that Bubbles was at the Passion Peak."

"Stinky could have known," I said, after a good, clearing swallow.

Mama wet her finger and wiped a smudge from the corner of my mouth. "How would Stinky have known?"

I smeared away Mama's spit. It's disgusting when she does that. "Through Roxanne. Didn't you tell her I was going to the Passion Peak?"

Mama fluttered her puny eyelashes. A sure indication of guilty as charged.

"I don't know," she said, trying to sound vague and old ladyish. "These days I can't remember what I say or who I talk to."

"Give it up, Mama. You're not riding any Goldwing motorcycle. I know how you gossip about me and Stiletto. You can admit it."

Mama opened her red lips to confess her sins, but Vilnia interrupted.

"Wait a minute, wait a minute." Vilnia was waving the cake knife around. "You telling me Bubbles got the fax when she was staying at the Passion Peak on her honeymoon?"

"No," Mama explained. "With Steve Stiletto, a news photographer. Her boyfriend."

"Bubbles! I'm shocked." Vilnia put down the knife and slid one index finger over the other, in the universal Pennsylvania sign language of warding off evil. "Oiii. Not married and—"

"Didn't you just tell me it's America in the twenty-first century?" Mama said.

"Guess it's none of my business. Not my soul that'll be languishing in purgatory." Vilnia sat down and plunged a fork into her own slice of cake. We all ate silently, pondering eternal damnation and Entenmann's.

"What made you think of Stinky, anyway, Bubbles?" Vilnia finally asked.

"Because his Lexus was at the mine when I got there. It was gone after Stiletto and I nearly blew up in the mine."

Vilnia held her fork in midair. "Seems like you left out a few details, LuLu."

"I need more ginkgo." Mama shrugged and pushed her plate away. "You got coffee?"

"Sure." Vilnia got up and plucked the pot from the coffeemaker. No. No. Not more coffee! Vilnia distributed the cups and frowned as she poured, deep in thought. She replaced the pot, brought a carton of milk from the refrigerator and plunked it on the table.

"If I were you, Bubbles, I'd go home," Vilnia said, folding her arms and sitting down again. "Go back to Lehigh."

"I can't go home," I said. "I need a new alternator."

"Why should she have to go home?" Mama asked. "Bubbles needs to write a big story that will get her a full-time job at her newspaper. Looks to me like this is it. This could be her Big Break. And, anyway, she can't leave without finding Stinky . . . or whoever it was that tried to kill her. She'll never get a decent night's sleep if she doesn't."

Vilnia regarded both of us. "It wasn't Stinky who tried to kill you." She lowered her voice and we had to lean over the table to hear her. "Whoever set you up, he's bigger than Stinky."

"Bigger than Stinky!" I exclaimed, as though this were an impossibility. "Who?"

She sighed. "Okay. You know about the casino, right?"

"Right."

"Well, someone very powerful doesn't want it to go through. He'll stop at nothing, including murdering Mr. Price, to make sure it stops. He does not want casinos to replace coal here in Pennsylvania."

Mama and I looked at each other. "Who is it?" I asked.

"Maybe Bud Price's murderer. I ain't sure." Vilnia sat back and plucked a toothpick from the toothpick holder. "But I bet Stinky knows. Stinky discovered something in his workplace he wasn't supposed to, Bubbles. That's what he told me when I ran into him at the library before he disappeared. That's why McMullen Coal fired him and that's why he's in hiding. You get Stinky and you'll get the straight poop."

"What poop?" Mama asked.

Vilnia shrugged. "I don't know. He didn't give me no poop particulars."

I tried to sort out the many stories Roxanne had prattled about this morning. She'd said her husband had quit his job because the maps at McMullen Coal hadn't been updated, making it look like less coal was being taken out than it was. But why would that result in Bud Price's murder?

"Are you sure Stinky's not crazy?" I asked.

"Not crazy." She tapped her temple with the toothpick. "Smart." She chewed on her toothpick and winked at me.

I didn't know whether to believe her. Vilnia might be another conspiracy nut like Genevieve, only shorter and with more plastic jewelry.

There was a faint shuffling and the door opened. Mr. Vilnia appeared. "I was thinking I might go out. You know. To the park. For a walk."

There was silence. Vilnia removed the toothpick. "And what, may I ask, have you done about the garbage? I told you this morning to take it out and still it's there."

"Oh, sorry." Mr. Vilnia scurried across the kitchen and removed the white plastic bag, tying it quickly.

"Don't forget to put in another liner. How many times have I opened the door under the sink to throw away coffee grounds only to have them land in the bare garbage pail. Do you know what a pain that is to clean?"

"Yes, dear," he said, shaking out a plastic bag.

"And I suppose the bathroom faucet's still dripping."

Mr. Vilnia dragged the garbage bag to the kitchen door. "It needs a new washer."

"I know *that*," Vilnia said, as Mr. Vilnia opened the door almost in relief. "That's why it's dripping."

As soon as he left, Vilnia jumped up and quickly opened the oven door. Mama, heeding some mysterious signal, also sprang to action, bringing down a white plate from the cupboard. Vilnia slipped on two oven mitts and brought out the apple crisp. She spooned out a section as Mama reached in the freezer and found some vanilla ice cream. The women worked silently.

Mr. Vilnia returned with resolve on his mind. "Listen, Vilnia. I have a right to go out if I want to. I'm retired. I've worked all my life—"

Vilnia handed him the plate of steaming cinnamon apple crisp with vanilla ice cream melting over it in rivulets.

"What's this?" he said, softening.

She gave him a spoon and he dug in. After two delectable mouthfuls he said, "Maybe I will stay home. It looks like it's going to rain and there's that documentary on fungi I've been wanting to see."

"Sounds good, tiger." The phone on the kitchen wall rang and no one budged.

"Phone's ringing, dear," Vilnia announced.

Mr. Vilnia snatched it off the wall and handed it to his wife without answering.

"I'll take it in the other room." She left through the swinging door. Mr. Vilnia followed dutifully.

After they were gone, Mama rested against the counter and fanned herself with an oven mitt. "Whew!"

"What the heck was that all about?"

"A rare treat. You have just witnessed the casting of the Nag 'N Feed spell, a local specialty."

"Nag 'N Feed?"

"It's how the women in this town keep their men folk in line. They nag them constantly about the garbage, watching too much sports on TV, you know the drill. Then, just when their husbands are about to blow their tops, they bring out the food and the men cave. The chores get done and the women remain in control. Flawless system."

"And the men put up with this?"

"They have no choice. They're enchanted." Mama hung the oven mitt on a hook by the stove. "These women aren't called the Sirens of Slagville for nothing."

I considered Vilnia with her support hose and Dentu-Crème whitened choppers. "Vilnia is a Slagville Siren?"

"Don't underestimate her. Women from coal country got powers that science can't explain."

Even Mama couldn't explain because the swinging door to the kitchen burst open, and Vilnia entered, face flushed, phone pressed to her ample bosom. "You better get over to the Number Nine mine quick, Bubbles," she said. "They found Price."

"Finally!" I shouted. "A scoop of my own."

"I don't know how much of a scoop it is," Vilnia said. "That was Esmeralda Greene on the line. She was there when they took out the body. She and that boyfriend of yours, Stiletto."

Chapter 7

"**I** told you to hit the pavement and dig up some dirt," Mama said, barely able to see above the steering wheel, "but nooo, you insisted on wasting your morning in gossip."

"What? Visiting Vilnia was your idea!"

"Bubbles, Bubbles, Bubbles. When are you going to face the fact that you're too soft for the big leagues. Unless you toughen up, honey, you'll be writing fluff pieces about strawberry festivals and high school graduations forever. I can't do your job for you, you know."

I would have throttled her dog-collared neck then and there except she was driving. Mama had insisted, claiming that her old race-car boyfriend had taught her a couple of tricks, including how to peel out of a neighborhood and take a turn on two wheels. Otherwise, it was little old lady as usual.

"If you're so perfect," I said, "then how come Stiletto was at the mine and not on Roxanne's couch like we'd left him?"

Mama turned a right onto the dirt road by the mine's entrance. "Slipup in the operation. Genevieve needs to check with her Sominex supplier. The stuff must have been cut with sugar. Holy mackerel. Talk about competition."

Ye gads! Monstrous white TV news vans with gigantic satellite dishes crowded the road in front of the exploded Number Nine mine shaft where I had frozen the night before. All were local affiliates of the major networks—Channels Three, Five and Six. There were so many reporters, in fact, that the lights from the cameras lit up the place like a county fair Ferris wheel.

"You're late!" Mama exclaimed, idling the Rambler. "Good thing I floored it."

Going forty miles per hour wasn't exactly breaking the sound barrier, but I didn't have time to argue.

"You want to come?" I asked, removing my reporter's notebook and testing my pen.

"No can do. Genevieve and I need to talk." Mama kept the engine running.

"About how come the Sominex dart didn't take hold?"

"Right," she said absently. "Now, this is what I mean about you being soft. Why are you here chatting with me about my schedule when you should be out there swimming with the sharks? Get going." And she gave me a little push out of the car.

My steps were leaden as I trudged toward the collection of cops and reporters. Perhaps Mama was right. Perhaps I was destined to be no more than a fluffy feature writer. Sure, I'd uncovered one major scandal—Henry Metzger, the ruthless chairman of Lehigh Steel. For decades Metzger had skimped on safety measures in the steel plant to rake in more profits for his own personal gain. And though numerous workers—like my own father—had died because of his cool disregard for life, no one in Lehigh had had enough guts to probe his evil doings.

Until I found his one weakness.

But in the end what had it mattered? Metzger had flown off to Central America and died in a plane crash, and that was that. No prosecution. No compensation for his victims. Within weeks Metzger's crimes were reduced to quaint, legendary tales. And somewhere my newspaper articles were yellowing with age, waiting to be committed to cyberspace and thrown in the incinerator.

Like they say in the newsroom, you're only as good as yesterday's story. Well, today was tomorrow's yesterday and I had better shape up, like Mama said.

Already a press conference was underway. Dolled-up TV reporters with their severely plucked eyebrows, bright lips and impeccable hair faced Donohue and two men I didn't recognize.

One was in a navy blue windbreaker that read MEDICAL EXAMINER on the back. The other was a business-suited type.

I searched the crowd for Stiletto, but he was nowhere to be seen. The other reporters wouldn't let me get closer to the podium, so I was forced to the back of the crowd where it was impossible to see or hear bupkis. Can you say loser?

"Loser," said a nasal voice. "Those big-city reporters make me feel like such a loser."

A reporter with curly brown hair, black glasses and a press pass that said MYRON FINKLE, *SLAGVILLE SENTINEL* was by my side. He was no taller than my shoulder and the sheen of his tan shirt, along with his baggy pants, indicated that the *Slagville Sentinel* didn't pay very well.

He squinted at the press pass around my neck. "Lehigh *News-Times?* Where's that?"

"About an hour or so from here," I whispered, trying to catch what Donohue was saying. "Lots of folks in Lehigh come from Slagville. Steel and all."

"Oh, yeah. The Lehigh Valley Railroad runs through town. Guess there's a coal connection." He lifted his chin toward the TV people. "We got TV reporters from Philly and New York here today. I bet they don't even know the difference between anthracite and bituminous."

"You can say that again." Bituminous was an eating disorder. Even I knew that. "How did they find out about Price's murder, anyway?"

"Are you kidding?" Myron pulled out a folded up newspaper from his back pocket. "It was in the morning papers all over the country."

Myron opened to a lead AP story from that morning's *Slagville Sentinel.* It was brief, but it delivered the essentials. Bud Price, who recently won unprecedented legislative approval to open a casino in Slagville, PA, was presumed dead after a portion of the Number Nine mine had exploded. Rescue workers were attempting to retrieve the body. No comment from Price's family or company, except confirmation he'd been in the area on business.

"Shoot!" I said. "He beat me to it. Son of a gun."

"Who beat you?" Myron asked, refolding the clipping.

"Steve Stiletto," I said. My mind raced. It was impossible. To get the story on the wire early enough for the morning newspapers, Stiletto would have had to call it in by 2 A.M. And he didn't get out of the mine until 2:30.

Or did he?

That dog. He must've found another exit after the cave-in and then somehow managed to get to a phone—a rescue worker's perhaps?—before returning to the ambulance where I had been crying about him suffocating, blah, blah, blah.

"Bastard," I hissed.

"Stiletto?" Myron said. "How do you think I feel? I'm the local cop reporter and I didn't even know about the explosion until my editor got me out of bed this morning, yelling that we'd been scooped by a New York AP photographer and his girlfriend. Biggest story to hit this town in a century and a prize-winning reporter and photographer happen to be here on a romantic weekend. Is that bad luck or what?"

I blushed. "That's nice of you, Myron, but I haven't won any prizes. Not yet."

"Not you," he said, pushing up his glasses. "Esmeralda Greene. She used to be the regional AP bureau chief here and then got promoted to New York after her coal region series was nominated for a Pulitzer. Kick ass babe-a-lonia." Myron stuck out his tongue like a panting dog. "That Stiletto is one lucky dude. Man, what I wouldn't give to be in his place."

"You mean Stiletto and Greene are . . . a couple?"

"That's the rumor. Supposedly they keep it hush-hush 'cause they work for the same organization. You know what the AP's nepotism policy is like." Myron said this with importance, as though he were tighty whitey with the AP honchos. "Management gets a whiff two employees are sleeping together and it's curtains. That's her over there, asking a question now."

A statuesque redhead towered above her colleagues. Even from the back of the press conference, I could tell that she was an arresting woman. Broad shoulders. Classic cheekbones. Her black suit lent a trim, stylish appearance and set off her shoulder-length, thick hair. She could have modeled more than women's underwear. Esmeralda Greene was a stunner.

"Chief Donohue," she said, her voice crisp and clear over the crowd, "what can you tell us about a former McMullen Coal employee named Carl Koolball whose car was spotted at the Number Nine mine entrance around the hour of Price's murder? From what my sources tell me, he had made numerous threats against his former employer and against Price. And, as an engineer, he would know how to set off a mine explosion. Is he a suspect in this case?"

Showoff. No decent reporter would ask a lengthy question like that in front of other reporters. She had just handed the competition tons of information she'd dug up. Perhaps she was trying to impress someone—Stiletto?

Donohue stepped to the podium, flushed and sweating. He looked like he hadn't had much sleep. "I am not at liberty to discuss an ongoing investigation with the press, Esmeralda. Suffice it to say that Carl Koolball is not a suspect. However, I would classify him as a 'person of interest.'"

Person of interest. I wrote that down. What the heck did that mean? He was either a suspect or he wasn't, right?

"Perhaps I can shed some light." The suit walked up to the microphone. "Hugh McMullen, owner of McMullen Coal Inc.," he said, removing a sheet of paper from his breast pocket.

My initial impression of Hugh McMullen could be summed up in three words: hungover Peter Pan. Although his wavy hair sported streaks of gray, it was boyishly (and, oh yes, expensively) cut and he had donned a spiffy pair of penny loafers. His posture was poor, he yawned as he prepared to speak and he seemed ill at ease, as though he were eager to return to the frat house.

The reporters crowded closer, shutting me out completely. No way I was going to miss McMullen. I expertly wedged my body between a Barbie and Ken from Channel Three in a move I like to call the "Bon Jovi Butt."

It requires years of grandstand seating at Jon Bon Jovi concerts to perfect the Bon Jovi Butt, and the feat is not for the petite or polite. The trick is to resist the urge to say, "Pardon me." Offers too much of a heads up. And once the butt is complete, never look back.

"Hey!" Barbie objected. I ignored her and kept my eyes straight ahead on McMullen.

"On Labor Day," McMullen began, reading stiffly from a prepared statement, "it came to my attention that one of our top engineers, Carl Koolball, was suffering from mental health issues. Our company offered him a generous leave and medical help, which he refused. We had no choice but to let him go—for the safety of our other employees."

I scribbled as fast as I could and recalled what Vilnia had said about Stinky being fired from McMullen. I sensed a plant. Esmeralda's question had been too detailed and McMullen's answer too pat to be a coincidence.

"Since then the Columbia County court has issued a restraining order barring Mr. Koolball from coming within fifty feet of the McMullen colliery and the Dead Zone, which we happen to be standing on right now. I'm not violating any confidentiality policies here. Everything I've just told you is in the public record. My primary goal is to be as upfront with you people as possible."

In unison, reporters whipped out their cell phones and dialed rapidly. I predicted that within an hour the oblivious clerks in the Columbia County Courthouse would be flooded with news interns requesting copies of the restraining order.

And then it struck me like an anvil falling on Wile E. Coyote. The Dead Zone. We were standing on it and it was right next to the Number Nine mine. I wiggled past Barbie, who threw me a darting look, to the back of the crowd where Myron waited, fed up.

"I hate these reporters," he said. "They're so mean. They won't let me get closer 'cause I'm from a dinky paper."

"You're not missing much." I smiled sympathetically. "Listen, Myron, if this is the Dead Zone, then where is Price's casino supposed to go?"

Myron pointed to a cluster of orange ribbons tied around a few trees. "There. Though the entire complex of swimming pools, hotels, theaters and a shopping mall will be much larger. Probably take up all two hundred acres."

"Hmm." I left Myron and hiked across the beaten grass, through the woods and over to the entrance of the mine, my heels slipping on the black slag scattered about. I was simply going to have to get new shoes if I was going to stick with this story. Nice if they made slingbacks with treads.

The exploded mine entrance was littered with burnt wood, rock and settled dust inside a perimeter of yellow police tape. Let's see now. Stiletto and I had entered here and then—I envisioned our underground path—we stopped there. I imagined a spot about a hundred feet away. That must have put us in the Dead Zone.

I thought back to the article I had read in Roxanne's bathtub. McMullen had sold the Dead Zone to Price because the coal company wasn't permitted to mine under that land for safety reasons—namely possible encroachment by the Limbo fire. But what if McMullen had been robbing coal from underneath the Dead Zone and not documenting it, to escape state scrutiny? And what if Stinky had found that out and that's why he'd been fired?

The wheels in my head spun. I needed to get back to Roxanne and convince her to let me break our pinky promise so I could track down what she told me about Stinky. This could be a big story, I thought, heading out of the clearing and toward the woods. Especially with Bud Price, owner of the Dead Zone, found shot through the chest in the Number Nine mine.

I scurried through the dappled light and around rotting tree trunks, my shoes not offering much traction on the fallen leaves. Which is why I nearly slid into a large figure who materialized in my path and grabbed my arm.

"Bubbles," he said gruffly. "Bubbles Yablonsky."

I caught my breath. He was a twenty-something man, tall, in a flannel shirt, jean jacket and a white baseball cap that sat on top of his ash blond hair. It was dark in the woods and I couldn't see his face that clearly. He had caught me off guard so I had no option except to say, "Yes?"

"Right." He let go and touched his finger to the brim of his hat. "Just wanted to know what you look like."

He took a few steps back and it wasn't until then that I noticed his hand had ever so slightly pushed aside his jacket to reveal a gun stuck in his belt. I lifted my eyes to his in total fright and comprehension of the message.

"Stay safe now," he said, smirking.

I was going to say something, but as soon as I opened my mouth, I was speechless. He apparently found my shock and obvious fear amusing because he kept on smirking. And kept on staring at me, the branches of the bare trees clicking in the wind, reminding me that he and I were alone. In the woods. Next to a murder scene.

"What are you waiting for?" he asked.

What *was* I waiting for? I slipped past him and ran as fast as I could, leaping over fallen branches and ducking tree branches, until I emerged in the clearing back at the press conference. I headed straight for the crowd of cameras, tape recorders and shouting journalists, Bon Jovi Butting my way with gusto, ticking off any number of people as I rudely bumped the coroner and kept on going.

I beelined for a satellite truck and turned the corner so that I was hidden by the open rear doors. My heart beat fast and I remembered that I didn't have wheels. Now how was I going to get back to Roxanne's?

"What was that about?" asked a woman's voice on the other side of the van door. There were footsteps on the gravel. Reporters leaving the press conference. "Did you see that crazy blonde in the low-cut number?"

I stared down at Roxanne's suggestive funeral dress.

"Who was she?"

"You don't know?" replied a different woman. "That's Stiletto's flavor of the month. Bubblegum. She's a hairdresser who goes around pretending to be a reporter."

Pretending? Why I'd . . . the two women had stopped just outside the van's doors. I remained statue still.

"A reporter? Where?"

"Some shopper called the *News-Times* on the Jersey border."

For her information, the *News-Times* was *not* a shopper.

"You'd think Stiletto would have matured beyond the sex kitten phase," the first woman said. "Anyway, he's too good to waste on a woman like that." A soda can popped open. There was a slight fizzing sound.

The other woman took a gulp. "It won't last," she said, burping slightly. "He just likes the conquest. That's all Stiletto has ever loved is the conquest."

My cheeks felt hot and I was tempted to turn the corner and give them a Liberty High School locker room special when the woman's friend said, "So how come he hasn't conquered you, Esmeralda?"

Esmeralda? Esmeralda Greene?

"He is damned good-looking, isn't he?" Esmeralda giggled. Funny. I hadn't pictured her as the giggling type.

"Are you kidding? And you know he's always had a thing for you. Remember that time when you two were assigned to cover the war crimes trials at the Hague and you had to share a hotel room?"

"That's not the kind of night I'd forget."

"And he had to—"

"Shhh," Esmeralda stifled her. "Here he comes."

"Hey, Esmeralda. Patty." Stiletto's voice was calm, coolly casual.

I rounded the van door.

"Bubbles."

Esmeralda and Patty's faces dropped to the basement. But while Patty's was pink with embarrassment, Esmeralda's remained as cool as her Clinique sand foundation. Her skin was strikingly flawless, not a blemish or dark spot on her face. She was a perfect porcelain doll.

"Have you guys met?" Stiletto asked. "I think you'd really like Bubbles. She's got a hell of a news streak in her."

Esmeralda and Patty smiled weakly, an expression Stiletto obviously took for kindness. God. Men were so off the planet half the time. Did they have even a spark of intuition?

"Uh, we better get back to New York, Steve," Esmeralda said. "The national desk wants us for the afternoon meeting. And, as it so happens, I've got the car."

"Aww shit," Stiletto said. "Bubbles, what are you going to do? You don't have a way to get into town."

"No problem," I said, hooking my arm in his. "You can drop me off at Roxanne's on the way. If that's all right with you, Esmeralda?"

"Hmmm. I don't know. It is a Miata and there's not much of a back seat." She frowned as though so very disappointed at not being able to help.

"Not to worry," I said. "I'll squeeze in. Just like a brand-new kitten."

Esmeralda's Potato and Green Tea Compress

Esmeralda may be a former model and big time New York City journalist, but she'll always be a Slagville girl at heart. Which is why she knows that sometimes the best beauty secrets involve potatoes. In this one the raw potato removes dark circles under the eyes while the moistened and cool green tea reduces the swelling—for that perfect porcelain doll look.

½ russet potato, grated raw
2 green tea bags
1 drop glycerin
2 pieces of cheesecloth, approximately 6 x 6 inches
2 rubber bands

Soak tea bags in cold water while you grate potato into bowl. Remove tea bags from water and shake off excess moisture. With scissors cut off top of tea bags and empty contents into potato mixture, along with glycerin. Stir.

Divide mixture in half and spoon each half onto center of cheesecloth. Scrunch up cheesecloth and secure with rubber bands. You should have two pads of potato and green tea in cloth. Place on closed eyes and relax for a few minutes.

Hint: For extra cooling and faster results, chill finished cheesecloth compresses overnight.

Chapter 8

It may have been my imagination, but I could swear Esmeralda was trying to kill me. Stiletto, ever the gentleman, had insisted on cramming his photo equipment and himself into the tight back while I sat in the death seat next to Esmeralda. Neither of us was pleased about that arrangement.

Mama's old race-car boyfriend would have applauded Esmeralda for zipping that bright blue Miata of hers up and down the back streets of Slagville, swerving occasionally toward a tree, lamppost or any convenient utility pole on her right. My palms were so sweaty they left marks on the butter-cream leather.

"So how long have you two kids been working together?" I asked, trying to mask the nervousness in my voice. I was dying to tell Stiletto about my visitor in the woods, but I wasn't eager to involve Esmeralda. She'd want to know why I was near the mine entrance to begin with. And that might tip her off to my simmering blockbuster.

"It hasn't all been work, has it Steve?" Esmeralda flipped down the visor and winked at Stiletto. I counted. Her eyes hadn't been on the road for a good two minutes and we, or I should say I, was headed straight for an oak tree. This is what I meant by the trying to kill me part.

"Might want to steer clear of that tree," Stiletto said.

"Whoops!" Esmeralda yanked the wheel. "Sorry about that, Bubbles."

"No problem," I said, gasping.

Finally, Esmeralda pulled up to the Main Mane. Stiletto

leaped out of the rear seat and opened the door for me—the result of my excellent training.

"I'll just be a minute, Esme," he said.

Esmeralda checked her lipstick like she couldn't give a hoot. But I sensed that deep down she was ticked.

Stiletto escorted me to the door of the salon. "I don't like leaving you, even if you do have Genevieve as a bodyguard." He put his hand to the back of his neck as a reminder. "I got out of your cousin's salon as soon as Genevieve's back was turned. I was afraid that if I didn't she'd club me with a baseball bat."

"Sorry about that. Listen, you know the woods by the Number Nine mine entrance? I was walking through there a few minutes ago and I ran into this guy, a—"

"What were you doing in the woods by the Number Nine mine?" Stiletto asked, curious.

"Uh . . ." Oh, that's right. I kept forgetting. Stiletto was working for the dark side. "Just, um, checking out where the explosion had been."

"*During* the press conference?" Stiletto squinted. "Really?"

Esmeralda beeped the horn. "Come on, lover boy!" she yelled. "If we don't get to the city soon we won't make the party."

"Party?" I asked. "You're leaving me in the hands of a killer because of a party?"

"Just a stupid get-together." Stiletto waved it off. "One of our entertainment reporters is throwing it. Esme wants to go because of all the celebrities and asked if I'd take her since I'd be in town."

I batted my eyelashes. Stiletto cleared his throat and gave it another shot.

"The real reason I've got to go back to New York is because of those damn editors. They're all hopped up about last night. I've got to meet with lawyers and write memos, you know how it is."

Not good enough.

"And then there's my exploded identity to repair," he continued. "I've got no license, no credit cards. Even the key to my apartment was attached to the one in the Jeep, so it's been blown up. I've got a lot of boring ends to tie up. Figured you'd rather stay here, get your car fixed, hang out with your cousin."

What? Stay in a run-down coal town? With someone out to kill me? With my black-leather-wearing Mama and her friend, the Sherman tank with breasts? Eating meat-loaf dinner at four-thirty and watching full-volume *Wheel of Fortune* and going to bed at eight? Yes. I'd much rather be here than at a celebrity party, I thought.

But all I said was, "I see."

"On the bright side," he said, "I talked to the Passion Peak folks. Since your stuff is there and you were nearly killed, they agreed to let you stay tonight for free."

"It won't be much fun alone." All those mirrors. All that cellulite.

"Why don't you invite your mother to stay? She might get a kick out of it."

Esmeralda leaned on the horn again and Stiletto kissed me quickly on the lips. Then he jogged back to Esmeralda's car. The two of them zipped off, Esmeralda's hair shimmering golden red in the breeze and me feeling like Cinderella. Then I thought, my *mother*? Why would I bring my mother to a lovers' hotel?

Instantly depressed, I opened the door to the Main Mane and stopped still. The place was a mess! It reeked of permanent solution and shampoo.

Through the white haze of hairspray, I counted three women on the couch with curlers, foil and caps. Another was dripping in the sink while Roxanne was busily finishing the comb-out on a client so wizened she looked more like a prune than a woman. But what was Genevieve doing at the manicure table with—no, Lord, say it's not true—an orangewood stick in her hand, pushing back some poor client's cuticles with short, sharp thrusts.

"Bubbles! Am I glad to see you!" Roxanne shouted, palming a sweaty frizz of hair from her forehead. She tossed a comb on the pink vanity and yanked the top off a jumbo-sized Final Net, spraying madly. "It's a zoo in here. The phone's been ringing off the hook. Genevieve's offered to do manicures, but I could sure do with another stylist."

"You bring that hunk Stiletto?" Roxanne's client the human prune asked. The three women on the couch lowered their magazines and the one at the sink raised her head.

"No," I said, closing the door. "He's gone back to New York."

"Damn." The prune snapped her fingers. "Darla Wychesko said he was bodacious."

"Oww!" yipped Genevieve's victim. She snatched back her hand and pinched her finger to stop the blood. "That's live skin."

"What do I know? I usually trim 'em with the vegetable peeler." Genevieve sighed and opened the Band-Aid box. "You want Elmo this time?"

Roxanne flew to the cash register and rang up the prune's bill. "I've got to talk to you, Bubbles, before Mrs. Manetti's timer goes off." The cash register binged and the prune handed Roxanne a twenty.

"Is it true what they're saying," Roxanne said, counting out change, "that Stinky's a murder suspect?"

"We should talk alone." I pulled Roxanne into her parlor and closed the door. There I gave her the lowdown from the press conference about how Stinky had been described by authorities as some disgruntled, homicidal ex-employee, and Roxanne started to cry.

"Reporters have been calling all morning. I had to remind myself that you were a reporter and that you were decent and some of them might be decent, too, but they're all bastards. I caught a photographer shooting photos in the front window. Like a Peeping Tom. The thing is that all the attention seems to have brought in business. I'm booked. It's like I'm a one-woman freak show."

I gathered Roxanne in my arms and let her head rest on my shoulder. After rubbing her back, I asked, "Do you remember what you told me this morning about Stinky having a fit over the Number Nine mine maps not being updated?"

She lifted her head and fumbled for a tissue. "You made a pinky promise not to tell."

"I know. But listen, Roxanne, I think you should let me write a story about that, before Stinky is completely discredited. I measured the distance from the Number Nine mine to the Dead Zone and I realized something. Is it possible McMullen was robbing coal from under the Dead Zone, the land Bud Price owned? Vilnia told me that Stinky was fired from McMullen because he discovered something there he wasn't supposed to. This could be it."

"Stinky wasn't fired." She blew her nose. "He quit."

"Details."

"I don't know," she said, sighing. "Let me check the box."

"The box?"

"Where Stinky keeps all his documents and correspondence and maps. You know Stinky. He was a stickler for documentation. I keep it in the guest bedroom dresser."

Holy hell, I thought. Mr. Salvo was going to pee in his pants. He lived for documents.

"I can get it when we get a break."

Mrs. Manetti's timer dinged.

"So you want me to write a story?" I ventured carefully. "A story that could be published tomorrow?"

Roxanne hesitated at the door and was silent for a minute. Then she said, "If it'll help my Stinky, absolutely."

Yes! I pictured Esmeralda boogying the night away with Stiletto and heard Mama's admonition: Slow and steady wins the race. Mama was big on slow and steady, being rather slow—if not always steady—herself.

Roxanne opened the door and Mrs. Manetti, who must have been eavesdropping, fell in. "I wondered when you were going to get to me," she said. "I don't want my hair turning orange."

Roxanne apologized and I dialed Mr. Salvo from the front desk phone as a heavyset woman entered. "I'm here for a makeover. I won the raffle." She handed me a blue raffle ticket from a Ladies Auxiliary fundraiser. "Louise Lamporini."

I glanced down at the scrawl on the appointment book. Sure enough. Louise Lamporini at one.

Mr. Salvo picked up the phone on his end. "Salvo," I heard in my ear.

I looked pleadingly over to Roxanne, who pointed to the other women on the couch and shrugged. "No way," she said. "It'll take me forty-five minutes to get to Louise. I'm way behind schedule."

"Uhh, can you wait," I said into the phone.

"That's not acceptable," Louise said, folding her large arms. Despite her extra weight, she was a striking woman. Strong, not fluffy. "I've got to get back to work."

"Who is this?" Mr. Salvo asked.

"It's Bubbles. I've got a hell of a story." I turned back to Louise. "I can do the basics. Foundation through eye shadow and a bang trim."

"Aww Christ." It irked Mr. Salvo when my other life as a hairdresser intruded. "Don't tell me you're doing that girlie stuff."

Louise glanced at her watch. "Okay. But we have to do it fast. I've got to be back at my desk in a half hour."

"I don't have time for this," Mr. Salvo said. "Call me back."

"Hold on." I led Louise over to an empty chair. Roxanne pulled open a drawer to reveal the makeup supplies. "You want bold or neutral?" I asked.

"What?" Mr. Salvo said.

"Not you. I'm doing a makeover."

"Neutral," Louise said. "I'm at work, remember?"

I pinned Louise's hair back and began to dab her face with a cotton ball to clean it. "You hear about what happened to me?"

"What happened to you?" Louise asked.

"Yeah, I heard," said Mr. Salvo. "A little tip? If I ever send you on assignment, it will never be by fax. I've been in this business for over twenty years and I never, not once, heard of an editor sending a reporter to cover a story by fax. What were you thinking?"

"So glad to know you're safe and sound, Bubbles," I said, shaking out foundation onto my fingertip. "What a horrible ordeal you went through."

"Oh, don't start with the guilt trip. I've left dozens of messages on your answering machine at home, making sure you were okay. So what's the big story?"

As I blended in the foundation lines, I filled in Mr. Salvo about the press conference and the documents Roxanne reportedly possessed. By the time I was finished, I had applied a transparent brown lipstick and mentally written the lead to the story.

"Wow," Louise said, examining herself in the mirror. "I want that lipstick."

"Next week. You can work on that story next week," Mr. Salvo said. "In the meantime, I want to inform you of a change in the schedule. You're on for Sunday day shift. I'm thinking of sending you to the Catasauqua Republicans' annual barbeque."

"What?"

"This lipstick," Louise said, holding up the tube. "I want it. How much?"

Roxanne, aware of my growing desperation, came to the rescue and led Louise over to the makeup counter. I focused my attention on Mr. Salvo.

"You're not going to tell me this story is out of our circulation area, are you?"

"No," he said. "Lehigh Steel has a historical connection to McMullen Coal and the other coal companies in that area. Hell, the Lehigh Valley Railroad physically connects the two. Our readers will definitely be interested in what you've got. Just not tomorrow."

This man was becoming impossible. Almost as bad as his evil boss, Dix Notch. "But we could run an exclusive proving that Carl Koolball was a bona fide whistleblower who is now being smeared by McMullen Coal who may have been robbing coal to avoid state oversight. Are you telling me you don't want that?"

Mr. Salvo sighed. "What I want, Yablonsky, is two more editors on the night desk. As it is, it's just me and Griffin tonight to handle three school board meetings and a profile that's as thick as mud on the mayoral candidates. I'll be damned if I have to unravel some overly complicated forty-inch saga you call in to Cora at the last minute."

I was silent. Fuming.

"Besides," he added, "Thursday is poker night. I missed last week and I told the guys I'd get there by eleven."

I spoke evenly into the phone. "Okay. So I was trapped in a mine, nearly blown up, and I don't get to write anything about that because you have to play cards."

"You can write a first-person account of the experience. Six inches only. We'll box it and run it as a column next to the AP story. Esmeralda Greene's a seasoned reporter. I'm sure her piece will be as airtight as all her stuff is."

Air wasn't all that was tight in Esmeralda Greene.

"Don't be too disappointed, Bubbles." Mr. Salvo's tone softened. "Just bring your notes and those documents your cousin supposedly has to the newsroom next week and we'll go over them together. See if there's credible material. Then we'll present them to Dix Notch and hear what he has to say. That way we won't encounter the same legal problems we came across when you wrote that Metzger story. As you know, if we get sued again, I'm out of a job. This time for good."

That Metzger story was only the most riveting piece of journalism the *News-Times* had run since it uncovered the ten most dangerous intersections in Lehigh the year before. And it wasn't my fault that Mr. Salvo's job security was sketchy. That he had brought on himself.

Still, seeing as how preppy managing editor Dix Notch was my sworn enemy, I didn't hold out hope that he'd be game to give me another go at investigative reporting. Even if this time I did have notes.

Already I was scheming. "Did you say Cora was on rewrite tonight?"

"Good old Careless Cora. So speak slowly and clearly. Otherwise she'll just screw it up."

Perfect.

Roxanne didn't realize the wealth hidden in her guest room undies drawer. Stinky, ever the meticulous geek, had retained every letter and memo on the subject of McMullen's coal robbing. There were two maps that he must have copied and sent to his superiors showing where coal had actually been removed. Since the maps were intended for those without degrees in geographical cartography from Carnegie Mellon, even I could understand them.

I was right. McMullen Coal had been violating federal and state regulations by entering the Number Nine mine and digging into the Dead Zone, possibly by as much as two-hundred-and-fifty feet. Stinky wrote in the letters that, although it was not his job to determine why the company had done this, he speculated that perhaps McMullen Coal did not want to wade through the lengthy regulatory process to receive approval to lift the mining ban. A process, he noted, that could take as long as ten years.

At the bottom, hidden underneath a collection of pink phone slips, was a letter to Stinky from Craig Sommerville of the State Bureau of Deep Mine Safety. It opened with Sommerville commenting on their long working relationship and his professional respect for Stinky, whom he called Carl, of course. He went on to thank Stinky for the letters and maps, which he had forwarded to his colleagues on the federal side. He added that he was planning on making a surprise state inspection of the Number Nine mine. This week.

Pay dirt. I dialed the number on the letterhead and got Craig on the second ring. Even though he was only a state bureaucrat, I was so excited to get hold of him he might as well have been Eddie Van Zandt. It was like a journalist's fairy tale come true.

I identified myself as a reporter and told him that I had his let-

ter in my hand, along with other documentation collected by
Stinky indicating that McMullen had been—I stopped myself
from using the inflammatory words "robbing coal."

". . . had extended its digging beyond the area of its permits."
There. That sounded innocuous enough.

Sommerville didn't say anything. I heard him flipping through
a Rolodex. "Here's the number for our public relations department—"

I was prepared for this dismissal. "The public relations department will tell me that they can't comment, which won't help
Carl Koolball. I just returned from a press conference where
Hugh McMullen himself publicly described Carl as a loose can-
non who was a danger to other employees and a likely murder
suspect."

"Jesus Christ." Sommerville sounded genuinely shocked. "I
had no idea."

I waited. Please, oh please talk. Say anything.

"Write this down," Sommerville said, new determination in
his voice. "Carl Koolball is one of the most thorough engineers
I've worked with in my twenty-two years on the job. He consid-
ers the safety of the miners and the environmental consequences
of mining above all. I spoke to him the day before Bud Price's
murder and he seemed perfectly reasonable to me."

It wasn't getting me what I needed. "To convince my editors
that Carl's concerns about the, uhm, overextension are valid, it
would help if you could, as a state inspector, validate them. Of
course, if you haven't visited the Number Nine—."

"I made a state inspection yesterday," he said. "And I have the
violation letter in my computer. McMullen Coal Inc. faces at
least one hundred thousand dollars in state fines alone and a possible shutdown for digging three hundred feet into the so-called
Dead Zone. I can fax you a copy if you want."

"You can do that?"

"I've apprised all the owners by telephone, why not? It's public record."

"Thanks," I said. "Hold on." I called over to Roxanne, who was smoking a cigarette and flipping through *Woman's World.* "You know of a fax machine anywhere?"

"Down at the stationery store." Roxy checked her watch. "But you better hurry. They close at five." She looked up the phone number, wrote it down and slid it to me.

I got back on and gave him the number. "We've got twenty minutes."

"Will do," Craig said. "By the way. You running this tomorrow?"

I told him I was, though the paper didn't know it yet.

Sommerville laughed. "Bubbles Yablonsky, huh? That's a name I won't soon forget. More ways than one, I expect."

A half hour later I had a copy of Sommerville's letter and a call in to McMullen Coal. As the company had closed at five, no one was available to speak with me. So I left a message for head honcho Hugh McMullen at The Inn in nearby Glen Ellen, a ritzy tourist town about thirty miles away. Roxanne had taken a stab that he might be there and she was right. Then again, did she expect him to be staying at the Red Roof?

Once I identified myself as a reporter, the inn's front desk clerk went icy cold.

"Don't you want to leave a message for Chrissy Price, too? Reporters have been calling all day for her."

"She's there?"

"Yes. But she won't talk to you. She's not taking any calls from the press."

Then why did he bring up her name?

"Put my name down, anyway, why dontcha," I said. "I'm feeling lucky."

As it turned out, I was anything but.

Chapter 9

Cora Rittenhouse answered the phone like I'd roused her from a deep sleep. "Rewrite," she droned. I pictured Cora at her *News-Times* desk—one hand in the bag of microwave popcorn, one hand on the keyboard and both eyes on the muted TV. One spongy brain on permanent vacation.

"Hi, it's me, Bubbles," I said with enough energy to be contagious. "I've got two stories for you. A six inch and a twenty-five."

"Ugh. You correspondents. So verbose," Cora said. "Give me the twenty-fiver first. Slug?"

The slug was what appeared in the night editor's computerized directory to identify a story. Had Mr. Salvo given me permission to write what I wanted, it would have been slugged something like McMullen.doc or coal.doc. Instead I slugged it—

"PMS." That should slip the attention of the average male editor.

"Huh?" Cora's fingers were tapping away on the other end. "You writing for the women's pages now?"

"Hmmm. Not quite. Ready?"

"Guess so."

I slowly and carefully read my story about how Stinky had been fired after persistently urging McMullen Coal to draw its maps correctly and how Hugh McMullen had then publicly painted him as a lunatic the day after a state inspector visited the Number Nine mine at Stinky's urging. It was good. At the last minute I'd managed to contact a United Mine Workers spokesman who provided a scathing quote about McMullen Coal Inc. being comfortable with putting miners' lives at risk just to avoid the tedium of regulation.

"Doesn't sound like it has much to do with PMS to me," Cora said when I was done.

"You ever meet an angry coal mining union boss?"

"See what you mean. What's the next story?"

The next story was the wimpy personal account of being trapped in the mine explosion. It was slugged coalmine.doc. As I read it over to Cora, Mama was in the next room shouting out incorrect answers to *Jeopardy!*—her "intellectual" moment of the day.

"What is toilet tissue?" screamed Mama, as though Alec Trebek could hear her.

"I'm sorry," Alec said. "The correct answer is, What is the capital of Tunisia?"

"Damn. Close, though."

Cora finished and I said good-bye and thanks. She asked if I wanted to speak to Mr. Salvo, but I said I needed to get my mother and her friend down to the Pocono Passion Peak Resort by their bedtime.

"Whatever flips their switch," she said. "Not my bag, but if that's what your mother and her friend are into, it's cool."

I hung up and turned to find Mama slipping into her black leather jacket. "I sure hope they got a decent bath at the Passion Peak," she said. "My bunions need a good soak after being in these boots all day."

Genevieve was right behind her, reloading the peashooter with refreshed Sominex darts.

"You're not bringing that, are you?" I said.

"Civilians," she snorted. "Always convinced they're out of range." She tucked the peashooter in her purse and pulled out a quarter. "Hey, I can use this in the auto massage at the Passion Peak. My back sure is sore after dragging your Stiletto around."

It was going to be a long, long night.

The first thing I did upon arriving at our scarlet suite at the Passion Peak was to put in a call to Jane. No luck. Since an inexplicable twist of genetics had rendered it impossible for me to comprehend how to check my messages on the answering machine remotely, I couldn't tell if she had left one.

I called Dan and Wendy, too, but they were out. I'd forgotten. Thursday night was their weekly marriage encounter session, which, as far as I could determine, required Dan to apologize to Wendy for forty-five minutes straight. Fine by me.

Still, I was worried about my daughter. It was not like her not to call. Jane's hair may be multicolored, her clothes tattered and grungy, but she was the most upfront, smart and loving kid around. She had never fallen into that snotty teenage girl routine. Personally, I had my doubts about whether most girls did— contrary to what TV would have you believe.

"Now what kind of bathtub is this, Genny?" Mama said, surveying the human-size champagne glass Jacuzzi. "How am I supposed to get in that?"

"Ladder." Genevieve lay on the bed, her mounded belly jiggling like a Jell-O centerpiece. "I could get used to this. It's orthopedic."

"Ortho-obscene is more like it." Mama cocked her chin at me. "This what Stiletto and you do in your spare time, Bubbles?"

We should be so lucky. I tried home again with no luck. "Where's Jane? I haven't spoken to her since jail."

"Wonder how many mothers get to say that?" Mama asked, stripping off her black leather and turning on the tub. "Well, here goes nothing."

Three hours later, Mama and Genevieve were sacked out on the red bed, while I, fully dressed, tossed and turned on the couch, constantly checking the digital clock and trying not to fall asleep. At eleven-fifteen I snuck out of the room and ran downstairs to the pay phone where I put in a toll-free call to the *News-Times* night desk.

"Griffin," answered Bob Griffin, the assistant night editor.

"Hi, this is Bubbles. Is Mr. Salvo there still?"

"Just left. But he edited your story. It's fine."

I paused for effect. "Story? Don't you mean *stories?* I filed two. A personal account of being trapped in the mine and a twenty-five inch piece on violations against McMullen Coal."

"Two? We don't even have space for twenty-five inches. Yours is supposed to run as a sidebar to the AP piece."

"I don't think so. It's supposed to run in place of the AP piece. Check the directory. I called it in around seven-thirty."

I waited nervously while Griffin checked the directory. "All that's here that's not edited is something slugged PMS. Careless Cora must have sent it to the wrong cue. I'll bounce it over to lifestyle."

"Why don't you open it just to make sure?" I tried to sound efficient.

Griffin opened it and read. "Yup. Guess that looks like your story. Geesh. That Cora. I'm gonna go over and ream her out. This is inexcusable."

"Don't do that, Bob. She probably has PMS and it was on her mind. Unless, of course, you'd like to listen to her cry about cramps and bloating and—"

"No, no, no. That's okay," he said quickly. "So, back to this story. Salvo wanted to run it in place of the AP, you sure?"

"Pretty sure."

He sighed. "Okay. Christ I wish he'd drop poker night. I'm all alone here. You know, one of these Thursdays something bad is gonna happen, some story's gonna get past me that's not supposed to, and I'm gonna get the flak."

"Don't worry," I said. "Tonight is not one of those nights. Trust me. This story is supposed to be in tomorrow's paper."

As I predicted, the phone began ringing shortly after 7 A.M. I lay on the foldout and let it, wagering mentally on who was calling. Mr. Salvo? Dix Notch? Stiletto? Unlikely since he had been up until all hours, probably, partying with Esmeralda Greene. Or maybe—

I snatched up the phone. "Hello?"

"Hey, Mom. Guess what?"

Jane.

"Where were you last night?" I said. "I called and called and there was no answer."

"Oh, it was sooo cool. You know Professor Tallow who's teaching my Local Celtic History course at Lehigh? The one who's leading the dig we've been working on?"

No. But that was okay. Jane didn't wait for my answer.

"He wore this head-to-toe shroud like a real Druid and led a midnight moonlight vigil around the rocks we found in the woods. It was awesome."

"Rocks?"

"Yeah. They're ancient Celtic. Baal and all that."

I didn't know what to say. It sounded *Star Trek*-ese.

"Like Stonehenge," Jane added.

"Oh."

"Anyway, I just wanted to ask if I can go back to the dig this morning. I have a couple of classes at Liberty High, gym and Latin, but I'm already through the Ovid due for next month, so is it okay if I miss them?"

Jane was most likely the only senior at Liberty who asked her mother if it was okay to skip school—and not to head over to the Delaware Water Gap or smoke pot behind the Hill to Hill, either.

"Fine by me. Anybody call this morning about my story?"

"That's how come I woke up so early. Salvo and that moron Notch called around five. Notch was bitching so loud I couldn't even make out what he was saying, so you must have done something right."

I rubbed my forehead. God, I hoped the risk I took was worth it. I'd never live with myself if Griffin, Cora and Salvo lost their jobs over this.

"There was one guy who phoned to say he really liked it, though."

"There was?" I sat up straight.

"Yeah, although he said you missed a really crucial point."

I despise nitpickers. "What crucial point?"

"I don't know. He said he's gonna stop by later this morning to explain it to you. But he doesn't want you to tell cousin Roxanne that, since he's in hiding."

I rolled off the couch. "Ohmigod. Stinky."

Chapter 10

While Mama and Genevieve hit the Morning After Breakfast Buffet downstairs, I took a shower, toweled off and stepped into a pair of black stirrup pants, a fuchsia top in a polyester/spandex blend and boots with heels. Lined my eyes with navy and enhanced my lashes with cobalt mascara. Next came foundation. Powder. Rose blush. A touch of orchid in the creases of my lids and matching color on my lips. Hung my head upside down and blew my hair dry, brushing it up so it cascaded down with body. Spritzed apple blossom spray from head to toe and added a few dabs of glitter powder.

Ready for another day of professional investigative journalism.

I packed all of my things and placed them by the door. I took a tray with a croissant and coffee Mama had brought up for me and called Roxanne to tell her that Stinky had called to say he'd be stopping by my home and I would be rushing back to Lehigh to meet him. The way I rationalized it, I hadn't made a pinky promise with Stinky not to tell and, besides, Roxanne needed to know that her husband was alive. Cousins who sneak into Journey concerts together don't keep that kind of info to themselves.

"I'm going back to Lehigh with you," she said as soon as I told her. "I have to see him and apologize. Stinky needs my support."

"No way, Roxy. Give him his space." I finished the buttery almond croissant and wiped my fingers on a paper napkin. "He may be staying away from you for other reasons."

"Like what? Deep down he adores me."

"Like your safety. Price was shot and left in a mine at the same spot and hour Stinky's car was there. Maybe the shooter meant to get Stinky, too?"

"My Stinky? No way. Everyone loves the Stinkster."

What was she, dreaming? Chief Donohue freely referred to Stinky as a blackmailing, homicidal vigilante, and from the way Hugh McMullen spoke at the press conference yesterday, Stinky might as well have been Charles Manson on a walkaway. "Think of what went down at the press conference, Roxanne. Stinky's a wanted man."

Roxanne exhaled from a cigarette. "Yeah. And no one wants him more than me."

On the off chance that the alternator was in, Genevieve dropped Mama off at Roxanne's and drove me back to the Texaco.

"It didn't come," squeaked the clerk. "Slagville must be last on the list in Detroit because it always takes us three weeks to get parts."

Three weeks! I could not live without my Camaro for three weeks. I'd lose my parking space on West Goepp Street.

Genevieve stomped forward and pounded the front counter so hard the cash register drawer opened. "Do you mean to tell me, Butch, that this girl is gonna have to wait three weeks for her car?"

The clerk gulped and quietly shut the drawer. "No, ma'am. Just that I fixed it myself, without the part."

And there wasn't a drop of oil on him. He slid a handwritten bill carefully past Genevieve and toward me. "That'll be twenty-five-ninety-nine. Sorry it's so expensive. There was a lot of labor."

I nearly kissed the blue pressed hanky in his breast pocket. Stiletto could make all the cracks he wanted about this place being stuck in time, but I did so like those 1935 prices. I wrote out a check, handed it to him and he sprinted out the door. He pulled the Camaro around to the front of the station and shifted the clutch into neutral, making sure to pull the seat forward be-

fore he got out. Cheap and considerate, too. It was even vac-
uumed and was that Windex on the dashboard I smelled?

"*Hasta la vista*, Genevieve," I said, revving the engine.

"Take the back roads. I don't like trucks," she said, waddling
toward her car. "And don't go over the speed limit. I ain't no law
breaker."

Hold on. Hold on. I leaned out the window and glared at her.
Genevieve was pulling out a musket from the backseat of her
Rambler and coming toward me.

"What are you doing?"

"Leaving the Rambler here for your mother," she said, opening my passenger-side door. "The Texaco's only a block away
from the Main Mane. She's got a spare key."

Genevieve heaved herself inside and slammed the door.
"What are you wasting gas for? Let's go."

"But?"

"You don't think I'd let you go back to Lehigh to meet up with
Stinky Koolball without a bodyguard, do you?" She patted the
musket that lay across her lap. "On the drive down I'll bring you
up to date on the Princess Diana crash investigation. Oh, and
there's also some new research out about Crest you should be
aware of. It could save your life."

Genevieve spent the next half hour explaining the imagined
evils of fluoride toothpaste and how Princess Diana had been
murdered by the powerful French cheese lobby. After wowing
me with Nostradamus's prediction of MTV, Genevieve revealed
that her bladder was not nearly as big as her mouth and she
needed a rest stop. That was doubly bad as we were on a wooded
back road in Nowheresville.

"Fiddlecock," Genevieve said, as I pulled onto the berm. "I'll
have to hike in."

Taking no chances, she slung the musket over her shoulder,
plunked on her camouflage cap, and produced a roll of Charmin
from her purse. Before she left, she pressed into my hand a
peashooter filled with Sominex darts.

"Don't be afraid to use it." She locked the door and left.

I placed the straw on the dash, zipped open a nail kit from my purse and began filing to keep the right brain occupied so the left brain could take a quick nap. That's when I noticed flashing lights in the rearview and saw a dark vehicle park at an angle behind me. Great. Just what I needed right now, a cop checking to see if the car had broken down. And me here with a Sominex peashooter on the dash.

The cop, wearing mirrored shades, stepped up to the passenger's side and motioned for me to roll down the window. I leaned over and rolled it down halfway.

"Problem?" he asked, zeroing in on the peashooter.

"No, no, officer," I stammered. "My friend just had to answer the call of nature. She's an older woman."

The cop stuck his hand through the crack in the window and yanked up the lock, opened the door and slid inside. As soon as he was next to me, I recognized him right off. He was about ten years younger than I, with all the muscle and confidence that youth bragged. Underneath his jeans and navy T-shirt was a gym-toned muscular body topped by a mop of windswept hair. Ash blond number six to be exact.

He wasn't a cop. He was the guy from the woods.

"Wha—?" My nail file shook. "Please, don't—"

"Aww, don't get hysterical or nothing." He removed his mirrored shades. Brown eyes. "I'm not here to hurt you. I guess I scared you back there by the Number Nine mine yesterday. Sorry."

Sunlight through the windshield glinted off the gun in his belt and I blanched.

"By the way," he said, "a woman should never roll down her window for a stranger. You never know who'll take advantage." He smiled wide.

Okay, it had finally happened. I was having my psychopathic encounter, just like the type you read about in *Redbook*. After all those years of being on high alert in poorly lit parking lots and back alleys, I'd been cornered. Cornered on a deserted country road miles from any sign of civilization. Without my keychain Mace or trusty travel-sized bottle of Final Net.

Deep breaths, Bubbles. Get your perfectly manicured fingers around that peashooter.

"You said you were a cop." I casually slid my hand up the dash, toward the African-style weaponry.

"I never said I was a cop. You assumed I was a cop." He leaned forward and pulled out the baseball cap from his back pocket, positioning it on his head and inspecting himself in the rearview.

"You have flashing lights."

"Nineteen ninety-nine at Wal-Mart. Anyone can buy 'em and stick 'em on their roof. All around America psychos are driving with those lights, cruising for unsuspecting women to do unspeakable things to. You should thank your lucky stars I'm not one of those."

My hand clutched the peashooter.

"Cut that out." He brushed it out of my hand. "What do I look like, a caribou?"

I stared at the broken peashooter lying on my shift case.

"I should introduce myself." He extended his hand, the good-sized, tanned hand of a man who hadn't spent his life in an office. I surprised myself by shaking it. "Ezekiel Allen," he said. "Like the Green Mountain Boys. Though I prefer Zeke."

"Green Mountain Boys? You're a Boy Scout?" I asked, relieved.

He slapped his forehead. "No, I'm the descendant of Ira Allen, who, although, yes, ended his life in jail, was nevertheless a patriot like his brother Ethan in Vermont. Few people are aware that the eight Allen brothers were a gnarly bunch of vigilantes until the Revolutionary War came and turned them into heroes."

"I can't believe it. You broke into my car to give me a history lesson. Is that why you tracked me into the woods, too?"

"No, way. I broke into your car to introduce myself. I'm your new bodyguard. Howdy do?" He touched the brim of his hat like a gentleman. "I would have told you so yesterday, but I was trying to be incognito. I'm kind of new at this Secret Service stuff."

"I already have a bodyguard."

"So I gather. Seventy-year-old woman with a peashooter. Little good that will do you." He nodded to the incapacitated straw. "My employer requested a more virile protector, you might say."

"Who's your employer?"

"Steve Stiletto."

I coughed. Stiletto? He hired someone to keep watch over me while he was in New York? That was so sweet. Wait. No, it wasn't. That was patronizing. "I don't need looking after," I said, bristling. "I'm not a dog, you know."

"So I've noticed." Zeke turned on the ignition to activate the battery and started fooling around with the knobs on the radio. "Let's see if we can find some Skynyrd. Rumor is Skynyrd makes you do crazy things."

"Only when there are Jell-O shots."

"I'll call Mom. Mom always has Jell-O and vodka on hand."

We were silent for a while as he searched the airwaves. "How do you know Stiletto?" I asked.

"Complicated story." He zeroed in on an easy-listening music station in Hazelton. "Let's just say if it hadn't been for Steve, I'd be in Mexico for a permanent vacation. And I ain't talking the Cancun Hilton."

Karen Carpenter came on and Zeke turned it up. "That's better. I hope you like the Carpenters because we'll be listening to a lot of them. So tragic what happened, with her not eating and all." He folded his arms behind his head, slouched down on the seat and leaned back. I stared at him in disbelief. Guy impersonates a cop and breaks into my car just to play the radio?

Where was that Genevieve? I rolled down the window. Not a sign.

"That was the toughest part about being in the Cerro Huerro jail. No Carpenters. No Pat or Debby Boone either. She really lights up my life, man. Gosh dang, but she's a good singer."

"Jail? You're a criminal!"

"Please. Criminal has such negative connotations. The better term is unreformed miscreant." He bobbed his head to the beat of "On Top of the World." I couldn't believe Stiletto had hired a former criminal to keep tabs on me. Probably came cheap.

"I don't like convicts in my car," I said after Karen stopped looking down on creation. "I try to avoid people who've been in the slammer, even if they are friends with Stiletto."

"Don't worry. I didn't get raped or nothing, if that's what you're worried about."

"I want you out now," I said. The fear was starting to wear off and irritation was taking its place.

"Really?" Zeke cracked his gum and thought about this. "What I want is world peace, a crisp Macintosh apple and unity with God. Okay, your turn."

From way far away there came a hearty whistling. "She'll Be Coming Around the Mountain." Perfect. Let Genevieve discover the Green Mountain Boy in her seat. She'd flatten his peaks.

"Okay. Let's say you are my backup bodyguard. Who, exactly, are you protecting me from?"

"I'm not crazy about that term, backup. But I'll let it slide." He turned down the radio, which had moved on to Barbara Streisand. "How to explain." He tapped his forefinger against his lip. "You know that story you wrote about McMullen Coal that ran in this morning's paper?"

"Yessss," I said slowly.

"And you know your ass?"

"Uh-huh." Not sure where this was going.

"Well, after that story, it's grass. Accusing a company of robbing coal is tantamount to signing your own death warrant in this part of Pennsylvania. We're not known for our doilies and afternoon tea, you know. This is the land of the Molly Maguires."

"Molly Maguire sounds like doilies and afternoon tea to me."

"I can't believe you don't know about the Green Mountain Boys or the Molly Maguires. Did you learn anything in high school?"

"How to dye my hair with peroxide and roll cigarettes. That's about it."

"For your information, the Molly Maguires were a group of Irish-American coal miners from this anthracite region who took up violent action in the 1860s when their working conditions became intolerable. Initially they were written up in history books as a secret terrorist organization and were blamed for committing a series of murders, for which a bunch of Molly Maguires were hanged. In recent years, though, historians have considered that maybe they were fighting the corrupt coal owners and their private police force. They were the nascent stage of America's labor movement."

"And this relates to my grass ass how?"

"Gum?" He held out a packet of Trident. I took a piece. "Thanks."

"Your ass is grass because coal country once was rougher than the wild, wild west, Bubbles. Being born and raised next to the anthracite fields, I can tell you that attitudes haven't changed much since 1860. Some people in town are of the opinion that arson, assault and murder are the only ways to get results."

"I see." I chewed the gum. "Even before I wrote that story, someone had been set up to kill me, you know. Me and Stiletto."

"Heard all about it. Got any idea who your enemy is?"

I shook my head. "Haven't a clue. Two days ago, the biggest worry on my mind was whether or not it was right for me to sleep. . . ." I stopped myself. This guy, whoever he was, didn't require knowledge of my private sex life. As opposed to a public sex life. "Anyway, two days ago I was under the impression I didn't have an enemy in the world."

Zeke shifted in the seat and stared out the front window. He had an impressive jaw line. I could picture him as a Revolutionary War patriot like his ancestors, shooting redcoats from behind rock walls. "This isn't a bad perm we're talking about or a dissatisfied client with an uneven trim," he said. "This is serious."

"I've seen some pretty bad perms." I folded my arms. "For your information, they're serious."

Boom! Clank!

"What the . . . ?" Zeke was out of the car lickety-split. "Holy . . . !" He hit the ground as another musket ball came flying where his head had been.

"I'll give you to the count of five to get into your vehicle and return to the cave you crawled out of," Genevieve hollered.

I stuck my head out the window. Zeke was slowly standing from his crouch, his arms high in the air.

"Okay. Don't shoot," he said. "Put the gun down, Genevieve."

Genevieve lifted the musket and put her eye to the sight. "I'll put the gun down when I'm damn good and ready."

"Some bodyguard," I said. "Can't even take an old lady with an antique."

"Did you see what that antique did to my truck?" He pointed to a deep dent on the front hood of his Ford F150. "That's body work. That's gonna cost me."

"I know a good mechanic," I said.

Genevieve was pounding down another musket ball. "This ain't the time to lolly about, boy. I'd move if I was you."

Boom! Whissshhhh. Another ball took out his front tire.

"Oh, man!" Zeke jogged toward his car with the musket trained on his butt. Genevieve refused to let up. He knelt down and inspected the damage. "It's flat!"

She lowered the musket. "That'll do ya, then."

When she stepped into the Camaro, she laid the musket in the backseat and patted my knee. "You okay, Sally?" Genevieve had a habit of calling all girls Sally and all boys Butch.

"Yes," I said, starting up the car, "though it kind of freaked me out."

Genevieve checked out Zeke in the rearview. "Who was that jerk?"

"A friend of Stiletto's. Stiletto sent him to look after me. For my safety."

"What for, when you got me?"

I gunned it down the road, to get away from Zeke as fast as I could. "You know men."

"No. Not really." Genevieve scowled. "But I know snakes. And, if you ask me, Stiletto sent that fella to spy on you while he's in New York dancing with Miss Fancy Pants. He wants to make sure you don't beat him on that story you two are racing each other for."

I hadn't thought of that. Granted, Genevieve saw conspiracies in toothpaste and municipal tap water, but she might have been right about this one.

"What should I do?"

"We'll think up a plan," Genevieve said, checking the rearview. "By the time you get home, you'll come up with something."

But by the time I dropped off Genevieve at her apartment and drove over to my own house, only one thing was clear. Namely, my smart and capable daughter Jane had been kidnapped.

Chapter 11

"**L**ook at this place, Mickey, it's a mess," I cried, picking up a couch cushion from the floor. "Jane's purse is on the kitchen counter, but she's gone. Oh, if I hadn't gone up to the Passion Peak to be with Stiletto Wednesday, this wouldn't have happened." The Lithuanian came out in me. I beat my chest like a crazed peasant. "What a lousy, selfish mother I am."

"You're a kind and loving mother, Bubbles," Mickey said calmly. "A selfish mother is one who abandons her children to seek a life without responsibility."

Lehigh Police Detective Mickey Sinkler spoke from experience. His wife had left him with a passel of kids, including a five-year-old still in diapers and a juvenile delinquent. But he had managed okay, transforming his string-bean body into a figure of steel and ordering his wife home to take care of the brood. Strutting around my wrecked living room, his leather belt crackling as he walked, Mickey was the model of leadership.

"Everything will work out just fine," he said. "Leave it to local law enforcement. We'll find her."

"I can't sit around twiddling my thumbs, Mickey. I've already called all her friends, the university, the high school, the ice cream shop, the library, even her boyfriend's father. Not a word," I said. "And my house . . ." Chairs were overturned. Paper was strewn about. There was even a rip in the plastic couch covering.

"Definitely not a break-in. Looks like the morning after your typical teenage party to me," Mickey said. "Take it from the father of a kid in juvie hall."

Juvie hall. That was reassuring. "Jane doesn't throw parties like these. At Jane's parties kids sit around playing these mathematical card games." I began to cry. "Something bad has happened. She's been kidnapped. Maybe the person who tried to kill me Wednesday took her."

"Who tried to kill you?" Mickey asked, alarmed. "I thought you said you were with Stiletto Wednesday at the Passion Peak."

"Didn't you read this morning's *News-Times?*" I asked.

"You know I only read sports."

I ignored the insult and told him the whole story of the fax, Price's body and the explosion. That Stinky's car was at the Number Nine mine during Price's murder and that Stinky was supposed to meet me here, at my home, this morning when Jane went missing, were not suspicious coincidences lost on me. I considered mentioning this to Mickey, but decided not to. Not just yet.

Mickey pulled me to him. "Jane's a smart cookie," he said, stroking my hair. "I'll call the department and spread the word. We'll have her back by lunch. Promise."

The door burst open and my ex, Dan the Man, entered in his usual morning golf attire—baby blue polo shirt, plaid pants and white shoes. Wendy, his cheeseball heiress wife, trotted in right behind him, her white tennis outfit hanging off her pretzel-stick body.

"Oh great. Super." Dan threw up his hands. "My daughter's missing and Bubbles is making out with Boy Wonder."

Mickey broke away from me to stand up to Dan. "Who you calling Boy Wonder?"

"Take it easy, Sinkler," Dan said, holding up his hands. "I don't want to have to file a police brutality action against you."

"Now, Chip," Wendy said, "let's focus on why we're here. Oh my." She lifted a T-shirt that had been slung over a mirror. "Looks like it was quite a night."

"What the hell happened?" Dan paced through the living room. "Jane hold a kegger or what?"

"I'm guessing Jane's been kidnapped after leaving your place," I said. "She must have put up quite a fight."

"Kidnapped!" Wendy gasped and Dan went pale.

"This is your fault," he said, pointing at me. "You and your stupid, worthless reporting. I read those stories you wrote this morning. They were crap. Crap stories that got our daughter snatched."

My cheeks burned. This was not what I needed right now. Mickey put a comforting hand on my shoulder.

"What if the kidnapper is after our money?" Wendy exclaimed. "What'll we do?"

"I don't have money to burn," Dan said. "Wendy's got all the money. It's not fair if the kidnappers hit her up just because they think I'm rich."

I was appalled. "Daniel Ritter. You should be ashamed of yourself."

"Chip! The name's Chip! How many gosh darn times do I have to remind you?" Dan, ahem, Chip's face was turning bright red. "Chip. Chip. Chip."

"That's even worse!" I screamed. "First you whine about paying a ransom, then you throw a temper tantrum because I didn't call you by your fake name."

Mickey stepped between us. "Cool it, you two. You're not helping matters by getting angry. This is your daughter we're talking about."

Exactly. I threw a dirty look at Wendy, who appeared to be calculating how much she could spare for the kidnappers and still afford a weekly facial at Helene's.

"My experience as a police officer is that it's never quite what it appears," Mickey said. "Frankly, the parents often imagine the worst. Forget that the house is torn apart, Bubbles. If you had come home and found everything in order and Jane gone, where would you have assumed she went?"

I studied my purple nails and recalled my last conversation

with her. Before she mentioned Stinky she spoke about going back to the dig.

"The dig," I said, snapping to. "It's a university class project at this farm in Emmaus. Maybe she got a ride."

"Digging for what?"

"Celtic rocks," I said, adding Jane's explainer, "like Stonehenge."

"Hippie love fest is what it is," Dan said. "Unwashed pagan punks staying up all night getting high and howling at the moon."

For the first time ever, Wendy leaped to Jane's defense. "Don't dismiss the rocks offhand, Chip. My crystal instructor is a staunch believer in the Celtic origins of this area. Do you know that those stones are aligned to the winter and summer solstices?"

Dan jerked a thumb at his wife. "Crystal instructor. Charges my wife fifty bucks a week to look through a piece of glass. I'll tell that instructor where he can shove his—"

Mickey opened the door. "Why don't we all go out to the dig. We'll find Jane and then everybody can relax."

"You can relax," Dan said. "I've got a tee time in thirty minutes with Fast Putt Herrick. How'd you like to be up against a two handicap in my state of mind?"

If Jane hadn't been kidnapped, she'd have vanished from pure mortification when she saw our caravan enter the farmer's field where the dig was underway. I led the pack in my rusted, two-toned Camaro, followed by Dan in Wendy's expensive midlife crisis special—an apple red BMW roadster—and Mickey in his Lehigh PD cruiser.

The cruiser caused an especially big stir among the muddy and energetic college students who were digging deep trenches in the field with shovels and picks. I assumed they were taking advantage of the morning's cooler hours to do the hard labor.

From the quick way the fog was burning off, it was shaping up to be another bright blue Indian summer day.

Neither Jane nor her boyfriend, G, was anywhere in sight.

"The fuzz!" shouted one kid, bare-chested except for a white line of puka beads around his neck. "Don't tell me it's a permit issue again."

Mickey slammed the door of his cruiser and strutted over to the edge of the pit. He stared down at the young, sweaty faces, dewy with the excitement of finding the past beneath their feet. "You guys see Jane Ritter today?"

"That high school girl?" Puka grinned at his partner, a woman in braids and a brown tank top. "I'm not sure you wanna know."

I did not like the sound of that.

"Let me handle this." Dan hitched up his plaid golf pants. "Now see here, junior, I've come for my daughter, Jane. If you potheads have absconded with her, I'll sue your parents for every dime of your absurdly inflated tuition. Where is she?"

Puka leaned on his shovel and regarded Dan with open distaste. "Okay, old man. If you really want to know, your daughter's in the woods with Professor Tallow. She follows him around like a puppy. If you ask me, she's got a crush and after meeting her father, I can understand why."

My poor, poor Jane. A crush on a professor. And she was just a baby. So vulnerable.

"A crush on a professor, eh? That's my girl," Dan said, beaming. "She knows how to suck up for an A. Connections, connections, connections. Get you there in half the time with half the effort." He winked at Wendy, who rolled her eyes and went off to examine a mound of grass.

Puka shook his head and returned to shoveling.

"Remarkable!" exclaimed Wendy, who was standing on top of a large mound where the field met the woods, her white pleated tennis skirt fluttering in the morning breeze. "Chip, come here."

The three of us trekked through the long, damp green grass

over to Wendy. "It's an ancient Celtic burial tomb. You can tell because the door is positioned east." She pointed to a hole at the side of the mound. "And check out this monolith." She hopped off the mound and ran to a tall pointed stone on which various indentations and lines were carved. "See the ancient ogam script? You can even make out the Eye of Bel."

We looked at the ancient ogam script.

"This site should definitely be designated an archaeological treasure," she said in a sort of bossy fifth-grader way. "I'll have to mention it to my historical society group."

"Too bad that rock's been marked up by plows, say?" Mickey squinted at what was supposed to be the Eye of Bel. "Now, where's this ogam you're talking about?"

Wendy ignored him. "Put your hand on this monolith, Chip. Can't you just feel the surge of energy?"

Dan put his hand on it and nodded dutifully.

"You know what it's supposed to be, don't you?" Wendy asked.

Dan blinked.

"A big stone penis."

He yanked off his hand and wiped it on his pants.

"I bet if I put a dowsing rod on top of this thing it would spin so fast it'd make you dizzy," Wendy said.

"Something's made you dizzy," Dan mumbled.

Mickey knelt by the hole in the mound. "I don't mean disrespect, but, gosh, this looks a heck of a lot like grandma's root cellar. Used to store pickles and moonshine during the summer months. Potatoes in the winter."

"Oh, you sound just like the state archaeologist," Wendy said. "Those academics refuse to accept the evidence that ancient Celts fished the Delaware and then journeyed northward to the Lehigh River around 300 B.C. . . ."

"And up the Monocacy where they sought refuge during a particularly harsh winter," added a man in a waxed green Barbour coat who was trudging out of the woods. Two college girls accompanied him, listening in rapt attention. Neither of them was

Jane. "You have a better than average grasp of local Celtic history, madam."

"Professor Fallow! I've seen your picture in the paper," cried Wendy.

"The name is Tallow," he corrected. "Although perhaps I've been in the dirt so long, Fallow might be a more appropriate surname."

The girls giggled.

Tallow had worked hard to perfect his Mick Jagger imitation. He was of slim build, medium height, in his late forties with shoulder-length, shagged brown hair that was unkempt enough to make him acceptable to younger generations. His khakis were slightly wrinkled and stuffed into black Wellingtons and the collar of his canvas shirt was unbuttoned to permit a glimpse of chest. He was the perfect English sportsman, rustic and effete at the same time. The type to cause the kind of crush a woman cherishes late at night, years after she's left his classroom.

"My crystal instructor has all your books." Wendy was getting giddy. "He's gonna die when he hears we met, Professor Tallow. He says you're a genius."

"Really?" Tallow's eyes dropped to Wendy's massive sapphire and diamond engagement ring that Dan had squandered Jane's college fund to buy. "I'm always open to private instruction for obviously intelligent students such as yourself. Why don't we meet for coffee sometime and, you know, I'll elucidate you?"

I wasn't exactly sure of the precise definition for elucidate, but in this case I think it meant, "Take you to bed and spend all your inheritance."

"Ooooh, I'd like that," Wendy gushed.

"Jesus Christmas," grumbled Dan, no fan of academics to begin with.

Enough of this. "Have you seen Jane?" I asked Professor Tallow.

"Come again?" Tallow put his hand to his ear.

"What in God's name have you done with my little girl?" Dan demanded.

"I apologize for my husband," Wendy said. "He's just concerned about his daughter, Jane Ritter. She's been—"

"Jane Ritter!" Professor Tallow's eyes brightened. "Of course, she's auditing my Local Celtic History course at Lehigh. A terribly bright student." He regarded Wendy warmly. "Don't tell me you're Bubbles. Jane talks about you all the time."

"Bubbles!" Wendy screeched as though a rat had run over her toes. "I should say not. That's Bubbles." She wagged a limp finger toward me.

"Brilliant," said Tallow, stepping away from Wendy and taking both of my hands in his soft ones. "Your daughter has been regaling us with stories of your adventures up in Slagville. What a nasty experience that must have been, although worse by far for Mrs. Price. How awful to wake up and find out that your very successful, very wealthy husband has been shot in a coal mine."

"Yes," I said, eager to get back to the topic of Jane. No point in "elucidating" him about how I had been a murder target, too.

"I want to know every detail of that incident. You must tell me. I have quite a connection to that area. As is widely known, I was the first to discover dolmens similar to those of Syrian design in Columbia County near Limbo, where I maintain a family getaway. My discovery was written up in *Modern Archaeologist.* Volume twenty. Perhaps you read it?"

"Sorry. Missed that issue," I said. "About Jane—"

"Yes, as Jane and I have discussed, I am very concerned about the plans for a casino there. That so-called Dead Zone is a gold mine of Celtic stone structures. My theory is that, later, Irish and Welsh immigrants were attracted to the anthracite region specifically because of the similarities in topography to their native—"

"We're very worried about Jane," I interrupted. "Please, if you know where she is, tell us."

"Haven't seen her at all this morning." Tallow seemed confused. "But you didn't let me finish—"

"Listen, Indiana Jones." Dan tapped him on the shoulder. "I happen to be a lawyer with some pretty influential connections at my alma mater, which is your place of employment. If I find you . . ."

The police scanner on Mickey's belt went off. All conversation stopped as Mickey listened to numbers and words that made no sense except for "teenage runaway . . . short royal-blue hair . . . black vest . . . numerous earrings . . . army boots." Last I recalled, Jane's hair was raspberry red and she'd tossed those Doc Martens months ago. But it was close enough.

"She's at the corner of Linden and Mulberry," Mickey said. "Hitching."

"I'm going with you," I said. "Jane's never hitchhiked before."

"Mothers." Mickey hooked the scanner back on his belt. "They're so naïve."

"I'll stay here and cross examine Doctor Crackpot," Dan said, pulling out his business card like it was a loaded gun.

We said goodbye to Tallow and company. I tagged after Mickey, the heels of my boots getting caught in the uncut hay and clumpy dirt. We skirted past the pits and budding archaeologists and made our way to the cruiser. Mickey got in and I had opened the passenger-side door when what should appear at the road into the field but my daughter stepping out of a truck.

Jane waved merrily at the driver and then proceeded to plow through the tall grass. What about all those lectures about not accepting rides from strangers? Hadn't she been listening?

Mickey surveyed the scene in the rearview. "I could bust her for that, you know. It's freaking insane of her to hitchhike. She could end up with her throat slit."

"Hey, Mom." She waved. "What're you doing here?" Not a care in the world.

"I had to find you. You were kidnapped."

Her brown Lehigh University backpack slid off her shoulder. She was wearing low-rider jeans and a white shirt that said HOT STUFF in pink glitter under her zippered black sweatshirt. What a combination.

"Kidnapped? What're you talking about?"

I took her by the elbow and escorted her over to the Camaro, so we could speak in private. "The house was torn apart when I came home. And the car was there and your purse. I figured Stinky grabbed you and you two were halfway to Canada."

"You have to be the most hysterical mother ever." Jane shifted her feet. "Stinky did stop by about an hour ago and stayed for a few minutes. When you didn't show, he gave me a message. He said it's important."

"What is it?" I asked eagerly.

But Jane's gaze had fallen on Wendy's apple red midlife-crisis special. "Oh, no. You didn't. Dad and Wendy are here?"

"Sorry," I said. "Your father loves you, too, you know."

Jane hid her face in her hands. "This is so embarrassing."

Embarrassing? Wait until she saw Dan's pants. Now that was embarrassing.

She ducked behind my Camaro. "Ohmigod. There's Thea Pippis. She's never gonna let me hear the end of this."

"I wouldn't have worried if I hadn't come home and found the place trashed."

Jane flinched. "Trashed? It was neater than when you'd left it. G found a pair of your underwear in the upstairs bathroom, by the way."

I looked down at my pierced and honest daughter. Most parents of teenagers might have rightly judged that their precious pumpkin was lying to cover up the previous night's bash. But Jane didn't lie. This was because I had adopted a "don't ask/don't tell" policy about her extracurricular activities. Like the hitchhiking, for example. Better not to ask.

"If what you're saying is true," I said, "then we need to get home, fast."

"Why? I just got here." Jane was about to argue further, but something behind me had caught her attention. She quickly stood, slipped her hands out her pockets and, I couldn't believe it, patted down her blue hair. She had gone all pink, staring in awe at Professor Tallow, who had mysteriously popped up by my side.

"Excuse me for eavesdropping," Tallow said. "I was drawn, intrigued actually, by the intense mother–adolescent daughter repartee. The natural maturation process as the offspring separates herself from the authority figure of a corresponding gender. So *Reviving Ophelia*. Did you know that in some African cultures it is common for teenage daughters to kill their mothers—at least in a simulated ritual?"

Creep, I thought.

"Wow," said Jane.

"You found the kid!" Dan jogged up to us, out of breath, his pot belly flopping under the baby blue polo shirt. He exhaled a sigh of relief when he saw Jane. "Great. Remind me to ground you later."

Jane gave a salute. "I'm already grounded, Dad, though shouldn't you be grounded for wearing those pants?"

"What's wrong with these?" Dan examined his pants. "Tiger Woods wears pants like these."

Really? I doubted that. Tiger Woods was a stud.

Dan checked his watch. "Let's get to the club, Wendy. I can make tee time if you speed."

Wendy stomped her foot. "I'm not going anywhere. I'm staying right here. These stones need to be declared historical monuments and this is a project I'm interested in backing. Financially, that is."

Tallow blew her a kiss. "You're a lovely woman, Mrs. Ritter. Simply gorgeous."

"Aw, get off it, Wendy," Dan said, wedging himself between Tallow and his wife. "Come with me and we'll buy you your own ogam stone. For the garden. Bigger than the neighbors' even."

She folded her arms and shook her head. "I want an authentic specimen dug with my own two hands."

"What will the tennis girls do without you?"

"Canadian doubles. And leave the car. It's mine."

Dan scratched the bald spot on his head. "Now what am I gonna do?"

"I can give you a ride to the country club, Dan," Mickey offered. "On Fridays I do a patrol near there."

"All right," Dan said with resignation. "But I'm playing all nineteen holes, Wendy. So who knows when I'll be home."

Wendy waved. When he was gone I said, "I thought there were eighteen holes in golf."

"Oh, Bubbles. Silly old Bubbles." Wendy patted my arm. "You really have been deprived, haven't you?"

Chapter *12*

Jane was still so angry with me that she kept her face plastered against the passenger-side window. After fifteen minutes of silence, I decided to break the ice by asking about her slack-jawed boyfriend G.

"How come G didn't drive you to the dig?" I said. "So you didn't have to hitch."

Jane shifted in her seat. "No car. It got totaled in an accident on Center Street last week. Don't freak."

My toes curled over the gas pedal as I stifled a freak.

"It wasn't G's fault. A stupid housewife in a minivan was handing out popsicles to her kids when she should have been paying attention to the road, and she just pulled out onto Mulberry. Broadsided him."

"She wasn't stupid, she was harried." I stopped at a red light and watched a mother trying to soothe a crying baby in a carriage. Oh, if you think these days are tough, honey, wait until your daughter's seventeen and her hair is blue and she hitchhikes and gets in cars driven by boys with one-letter names and one-cell brains. "You'll see when you have children and you're driving your own minivan."

"I'll never drive a minivan. They remind me too much of hearses. Anyway, even though she was at fault, the insurance company was gonna charge G fifteen hundred dollars a year unless he agreed to lease a Teen Safety Car."

"What's a Teen Safety Car?" I asked as we turned onto West Goepp Street.

Jane shook her head. "I don't know, but it sounds goofy, doesn't it?"

I slowed down and surveyed the cars parked in front of the tidy brick and aluminum-sided houses for which my neighborhood is famous. Ford Escort. Three Chevy Impalas. One Toyota. Must be a visitor from out of town. Japanese cars were not appreciated here in the home of Lehigh Steel. Japanese cars parked overnight on West Goepp had a tendency to end up dented and deflated by morning.

Jane was as shocked as I had been when we opened the front door. However, the strewn lamps and ripped plastic on the seat cushions didn't appear as horrifying as they had a few hours ago, now that I knew my daughter was safe and sound. There hadn't been any serious property damage. No smashed dishes or kicked in televisions.

"I did not do this," Jane said. "If I had I'd be the most popular kid in school."

Jane surveyed the back of the house where the kitchen was. I went upstairs. Every drawer was open with clothes tossed about except, oddly enough, for our underwear drawers. Those were shut and as disorganized as always. Untrifled with. My few possessions of value—the china Princess Diana plates, Hummel figurines and a commemorative porcelain Scartlett O'Hara that I had ordered from the back of *Family Circle* magazine—were still intact. So was my stash of expensive Clinique makeup.

"The leftovers!" Jane shouted from the kitchen. "We've been wiped out." I ran downstairs. Jane had lined up my square Tupperware containers along the kitchen counter. They were next to her purse, which also, I noted, had not been stolen.

"They were empty except maybe for one bite in each and placed back in the refrigerator," she said. "What does that tell you?"

"I got a theory," I said. "Check the O.J."

Jane shook the Minute Maid. Barely a splash. "But see here. The vegetables are untouched." She displayed a bunch of broccoli and then opened another drawer. "Although the ham and cheese are eaten up. And that summer sausage that's been floating around since last Christmas, it's gone, too." She held up a plastic wrapper that once held the summer sausage. "Along with all the mustard."

"Men," I said. "Middle-aged men to be precise."

"You mean someone broke into our house just to eat our cold cuts?" Jane was incredulous.

"Good thing you weren't here," I said. "Otherwise you would have been forced to make them sandwiches. I'm not too worried. At least they weren't real criminals." I did not want to alarm my sensitive daughter. "Did Stinky seem hungry?"

"I offered him some toast and coffee, but he said no thanks. He was really nervous, pacing the floor, waiting for you."

"What did you two talk about?"

Jane twirled a white key chain around her finger. "Mostly we talked about carbon dioxide and its properties."

I winced. "Anything else?"

She removed a small tablet from the back pocket of her jeans. "Let's see."

"You have notes?"

"Notes are good, remember, Mom?" She flipped through several pages and started reading. "He said he didn't have anything to do with Bud Price's murder, but that he wanted to talk directly to you about Wednesday night. Something about not burdening me with that information. Oh, yeah. He kept saying that you'd missed it, you'd missed the real story. Since I hadn't read the article in the *News-Times*, I couldn't talk to him about it intelligently."

I tapped my knuckles to my forehead. What had I missed? I'd used all the documents he had left behind. "What was the message he gave you?"

"He said it was very important that you talk to a Pete Zidukis in Limbo before you do a follow-up to today's story. And Stinky said if you need to get hold of him, you should try the Hoagie

Ho. It's a hoagie place or something." She closed the tablet.
"Stinky indicated that that's where he's been holed up."

At a hoagie shop?

"This yours?" Jane held up the white key chain.

"No. Where'd you get it?

She shrugged. "Found it lying on the kitchen counter. I've
never seen it before."

It was clean white plastic with bright green lettering. A promotional item retailers like to hand out to prospective customers.

This particular one said Price Family Ford.

One might have expected that Price Family Ford, having been
run by the family of Bud Price, would have been closed the days
following his untimely death. So Jane and I were slightly shocked
to see "No Interest/No Payment Down/$100 Off Sticker Price
One-Day Sale" as we toured the large lot of Ford F150s, mini-
vans, SUVs and Tauruses.

"Do you know the gas mileage one of these oversized heaps
gets?" Jane asked, inspecting a sticker on a Ford F150. "Seventeen miles city, twenty-one miles highway. That's criminal, Mom.
That's global suicide."

I scanned the premises looking for salesmen. I still didn't
know how I was going to begin finding who had raided my home.
I certainly wasn't going to give anyone from the Price company
my name, which they'd recognize from this morning's story in
the *News-Times*. And what if the Prices had been the ones to bur-
glarize my house? Though why would they have left behind a key
chain?

"Look at this Ford Expedition. Twelve miles city, sixteen
highway. Is that a misprint? Haven't these people ever heard of
greenhouse gasses?" Jane's voice was getting louder. Other customers were rereading the stickers and clucking their tongues.
"No wonder we don't have white Christmases, anymore. Thank
you Henry Ford for single-handedly ending civilization."

Jane's Earth First outrage caught the attention of a salesman in a navy jacket. He jogged out of the dealership, his lapels flapping.

"Looking for a large, safe vehicle for your daughter?" He put his hands on his hips and nodded toward the SUV. "Listen, I put my own kid in an Expedition. My wife wouldn't have it any other way. Between you and me on the QT, I sleep better at night knowing that if she hits somebody on some highway, they're dead, not her."

Behind him Jane gave him devil horns with two fingers.

"I'm Frank," he said, extending his hand, which I shook because it would be rude not to. "And you are?"

"Uh, looking for some men who maybe came in for a car today."

Frank lowered his hand. "Excuse me?"

I held up the white plastic key chain with the Price Family Ford lettering. "They left this in my house. I wonder if you might know how I could find them so I could return it."

Frank still looked nonplussed.

"And I, uh, assumed they must be searching high and low for it. These are pretty nice key chains." I dangled the chain. "Yessiree. If I lost one of these, I'd be mighty bummed. So sturdy and easy to find in your purse—"

"So plastic," Jane interrupted. "Not that you gas guzzlers care."

Frank, not sure whether I was a prospective customer or not, but eager to get Jane and me off the lot—especially Jane—ushered us into the dealership.

Jane can rant and rave as much as she wants about how evil fossil-fuel-burning vehicles are, but I love showroom cars with the hoods open to reveal sparkling clean engines. I love the smell of genuine leather and fake leather, the feeling that if I just had this perfect automobile, everything else in my life would come together.

Frank led us into a large wood-paneled office, which was

pasted floor to ceiling with framed photos, every one showing a celebrity and Bud Price in a tuxedo grinning so hard his face was about to split open. Liza and Bud in front of the Sands Casino, arms around each other's waists. Bud and Bob Hope in a hospital bed. On the stage with Bill Cosby and Billy Crystal in Las Vegas. With Charo and Bo Derek by a pool.

It was hard not to recall the last time I saw Bud's smiling face, pasty white and shocked dead, at the bottom of a mine.

"Who is this lucky guy?"

"It's my brother-in-law. It's his office," Frank said, slipping behind a large mahogany desk. "And he's not so lucky." His voice took on a somber tone. "He was killed Wednesday night in a mine explosion. The whole family was at a reunion in Bermuda when they got the word, except for his wife, Chrissy. She was in town 'cause her kid had school. I flew back last night to run the dealership. Chrissy, I guess, is going up to visit the site where he was killed."

"Oh, that's terrible," I said, sitting on a red leather chair. I flashed a look at Jane to *keep . . . her . . . mouth . . . shut.*

"That's why I decided to have the big sale." Frank clapped his hands. "No money down. Interest-free financing if you drive off the lot today. Bud would have wanted it that way. His last big closeout deal."

Jane coughed. I slid my foot over and stepped on her toes. Damn those Doc Martens. Impenetrable.

"Where was the explosion?" I asked.

"Slagville. Bud owned land up there."

"Get out!" I said, slapping my knee. "I bet that's where those men were from who left the key chain." It was a gamble, but I was hoping to smoke out more info.

"Oh, those men." Frank opened the top drawer and rummaged around. "Come to think of it, they did catch my attention 'cause they were from where Bud blew up. Now, where is it? I swear one of them left his name. I remember asking where they worked and they said they were retired coal miners." He pulled the drawer out another inch. "One of the gentlemen said a hairdresser here in Lehigh recommended he talk to Bud. She told him Bud could get him a good deal on a trade-in if he just mentioned her name. They drove a pretty decent F1 Ford. Still had the old Fordomatic."

"That hairdresser wouldn't have happened to have been Bubbles Yablonsky?" Jane asked before I could stop her.

I froze, sweating on the red leather. Frank stopped searching the drawer. "You know, I think it was a Bubbles something. Those fellows were real interested in her. How she knew Bud. Where they'd met. They made it seem like Bud and Bubbles were," he glanced behind each shoulder, "kind of intimate, if you get my drift."

Jane folded her arms. "Don't you know Bubbles Yablonsky is a reporter at the *News-Times*, too? Wrote that front page story today about McMullen Coal digging under the casino Bud wanted to build."

She hadn't even read the story. What had gotten into this kid?

Frank sat back and eyed her. "And you read that newspaper article and got it into your pretty head to visit Price Family Ford and get yourself a brand new vehicle?"

I swallowed. He was onto us.

Jane played it cool. She popped her bubble gum and said, "Yup. How about that?"

He leaned forward. "How about three percent off on today's purchase? Honey, you can't buy advertising like this. Bud must be rolling over in his grave or wherever he is." He shut the drawer. "Well, I can't find that damn name and number. Why don't you tell me yours? Let's start with your mother, here." He poised a pen over paper and winked at me.

I, however, was speechless, totally and completely confused. Why would a couple of retired coal miners invade my home? Zeke Allen had said not much had changed since the 1860s. Arson, assault and murder were still the ultimate tools for change. Did that mean that these coal miners, whoever they were, were the ones who had set up Stiletto and me to die? I didn't even know any coal miners.

Frank coughed and tapped his pen. "Miss?"

"My mother appears to be having one of her episodes," Jane answered. "Just put down that her name is Sally Hansen, like the manicure maven. That'll be close enough."

We stopped by Genevieve's apartment and found her waiting on the sidewalk, repacked suitcase and polished musket in hand. Jane climbed in the back and Genevieve sardined herself in the front again. She was ecstatic to hear that we were off to Limbo, to stop by the home of one Pete Zidukis.

"Pete Zidukis? *The* Pete Zidukis?"

"I think so," I said. "Is he . . . somebody?"

"Only the most respected conspiracy theorist in Eastern Pennsylvania," Genevieve said, clapping her big paws together. "His nickname's Stay Put Pete 'cause he's the one resident of Limbo who refused to leave when the U.S. government bought everyone else out of their homes after the fire started. He's a celebrity. I've got to meet him."

I headed east on Route 22. "That might not be a good idea, Genny. We have—"

"You'll never find Limbo without me. The government's rerouted the highway and put up road signs to trick you. They've even ordered all the mapmakers to erase the town off the maps."

"Let me check," Jane said, opening a Pennsylvania/New Jersey AAA map. "Sure enough, there's no Limbo where it's supposed to be. You're right."

"Of course I'm right, dear," Genevieve said, punctuating her comment with a snort.

Since we'd been cleaned out of leftovers and cold cuts, Jane and I stopped at Mona's Lunch in Pottstown. Genevieve, who had chowed down on pickled beets, pickled herring and coleslaw at home, said she'd stay in the car and keep a lookout for any trigger-happy coal miners, or whoever it was who was supposed to be after me.

Inside Mona's I ordered a turkey and bacon on toasted white with extra mayo, a little lettuce, a bag of potato chips and a diet A-Treat with a double chocolate brownie chaser. Jane ordered a salad with extra carrots and broccoli, vinaigrette on the side and a mineral water.

While Mona made our lunch, Jane tapped her black nails on the glass counter and studied me. I could feel it coming, the same old lecture, and I pretended to be very interested in a notice about a garage sale held last Saturday that was still left on Mona's bulletin board.

"You're killing yourself, you know," she finally blurted. "What did you have to eat today? No. Let me take a shot." Jane closed her eyes while I concentrated on an antique china hutch, baby carriage and assorted Fisher Price toys. No sales before 8 A.M. No kidding. "Coffee, pastry, chips. Tastykakes and soda, soda, soda."

"Croissant." I patted my thighs. "And see? Not an ounce of fat." I also took a "don't look/don't tell" approach when it came to cellulite. That is, when I wasn't staring at an overhead mirror.

"It's not just about beauty, Mom, it's about health." Jane slid down the counter toward me. "Nitrates in the bacon, saturated fat, coconut oil, and white death in those brownies."

"White death?" I asked, suddenly alarmed. "Cocaine?"

"No. Sugar. Tons of it. You'll have diabetes by forty."

I waved her off and returned to the garage sale. "By forty I'll either be married to Stiletto or I never will."

"Unbelievable." Jane slapped the counter. "You and men. Left to your own devices, you'd guide your entire life according to some man. They're not our compasses you know."

Goody. I'd been waiting for this opening ever since Jane had announced via Mama that she was holding off on higher education after graduation so she could pick grapes with G in France. It probably wouldn't have bothered me so much if she hadn't had a 3.8 average, near 1600 SATs and offers from universities being mailed to our house daily.

"Really," I said. "So I guess you bypassing college because of what G wants wouldn't be following a man. Per se."

Her expression soured. "Not per se. Anyway." She looked off. "G and I are kind of shaky these days."

What! What was that? Did I sense a split? I bit the insides of my cheek to keep from grinning.

"Is that so?" I said casually.

Jane's glance flittered toward me with doubt. The next few minutes were crucial. How I played this could well determine my daughter's entire future. "I suppose you're glad about that, huh?"

"Wonder Bread Gobbler and Pig with extra Slime!" Mona slapped my sandwich on the counter. "Your Compost Heap is coming up, hon." She smiled at Jane.

"Glad's not the right word," I said, grabbing the sandwich and chips. Ecstatic was. "But you guys seemed so close. What changed?" I asked with feigned concern.

Jane batted her eyes. "It's difficult to explain. I've read that people who are intellectually curious are less likely to bond permanently with another individual because they tend to grow and evolve whereas their partners don't. This has been a topic of serious discourse at my Mensa meetings."

"You met a hunk," I translated.

"Not just a hunk." Jane gripped my arm. "A mature man. A man who understands me, who can discuss Plato and black holes without cracking butt jokes."

"Compost Heap!" Mona plunked the salad onto the counter, but Jane didn't even notice.

"I think it might be love."

"Christ," Mona said, wiping her hands on her apron. "They're all like that. All the Compost Heap orders. Just wait until the sex goes bad, then you'll be adding extra mayo like your ma."

Mona and I exchanged knowing, appreciative looks about the comforts of rich, satisfying mayonnaise and crispy bacon.

"Sex!" said Jane. "We can't have sex. I'm underage. He'd get fired."

Mona quit wiping her hands. "That'll be six forty-five," she said, rushing to the cash register.

I counted out the change, my hands shaking. Mona returned a nickel and clasped my hand sympathetically. "My heart goes out to you, dear. If it's any consolation, these crushes usually last only a week. Maybe someone decent will come along to take her mind off the scum."

"I don't think her mind is the problem," I said.

"Ain't that the truth."

I smiled at her weakly and handed Jane her salad.

"He's older than you?" I said, opening the door for her.

Jane walked ahead of me. "He teaches at Lehigh. He's European."

European? Professor? The door slapped me on the back. Professor Tallow. It must be Professor Tallow. That's what all the college kids at the dig had been snickering about. Jane with her puppy love crush on Tallow.

Jane waited for Genevieve to heave herself out so she could get in the back. "I got a question to ask," I said when we were all settled in.

"If this is about him being older than me, forget it. I've always been adult for my age. I'm very responsible."

"How long has," I cleared my throat, "this guy been interested in you?"

Jane lifted the Saran Wrap off her salad and stirred it with a plastic fork. "We've known each other since the beginning of the semester, since August, when I started auditing his course." She bit into a lettuce leaf and thought about it. "But I'd say it's only been a few days since we've really gotten close."

"Close?"

"Remember when I told you this morning about the Druid thingy last night, well that wasn't all." She cracked open the mineral water, carefully avoiding my searing gaze. "Don't tell Dad, but we spent hours afterward curled on a blanket in the field, talking, until the sun rose through the mist. It was pure Shakespeare."

Shakespeare, huh? Did Shakespeare ever write a play about a forty-something professor taking advantage of a high school crush?

"We just talked," Jane insisted. "He didn't kiss me or anything. He didn't even touch me."

Genevieve and I exchanged sidewise glances. "Leave me out of this," Genny said, raising one hand in protest. "If I was you, I'd just shoot the S.O.B. and be done with it."

The author of *Reviving Ophelia* would be pleased to know that I did not probe further into Jane's relationship with Professor Tallow. I did not point out that there is no conceivable reason why a normal man who was a decade older than myself would be interested in my daughter. I did not ask what they discussed or in any way forbid her from seeing him again.

If Jane had Shakespeare in mind, she was thinking *Romeo and Juliet*. And from my Shakespeare for Dummies course at the Two Guys Community College, I knew that Juliet's pushy parents had ended up with the crummy end of that deal.

Except in this case I was willing to bet my pointy-toed slingbacks that Jane was going to end up the worse for wear. Her heart was going to be broken and the bright beacon of higher education would dim forever when she discovered she had been used by a professor she worshipped.

It was time to don my imaginary red cape and morph into Super Mom of a Vulnerable Teenager. I pulled into a 7-Eleven, threw a bunch of quarters into the pay phone and forced myself not to hang up when G answered.

"Eh," he grunted. "Talk to me." A TV blared in the background. *SpongeBob SquarePants*.

I swallowed hard. "Hello, G, this is Bubbles Yablonsky. Jane's mom."

"Mrs. Y! Uh-oh. What have I done wrong now?" The TV went on mute.

"It's not what you've done, it's what you're going to do," I said before diving into a lengthy explanation that if G didn't get his flabby butt to Roxanne's Slagville salon pronto there was a good chance Jane was going to fall in love with Professor Tallow.

"Who? That dinosaur? He's, like, old. Older than Stiletto even."

I clenched my teeth. "He's not old. He's English."

"Yeah. Chicks go for that British stuff, don't they? Wait. How's this sound? Blimey, eh? Pretty good. Though that might be Australian."

G simply wasn't grasping the gravity of the matter.

"It's up to you, G," I said. "I'm just giving you a heads up."

"And to think I always thought you hated me."

"Now where ever would you get that idea?"

There was a pause. " 'Cause like those were your exact words. I hate you, G."

"You must've misunderstood."

"Okay. But I'll only get up there on certain conditions."

Demanding little bugger. "And those are?"

"That you'll be nice to me. Make me sandwiches and stuff and don't disrespect me."

"Perhaps." I wasn't too sure about making sandwiches.

"And I get to call you Bub."

"Bub?"

"Like, hey, Bub, wassup. Or could you get me a Coke, Bub? Or turn the channel, Bub, this is 'Animal Planet.'"

"Whatever," I said, hanging up and looking over at Jane, who was passionately arguing with the 7-Eleven clerk about why they didn't have a system for recycling her plastic salad container.

Still, having taken steps to wean my daughter off Tallow, I was feeling a whole lot better. If I could manage the challenges of motherhood, what was there that I couldn't handle, I thought, pulling back onto the highway. Jane was in the backseat, passed out for an afternoon nap, and Genevieve was snoring beside me.

Yup. Everything was going to work out fine, like Mickey said. I'd do my due diligence with Pete Zidukis, perhaps write a follow-up and then Jane and I would drive home.

So what that I never found out who sent us to the Number Nine mine? Maybe that person had learned his lesson and I'd never hear from him again. Maybe it was merely a fluke.

But in my self absorption, I had neglected to consider my cousin. When we arrived at the Main Mane and found her crying, I realized that my unknown enemy meant business.

Chapter 13

"It's just so weird." Roxanne was sitting by the cash register, squeezing Visine into her red-rimmed eyes. "I mean, the salon's untouched and they didn't break into the cash register."

"Am I done yet?" a client under the dryer yelled.

Roxanne checked her watch. "Two more minutes, Mrs. Foster." Turning to me she said, "Even so, I don't want to sleep alone tonight. I saw your mother this morning before she left to look for the Nana diary and she promised she'd stay, but I'd feel better if you were here, too. What kind of gun is that, anyway?"

She nodded toward Genevieve who was on the job, marching through the house and preparing for "lockdown," as she called it.

"It's a musket," I said. "Don't ask." I took out my reporter's notebook. "You got two minutes to tell me exactly what happened. I need details."

Roxanne explained that she had fallen asleep on the living room couch while watching TV the night before. It was shortly after six that morning when she woke. She got dressed and went about her day. Later, when she got a break from the salon, she went into the guest bedroom to change the sheets, in case I wanted to stay the night, and found the top drawer of the dresser open and dumped on the bed.

"You call Donohue?"

"To tell him a dresser drawer had been overturned?" Mrs. Foster's timer went *bing!* "Even if this is only Slagville, I think the police have more important matters to take care of."

I told her about our own burglary back in Lehigh where the

dresser drawer had been the one place our snoopers *hadn't* touched.

"Maybe there's a connection." Roxanne was running over to turn off Mrs. Foster's timer.

"I can't tell without having a clue as to what they're searching for." Then I had an awful thought. "What happened to the box of Stinky's documents?"

"Gone, of course." Roxanne lifted the dryer hood and unrolled one of Mrs. Foster's curlers. "Stinky's gonna kill me."

So was Mr. Salvo. After the move I pulled, lying to Griffin to get my story in the paper, Mr. Salvo was not going to be pleased to discover that there weren't any supporting documents available. Oh, no. What if we got sued? Mr. Salvo said that'd be the end of his career. And I'd have no evidence to pull him out of hot water.

"Premises secure, Roxanne," Genevieve announced. "In the meantime, I suggest you survey the surroundings. Familiarize yourself with what weapons are at hand for your defense." She pointed to a green bottle of Sani-Bac, which we beauticians use to delouse combs. "That stuff'll kill a two-hundred-pound man with one swallow. Know it. Love it. Make it your best friend."

Mrs. Foster visibly cringed as Roxanne examined the bottle with new appreciation.

"We better get a move on, Bubbles. Jane's been waiting in the car for at least a half hour."

Armed with Sani-Bac, Roxanne waved a reluctant farewell. Genevieve, Jane and I drove to the burning town of Limbo to meet Pete Zidukis. We took a right at Slagville's baseball field located next to the fire department at the top of the hill and passed a closed ice-cream stand. Jane kept an eye out for the Hoagie Ho place where I was supposed to meet Stinky until we jogged left, blatantly disregarding yellow *Do Not Enter* signs.

"Stop here," Genevieve ordered. I parked the car next to a large federal warning outlining the dangers and liabilities of entering the area. We got out, read the U.S. government's disclaimer and then studied the view in awe.

Had I not driven through Limbo as a child for Thanksgiving dinner with Roxanne's family, I would never have known that the deserted grassy valley that lay before us had once been a thriving working-class town famous for its St. Patrick's Day festivities and Fourth of July fireworks.

Thirty years before, children had dragged their sleds to the top of Troutwine Hill on winter days, played softball in the overgrown park and roller skated over leaves in St. Ignatius's yard on fall afternoons. There had been dances at the American Legion Hall on Friday nights and lines at the post office on Saturday mornings where neighbors caught up on gossip.

Now there was nothing but a grid of cracked and barren streets that went nowhere. Sidewalks bordered vacant lots and driveways led to homes that long ago had been reduced to rubble and carted off. Every school, store and gas station had vanished, as though they had been sucked up by space ships. It was eerily quiet. Not even a bird chirped.

"I don't see any smoke," Jane said.

"Yeah? Put your hand on the ground." Genevieve bent over and touched the sidewalk.

"I can't believe it," Jane said, her eyes wide. "It's actually hot. From the sun maybe?"

"Not from above, Sally," Genevieve said, "from below. Underneath where we're standing right now is a fire with temperatures that reach seven hundred degrees Fahrenheit. On the surface."

"Get out," said Jane.

"How come this fire was never put out?" I asked.

"Local municipalities couldn't figure out who had the responsibility for putting it out. They bickered and bickered. They bickered so much that the fire spread so far it was out of control."

"That's it?" Jane asked. "Bureaucratic squabbling led to one of the worst environmental disasters in American history?"

"There's more," Genevieve said. "But I'll let Pete tell you about that."

We got back in the Camaro and drove through deserted

streets to one of the few houses left standing in Limbo. It was situated on a lovely tree-lined lot and was an impeccably maintained half of a double. As with every other home in Limbo, the other half had been razed and supports had been constructed to keep its twin from falling over. The outline of the former half's stairway remained like a shadow on the external wall of the standing home.

We found Pete in the backyard raking leaves. He was more ancient than Mama and Genevieve, dressed in the kind of dull green shirt and pants that school janitors wear. His posture was stooped, his hair was thinning and snow white, but the vigor with which he raked proved he hadn't given in to old age yet.

Genevieve was so starstruck she was speechless. She could only stand a few feet away, clutching her purse and gaping like a teenybopper meeting 'N Sync.

I introduced myself as Bubbles Yablonsky, a reporter from a newspaper in Lehigh.

"Lehigh." Pete scratched his head. "I haven't been there in a century."

"You can't be over a hundred years old," I said. "You don't look a day over eighty."

Pete chuckled. "You're somewhat literal, I gather."

"Thank you. I do read a lot." Nice, finally, to be complimented for something besides my excellent makeup choices and spandex selection.

Jane stepped in, employing her new boldness. "My mother wrote a story today revealing that McMullen Coal had violated its permits by digging under the Dead Zone. Carl Koolball stopped by our house this morning and suggested that my mother speak to you."

"He told Jane you would know what was missing from my story," I added.

"Did he now." Pete placed the rake against the house. "I ain't seen your story, but Stinky's been by the house a lot recently. Measuring and asking about the Mammoth Basin."

"Mammoth Basin?" I asked. "What's that?"

"A gigantic deposit of anthracite worth close to one hundred billion dollars," Genevieve said, breaking her trance. "It's located right under our feet."

"My, my, my," Pete said. "And where did you pick up this information, lovely lady?"

"*The Daily Conspiracy Newsletter.* 'On Why I Stay in Limbo,' by one Peter Zidukis." Genevieve blushed and modestly bowed her head. "I read it five times."

Pete smiled and his watery blue eyes twinkled slightly. "Impressive. Seems to me we may have met before."

"Y2K conference in Schnecksville," Genevieve gushed. "Dried foods and generators seminar. You gave a speech on surviving underground in broiling temperatures."

"You live eighty years in Limbo, you know about broiling temperatures."

"Yeah?" piped up Jane. "Where is this so-called underground fire? I thought this place was supposed to be ablaze."

"Oh, it is," Pete said, hobbling past her. "Follow me."

"Isn't he fantastic?" Genevieve whispered in my ear as we marched up the street to St. Ignatius Church and cemetery, my tiny heels taking a pounding on the pavement. "What a hunk, say?"

"He could be crazy from the underground gasses," Jane said to me when Genevieve caught up with Pete. "He's like exhibit A, why no one should still be living here."

Twenty minutes later Pete, Jane and I were staring at an expanse of charcoal-gray, scorched earth framed by leafless white trees, bleached from the underground fires. Behind us was St. Ignatius Church. Above us on the hill was the cemetery, precariously close to the smoldering wasteland before us.

The scene reminded me of movie battlefields after the battles. Wisps of white smoke rose from the charred ground, which was so hot in places that it had melted pieces of smashed beer bottles into brown lumps. The inside of my nose stung and the air was heavy with a biting stench similar to oven cleaner.

"Stand here any longer and pretty soon I'll be spouting conspiracies," Jane said, covering her nose with her hand.

"This is as bad as it gets, ladies," Pete said, waving his arms. "As you may have noticed, the rest of Limbo is untouched, except for a few potholes here and there. So why did the government spend forty-two million of your taxpaying dollars to move everyone out?"

"Logically, because living on top of a fire is unsafe," Jane said. "But, again, that would be the logical explanation so I'm not sure it'd play in Limbo."

"That's because it'd be wrong," Pete said. "The U.S. government doesn't give a pig's snout about our safety. All it cares about is acquiring the rights to the Mammoth Basin—the rights that are currently held by the town of Limbo. Once they accomplish that, they'll sell the rights off to some American coal company that donated heavily to the president's reelection campaign."

"Where exactly is the Mammoth Basin?" Jane asked.

Pete spread his arms. "It runs under all of Limbo straight through to the Dead Zone. That's why the government banned mining in the Dead Zone, because it connects to Limbo through the Mammoth Basin. Too much of a risk with the fire burning there."

That put the Mammoth Basin directly below where Bud wanted to build the casino.

"The coal from the Mammoth Basin would be worth billions if it could be removed efficiently," Pete said. "But 'efficiently' means literally ripping off the town and dumping it in a valley like coal companies do in West Virginia.

"Can't strip here, that's the thing," he went on. "If you did, you'd expose that smoldering anthracite to oxygen and this whole county would explode in flames. It's driving the collieries nuts to have this incredible deposit of coal and no way to get at it."

"So why pay to move everyone out?" I asked.

"Think, Bubbles. You're not thinking." Pete hitched his pants. "Let's say the fire is put out. All my neighbors and relatives and nieces and nephews can move back to the town where they were born. Can the coal company come in, rip the top off and mine then?"

"It'd be difficult, I suppose."

"But with the fire burning, the government has an excuse to force everyone out because of our reported safety. Let me tell you, no one ever died in Limbo from the gasses or the fire. Not one person. It's a scam. The government's been pressured by the coal industry to evacuate the town. Once Limbo ceases to exist, the mining rights are up for grabs. So, when—and I think it is when, not if—a method of extinguishing this fire comes along, that company with the rights will have carte blanche to rip up this town and make billions."

"Do you think McMullen Coal is that company?" I asked.

Pete frowned. "Unlikely. Too small an operation. Besides, why would they have sold the mining rights to the Dead Zone, at a loss, to Price if they had been planning with the government to tear up Limbo and mine under there, too?"

"I'm surprised you haven't been offered millions to move out," Jane said.

"Oh, I have. And I've turned them all down. There was a time there when a lawyer a day representing some party or another came knocking at my door with a big fat check. That stopped, though. My hunch is that the coal companies have given up on trying to find ways to extinguish the fire. And as long as that fire burns, that coal can't be touched."

"Aren't you afraid for your life?" Genevieve asked. "If they kill you, that's one less obstacle to getting the mining rights."

"If they kill me, ma'am, they're gonna have to answer to a trained militia of my buddies. We're prepared for that event. Believe you me."

"I think I'm in love," Genevieve moaned.

"I think I need to leave," said Jane, who was turning green. "These gasses are making me sick."

Jane and Genevieve returned to Pete's house while I poked

around the burning landscape. It fascinated me, the way the earth was literally on fire. I tried to relate what Pete had just said to Stinky's claim that my story had missed the crucial point. Had McMullen violated its permits so it could dip into the Mammoth Basin? Perhaps. I was more intrigued by the location of Price's casino over this humongous coal deposit, the fact that Price had bought the land and its mining rights from McMullen at a discount and that Price was now dead, murdered in one of McMullen's own mines.

I strolled up to St. Ignatius Church for a better view. The church must have been abandoned years ago. The stained glass in the front windows had been smashed by rocks. Faded red, blue and green pieces lay on the burnt grass, also melted into lumps like the beer bottle shards a few feet away. In happier days, Limbo couples had been married here; they'd baptized their children in this church and memorialized their dead. And now . . . now it was such a waste. All because bureaucrats were too petty to take responsibility.

A car door slammed behind me. I turned to see a man locking his blue Saab and walking in my direction, almost stumbling. His tie was askew, his beautiful tan Burberry coat was seriously creased and his eyes were wild.

Hugh McMullen on a bender.

Chapter 14

"**N**ot here," he said, stepping into the church. "In here. Sanctuary."

I hesitated, not sure what to do, and then I found myself trailing behind him. As my eyes adjusted to the dim light inside, I distinguished the crucifix over the altar and a blue and pink statue of Mary weeping by its side.

What I did not see was Hugh McMullen.

"Hello?" I called out.

"Use the stairs," he replied. He must have entered the door by the altar. I took a few steps and tripped on a deep crevice that ran straight down the middle aisle between the worn pews, as though the church had been ripped in two by an earthquake.

"Jesus Christ," I exclaimed, grabbing a pew to stop myself from falling. The disheartened figure on the crucifix hung forlornly, severely disappointed by my language.

"Whoops!" I covered my mouth. "Sorry."

I traced the fissure to where it opened widest in the middle. Kneeling down, I carefully extended my hand, only to pull it out quickly in pain. The crack was steaming. A very faint stream of white smoke rose from its interior, sending up a foul incense of fuming sulfur and wood. It was a miracle that the entire church wasn't ablaze.

The saints who had remained intact smiled benevolently from the stained glass windows, their fingers held up in signs of peace and patience—attributes of which I suddenly felt in mighty short supply.

Keeping a lookout for more cracks and potholes, I tiptoed

toward the door by the altar and descended the carpeted stairs. It was even darker down here. Warmer, too.

At the bottom I could make out several closed doors off a short hallway. There was the smell of chalk and crayons, poster paint, paste and paper. Sunday school rooms. At last I arrived at a door with a faint golden glow underneath.

Gently pushing the door open, I was surprised to find Hugh praying in a tiny chapel, his back turned toward me. Two candles were lit. It was stifling hot in there. And it reeked of cigarettes.

"Mr. McMullen?" I asked softly.

Hugh McMullen pivoted mechanically. The candlelight had done nothing to soften his appearance. His hair was ragged and his face unshaven. He had tossed his rain coat carelessly over the pew and thrown the tie there with it. My eyes dropped to his preppy loafers.

"What happened to you?"

Hugh McMullen pushed back a lock of wavy hair that had fallen over his forehead. "I've been through the ringer, that's what's happened to me." He fumbled in his khakis and brought out a maroon box of Dunhill cigarettes. Give me a break. Dunhills?

"Did anyone come with you?" he asked. His hand shook as he tried to light the cigarette with a silver lighter.

"Why?" I said. "And why are your clothes a mess and why did you want me to follow you here?"

"I had to talk to you. In private. Without the other reporters finding out."

"You had your chance last night when I left a message at The Inn in Glen Ellen asking for a comment." I stepped back to get some air. Ugh. I waved the smoke away. "If you have a problem with my story today, call my editors at the *News-Times*."

Wait. What was I saying? Bad idea. The editors were probably drafting my pink slip right now. Drafting it with glee and permanent ink.

"I don't give a damn about that story." McMullen perched his butt on the communion rail. "I don't give a damn about mining permits or union contracts or coal. Period. I detest this business. I inherited this company from my father and he inherited it from his father who inherited it from his father. I never asked to be a coal baron."

I watched him suck on the cigarette. Spoiled child, I thought. Life handed to him on a silver platter and it wasn't good enough. He should be spanked and sent to his room. "So, you didn't know about your own company digging beyond its permits? Or fudging maps to escape the regulators?"

"I could care less. That's why I have people working for me, to keep an eye on shit like that. You know what I told the state when they asked me why the company dug three hundred feet into the Dead Zone? I told them maybe the miners didn't know they'd gone that far. It's dark down there."

I choked back a laugh, appalled as well that he was blaming his company's crime on the workers.

"Lookit, I have to get in touch with Carl Koolball," he said, tossing the cigarette onto the chapel floor. (The chapel floor!) "You're the only one who's had contact with him since Price's murder. How do I find him?"

My jaw dropped. "How did you know that—?"

"If I don't get hold of Koolball," he interrupted impatiently. "I am in some deep, deep shit."

"For digging under the Dead Zone?"

"Nooo." McMullen massaged his temples. He was barely, barely tolerating me. "For a separate matter altogether. For something that I am absolutely not discussing with a two-bit, Podunk reporter named Bubbles Yablonsky."

"For shooting Bud Price in the chest." I held my breath and mentally crossed my fingers.

McMullen dropped his hands. "Don't tell me the press knows already. Donohue said he wouldn't make it public."

It was my turn to say, "Nooo. I guessed. And you fell for it."

"Bitch."

"You say that like it's a bad thing." I'd seen that on a bumper sticker once and I'd been waiting to use it on the next man who cursed me out. "Why don't you fill me in on what's going on and, when we're done, we'll talk about Stinky."

"Hard ass," he said.

I patted my rear. "Thank you. Now that you mention it, I have been Sommersizing." I pulled out my reporter's notebook and pen. "Let's start with the first question. Did you murder Bud Price?"

"If my lawyer were here—"

"You wouldn't have a chance in hell of getting hold of Stinky Koolball."

He folded his arms and glared at me. "No, I did not murder Bud Price. Like I said, I don't give a damn about the coal business. I just stay in it because it earns me over a million dollars a year. Tell me, would you give up a million-dollar paycheck for doing nothing?"

I ignored that. It was insulting to a hardworking single mother like myself who was barely raking in twenty grand despite two jobs. "Then, why does Donohue suspect you?"

Hugh got out that pack of Dunhills again. "Because—and I have no clue as to how this happened—the Keystone cops here claim that the bullet that killed Price allegedly came from my gun, a Smith and Wesson, which last I knew was locked up in my house back in Pittsburgh."

"Where is it now?"

"Out of the case. Missing. Wouldn't be surprised if Chief Donohue took it himself."

"Yup." I wrote this down. They were going to have to start calling me Bubbles Blockbuster Yablonsky around the newsroom.

"Were you in Pittsburgh the night of the murder?"

"Actually, there's been some misunderstanding about that. I was here in town, staying with a friend I've known for years."

"Friend's name?" I positioned my pen.

"Is none of your business."

"Funny name, 'none of your business.' Isn't none of your business providing you with an alibi?"

"That's why I'm in this hell hole with you." He lit another cigarette and exhaled. "That's why I look this way. That's why I need Koolball. My friend is scared. The cops in this town have threatened to lock her up in jail if she sticks by me. So she finked. Friends will do that, you know."

Not mine. "How can Stinky save you?"

"You figure it out." He approached me, his mouth set and mean in a schoolboy-tantrum way. "I've answered enough of your stupid questions. You said you'd tell me how to find Koolball." He grabbed the back of my neck. "Now tell me where he is."

I blinked and tried to remain peaceful. McMullen had just crossed into the brink of some psychotic hostile territory. In short, he was flipping out.

"Calm down, Hugh," I said, putting my hand on his. "Calm down. I'm not exactly sure how to find Stinky myself. Not right now."

"What?" He shook off my hand and raised his fist. I covered my face and prayed he wouldn't hit me. I don't like getting hit. It's so . . . painful.

There was a crash as one of the wooden chairs went flying.

"You bitch! And I mean that like it's a bad thing."

"Hit me, Hugh. Lay one finger on me," I said, lowering my hands, "and Donohue has a legitimate reason to throw you in jail right now. I never said I'd bring Stinky to you, only that we could talk about him. Stinky's in hiding. If I see him, I'll tell him you need to speak with him."

Hugh stamped out his cigarette and snatched up his coat and tie. "I'll find him myself." He gave another chair a kick and then put his fist into the chapel wall before flinging open the door and stomping out, making sure to slam it hard as he left.

Whew! I let out a long sigh and collapsed onto one of the hard wooden chairs that McMullen hadn't broken. What a brat. My knees were shaking so hard the chair was rocking.

Outside the door came the shuffling of footsteps. Oh, super. Baby Hughey was back to lay into me. The shuffling stopped. There was a sound by the floor, as though someone were trying to slip something under it. And then came the click. I don't like clicks.

I blew out the candles, felt my way along the wall and put my hand on the knob. Just as I feared. Not only was the knob locked—it was hot.

"When in danger or in doubt, run in circles, scream and shout."

That was the children's rhyme that ran through my mind as I broke two nails and completely ruined my fifteen-dollar manicure for nothing while attempting to pry open the door. It was sealed shut. I deduced that some evil devil had stuffed the space between the bottom of the door and the basement floor with a heavy cloth. Perhaps a coat.

A coat like the one McMullen had been wearing.

I put my trusty old cheerleading talents to good work by screaming my head off until my throat burned. Then I began to get lightheaded and dizzy. A distinct buzz grew in my ears. It was sickening and at times I was close to throwing up Mona's Wonder Gobbler with Slime. I grabbed a chair, sat down and put my head between my knees, which were shaking and weak.

Carbon monoxide poisoning. Odorless. Invisible. CO. Who had told me about its symptoms? Donohue. Donohue had listed all the ills—headache, dizziness, nausea. He said it started off like the flu and you ended up either dead or debilitated. I did not want to be spoon-fed pudding at the nursing home. I did not want to die, either, for the record. All I wanted was sleep.

My eyelids drooped heavily and a nap became a top priority. I could assess this situation much better after a few winks. That's dangerous, Bubbles. Go to sleep and you may never wake up, a voice in my head said.

She was right, that voice in my head. She'd been right eighteen years ago about not skipping up to that Lehigh fraternity party where Dan the Man lay in wait, slurping on a funnel of beer. She'd been right about the Radio Shack clerk with whom I shared five minutes of sexual deviance in the back of my Camaro.

Even though she was right, I had to sleep.

Leaning against the wall for support, I shoved my hand into my purse and pulled out my wallet. Okay, credit cards were a long shot, but I'd seen Stiletto work them on a door in Dutch Country. I yanked out the infamous Visa and tried to focus.

Rolling along the wall, my hands slid down the crack in the doorjamb. Wiggling the card into the slim space, I let out a weak cry of joy when the Visa, so flexible after years of overuse, broke the seal in the lock. The door popped open.

Vaguely, I was aware that whatever had been stuffed against the door was not a coat. It was a blue plastic tarp. Super, I thought, not really caring, just wanting to sleep.

The hallway outside had fresh air but even so I couldn't take another step. A little nap wouldn't hurt now that I was out of danger. I threw my purse on a musty smelling loveseat in the hall and collapsed, drifting into a haze of worries. Where was Jane? What had happened to McMullen? Why wasn't Stiletto here? And finally, what was my name?

My name. I could not remember my name. What was my name? It was something sophisticated that befitted a journalist like myself, Diane Sawyer or Maureen Dowd. Of that I was pretty positive.

Chapter 15

"**B**ubbles! Bubbles Yablonsky!"

Oh, that's right. It was Bubbles. Well, that wasn't very sophisticated, was it? Strippers and cartoon characters were named Bubbles. What genius had given me that annoying name, I'd like to know.

"We need to get you out of here."

Yes we do, I agreed mentally. Right after this snooze. "Let me sleep."

Muscular arms surrounded my chest and lifted me up. A man began praying out loud, "Dear Lord. Please save this lamb in your flock from an untimely end. Give me the strength to carry her to safety as you have given so many in your flock the power to do great feats in times of hardship. Amen."

My head fell back and I let out a loud snore. That roused me a bit, enough to be conscious of the baseball cap and tousled blond hair. Zeke Allen.

"Hey, sleeping beauty." He slapped my cheeks gently. "Wake up. Wake up or you're history. And we know how you are with history." He threw me over his shoulder. "How much do you weigh?" he asked.

"One-eighteen." Like most women, I could lie about my weight under any condition, CO poisoning, fire, crashing airplane, you name it. I was one-eighteen, come hell or high water. "Don't forget my purse."

"Leave it."

"Get it. It's my purse. A girl's gotta have her purse."

He knelt slowly and picked up my purse.

"And my shoes," I added, since they had slipped off my feet when I lay on the couch.

"Man, no one would have gotten off the *Titanic* if you'd been around."

A few minutes later Zeke carried me up the stairs and into the church. The air was better, but my head was still splitting. Oww.

"Was that you praying?" I asked.

"Never hurts, does it?"

He took me outside where there was bright sunshine, blue sky and plenty of clean air—at least as clean as it gets in Limbo, PA—and laid me carefully on the dry grass. I clamped my head between my hands and wished for sleep. Why won't people let me sleep? Always moving me from this place to that place.

Zeke bent over me. He leaned down and pressed his soft lips against mine. They were full and alive. For the teeniest, tiniest moment, I felt twenty-two again. Vibrant. Carefree. A virile man caressing me. My chest rose into his and I let go. Breathless. Choking. . . .

"Get off!" I said, pushing him away and coughing. "What are you doing?"

"Mouth-to-mouth." He sat back, offended. "You stopped breathing."

My heart was racing. Whatever Zeke's motivations, I had to admit he had stirred my juices either by pumping in oxygen or, well, you know. . . . My lungs were now working and blood pounded in my brain so hard I could hear my pulse.

"You didn't have to give me mouth-to-mouth," I whispered.

"Are you kidding? When I found you in the church you were nearly dead. Although you wouldn't have been in there in the first place if I'd been able to do my job as your bodyguard."

There was a sound like an amplified mosquito in my ears. *Eeeeee.* "What happened?" My question came out like a wheeze.

"Darned if I know. I stopped by the bank to cash a check while you were at the Main Mane. When I left the bank, I found all this white junk in my tailpipe. It was stuffed in my carburetor, too."

Zeke took off his baseball cap and ran his fingers through his sandy hair. He was tan and healthy from life in the outdoors. He would've made a great surfer—if the Pacific Ocean ever moved to Eastern Pennsylvania. "I may be crazy, but I swear it was mashed potatoes."

Genevieve strikes again. Guess she was securing more than Roxanne's home when we were at the Main Mane.

"By the time I went home and got my Dad's tow truck, your car was gone from the salon. I sweet-talked your cousin Roxanne into telling me you went to Limbo. Located your car parked on Elm Street and ran into Pete Zidukis, who said you were up by the church. That's where I found you, passed out and half dead. All because of mashed potatoes."

"Guess that should teach you not to spy on people."

Zeke plucked a blade of grass. "Spying on you?"

"Confess," I said, still too woozy to raise my head. "The only reason Steve Stiletto hired you was so that you could report back to him on what kind of progress I was making on this story while he was in New York."

"No, ma'am. I'd never do something like that and Steve doesn't pry. All he asks me are a few questions about how you're doing. I say 'fine.' He asks what you did during the day. Sometimes we talk about his stint in India and his plans to open another AP bureau in England. For that he pays me five hundred bucks a day. Never made money so easy in my life."

I started coughing again, this time out of shock. "Five hundred bucks a day. That's—"

"Almost one thousand bucks so far. I didn't set the price, he did. He said if I kept a bead on you for a week he'd pay thirty-five hundred bucks wired straight into my checking account."

Hey, that could buy an engagement ring.

I put out my hand and Zeke helped me up. I swooned in dizziness and had to lean against him to get my balance. I was surprised by how tall he was, how his shoulders were so well built. How he smelled like cut hay. He was a hick. A cute hick, but a hick nonetheless. I couldn't help comparing him to Stiletto, who was so worldly, so sure of himself. Zeke was more like a rough piece of marble, ready to be chiseled into David by the right hands.

He supported me around the waist as I attempted to take a few baby steps.

"The thing is, my gravy train's not gonna pull into the station if my boat keeps getting plugged with spuds," he said. "Over forty now, my car smells like french fries. I'm just glad I've got the tow truck as backup. Otherwise no self-respecting woman would go out with me."

"And I suppose you're lousy with women?" I asked.

"Afraid not." He held me steady. "The ones around here are too silly. I'm looking for a woman of strong moral character. A woman who's more mature—like you."

Had he just called me old? I closed my eyes and opened them deliberately. Each time the earth swiveled a bit. "I'm, ahem, mature enough to be your babysitter, Zeke."

"Since when do you babysit twenty-three-year-olds?"

I tried to take longer steps, but my knees buckled.

"Are you okay?" His grip tightened. "All joking aside, CO poisoning is dangerous business. You're still not out of the woods. It can take hours, even days to flush it from your system. Maybe we should get you to the hospital. They got a pressure tank there just to remove the CO from your bloodstream."

"No, thanks." I took another step. Instinct told me that the more I moved, the faster the CO would leave my body. I had to find Jane. I had to track down McMullen and ask him why he locked me in the chapel. I took another step, which was easier than the one before. "I think I'm getting better." Though my head still hurt like hell.

Zeke gave my shoulder a quick squeeze. "Glad to hear it. Stiletto would kill me if you bit the dust on my watch. Okay, now spill. What happened in the church?"

"Promise you won't tell Stiletto?"

"And admit that I let you slip out of my sight? What do you think?"

So as Zeke and I circled St. Ignatius's, I told him everything, including, for some reason, the part about Jane and my fears that she had a crush on Professor Tallow. Zeke was an amazingly rapt listener. Occasionally he asked me a few questions when I drifted off topic, but mostly he kept his mouth shut. The only comment he made referred to Pete Zidukis's claim that Limbo sat on a gazillion dollars worth of coal.

"That's a load of horse hockey. That rumor about the Mammoth Basin is a tall tale I've heard since childhood. The town never owned the rights to that coal, anyway."

"Then the government didn't move everyone out just so they could sell the land to a coal company?" We had reached Zeke's tow truck.

"The government moved everyone out so they could dig up the town and stop the fire," he said. "As long as there are holdouts, they can't do that and the fire burns on and on. But what does a crazy old fart like Zidukis care? He'll be dead in twenty years and by that time the whole town will have caved in."

That's when we heard the shouts from over the hill. At first they were faint and then louder. It was clearly a desperate call for help.

"That's my daughter," I said. "She's in trouble."

Zeke opened my door in the tow truck. "It's coming from old Route 61, the portion that's been closed off because of the fire," he said, helping me in. "We better hurry. There are some huge craters on that road. You can go straight down into the pits if you step on the wrong spot."

I had prepared myself for a gruesome scene. Jane submerged below smoldering macadam, only her blue-topped head sticking out among the steam and smoke.

What we found instead was G, headphones on, in a bright yellow, egg-shaped vehicle completely surrounded by black rubber bumpers about a foot thick. From each of its two windows bulged white airbags, which must have been activated when it drove into a pothole the size of a wading pool.

Jane was jumping up and down, hollering and pointing at the goof, who was stuck in the driver's seat. Stuck not by crushed metal, for I didn't think this kind of metal could crush, but by his nose ring, which had punctured the airbag and gotten caught.

"You have to get him out," Jane said. "If the battery inside the car reaches four-hundred degrees centigrade it will explode! I've been trying and trying, but I can't push the car alone and G can't get out. Quick."

Zeke swung the tow truck around so that its rear touched the end of G's car. We both got out and I helped him with the winch in the back, thankful that my headache had temporarily subsided in the mayhem.

"Yo! Wassup, Mrs. Y?" G said, moving the airbag aside a bit and leaning out the window as much as the airbag would allow.

"Who's that?" Zeke asked as we attached the hook to the bumper.

"My daughter's boyfriend."

G, apparently unaware that he was about to blow up in an Armageddon mixture of battery acid and mine fire, bobbed his head to the music in the headphones.

"That's the professor you're worried about?"

"No. That's the guy I want her to get back together with. I called him and asked him to join us in Limbo."

"I can see why. He sure is a keeper."

I joined Jane by the side of the road.

"What happened?"

"Roxy gave G directions to Pete Zidukis's and when he got there I told him about this closed highway. So we took a drive up here and this is what happened."

Zeke gunned the tow truck and pulled out G. G let his head hang out the window like a dog, smiling and hooting as the car emerged from the sinkhole.

"Yahoo!" he yelled. "One more time!"

I covered my eyes.

"Thanks, Mom," Jane said. "It would've been awful if you hadn't come. Who's driving the truck?"

Zeke was out now, strolling up the road in his cowboy boots, all lean and brawn. G was busy trying to unhook the airbag from his nose ring, his double chin getting in the way. Zeke regarded him with open scorn.

"City kids," he said, under his breath.

I introduced him to Jane and vice versa.

"Thanks for showing up in the nick of time," Jane said.

"De nada. What's wrong with your hair?"

Jane brushed back a raspberry blue spike. "People make too much fuss over hair. I think this color's artistic. Anyway, it's only cuticle."

"Cuticle?" Zeke wrinkled his nose. "Your mother lets you do that?"

"My mother," Jane answered, "doesn't *let* me do anything. I'm old enough to do what I want. I'm auditing courses at a university, you know."

"Ahhh." Zeke brought his hand to his mouth in an effort to keep a straight face. "Well then, you are grown up. My mistake."

"Stiletto hired Zeke to be my bodyguard while he's in New York City," I explained.

"Really?" Jane asked. "How do you know Steve?"

Uh-oh, I thought, as Zeke revealed that Stiletto had bailed him out of a jail in Mexico. Nothing more intriguing to a teenage girl than a hunk unjustifiably imprisoned.

"Cerro Huerro?" she asked.

"That's the one. I'm surprised you've heard of it."

"What were you in for? Drugs?"

Zeke kicked some melted macadam with his toe. "Actually, I was in Chiapas building houses with my church group."

Church group? So that explained the praying. This was a regular John Boy Walton we had here.

"And they put you in jail for that?" Jane was suspicious. "My understanding was that the Mexican law pertaining to tourists engaging in nontourist activities only resulted in a permanent expulsion."

"See now, when they permanently expelled me they found a shotgun in my truck. For rattlesnake hunting."

"That was stupid. That could get you fifteen years in jail."

Zeke turned toward me. "She always this way?"

"Exhausting, isn't it?"

We were saved by G, who had given up on the nose ring. It hung forlornly from the airbag and G had shoved a wad of Burger King napkins into his nose to stem the bleeding. He was some sight with the orange crew cut and baggy jeans that hung so low on his hips, his red plaid boxers peeked out. He kept having to pull up his jeans with one hand while keeping his other hand on his nose.

"This place is awesome. Dead trees. Smoking earth," G said. "It's so Blair Witch." Crimson patches were spreading across the Burger King napkin.

"You know," Zeke said, "you could've pushed that car out of the hole yourself. It wasn't that hard."

"No way, man. I could never have pushed that thing."

"Strapping boy like yourself. Go on." Zeke reached out and squeezed his muscle. "How much can you bench? At your age I was pressing five hundred."

G gazed dully. "I don't know. I've never lifted weights."

"That's pitiful. We're gonna work on that, starting with a three-mile run at six a.m. tomorrow."

His eyes widened in total terror.

"Now let's see about that car." Zeke put his arm around G's shoulder, leading him off. "What is it exactly? I don't believe I've ever come across that model before."

G sheepishly admitted that it was a Teen Safety Car designed to carry only one passenger, run on electricity and not to exceed fifty-five miles on the highway. He had leased it from the insurance company.

Zeke launched into a tirade about the namby-pamby, overregulated society of car seats, bicycle helmets and safety belts while G accidentally gave himself a wedgie by pulling up his boxers instead of his jeans.

When they were out of earshot, I asked Jane how she knew so much about Mexican jails.

" 'Cause of G," she said. "G's decided against going to Europe to pick grapes because he thinks it's been done. So we were looking into harvesting coffee in Mexico. Then my research showed that there are four thousand Americans in Mexican jails on charges ranging from possessing a thimble of pot to waving an American flag. That's tough because Mexico's governed by Napoleonic law, which means you're guilty until proven innocent, which also means that once you're thrown in jail you can languish there for years, even decades."

"And?"

"And G said he wasn't worried. He never waves an American flag."

My stomach lurched.

"By the way," Jane prattled on, "thanks for calling him up here to help out with the investigation. G was really flattered."

"Excuse me?" I said, glancing over at G who was leaning against the Teen Safety Car, adjusting his underwear.

"That's what G said, that you called him to Limbo because he was so good in finding things. Like the marijuana plants, remember that? Of course, when it comes to marijuana, G could find it blindfolded."

I considered Professor Tallow. Stable. Mature. European. Good job. Great benefits. No indication of hallucinogenic drug use. So what if he was a little creepy and thirty years older than my daughter? Women do better with men who are a little older.

Chapter **16**

I wasn't too confident that they'd actually ever seen airbags before at the Slagville Texaco, where we dropped off Jane and G to repair the Teen Safety Car. After a few telephone consultations with the automaker in Detroit, the Slagville mechanics had a vague notion of what to do. Whether or not the bags would ever work again was another matter.

There was still the outstanding issue of my editors and what one might call their silent fury. Silent because I hadn't called the *News-Times* yet. But no matter how angry Mr. Salvo might be about my story switch, he would have to be pleased that I had conducted an exclusive interview—including notes, thank you very much—with Hugh McMullen. McMullen's own confirmation that he was a murder suspect was the icing on the cake.

Genevieve took my Camaro to the A&P to pick up groceries for dinner after she and Zeke had decided it wasn't safe for me to get behind the wheel. Not that it's ever safe for me to get behind the wheel. While Zeke drove me back to the Main Mane, I considered how best to break the news to Mr. Salvo.

"Boy, you were quiet," Zeke said as he helped me out of the tow truck and onto the sidewalk in front of Roxanne's salon. "Maybe I should take you to the hospital, anyway."

"I'm fine," I said, climbing the steps. "I was just thinking."

"Thinking, huh." Zeke stopped me at the door and lay his arm casually across my shoulder. "Just what I've been searching for. A woman with beauty and brains. Not to mention guts."

In the late afternoon light Zeke's flawless features glowed with the kind of vigor that only the young, virile and testosterone-laden possess, but rarely appreciate. This man could turn on granite. He was pure sex, from his wild hair and capable shoulders to the faded outline of his wallet in his back jeans pocket. I wasn't too tempted. After all, I was chaste, a model of perfect feminine control. And I had other romantic interests worth waiting for. At least I hoped I did.

I politely removed Zeke's arm. "Stiletto. Remember him?"

"Hey, I wasn't making a move." He held up both hands. "Anyway, it's not like you're his property, right?"

"True."

"If you were married, absolutely." He moved in closer. "But you're not. You're free. Or . . . are you?"

Damn, this kid was good for a church boy. I didn't recall men with lines like that when I was twenty-three. Then again, when I was twenty-three I was working two jobs and caring for a self-centered husband and a five-year-old.

"Listen, Zeke . . ."

The front door flew open. Roxanne stood there wearing a hot pink chiffon blouse, skin-tight pants and cleavage, cleavage, cleavage. This outfit didn't just happen. It had been concocted. She must've seen Zeke through the side window, checked a catalogue to see what all the well-dressed hookers were wearing these days, and done a quick change.

"Hell-o handsome," she cried, grabbing Zeke by the hand and yanking him inside. "Don't just let him stand there. Invite the gentleman in, cousin."

I traipsed behind her into the salon where Mama was waiting—an oversized rolling pin in her hand.

"Oh, no. Don't tell me you're on safety patrol now, too?" I asked.

Mama jutted her chin at Zeke. "Who's the cowhand? You want I should clock him?"

"No way, Aunt LuLu," Roxanne protested. "He's the bodyguard Steve Stiletto hired to protect Bubbles. He stopped by this afternoon and we had a perfectly delightful chat. Seems some hideous individual stuffed mashed potatoes in this poor fellow's tail end."

"Tailpipe," Zeke corrected.

"Tail whatever." Roxanne snuck a quick glance at Zeke's behind.

"Roxanne's right," I said before leaping into a detailed explanation about how Zeke had pulled me out of the church. My head was pounding by the time I finished, as though my body remembered the CO poisoning and decided to play the part.

"Aw, shucks," said Mama. "Anyone who sticks his neck out for Bubbles is like family." She lowered the rolling pin.

"Practically kissing cousin," agreed Roxanne. "Won't you stay for dinner, Zeke?"

As though she thought this would be tempting, Mama rattled off the night's menu: meat loaf with ketchup sauce, frozen green beans, the always present applesauce, milk (iced tea for the adults) and, ahem, mashed potatoes.

"No, thanks," said Zeke. "I think I've had enough mashed potatoes."

But Mama wouldn't take no for an answer and despite his polite declines, Zeke ended up literally picking Roxanne's fingers off his wrist so he could leave. Roxanne watched him from the storefront window and pouted when he climbed into the truck.

I went upstairs to take a detoxifying shower with Mama's homemade rose-scented glycerin soap. When I emerged clean, wet and naked, I found Roxanne sitting on the vanity in a veil of steam.

"Pardon me for busting in like this," she said, swinging her legs, "but I gotta know if I have carte blanche."

I modestly held a towel to my chest. "Carte blanche for what?"

"Like you don't know. Zeke. I wanna date him."

I slipped into pink thong underwear I'd brought for my night with Stiletto and felt sad. It was so wasted on Roxanne. "You can't date Zeke. You're married."

"Doesn't feel that way. Stinky's been gone for weeks. I have got to get me some loving or I am going to burst."

I snapped the elastic of my thong. "You're not even divorced . . . or separated."

"I'm not talking about getting remarried. I'm talking about getting me a man to hang around the house. After the break-in today, I realized I need Stinky for more than the sex. Having him around made me feel safe, Bub. Even if all he did was gnash his teeth about McMullen."

"He was wasting his gnashing. McMullen doesn't give a hoot about coal." I told her about McMullen's immature temper tantrum in the church. "I think it might have been him who locked me in the chapel."

"Boss boy." Roxy hopped off the counter. "They're all that way, aren't they? I remember when McMullen's brothers used to come back from college every Christmas and strut around town like they owned the place, even though they hadn't done a lick of mining in their lives. That's why I love Stinky. He's college educated, but he's real, you know? Down-to-earth."

"He's coming back, Roxanne. Heck, I bet he's already back in Slagville. He told Jane that I was to meet him at some hoagie joint. Is there a hoagie joint in town?"

"Not that I know of. Is that a matching bra?"

"Ten ninety-nine for the complete set at JC Penney," I said, shifting the pink cups. "One more reason you can't date Zeke. He's too young for you."

"Like hell that stud's too young. I'm forty—just hitting my sexual prime and Zeke's on the downside of his. Oh, you're not going to wear that, are you? It is Mrs. Price you're meeting, you know."

"Mrs. Price?" I zipped up the side of my beige leatherette miniskirt. "What're you talking about?"

"Didn't you get the message?" Roxanne leaned into the mirror and inspected her eyebrows. "You're supposed to meet her at eight p.m. tonight at the inn, room 500. She said she was returning your call."

"Shoot. And here I was looking forward to calling in my story and hitting the hay. I'm beat."

As soon as the words left my mouth, I knew they were heresy. Everyone had been clamoring for an interview with Chrissy Price. Those other reporters would have jumped at the chance. Then again, those other reporters hadn't slept on an uncomfortable steel foldout cot next to two snoring broads in a sex hotel the night before and on a jailhouse bed the night before that.

"You sure it was Mrs. Price, Roxanne?"

"Most definitely. Said you had to come. Said she didn't know who else to call. If you ask me, she sounded absolutely panicked. You have to go see that woman, no matter how tired you are."

After I was dressed, with a tasteful application of fawn eyeliner, black-brown waterproof mascara and blushing pink on my lips, I went downstairs and called Mr. Salvo with an update. This was not a phone call I looked forward to making.

"Salvo," is how he answered the phone.

I cleared my throat. "Hi, Mr. Salvo. It's me, Bubbles."

"Bubbles?"

"Bubbles."

"Wait. I gotta put you on hold." The next thing I knew I was listening to an a cappella version of "More Than a Woman."

In the next room, Jane, G, Mama and Genevieve were setting the dinner table and engaging in an argument about Celtic stones and dowsing. Mama insisted that the so-called Celtic rocks had been merely left over by farmers a few generations before and that Professor Tallow was a hysterical ignoramus.

Jane countered by pointing out that the dowsing rods had spun furiously when they were placed on top of the pointed standing stones or directed toward the opening of the cellars so their placement couldn't have been haphazard.

"Professor Tallow has a theory that it's a magnetic field," Jane said, placing a dish of baked tofu on the table. Her substitute for meat loaf. "That's why the Celts arranged divining stones on those spots, for purposes of spiritual observance and astronomy."

"Like that Jamaican fortune-teller on TV," G declared, his nose still slightly bloody from the afternoon's mishap.

Mama brought over the bowl of beans. "That's astrology, genius, though dowsing is just as kooky, if you ask me."

"I beg your pardon." Genevieve stopped pouring iced tea. "I'll have you know that dowsing is a perfectly respectable science. I used a dowser to find my first well. The cherry branch in his hand bent so low to the ground that the bark ripped right off."

"Ah, you're lame-brained, too," Mama said, motioning for everyone to sit down. I signaled for them to eat without me.

Mr. Salvo was back on. "You still there, Bubbles?"

"Yeah."

"You're fired."

I gripped the edge of the phone table. "Okay."

"And you're working Sunday. No one gets out of the Sunday shift. I don't care if they're dead, their corpse still has to call all the police departments and find out what's going on. Understand? You're working, but you're fired."

"Makes sense."

"Don't you ever, ever, ever pull that stunt on me again," he said. "Where did you learn a trick like that? Six months ago, you didn't even know what a slug was. You were some clueless hairdresser clicking around the newsroom. Now you're using our computerized editorial system to sneak your story onto the front page. I'm just waiting for McMullen's lawyers to sue us."

"I think they're preoccupied with other matters."

"Like what?"

"Like Hugh McMullen is the prime murder suspect. The bullet that killed Price came from his gun, a Smith and Wesson he kept in Pittsburgh, and McMullen was in Slagville when Price was murdered, although he doesn't have an alibi."

Mr. Salvo was quiet. Roxanne was up from the table. She

opened the coat closet and handed Genevieve two metal coat hangers for cutting and bending into dowsing rods.

"Of course, you'll have to call him for a reaction," Mr. Salvo said, clearly reining in his enthusiasm. "Can't just say the company was closed so McMullen wasn't available for comment, like you did in today's story. I'd have never let that cheap shot slip past if I'd been on the desk."

"I did get McMullen's comment about the murder investigation. In fact," I paused for dramatic effect, "*he* was the one who told me he's a suspect."

"You're yanking my chain."

"I am not. McMullen's a mess. He looks like death warmed over and the only reason he spilled his guts was because he thought I could put him in touch with Stinky Koolball."

"Why would he think that?"

"Uh . . ." I was loathe to tell Mr. Salvo that Stinky had stopped by my house in Lehigh. Brought up so many icky legal and ethical questions. "Because I'm the cousin of Stinky's wife."

"Oh, yeah. Okay. Twelve inches and no more. Keep it short, sweet and accurate," Mr. Salvo said. "Get that Chief Donohue at home and tell him you're going with the story no matter what. He'll have to either confirm or deny that McMullen's a suspect. Call it in and let's talk at eight-thirty."

Genevieve had started a slow march across Roxanne's living room floor, holding the dowsing rods in front of her like they were loaded pistols.

"Can't talk at eight-thirty. I've got an exclusive interview with Chrissy Price over at The Inn in Glen Ellen."

Pound. Mr. Salvo's fist hit the news desk. "Why didn't you say so? What's gotten into you up there in Slagville? First you get privileged documents, then the head of a major coal company admits to you he's a murder suspect and now you're meeting with Bud Price's widow? You handing out the payola or what?"

"Mr. Salvo! I hardly think a millionaire like Hugh McMullen needs to be paid off."

"Just don't let it go to your head. Journalism is like baseball. You get a streak where all you can hit are homers and then you spend the rest of the summer on the bench. Speaking of which . . ." There was shuffling from his end. "Looks like I will be sending you to the Catasauqua Republicans' barbecue after all. You should make advance calls before Sunday. Find out if one of those Heinz politicos is gonna stage a surprise appearance."

My headache was returning because of the CO. Either that or the GOP. I couldn't imagine spending a crisp, fall Sunday afternoon interviewing Republicans with rib sauce on their chins and Michelob on their breath, spouting off about school choice and flag burning.

"By the way," Salvo added. His mood was improving. "You happen to see the *New York Times* Style section?"

"They do a feature on the new Frederick's of Hollywood fall collection?"

"That'll be the day. No, I'm talking about the pictures of Stiletto and Esmeralda Greene at that society party."

Genevieve had walked over a spot on the floor that caused the dowsing rods to part and swing madly. Everyone was out of their chairs and running to the basement to see what was below. There were shouts about some incredible discovery and calls for me to join them.

"Oh?" I affected a devil-may-care tone. "What about Stiletto and Esmeralda Greene?"

"Whoa, man, that Esmeralda Greene is gor-gee-ous. You know, you work with the wire reporters for years and you never know what they look like 'cause your only contact with them is over the phone. If I were Stiletto, I'd be . . ."

"What?" I clicked my Bic. "What would you be?"

"Christ. Don't tell me you're still after him."

"I'm not after anyone, Mr. Salvo."

"Listen. What did I tell you the first day you went out on assignment with Stiletto? Steer clear. He's a playboy, Bubbles. He's been that way since we were teenagers and I don't think that after twenty years of women throwing themselves at him, he's going to change. Why should he? He's living the kind of life the rest of us schmoes can only dream of."

I thought about this, clicking my Bic rapidly. "Bruce Springsteen settled down. He used to run around with lots of women and now all he wants to do is hang out with Patty Scialfa and the kids."

"Patty's from Jersey. You don't mess around on Jersey girls. They're too tough. I'm sorry, Bubbles, but being from Pennsylvania, you're no match. You're just too damned nice to keep a man by hinting at physical retaliation."

Mama's Homemade Glycerin Rose Soap

There is nothing more satisfying to make and use than homemade glycerin soap. And it has never been easier to make, thanks to all the wonderful products found in craft shops. Mama used to save old soap pieces, melt them down in a double boiler, and mush them together for one usable soap bar. But this method is faster and prettier. So pretty you can give the soaps as gifts, scenting them with rose, citrus or lavender and filling them with dried flowers, oatmeal or even—for kids—plastic bugs. Enjoy!

1 eight-ounce bar of glycerin*
**2 drops of red or purple color formulated for dying
    soaps***
10 drops of rose perfume*
2 plastic ice cube trays
Spray nonstick coating

Spray ice cube trays with nonstick coating. Cut glycerin into chunks and put chunks in microwave-safe bowl. Heat at 80 per-

---

* Can be found in most craft sections of department stores or in craft shops. If you can't find glycerin, you can cut up an unscented bar of Neutrogena.

cent power for one minute. Check and heat at same power level in 10-second increments until all is melted. Stir in color and perfume, adding more depending on your preference. Pour into trays. This is the time to stir in dried rose petals or oatmeal or to drop in tiny plastic items for kids. (Kids are supposed to use the hardened soap all up to get to the plastic bug, etc. But mostly they dig it out with their fingers. Don't let babies who might put objects into their mouths use this.)

Remove from trays in two hours and let sit for six hours more. Wrap with ribbons and give as gifts!

Chapter 17

I made a couple of calls before I wrote the twelve-inch story on "Hugh McMullen: Murder Suspect." One of the calls was to Chief Donohue.

Donohue confirmed that Hugh McMullen was a "person of interest, though not a suspect at this time." What was this "person of interest" stuff? He declined to comment on the Smith & Wesson or the Smith & Wesson bullet found in Price's body and he mumbled something about reporters knowing too much too soon and screwing everything up. I called in the story to Mr. Salvo with the caveat that I would add a response from Chrissy Price when I spoke to her.

I was a little early to meet with Chrissy, so I thought I'd pay a surprise "guess what? I survived the kiln" visit to Hugh McMullen at the inn.

Now, I've read in certain women's magazines that to be treated like a professional, a career girl has to dress like a professional. Charcoal, black or navy suits. Sensible, expensive shoes. A tasteful scarf, perhaps. Discreet gold earrings and nail polish of a neutral color.

Then again, that depends on the profession.

I sauntered up to the counter in my beige leatherette miniskirt, my bare, smoothly shaven legs, red pumps and a black tank sweater that was so tight you could make out my internal organs. Leaning invitingly and, okay, I was putting on the slut, revealingly, over the front counter, I asked the white-suited clerk with the yellow bow tie if he could direct me to Mr. McMullen's room.

"Oh, aren't you adorable." He bit the end of his pen. "Don't tell me, let me guess. You're a reporter trying to pass as a quote-unquote lady of the night."

"No, I'm, I'm . . ."

"Speechless, I know." The clerk flapped his hand. "Honey, if you only knew how many reporters have tried that shtick. We had George Hamilton stay here last week doing dinner theater and twice the food editor of the local rag walked in wearing 'come fun me' shoes and . . . Well, let me just stress that this woman was the food editor. Two-hundred-fifty-pounds on spiked mules is not an appetizing sight. I've been served escargot that was more attractive."

I was crestfallen. I was so certain I looked like a bona fide hooker. Where had I gone wrong?

"Buck up," he said. "I had an unfair advantage. Mr. McMullen left the building for dinner an hour ago. I wouldn't have let you up to his room, anyway."

"Ahhh."

"Now run along," he said, "it's still early. I've got many more members of the press to fend off after you."

Down, but not out, I walked over to a map by the elevator to locate Room 500, the temporary residence of Chrissy Price. I had just found the spot when I heard someone behind me say, "Bubbles? Is that you?"

Myron Finkle, my short, curly-headed friend from the *Slagville Sentinel*, stood behind me holding a Diet Pepsi and looking glum.

"Hi, Myron, what are you doing here?"

"Babysitting the Price story. I'm supposed to hang around on this, a Friday night, and watch who goes in, who goes out. It totally sucks. No wonder I don't have a social life." He took me in from head to toe. "What are you doing?"

To tell Myron that I was on my way to an exclusive interview with Chrissy Price would have been cruel and unusual treatment of a cub reporter. "Thought I'd take a shot at McMullen," I jerked my thumb to the clerk, "though Mr. Bald Spot wouldn't tell me what room he's in."

"No problemo." Myron took a sip of Diet Pepsi. "He's right under the Prices. Room 400, Tower Two. I practically live there. Or, rather, the hallway outside his door. I once counted the carpet stains, I got so bored hanging around. I'll show you where to go."

He led me by the elbow to two elevators. "I use the second one. It's faster."

"So," I said after the door closed, "how many carpet stains are there?"

"Six." Myron raised his eyebrows. "And one's mustard."

The elevators opened on floor four. "This way," Myron said, leading me through the maze of hallways. "It took me an hour to find his room. Whoever designed this place must've been a rat."

"Kinda funny how he's right under Chrissy Price."

"Hugh wouldn't have to stay in a hotel if he hadn't sold the family mansion here last year. Supposedly he didn't want it because he spent most of his time back in Pittsburgh. But I'd heard he'd been having serious financial problems. He unloaded it for less than its tax-assessed value."

Room 400 was at the end of the hall and private. Myron rapped on the door.

"Sounds like voices," I whispered.

"CNN," Myron said. "It's on all the time. I don't know how room service gets through. He never answers his door."

This time I tried knocking, hard. Still no answer. I checked my Timex. Shoot. It was 8:05. Chrissy Price was probably wondering where I was. Maybe she only had a few minutes to spare and I was blowing my Big Break. "Gotta go, Myron. I'm late."

"For what?"

I thought fast. I didn't want Myron tagging along stealing my exclusive, even if he was a nice guy. "Got to meet someone at the bar across the street. An old newspaper buddy in town for the story." I headed down the hall.

"Wait. I'll join you." Myron ran up to me. "I've been here for twenty hours. I deserve some R&R. I'd love to meet some newspaper buddies."

"Oh, no, no, no." I spun around and put my hands on Myron's shoulders. "You've got to stay. It's your assignment. What if your editor found out that you'd gone to a bar and then McMullen entered the hotel, looking to chat. That's grounds for automatic firing."

Myron bit his lip. "I guess you're right. I am still on probation. I just graduated from school in May."

"So they don't even need a reason to can you."

"Maybe you're just saying that because you don't want to be seen with me." Myron pushed up his glasses. "I'm not much of a player, you know."

"A talented, ambitious college man like yourself? Why, I'd be honored." I traced his baby smooth face with a baby pink nail. "And perhaps when you're off shift we can get together. Later, at my place." I winked and Myron went all to goo.

"Sure," he said as I walked slowly backward down the hall.

As soon as I turned the corner, I dashed to the elevator, praying fervently that he hadn't come to his senses.

One floor up, I followed the same maze pattern to find Chrissy Price's penthouse suite. This time I had barely knocked before the door flew open.

"Finally!" shrieked a teenage girl with long brown hair. She grabbed my hand and yanked me into a spacious, airy hotel suite decorated in various shades of white and mauve.

"I was so dying for you to get here. I'm Sasha by the way. I don't know if Chrissy mentioned me. I'm her daughter."

"Sorry I'm late," I said. "She left a message for me at the salon."

Sasha was already at the end of the short hallway. "We were so glad you called. I was like desperate. I set up a spot for you right here, if that's okay."

I followed her into a typical hotel master bedroom that had

been personalized with big white and gray feathers taped above the bed and around the mirrors. Several rock and sand displays were scattered about, along with a tiny waterfall that cascaded in a plastic pool by the telephone. A tape of breezes rustling through leaves played from a small boom box on the TV and the room reeked of the many eucalyptus branches stuck here and there. It must have taken Chrissy hours to unpack and arrange this stuff.

"My mother." Sasha rolled her eyes and twirled a shiny black rock. "She is like totally into this desert Native American stuff. Hawks and rocks, I call it. Especially after Bud's death. I think she's trying to find spiritual meaning or something."

Spiritual meaning after her husband's murder? How dare she.

Sasha, in contrast, seemed unaffected by Bud's death as she plunked herself before a well-lighted vanity. A comb, hairbrush, and flat iron lay waiting along with several magazine photos of models that had been ripped out and displayed. She started sorting through the magazine pictures. "I assume you brought your own scissors. You guys usually do."

"Us guys?" I threw my purse down.

"Yeah, hairdressers." She held up a photo of Jennifer Aniston. "She's totally Pixie Stix but her hair is killer. Think you can pull it off?"

I sat on a Navajo blanket on the bed and studied Sasha in the mirror. She was about Jane's age, though tanner and slenderer in a sleek country club kind of way. She wore a black J. Crew sweater, Juicy Couture jeans and a silver Tiffany heart bracelet that cost about my monthly payment on the Camaro. Her straight brown hair lay neatly on her shoulders and hardly seemed in need of a trim. At least not forty-eight hours after her father had been murdered.

Unless—unless her desperation was more than vanity. Once I had a client named Emma Herman make a hair appointment the day her mother died suddenly of a heart attack. All she wanted was for me to brush her hair over and over. For one hour I brushed while she cried and reminisced. At the end of her appointment she was purged, refreshed and, it sounds crass, pretty conditioned. Hair care can be very therapeutic. There should be a clause in health insurance for it.

"Sasha," I said softly, "I think there's been a mistake. I was under the impression your mother was returning my request for a newspaper interview."

Sasha put down Jennifer and eyed me in the mirror. "Newspaper interview?"

"I'm a reporter."

"But you're also a hairdresser, right? When your message said to call you at the salon, we figured you were a hairdresser."

"Oh I see." Shoot. I hadn't been called to the inn to interview Chrissy at all.

"Okay, so no brainer. Chrissy's not even here. She's out planning Bud's memorial service next week in the woods or whatever it is she's been doing every night. I've hardly seen her since Bud corked. Anyway, she totally hates reporters." Sasha nodded, satisfied. "So, how about an inch off the bottom? And these bangs. I can't take them anymore. You can straighten afterward."

Straighten? Her hair didn't have so much as a wave, not even a tiny ripple.

"I like it jet straight," she said, reading my mind.

What the hell. I opened my purse and pulled out the plastic sheath that holds my $400 scissors to prepare for my good deed of the day.

"I'm awfully sorry about your father," I said, combing out her hair.

"Oh, he's not my father." Sasha thumbed through a *Cosmo*. "My mother married him when I was like ten. I barely knew him. He would have nothing to do with me. Even refused to let me eat dinner with them."

"You're kidding?"

"No. He despises—I guess that's despised—kids. Part of their prenup was that I could live under the same roof and he would pay for anything Mom wanted me to have—clothes, boarding school, a horse, *Sail Caribbean*—as long as Bud didn't have to act like a parent. You didn't bring any Miracle Whip, did you?"

"What for?"

"To put on my face." Sasha ran her fingers over her cheeks. "I do it at home. Sounds gross but it really exfoliates your skin. Do you think I should get highlights?"

"Your hair is beautiful. My daughter Jane's hair is like this, except, uh, bluer."

"My mother won't let me go blue. Though one of these days I'm going to do it. I'm very impulsive. Everyone says so." She licked her finger and flipped rapidly past the articles to more photos while I pinned up her hair. She must mainline Starbucks, this kid.

"But then Donatello, that's my boyfriend, threatened to dump me if I went blue or pink and you know, that was that." She let out a long, lovelorn sigh. "I can't wait to get back to Donatello. He's picking me up Sunday and taking me back to school."

I bent over and began cutting away.

"Your daughter have a boyfriend?" she asked, not really paying attention to the *Cosmo*. "What's her name again?"

"Jane." I unclipped another swatch of hair so that it fell down in one loop. "Her boyfriend's name is G. He wants her to go grape picking in France."

"Tight." Sasha gave me a thumbs up in approval. "Sounds like they're hot 'n heavy."

I pulled out my razor. "Too hot 'n heavy. Although at her age I was married."

"Preggers?"

"Yup." I combed up some hair and began razoring. "One night stand at a fraternity party. Let that be a lesson to you."

"Oh, I don't have to worry. Donatello and I don't have sex. At least," she crossed her legs, "not, you know, that way. More like in a President Clinton, Monica Lewinsky way."

Testing. Testing. One. Two. Three. Teenager testing. I

dropped the strand and moved onto the next, pretending that I hadn't heard this classic shocker. "These bangs too short?"

"Just fine." She eyed me in the mirror to get a bead on whether I was up for another zinger. "You think your daughter is having sex?"

I removed a bobby pin from my mouth. "She tells me she's not."

"Then she is."

"Hmmm."

"Most of my friends would die rather than tell their mothers they were sleeping around. We'd much rather get on our knees."

"Ouch." I had touched the iron to see if it was hot and nearly burned myself. "That sounds uncomfortable." I clamped a plait of hair in the iron and slid it through. I did not want to imagine Jane on her knees to G. Frankly, Jane was too smart and beautiful and dignified to be on her knees for any man, much less a potbellied couch potato with an addiction to chocolate frosted Pop Tarts.

"It's safe. Can't get pregnant and he's happy. Plus, I get to remain a virgin. Technically."

"And that's important?" I moved on to another swath of hair. This was all going to be ruined when she slept, anyway.

"I'll say it's important." Sasha nodded. "Abstinence is very big these days. We all signed abstinence pledges back in ninth grade." Giggle.

When I was done with her, Sasha looked much the same as when I had arrived, except a few split ends were missing and her hair hung like sheet metal. She seemed not at all interested in the cut she had so desperately desired a half hour before.

"If you want, I can find out for you about Jane. I'm an excellent detective." Her eyes glistened. Finally, some drama to break the monotony of sitting in a hotel room while her mother gallivanted about. "You wanna give me Jane's number?"

Might not be a bad idea for Jane and Sasha to get together. Of course, Sasha would drive Jane up a wall, but my motherly instincts told me Sasha wasn't as blasé about Bud's death or her mother's absence as she'd like me to believe. She needed a peer to talk with. A normal teenager with Kool-Aid colored hair and cartilage piercings and a *que sera sera* attitude about higher education. I wrote down the number and address of the Main Mane and picked up some of the hair.

"Don't worry, maid service will get it in the morning," she said. "I never pick up anything. Never have. Never will."

The phone rang and Sasha rushed to get it. "Donatello? Oh, hi, Mom," she said with exaggerated disappointment.

I cleaned the vanity and threw the ends in the trash while Sasha answered her mother with clipped yeses and nos.

"That was my Mom," she said, hanging up. "She won't be in tonight so I guess that's ixnay on the intervieway."

Great. An entire evening wasted. I could have been in bed where my aching body longed to be. Instead I'd cut a rich kid's hair for free and was made to look like a chump. I gathered my purse and was considering leaving a sharp message for Chrissy Price when I thought better of it. She'd lost her husband this week. This was no time for lectures.

"Maybe I'll call your daughter tomorrow," Sasha said at the door. "I can't take another day in this hotel. I've seen the same *Sex and the City* episode five times."

In the elevator, I took off my shoes and rubbed my aching feet. When I got back to Roxanne's I was gonna make me one of those mouthwatering meat-loaf sandwiches on Wonder Bread dripping with mayonnaise and ketchup. Get me a can of Diet Pepsi, a bag of chips and a perfect position in the Barcalounger to watch some brain-numbing television. Most important, I was gonna put my feet up.

"Ah, Miss Yablonsky?" The desk clerk flagged me down as I walked through the lobby. "There's a message for you."

Cripes. Probably Hugh McMullen. Back from dinner and anxious to get hold of Stinky. The clerk slid the message over to me. It said simply *Meet me in room 315. I've got what you want.*

"Who's in room 315?" I asked.

The clerk shrugged. "I have no idea."

"Man or a woman?"

"Man. You'll just have to take your chances, dear." The clerk returned to flipping through a Rolodex.

"What am I, James Bond?" I asked, waving the message. "I don't want to go up to a strange man's hotel room."

The clerk glanced up from his filing. "And here I thought you wanted to become a hooker."

The door to room 315 was slightly ajar when I arrived. I knocked twice and clutched my purse. I'd knock one more time and then leave. With the third knock the door opened wider to a pitch black room. Forget it. No story, no scoop was worth this.

I turned on my heels and was grabbed from behind, a hand over my mouth. The door was kicked shut and my attacker held me firm. Nuh-uh. No way was I going to be attacked. Not before getting the first decent night's sleep in two days.

I brought up my heel and back kicked him in the nuts. There was an expulsion of air. *Oof.* As he buckled, his grip loosened enough for me to elbow him hard, yes, in the ribs. Twice for good measure. That self-defense lesson at the YWCA had paid for itself and then some.

He let go and his back hit the wall. I swung my purse and hit the shadow of his head as hard as I could. The purse opened, spilling my wallet and car keys and cosmetics everyplace. I reached inside and pulled out the can of Final Net at the bottom, then gave him a good long spray in the face.

"Take that, you scum."

"Stop it!" he said, gasping. "What the hell do you think you're doing?"

I ran my hand over the wall and found the light switch. Stiletto was leaning against the wall, clutching his sides. His hair glistened with fresh shellac. Definitely Mel Gibson in the *What Women Want* stage.

"I'm so sorry," I said. "I didn't know it was you." Then I got ticked. "What was that with the hand over my mouth, anyway? And the darkness?"

"Didn't you see the candles?" He pointed over to the living room at the rear of the suite. It was filled with candles and fresh flowers. A bottle of champagne sat in an ice bucket next to two crystal flutes.

"But how did you find out I was here?"

"I called Salvo. He told me about your meeting with Hugh McMullen in the chapel and how he was worried that he had upset you by pointing out that stupid photo in the *New York Times* Style section." Stiletto coughed and straightened. "I decided it was time I paid you extra attention before you ran off with some brawny coal miner. Though I'm not sure I should try to surprise you anymore."

Stiletto's trademark white oxford shirt was unbuttoned. I slid my arms around his neck. He smelled the way I liked him. Ivory soap and freshly ironed cotton.

"I love your surprises," I whispered. "I'm knocked off my feet."

"Too late now," he grumbled, "you've ruined it."

"Oh, have I?" I kissed him right below the ear.

"Lower."

I kissed him on the neck, by his pulsing carotid.

"Keep going."

And on his collarbone, parting his shirt to run my lips down his sternum to his navel.

"That's okay," he said, closing his eyes in anticipation, "you don't have to stop."

"I think before that I deserve some champagne, don't you?"

"At least." And he brought me to him, wrapping me in his arms so that his bare chest was hard against mine. "Regarding the *New York Times* Style section, don't listen to Tony Salvo, okay?"

"I never listen to editors. You taught me that. Editors are finks."

He cupped my chin and kissed me long and slow. "Editors are the human equivalent of vampires," he murmured. "They will suck out every good story idea and every creative approach to getting a good story until you're nothing but a hack."

"I like the sucking part, but what does this have to do with us?"

Stiletto led me over to the couch and candles and flowers. He sat me down and unwrapped a ten-year-old bottle of Moët & Chandon champagne. "Newspaper editors also expect the worst out of life. They crave it. They want buildings to burn and people to get shot. Makes their jobs a lot easier. After twenty years of hoping for the worst, they expect the same about people in love. It's habit."

I watched as Stiletto expertly tipped the champagne into the glass. How many women had sat next to him with their glasses ready, his shirt open, and their mutual expectations high?

"Bubbles for Bubbles," Stiletto said, clinking his glass against mine.

The champagne went down cold and delicious. I hadn't really eaten anything since Mona's Wonder Gobbler with Slime and knew that I had to watch it. I could get tipsy.

"But, you know, Mr. Salvo does have a point," I said, placing my glass far away from me on the coffee table.

"I have a point," Stiletto said, grinning like a schoolboy. "Would you like to see it?"

"I'm sure plenty of other women have."

"Ouch." Stiletto sat back. "What's gotten into you? First you beat me up physically and then you batter me about verbally? What did I do wrong?"

Ran off with Esmeralda Greene for one thing. I kept mum about that, though. Some men, men like Stiletto, do not respond well to what might be misinterpreted as jealousy. It either makes them mad or goes to their heads or both.

"You didn't do anything wrong. You can't help it that every woman in Slagville from the old ladies sweeping their sidewalks to the clients in Roxanne's salon drool after you."

"Bubbles. In case you haven't noticed," Stiletto slid his arm along the back of the couch behind me, "men drool after you, too. Do you know what it's like to walk down a street with Bubbles Yablonsky? I've witnessed near car crashes because men behind the wheel cannot keep their eyes on the road when you strut by."

I leaned forward and took another teensy weensy bit of that champagne. "Go on."

Stiletto smiled and stroked my chin. "That goes for me, too. It's all I can do to keep my hands off you when you're around. We're in a coal mine after surviving an explosion and I think, 'I've got to kiss her.' "

And he did just that, pushing me back on the couch as he did so. "You were lying on the cot when I got out of the mine and the first thought that ran across my mind was, 'Maybe I can lock the doors and get her alone.' "

He bent closer. His blue eyes were no longer twinkling, but piercing. The crow's feet were deep with age and experience, but every part of him felt strong and hard under my hands. And I mean every part.

"I have got to have you, Bubbles," he said, his hand sliding over my arms. "I can't stand it a minute longer. These aren't just words to get you into bed. This isn't curiosity. I've been through that, Bubbles. I'm done with that. This is—"

I couldn't take it. I gripped his shoulders and brought him to me. Our tongues entwined, hot and crazy. I kicked off my shoes and wrapped my legs around his calves, sinking deep into the couch. I tore off his shirt and he pulled off mine.

"Christ, Bubbles," was all he said before letting his head drop to my chest. His lips were maddening, purposefully caressing every spot except that one. I let out a stifled scream as his thumbs explored under my bra and ripped it off. Hooks went flying.

"Yessss," I hissed.

"I love you," he said.

Don't talk, I thought. Don't stop! The skirt. The skirt. Take . . . off . . . the skirt.

Mind reader that Stiletto has always been, his hands slid up my thighs and then stopped at the very top, his fingers playfully tormenting me. The only satisfaction was in feeling the pressure of his own unleashed desire, which appeared to support Stiletto's frequent claims of abundance.

Let's help that boy out. My own fingers worked the belt buckle and slid down the zipper. Naughty, naughty, Stiletto. What was it with him and no underwear? My palms slid underneath his jeans and over his smooth skin and this time it was Stiletto's turn to moan, "Yesss."

And that's when the sirens came. Not portly little Slagville housewives. Real ones. Screaming right outside Stiletto's window.

"No," I cried, as Stiletto sat up and cocked an ear.

"Sounds major, Bubbles. Especially considering who's staying in this hotel."

He zipped up his jeans and opened the curtains while I adjusted my skirt and pulled on my top without the bra, which lay stretched and ripped on the floor.

Stiletto cranked open a window. I peeked over his shoulder. "Hey, there's Myron Finkle," I said, leaning out. Myron was running across the parking lot toward an opened car that was surrounded by two police cruisers and blindingly bright klieg lights. It was a Saab sports car and there was a person in the front seat, slumped over.

Hotel employees were gathering along the side of the lot and other guests were hanging out their windows to watch the action.

"Myron!" I shouted. "Myron, what's going on?"

Myron stopped running. He pushed up his glasses and waved. "Hi, Bubbles. Can you see anything up there?"

"Cops around a Saab and a man in the front seat. What is it?"

"That's Hugh McMullen. Someone told me he's been shot." There were gasps from the hotel employees and the other guests. "In the head." And Myron ran off to catch up with the cops, who were taking their own slow time. An ominous signal. If McMullen had been alive, he'd be in an ambulance speeding off to the hospital. But he wasn't alive. His corpse was merely one part of a crime scene now.

I closed my eyes and murmured a quick prayer, but all I kept thinking was Hugh McMullen dead? My mind raced, leaping from image to image. Hugh nervous at the press conference reading stiffly from a prepared statement. Hugh in the church, rumpled and mad to find Stinky.

Uh-oh, Stinky. If Hugh McMullen was dead, shot like Price, and if McMullen had been Price's murderer, then what did that mean for Stinky?

"Come on, Bubbles." Stiletto had his camera equipment together, was dressed and ready to go. "This is going to be another media zoo."

I slipped into my shoes and pulled out my notebook. I stuffed my broken bra in my purse and gathered up my cosmetics from the floor. We didn't say anything to each other except bye as I headed out the door to the parking lot.

Sometimes I hate this business. I really do. When you're a hairdresser and you want to have sex, you just have sex. You don't have to stop for sirens.

Sasha's Miracle-Whip Facial (Slightly Improved)

Miracle Whip has less fat than regular mayonnaise and the vinegar in it does wonders for skin. My advice is to apply a thin layer and rub it off before a shower so you don't smell like chicken salad all day. It really does exfoliate, though, like Sasha says, it is kind of gross.

2 tablespoons Miracle Whip
½ teaspoon ground, uncooked oatmeal

Mix Miracle Whip and oatmeal. Spread thinly on clean, dry face. Leave on for thirty minutes. Wipe off with moistened face-cloth and wash and moisturize as usual.

Chapter 18

The preliminary word from Chief Donohue was that Hugh McMullen had committed suicide with a Smith & Wesson to the temple. This did not register with the other reporters, but it certainly registered with me. I suppose if I had been Esmeralda Greene and had been eager to impress the Barbie and Ken of Channel Three, I would have asked at the press conference if that was the same Smith & Wesson that had blown away Bud Price.

But my ego didn't need stroking. My ego had been stroked enough tonight.

I approached Donohue as he stepped into his cruiser. "Is that the same Smith and Wesson that—?"

"Won't know until the ballistics tests get back," he said, sliding his paunch behind the wheel. "But it appears likely. The bullets in Price came from a forty-four magnum S and W revolver and that's what was in McMullen's hand tonight."

I wrote this down. Why was Donohue being so nice to me? Usually cops fresh from a suicide tell reporters to buzz off. Half the time they refuse to release police reports on suicides, even public ones. Gosh. I hoped Donohue's kindness wasn't because I didn't have a bra on.

"You think he shot himself because he was going to be arrested for murder?"

"His lawyer was informed this evening that he had twenty-four hours to bring his client in or we were going to come for him." Donohue shut the door and leaned out the window. He looked over my shoulder. "Aw, shit. Myron Finkle. That twerp bugs the hell out of me."

I folded up my notebook.

"What were you and Donohue talking about?" Myron asked after Donohue peeled out of the hotel parking lot.

It was fun to thumb one's perfectly powdered nose at Channel Three, but Myron was just a kid. He needed a break. "What time do you publish, Myron?"

"I don't know. I think the paper gets delivered at four a.m. Why?"

"When you get back to the newsroom, give Donohue a call. Ask him about the weapon."

"The gun McMullen used to shoot himself?" Myron exclaimed. "How come?"

"Shhh." I put my finger to my lips. News-Nine-All-The-Time walked by, pretending like he wasn't eavesdropping. "Keep a lid on it, Myron. I'm giving you a tip."

Myron smiled. "Thanks, Bubbles. No one ever gives me tips. Not even my father and he's a state trooper."

"Awww." I resisted the urge to pat him on the head. "Hopefully this will be the first of many scoops, hon."

Stiletto was reloading his camera and talking on a cell phone when I walked up to him at the other end of the parking lot. "Give me an hour," he told me, tucking the phone under his chin. "I'll find some place to develop this and then we'll take up where we left off. You can stay with me tonight."

"Can't. I've got to get back to Roxanne."

"Roxy's a big girl. She can stay with herself."

"Not tonight," I said, "though, knowing her, she'll be spending the night with Zeke Allen. Next time you assign me a bodyguard, make him short, fat and ugly, okay?"

"Bodyguard? I assigned you a bodyguard?"

"Uh . . . that's what I understand."

Stiletto got back on the phone and told his editor he had to get off, quick. He had an emergency. He shut the phone and turned to me. "What's this about a bodyguard?"

"Give it up, Stiletto. I know all about how you hired Zeke to look after me. Genevieve said you wanted him to spy, but he's such a squeaky clean—"

"Zeke Allen from Slagville?"

Stiletto was not joking. He was not trying to pull my leg. He had the look that made my mouth go dry. That this-is-not-funny-this-is-serious look. "Okay. There's this guy," I said slowly, "Zeke Allen—"

"Yeah, yeah, I know Zeke. He was thrown in the slammer for building a church in Mexico. I ran into him when I was doing a story on jailed American kids in Cerro Huerro. I ended up bribing a judge to spring the poor bastard."

"And then," I said, keeping my voice calm, "you hired him to look after me while I was here working on this story."

"No, Bubbles." Stiletto placed his hand firmly on my shoulder. "I didn't. I haven't talked to Zeke Allen in at least a year."

For a few minutes we didn't say anything, just stared at each other.

"Then what's going on?" I said. "He said every night you call him and ask a few innocuous questions about me. You've apparently paid him a thousand bucks with the promise of twenty-five-hundred more. Directly wired into his bank account."

"Shit!" Stiletto slid his phone into his pocket. "This is too much like the fax you got at the Passion Peak and my e-mail message. It's got to be the work of the same guy. He knows every detail about us, that I was in New York yesterday, that you were at the Passion Peak on Wednesday, what my e-mail address is."

We were silent, pondering. "What happened when you traced the e-mail?" I asked.

"That phone got blown up in the Jeep, remember?"

"Oh, yeah. So, what are we going to do?"

"I've got to get this film developed and find out what's going on. Until then, Bubbles, I want you to lock and bolt the doors when you get back to Roxanne's. And stay away from Zeke."

*   *   *

It was a long, dangerous drive back to the Main Mane and not because I imagined menacing headlights in my rearview at each twist and turn. (For I did repeatedly imagine menacing headlights.) No. The drive was dangerous because I was beat. So tired that I almost didn't care if I crashed.

I had called in my update about McMullen's murder from the inn well in time for the *News-Times* deadline and after that I was ready to collapse. For a fleeting second I considered joining Stiletto in his room, but then my conscience got the better of me. I remembered Roxanne and how panicked she'd been after the burglary. So I got in the Camaro and did my duty.

My heavy eyelids flickered as I negotiated the pitch black back roads. This was torture. Absolute torture. I should have pulled over and slept. But I kept on until I pulled up to the Main Mane and put on the parking break. I'd made it. I'd never felt so relieved.

It was after one A.M. and Roxanne's house was quiet and dark. There were no lights on in the three bedrooms upstairs. Mama and Genevieve had been assigned twin beds in the guest room. The door to Roxanne's room was closed and Jane was on a couch in the office.

I tiptoed in and kissed her like I have every night since she was one day old. Her cheek still had a trace of baby-girl fat and she clutched the sheet protectively about her. If I squinted, I could picture what she looked like at four years old, hugging her blue Smurf.

I went into the kitchen and made myself a meat-loaf sandwich, consuming it in four bites. Downed a glass of milk. Washed up. Brushed my teeth and slipped into a black Journey T-shirt with matching thong. What a night. Sex. Death. Myron Finkle and Sasha with the straight, straight hair. Like the old feminine hygiene commercial used to taunt, "So you wanted the busy life of a reporter."

Roxanne had been kind enough to make up the foldout downstairs. I slipped in between the cool sheets and wiggled my toes.

I didn't mind the thin mattress or the iron bar that ran under my back. I kind of liked it. It massaged out the kinks. Needless to say I was asleep as soon as I clicked on my Donald Duck night-light.

Asleep, but not at peace. My dreams were so vivid and frightening it was like having a front row seat at IMAX. Flames spewed from St. Ignatius Church with its red and blue broken stained glass. Hugh McMullen's bloodied face warned me in silent urgency about a monster who was after me. Who was it?

"You should know," McMullen kept saying. "You've met him. He knows who you are."

And then there was Professor Tallow, his thin white finger slowly tracing the multiple pierced ear of a helplessly enthralled Jane. For some reason Keith Richards was nearby with an electric guitar and a bandana around his forehead, a cigarette dangling from his lip as he crooned with . . . G.

G?

"Wassup, Bub?" an imaginary G called out to me through the smoke, which seemed to be billowing from everywhere, choking me, stinging my eyes, filling my nose. "Hey, Bub. Is there more meat loaf? I sure could do with a sandwich."

I sat up groggily. My chest hurt and the Donald Duck nightlight illuminated waves of smoke filling the living room. It was coming from the kitchen. It smelled like grilled cheese out of control.

I slid off the bed onto the floor and crawled my way toward the kitchen door. Remember, Bubbles, lay low to the ground where the air is good. If there is a fire, get everyone out of the house first, then call the fire department. Not vice versa. There weren't flames, I was relieved to see. But as the saying goes, where there's smoke there's . . .

"Bubbles Yablonsky! What are you doing on the floor with your naked bottom in the air?" Mama's voice screeched. I was eye level with a pair of fluffy pink slippers and the bottom of a chenille zipper robe.

"Hot damn! My girlfriend's mom." G was jumping up and

down in the smoky haze. "I saw my girlfriend's mom's naked butt!"

I gripped the green Formica kitchen counter and pulled myself up. Mama was by the stove while Genevieve was at the sink scrubbing out a pan. G was in his street clothes and holding a gray metal canister. A fire extinguisher, I supposed. All of us were shrouded in a mist.

"What happened?" I asked between coughs.

"There's been a fire. Obviously," said Mama. "Genevieve and I came home and thought we'd brew us some Sleepytime before bed and Genevieve forgot—"

"I did not forget." Genevieve paused from her scrubbing. "I turned off the burner. Anyway, it wasn't the teapot, it was this pan that caught fire. It had grease in it. If you ask me, those Kenmore people are to blame. Planned obsolescence so you'll have to buy a new stove every five years."

Mama dismissed her with a wave and Genevieve turned her attention back to the pan. "Point is, G is a hero. He grabbed a fire extinguisher from the basement and saved us all."

"Hear that, Bub. I'm a hero." G pumped his fist. "Now you definitely gotta treat me right. We're talking me getting the fold-out bed. And I got some underwear that needs washing. It hasn't been washed in weeks."

Oh joy, I thought. Dirty G underwear. Except I didn't remember a pan of grease being on the stove before. When I had made the meat-loaf sandwich, the kitchen had been entirely cleaned up. Jane, being a vegetarian, doesn't cook with grease and G, well, G doesn't cook.

"I didn't use the stove tonight," I said. "What time did you two ladies get in?"

Genevieve and Mama exchanged guilty looks. Mama checked her watch. "About two hours ago."

The Home Sweet Home kitchen clock said 5:15. "You were out until three?"

Mama cleared her throat and started rubbing a Brillo pad

around the charred burner. "We're grown women. We can stay out as late as we want. Anyway, we were working."

"You go, granny!" G exclaimed.

Mama turned on him like a lioness on an antelope. "For your information, junior, I am the undisputed billiards champion in the South Side Seniors league, I can lift seventy pounds in sixteen reps and got my sights set on eighty. No one calls me 'granny.' No one."

G looked humbled. "Sorr-ee."

"Ignore him," I said. "What's this, we-were-working-until-three-a.m. business?"

Genevieve pointed to a plastic garbage bag in the corner. "We were looking for Nana Yablonsky's diary—in the trash."

"Cool." G lifted the bag onto the counter and began sorting through its contents.

Mama returned to her scrubbing until I snatched the now rusted Brillo pad out of her hands. "Hold on. You've been roaming the streets of Slagville searching garbage cans?"

"Pharmaceutical companies do it all the time, Bubbles," Genevieve said. "It's how they discover the research secrets of competing companies. Good old dumpster fishing. Only difference is we don't get paid fifty-thousand dollars a year with two weeks at the shore. Then again, we aren't paid by the government not to cure cancer, either."

"And besides, they weren't any old garbage cans," Mama said. "They were Vilnia's."

"Vilnia, the gossip?"

"Vilnia the thief is more like it."

"Broken comb. Lots of dirty paper napkins. Opened can of Comstock blueberry filling." G was announcing the bag's goodies. "An empty box of Pillsbury ready-made piecrust—"

"Knew it," Mama said to Genevieve. "Vilnia's probably the type to do slice-and-bake, too."

Genevieve snorted in self-righteous disgust. "Hamburger Helper, I'm betting."

"Black bra. Tan in a can. Printer ink cartridges." G popped his head out of the trash. "No diary."

"That's because I've got it right here, G is for genius." Mama reached into her robe and pulled out a small, weathered black leather diary. She handed it to me and I flipped through the pages. It was all in Polish.

"How did you know?" I asked, handing her the book.

"Potato soup. Remember when we were at Vilnia's? There is only one woman in the world who put mint in potato soup and that was Nana Yablonsky. Once I saw that recipe cooking on Vilnia's stove, I knew we had our woman. I also knew she'd toss the evidence. Genny and I been through her garbage every day and night since."

Genevieve yawned so loud it sounded like a B-47 overhead. " 'Cept tonight Vilnia was up awful late with guests. She got to bed way after two. We had to wait until everyone was asleep to go through the trash."

"Looked like a secret meeting of the Slagville Sirens to me," Mama said. "I'm telling you, those sirens are up to something. And if I know them, it's no good."

"Man, these old ladies. Sirens. Prowling the neighborhoods until three rustling through other people's trash," G said. "Wilder than I ever imagined. You guys should get a website."

Roxanne appeared in the doorway. She was wearing a fluffy green robe and an eye mask around her neck. Her hair was a mass of red, rumpled curls.

"Heavens!" She clamped her hand to her mouth. "So it was a fire. I knew I shouldn't have taken those batteries out of the smoke alarms. It's just that I can't stand those things when they go off. So loud."

"It's okay. I put it out," G boasted, patting the fire extinguisher, "with this."

"Really? One of those cylinders Jane found in the basement tonight?" Roxanne yawned.

"Jane said she thought it was a fire extinguisher and she was right."

"Still say the dang-fool boy could've blown the top off the house," Genevieve said. "Even if it is just CO-two in them cylinders, you can't mix your chemicals. Fire extinguishers are not a one-size-fits-all kinda deal."

My brain was busy taking all this in. Fire extinguisher. Basement. Stinky's visit to Limbo with his maps and measurements. Interesting. "How many of those tubes are down there?" I asked.

Roxanne shrugged. "I don't remember. Dozens. Jane found them after Genevieve's dowsing rods went crazy over this one spot. I'd tell you to ask Jane, except she's not here."

"Yes, she is. I kissed her goodnight," I said.

"She's not there now. I checked before I came downstairs."

"Where could she be?" I was slightly alarmed, given tonight's events. A missing daughter was not what I needed right now.

"Don't get your knickers in a twist, Mrs. Y," G said, tying up the garbage bag and tossing it back into the corner. "She's run out with that old geezer Tallow. Something about watching the sun come up through a bunch of rocks."

Now I was really alarmed. "She went all the way back to Lehigh?"

"Nah. Right here," G said. "Tallow's got a camp in that Blair Witch place I was at yesterday. What was it called again?"

"Limbo." I was stunned. "But why didn't she tell me? Why didn't she even leave a note?"

Mama shook her head. "You gotta have a talk with that girl, Bubbles. Forget Limbo. She's gonna put you through hell."

Chapter 19

I awoke sometime later to a piercing *Beep! Beep! Beep!* and the smell of rotting grapefruit and spoiled milk.

"Hey, lady. Move it. You're blocking the driveway." A garbage worker in navy overalls was pounding on the windshield, through which I had a full view of the trash-strewn rear end of a waste management truck. McDonald's wrappers, moldy cucumbers and eggshells galore up close and personal. "I can't get to the dumpster, lady, if you don't move."

"Okay, okay." I yawned and wiggled up on the seat. My legs, having been stuffed under the dashboard, felt like they'd been squished in a tuna can and my shoulder, ouch. I tried to rotate it but I feared it was permanently damaged from hugging the stick shift all morning.

Thank you, G, I thought as I started up the car and parked it down the block. After saving the house from fire, G had demanded the pullout bed in the living room. And since I was afraid that denying Prince Precious any little whim would result in him going back to Lehigh and my daughter being abducted by a cradle snatcher, I agreed to sleep in the Camaro. The front seat made the so-called mattress at the Slagville lockup a heated water bed in comparison.

I got out and stumbled toward the salon in the freezing gray dawn. It was not until I was halfway up the walk that I remembered I was wearing a thong and a T-shirt that came down an inch past my navel. Oh, what the heck. So I had made some garbageman's morning. Call it a public service.

All was quiet inside except for G's nasal snoring in the living room. I picked up my skirt that I'd tossed on the floor the night before and found a note from Jane. She had left with Professor Tallow and would return later in the morning. To the note she had taped a press release written by Tallow himself.

The press release invited members of the media to join him at a sunrise gathering Saturday morning around an "historically significant menatol standing stone" (whatever that was) in the so-called Dead Zone. Tallow wrote that his goal was to have the entire zone declared a historical site before a casino could be built there. After the sunrise gathering, the press was encouraged to return with him to Tallow's Limbo cabin where they could view—and photograph—other Celtic artifacts he had gathered from the area.

"Isn't he *amazing*!" Jane wrote in loopy cursive right below the directions to Tallow's cabin. "Maybe *you* should do a story on him."

Right. Considering every reporter in a fifty-mile radius had been up past midnight covering Hugh McMullen's suicide, I doubted Tallow was going to get much of a turnout. I should go, though, I thought, looking out the window. Darn. The sun was already up.

So was Stiletto—hopping out of his spanking new black Jeep. He was carrying a pair of running shoes and what appeared to be blue spandex bike shorts and a jogging bra. Boy, I sincerely hoped those weren't for me. I don't do running. It's against my religion.

"Hi," he said when I opened the door. "How about breakfast?" Stiletto was wearing a gray T-shirt and black shorts composed of a filmy, athletic nylon that hung—and that is the operative word here—well from his hips.

"My, oh my," I said, trying to maintain eye contact at a lady-like level. "What do those have to do with breakfast?" I pointed to the athletic wear.

"Breakfast is going to be at Lou's Eggs." Stiletto stepped in and closed the door gently behind him. He held up the clothes.

"These are what you're going to wear and," he held up the Nikes, "these are going to get you there. Three miles away. Piece of cake."

"Piece of cake, my ass!" I exclaimed, forgetting about G and the rest of the snoozing household. "I can't wear arch-supported rubber-based footwear."

Stiletto tossed me the running gear. "Unlike cake, running does your ass wonders. Reduces the stress of being a reporter and it keeps you on your toes, so I don't have to worry about whether you can out distance creeps like Zeke Allen."

"Zeke Allen is a creep? He seemed so goody-two-shoes."

"We'll discuss it over coffee." He threw me the shoes. "C'mon, I want to beat the crowd."

"But I . . . my toes . . . all those years of high-heeled shoes."

"Bubbles. Excuses aren't going to get you anywhere but prematurely dead."

Ten minutes later there I was, Bubbles Yablonsky, she of "get the closest parking space to the mall and drive the car around the block for a quart of milk," on the sidewalk in her dazzling running gear. I ran my hands over my smooth and silky tight blue hips.

"Not bad. Shiny spandex. I like these."

Stiletto grinned. "I thought you would. Seemed like your style. Ready?"

"As ready as ever." I smiled like a brave soldier and started a gentle jog down the sidewalk.

"I'll go slow, your pace this time, but as we continue to run we'll increase the speed, okay?" He kept a few paces ahead of me.

"Okay." I couldn't get over Stiletto's leg muscles. Such definition. Such rock.

I leaped over a sidewalk crack and waved to a woman running an old-fashioned mower on her lawn. My legs were beginning to feel heavy, but I took a deep breath of air, pushed out my chest and pretended my feet were big marshmallows padding along in the cool autumn morning.

"Watch out for leaves, they can be slippery." Stiletto pointed to a pile ahead and I charged right through it. "How you doing? You should concentrate on even breathing. In through the nose, out through the mouth."

"I'm doing fine." I took in another lungful. Hey, this wasn't so bad. I flapped my arms to loosen the muscle tension. In fact, it felt pretty good. The morning mist was clearing to reveal a blue sky. The scent of freshly mown grass and fallen leaves was in the air. What wasn't to love? "I think I'm getting my second wind."

Stiletto, who was slightly behind me, warned that we were approaching one of Slagville's famous vertical hills. "If you want to stop, slow to a walk. Whatever you do, don't stop completely."

"How about you run in front of me?"

Stiletto charged past. "How come?"

"I'm a sucker for a scenic view."

"You're not going to pull a trick and duck into a bus or something?"

"Me? Please, a bit farther."

Stiletto was now six feet away, his strong legs propelling him up the hill with effortless ease. He moved like an animal, shoulders first, as though his whole body were being lifted by his pecs. I fixated on his figure and was surprised when we reached the top of the hill and Lou's Eggs.

"Jesus." Sweat was dripping from his head and neck, soaking his T-shirt and he was breathing heavily. "Not bad. For a novice." He bent down and held his knees. "Man. That was some hill."

I hopped onto the cement wall outside Lou's Eggs and waited for him to finish with the post-marathon dramatics.

"You're not even," pant, pant, "sweating." Stiletto was pacing, hands on hips.

"Glowing. Men sweat, Stiletto. Women glow."

"It's unbelievable. You shot right up that incline. I bet you ran a four-minute mile. Straight up a hill."

"Four minutes, huh." I jumped down. "Is that good?"

"Four-minute mile is that good." He punched me playfully on the arm and we entered Lou's Eggs.

Nearly every window in Lou's Eggs had its own personal fan to force out the airborne grease. We passed the counter of men, their arms protectively encircling massive white plates of fried substances, and sat down at a table covered by a floral cloth topped with a sheet of clear plastic. We were the only ones not smoking. And that included the customers in mid-meal.

"Talk about tobacco road," Stiletto said, opening a plastic menu. "You've stopped smoking, right?"

"Absolutely. Smoking. Yuck." I furrowed my brows at the all-day breakfast offerings. Of course, that may have been a teensy tiny lie about me not smoking, but I highly doubted a cigarette now and then would hurt me. Then again, there are horror stories. Grapefruit looked good. But not as good as a chocolate doughnut. Then again, doughnuts are chock-full of B vitamins. Decisions. Decisions.

"Where's Esmeralda?" I asked casually.

"Esmeralda? Esme's back in New York. Forget Esmeralda."

"So, she's not working on the Hugh McMullen suicide?"

"What's to cover? A suicide is a suicide." Stiletto eyed me suspiciously over the menu. "*Right*, Bubbles?"

"Uh-huh."

"Unless you know different."

"Who, me?" I flagged over a waitress. No freaking way was I telling him about the Smith & Wesson.

A waitress with flyaway hair wiped our table with a wet cloth, stuck it in her apron pocket, removed her cigarette from her mouth and asked for our order. I chose blinis, grapefruit and coffee. Stiletto ordered two eggs over easy, hash browns, scrapple (oh, please, not that), bacon and orange juice. He was going to be sorry. His eyes were bigger than his stomach was Teflon coated.

"So what's this about our mutual missionary being a creep?" I asked, to change the subject from Hugh McMullen.

"I went over to Zeke's apartment last night and then again around dawn. He wasn't in."

"Maybe he has a girlfriend and was spending the night?"

"I don't think so." Stiletto touched my fingers thoughtfully. "His car was in the driveway. But there was all this crusted white junk around the tailpipe. Funny. I could've sworn it was mashed potatoes."

Dum, de dum, dum, dum.

"What did Zeke tell you about me again?" he asked.

I recounted in more detail than last night what Zeke had said, that Stiletto had called him shortly after the explosion and asked him to keep a watch on me, that the two of them spoke about what Stiletto had been up to in the past year, including the stint on the India/Pakistan border and his plans to move to England.

As though bowled over by this, Stiletto sat back and folded his arms. "Fascinating. How would he have known that? I haven't spoken to Zeke's parents since last Christmas."

"His parents?"

"Earl and Martha Allen. Nicer folks you'll never meet. They moved from Limbo to Slagville two years ago after the government buyout, but insisted on returning the money. Wouldn't take a dime of someone else's tax dollars. They send me birthday presents and Christmas cards because I sprang their son from a Mexican jail."

The waitress plunked down our dishes. Hmmm. Blinis. Grated potato pancakes fried crisp. You can't make them at home—well you can, but they put out such smoke that you might as well invite the entire fire department if you do. I emptied a packet of Sweet 'N Low into my coffee and dug in.

"What do Zeke's parents say?"

"I don't know." Stiletto chowed down on his eggs. "I didn't go over to their house."

"You mean you, experienced photojournalist, forgot the old newspaper trick of just asking?"

Stiletto smirked at me over his juice. "Cute. I didn't want to worry them."

"That's silly." I sipped my coffee. "If you won't ask them, I will, though I think since you saved their son you might make more headway than I would."

"How about we go together?"

"Should we run?"

Stiletto glanced down at his half-eaten breakfast. "I feel like I just ate a bucket of lead. Next time I order scrapple stop me. This stuff should be banned by the FDA."

Stiletto's Jeep had the new-car smell that made me swoon with delight. There were even paper mats on the floor, which hadn't been saturated by Diet Coke and coffee like mine. Boy, did I envy his ability to walk into a dealership, purchase a $28,000 car with cash and drive off the same day. I had paid cash for a car once. That was five hundred bucks for a rusted Chevy Impala and it was as illegal to operate on the road as a hijacked armored vehicle.

"No top again, I see." We whizzed through Slagville, the wind breezing through my unwashed hair. It was October, not August, and a tad chilly for driving around without a top but I didn't want to come across as a poor sport. "You ever think of buying a different model besides a Jeep?"

"Like a Crown Victoria with cruise control?"

"Cute."

As it was Saturday morning, the normally quiet town was buzzing with activity. A Cub Scout troop in blue uniforms was conducting a bottle drive, hauling around red wagons full of glass and soda cans as they went door to door along the immaculate row of homes. A father and son, rod and tackle boxes in hand, were heading down to the creek to catch the last of the fishing season. Freshly washed sheets flapped on laundry lines near piles of burning leaves and the local high school band practiced "Louie, Louie" high up on the hill.

Small-town bliss.

Life in Slagville hadn't stopped because a builder of family-friendly casinos had been murdered a few miles away or because the bratty owner of a colliery had shot himself. What was important—love, family, spotless lawns, clean sheets, Saturday morning soccer and Saturday evening Mass—were forever here.

A fireman was replacing the letters on the sign advertising tonight's get together at the Slagville Union Hall and I almost fell out of the Jeep.

"Hoagie Ho!" I shouted before I could catch myself. Actually so far the sign just said Hoagie H, but I got the idea. Stinky had told Jane he'd meet me at the Hoagie Ho and here I'd been keeping an eye out for hoagie shops when all along it had been the name of the next festival. No wonder it hadn't been in the phone book. I had to get over to that Union Hall, pronto.

"What're you so excited about?" Stiletto turned the corner and parked in front of a new vinyl-sided beige doublewide that was landscaped like it was Windsor Castle. Pruned bushes, hearty mums and fountains galore. "The Union Hall party?"

Shoot. I'd forgotten that Stiletto knew nothing of Stinky's surprise visit to me in Lehigh.

"Uh, Genevieve," I said, not completely fibbing. "I've been racking my brain trying to think of a way to get her together with a nutty conspiracy theorist in Limbo named Pete Zidukis. They'd be perfect for each other. I think maybe the Hoagie Ho might be the ticket."

Stiletto killed the engine. "Genevieve likes men?"

"Of course she likes men." I frowned at him reproachfully. "She's been married twice."

"And they left her?"

"No, she killed them. . . ."

"With her musket? Or a peashooter?" Stiletto said.

"With love," I finished. "They died of heart attacks in the sack. Smiles on their faces, if you get my drift."

"Talk about your conspiracy theories." Stiletto opened the door and hopped out.

I joined Stiletto, who immediately launched into a speech about how we should not alarm Mr. and Mrs. Allen. They were simple, church-going people who ladled up food in soup kitchens and visited the elderly and sick. It would never occur to them that their son might have fallen to the dark side. We must be careful what questions we asked.

We found Mr. Allen in a cement garage that was more spotless than a biotech laboratory. Rakes hung on hooks. Green hose lay perfectly coiled. Even the dark plastic garbage cans were shiny clean like they'd been buffed. The place smelled faintly of Tide detergent and gasoline.

"Hey, hey, hey. If it isn't Steve Stiletto. How go things old champ?" Mr. Allen pulled his head out of the toolbox he'd been organizing and shook Stiletto's hand with both of his. "Mother! It's Steve. Champ's come to visit."

Champ?

"Oh my," a maternal voice replied from inside.

Steve introduced me as Bubbles Yablonsky, his "friend." I flashed him a dirty, dirty look before I extended my hand, smiling sweetly.

Mr. Allen smiled back. "And look, honeybunch, he's brought his tart!"

I was stunned, to say the least, but Mr. Allen didn't seem to think he'd said anything, ah, inappropriate, as the guidance counselor at Jane's school would put it.

"Pardon?" I said. Mr. Allen ignored me and opened the door to the kitchen to call Mother one more time.

Stiletto poked me with his elbow. "That's the way they talk. I told you they were simple. Don't take it personally. They mean only the best."

Easy for "Champ" to say. He hadn't just been called a slut.

Mother appeared looking every inch the part. Blue dress, flowered apron, permed and sprayed brunette hair with not a strand out of place. "This must be Bubbles."

Mrs. Allen hugged me delicately, my eau de morning's jog,

smoke and grease from Lou's Eggs and last night's fire making for an oh-so-pleasant perfume. "How wonderful to meet you. She's not too much of a Jezebel, Earl."

"These are running clothes," I said for some inexplicable reason. "Champ bought them."

Mr. Allen winked. "Thatta boy. Get it while you can before you find yourself an old-fashioned girl and settle down."

My bottom jaw dropped.

"I'm sure Bubbles is old-fashioned." Mrs. Allen rose to my defense. "Aren't you, dear?"

"I better be. I'm a single mother of a teenager." My face felt hot and it didn't help when Stiletto put his hand on my shoulder to calm me down. "Not that it's anyone's business."

"That's the hussy in her speaking." Earl Allen slapped Stiletto on the back. "Say, who's up for a tour? I just redid the paneling in the rumpus room. Let's take a look-see." And he escorted Stiletto out of the garage, leaving me alone to do battle with Betty Crocker on overload.

I said, "Before we join the men folk—" (Mama has an old Polish saying: When flying with crows, fly like a crow. Deep. Very Deep.) "I wonder if you might know how I can locate your son, Zeke?"

She smoothed her apron. "I think one man at a time is enough, don't you?"

"This is for professional reasons."

Mrs. Allen blinked.

"I'm a reporter. Like Lois Lane." She was a virgin.

"Why don't you ask Steve? He sent Zeke off to Colorado or some such place yesterday afternoon. Chartered a personal plane for him at the Allegheny Airport even." She led me out of the garage. "To tell you the truth, I'm surprised to see Steve here. Zeke said he was in New York."

Holy mackerel. Stiletto chartered a plane to Colorado? What the heck was going on?

"I see," I said, keeping my voice normal, "and what is it exactly that your son does for a living?" We had entered the kitchen, all yellow with checked curtains and matching place mats. Straight out of the Sears catalogue "Homemaker On Valium" section.

"Zeke's a dick." Mrs. Allen slipped on yellow checked mitts and opened the oven door.

I thought about this. "A dick?"

"Yes. A private dick." She proudly displayed a pan of cinnamon rolls that had just happened to be in the oven and had just happened to be ready when two impromptu guests arrived. "With your profession you should know all about that."

Stiletto returned just in time to stop me from socking her. "What Martha means is that Zeke is a private detective. 'Dick' is just slang for that."

"Apparently, Champ, you chartered a private plane for Zeke, which he flew to Colorado yesterday," I said.

Stiletto stifled a look of shock. "Yes."

"Is there some problem?" Mr. Allen asked. Perhaps it had dawned on Earl that things were amiss when the client who had hired his son to fly three thousand miles away was suddenly in town looking for him.

"No problem. Just doing a bit of checking." Stiletto rocked on his heels. "Well, we better be going. I need to get back to New York and wait for Zeke's call."

Mrs. Allen put down the spatula, which she had been using to drizzle perfect curly-cues of white frosting onto the cinnamon rolls. "Don't you usually call him at eleven every night?"

"Ahh," Stiletto said. "Right."

"And, besides, you've obviously found Bubbles, so what do you need Zeke for?"

That was my cue. "You mean to tell me, Champ, that you hired a private dick to tag me? Is there no trust between us?" I pretended to be getting a head of steam. Hands on hips. Eyes flashing. Etcetera, etcetera.

"Don't get mad, babe. I was only concerned about your safety."

"Sure. And with a loose goose like Bubbles for a girlfriend, you never can tell what sailor she's brought home, eh boy?" Mr. Allen nudged Stiletto in the ribs. "In this day and age with all them diseases around it's your safety, too, that's at stake."

"I wouldn't know," Stiletto said. "Bubbles is the most honorable woman I've ever met. Sorry to have disturbed you." And, bowing slightly with respect, he put his arm around me and ushered me out the door.

"Doesn't that beat all," I heard Mr. Allen remark to his wife. "I think he actually loves the floozy."

Back in the Jeep I was frothing at the mouth. Let me at 'em. Let me at 'em. Stiletto had the good sense to get out of there hell for leather.

"I don't blame you, Bubbles. I got a bit ticked off in the end there, too. But you have to remember that the Allens are very basic people. What you see is what you get."

"What I see is my running shoe in Mr. Allen's—"

"So, did Mrs. Allen tell you anything of worth?" Stiletto stepped on the gas. "Her husband kept yapping about his hand-hewn paneling. I could barely get a word in edgewise."

When I told him what Mrs. Allen had said, it was Stiletto's turn to froth at the mouth. "The temerity!" He pounded the steering wheel. When Stiletto got mad he occasionally slipped into English Twit Speak. Some tic left over from years of boarding school. "Who in heaven's name had the audacity to pose as me? Right down to the most minute detail of my schedule."

"Whoever had the audacity also had the bucks," I said. "Think how much a chartered flight to Colorado costs."

Stiletto leaned back and steered with one hand. "We're not using our brains. What's the key distinction of the person who set us up Wednesday night?"

"He knows us. He knows where we work, our pasts, or at least your past, and all about our relationship," I said. "Though it could be a she."

"A she?" Stiletto grunted. "No woman could imitate a voice as deep as mine. Certainly not with my timbre. I've just got too much testosterone flowing through my veins."

I tapped my head. "Sorry. What could I have been thinking."

"I'm going to go back to the inn and make some phone calls. Maybe I can track down Zeke in Colorado," Stiletto said, pulling up to the Main Mane. "What are you going to do?"

"Take a shower. I don't care if someone's watching me, planning an ambush. At least my corpse won't smell like scrapple and B.O."

"Until next time," he said as we stood on the stoop of Roxanne's, where I could hear the buzz of blow-dryers going full steam inside.

He bent down and, despite my sweat and grime, kissed me softly. I sensed a depth of concern I hadn't felt before. Stiletto was really worried about me. And that made me worried about me. "Do me a favor and don't go outside today, okay?" he said. "Not that I expect anything will happen."

"Sure, Champ." Although I was thinking, fat chance I'm staying in. I'm going to find Stinky at the Union Hall.

He kissed me again. "Champ. I like that." And he was off, filled with more determination than I had ever seen in him before. Stiletto knew something I didn't and whatever it was I didn't know was something I knew I'd want to know.

You have to be a blonde to understand.

Chapter 20

I opened the door to find Roxanne catering to two clients at the same time. "Thank God you're back," she said, holding out a tray of bleach. "I took on a last-minute walk-in. Can you do Tammy?"

The bleach secure in my hands, Roxanne dashed to the rear of the salon to towel off a woman dripping in the sink. I turned to Tammy. Tammy's hair was a dull, faded brown and badly in need of highlights that weren't too garish. Only the most experienced stylist could freshen up hair like this.

"Thank God you're back," G said, entering from the living room and rubbing sleep from his eyes. "I want you to make me pancakes."

"Can't now," I said, painting on a strip of bleach. "If I don't finish this pronto, this woman's gonna be two-toned."

"I'll tell Jane if you don't," he threatened. "I'll tell her that she and I can't go out anymore. That I don't even like her."

I combed out another section. "She back yet?"

"No. Her friend's here, though." He handed me a strip of foil as I moved on. "That looks cool. Can I do it?"

"It's very technical, G. Too much bleach and she'll end up looking ridiculous. Too little and this woman doesn't get what she paid sixty-five bucks for. What friend?" Professor Tallow?

G thumbed over his shoulder, his eyes never leaving my hands for a minute. "Some girl. She's in the kitchen crying with your mother and Genevieve. How do you know where to paint it?"

Roxanne escorted her wet-headed client over to the chair next to us. "Thanks, Bubbles. I guess I've been a little preoccupied these days, what with Stinky gone and all. I should never have taken on the walk-in."

"There's some friend of Jane's in the kitchen, upset," I said, pulling out another piece of foil. "I think she's crying."

"Go, go see her. That's much more important." Roxanne shushed me out. "I'll handle the foil . . . somehow."

I hesitated. "That's too much work for you, Roxanne."

"I can do it. I can do highlights," G piped up. "C'mon. Pleeease."

"Sure, why not? I'll direct him," Roxanne said, motioning for me to hand G the bleach. "You run along."

"Thanks, Roxanne." To G I flashed an I've-got-my-eye-on-you look. He turned his back to me and began painting away merrily.

In the kitchen Mama and Genevieve were clucking over a red-eyed Sasha whose hair was as straight as I'd left it, sure proof that she hadn't slept a wink. Genevieve held her hand and Mama slid a cup of tea toward the poor girl, who merely looked at it glumly.

"Thank God you're back," Mama said as I entered.

"I've never been so needed in my life. Everyone's thanking God that I'm back." I sat down opposite Sasha. She wouldn't make eye contact with me. "What's wrong?"

"Mom's gone," she blurted. "She didn't come back to the hotel last night and I don't know how to find her. You were the only person I could think of. I . . . want . . . my . . . mom." A torrent of tears followed.

Mama handed her another Kleenex and I patted Sasha's other hand. "Did you call the police?"

"I'm afraid to," she said. "What if they arrest her?"

"Arrest her?" Genevieve said. "What in tarnation for?"

Sasha blew her nose and patted her eyes with the same tissue. Black mascara was smeared all over her face. "For shooting Mr. McMullen."

That shut us up.

"Uh, we better let you handle this, Bubbles," Mama said, getting up and nodding for Genevieve to join her. "I don't want to get involved in no murder stuff."

I waited until they left, closing the swinging door silently behind them. When they were gone, I asked Sasha how she'd gotten it into her head that her mother was a killer.

"I don't know that for sure. It's just that, well . . ." She twirled the tissue in her lap. "Mr. McMullen had been bugging us a lot. He used to phone Bud at home almost every night and after Bud died he started calling Mom."

She leaned forward and stirred the spoon in the cup. "Mom told me never to talk to Mr. McMullen and to hang up if he called. He phoned all last night, right up until you came and then . . . then he was shot and Mom didn't come back."

Nothing like mother-daughter trust. "You'll be relieved to know," I said, "that McMullen wasn't murdered. He committed suicide."

"You mean it?"

"That's what the cops say."

"Oh." Sasha nodded. "That is a relief."

Not really, but why belabor a moral issue. "As for your mother not returning to the hotel . . . maybe she got stuck in traffic?" Hey, it was all I could think of on the spot. "Though you'd expect her to call if that had happened."

"She called," Sasha said matter-of-factly. "She called me last night and then this morning."

"Your mom called?"

I was gonna strangle this kid. If this was some passive/aggressive attention-getting teenage girl maneuver, she was going right over my knee.

"Yeah. Mom said she was okay, but that she needed to take a break. She told me to stay at the hotel until Donatello picked me up on Sunday. Charge everything to room service and not to leave under any circumstances. She said that like fifty times. When I heard that Mr. McMullen was shot, I kind of freaked out, though."

I had to admit, it was an odd "fact pattern," as the cops term it. Then again, Sasha was only seventeen. Her stepfather had been murdered and her mother was off on a lark.

Sasha downed her tea. "Whew! I feel so much better. I guess I just needed to get that off my chest." She opened her purse and pulled out a green Clinique compact and began rubbing at the mascara patches.

"Everything will be fine, I'm sure." I took her cup to the sink.

"It just occurred to me. You don't suppose my mom's been kidnapped, do you?" Sasha asked, wide-eyed. "I saw a *Law and Order* show on that once. The woman was kept in a hole in the basement."

I smiled to myself and turned on the water. "No. I don't think so."

"Then I wonder how come her Jag is still at the Le Circe Restaurant."

I flipped off the water. "Her Jag is still at Le Circe?"

"Yeah. In Wilkes-Barre. There was a message on our home answering machine about it. The manager said it was going to be towed if Mom didn't pick it up."

What to do? What to do? "I think you better go back to the hotel, Sasha, in case your mother calls again. She might get worried if you're not there."

Kidnapped, I was thinking. Chrissy Price had been kidnapped. No. Couldn't be. Why would she have called to say she was okay?

"But I took a taxi," Sasha whined, "and I'm out of cash. There's no way for me to get back to the hotel."

"I'll get G to drive you. In the meantime, promise to call us as soon as you hear from her. If your mom doesn't call by this evening, we might want to contact the police just to, uhm, cover all our bases."

This did not go over well with Sasha, who promptly started crying again. I ran into the salon in search of G.

He was standing by the hairdryer studying his watch. Roxanne was barking instructions to him as she swept up from her last customer.

"Bubbles. This boy is a natural!" she exclaimed, leaning on her broom. "The way he applied that bleach, it was artistic. I was in awe. Such delicate handiwork. Such instinctive layering. He knows all the terms. Chunky. Buttery. He's a genius."

Just like G always claimed.

"Thirty more seconds should do it," he announced.

Tammy flipped through the *Family Circle*, unaware that she was being handled by a junior Vidal Sassoon. I asked G if his car was back from the Texaco.

"Yeah. But it's got a funny smell. I think they just Elmer-glued the airbags in."

"Can you take Jane's friend Sasha back to her hotel in Glen Ellen?"

He lifted up the dryer hood and unwrapped a foil for a peek. "Not bad, *n'est-ce pas?*" he asked, holding up a strand for Roxanne's inspection.

"*Oui, oui!*" said Roxanne. "*C'est magnifique.*" Turning to me she said, "I'm sorry, Bubbles, he can't go."

"We're in the moment," he said, gently helping Tammy out of the chair.

"Is he ready?" Sasha stepped into the salon, her lips pouty enough to make Liz Hurley jealous.

G let go of Tammy and wolf whistled. "Sweeet."

"This is Sasha," I said. "She's the one who needs a ride."

"For that bodacious babe, I'd drive to Mars." He wiped his hands and sauntered over to her. "Let me finish up with this client and then I'll be at your service. Just as soon as I, uh, unplug my car."

"A guy who does hair. Awesome," Sasha said. "And you drive an electric car? Cool. It's like so Ed Begley Junior."

G, the hairdressing, battery-powered stud muffin. Would wonders never cease?

After a thorough, hot shower, I grabbed my favorite jeans and a bateau-neck, three-quarter sleeve top in purple spandex. Perfect for a day of kicking around town. I slipped into my high-heeled boots with the little zipper on the side and pulled my hair up into a ponytail. Plucked a few stray eyebrow hairs, applied a tasteful line of midnight blue liner, jet black mascara (triple coat, of course) with eyelash curler, Plum Passion shadow and I was done except for the lipstick.

I ran down the stairs and was turning into the salon when I bumped into Mama and Genevieve heading out the door, suitcases in hand. Genevieve was in the black-and-white striped dress that made her look like a referee. Mama was wearing faded dungarees, a black Harley shirt and a hairnet.

"Going back to Lehigh?" I asked, taking their suitcases from them.

"First, we're off to make hoagies at St. Stanislaw's Church," Mama said. "They're selling them at the Hoagie Ho tonight as a fund-raiser to buy new carpeting for the parish hall."

Mama and community service? Not likely.

"Hold on, Rambette." I plunked the suitcases down on the sidewalk. "Since when do you care about fund-raisers for a church parish hall?"

"Since Vilnia's showing up. We've got to find out what she plans to do with the Nana diary," Genevieve said, tossing the two suitcases with ease into the back of her Rambler. "I bet she photocopied it cover to cover."

"And if she did," Mama opened her jeans jacket and pulled out a wooden rolling pin. "We're going to war."

I gasped. "A rolling pin? You won't go to war, you'll go to jail. You'll kill someone."

"Nah. Women in these parts of PA got hard heads, say Genevieve?"

"Say." Genevieve opened the driver's side door and got in.

"No way." I tried to grab the rolling pin from my mother's shriveled and newly tattooed hands, but she was stronger. "You two old dames can't waltz into town and pick a fight."

"They started it," Mama said, getting in and slamming the

door. "Those Slagville Sirens stole the Nana diary and I can tell they're cooking up something."

"Literally," Genevieve added, revving the engine. "Now listen up, Bubbles. If we don't come back alive, don't forget to demand Charlaine at Gupka's Funeral Home. She's the only one who knows how to do decent makeup at that place." And off they went.

Ugh. I stamped my foot on the sidewalk in frustration. More trouble. Here I had one day left in Slagville to find Stinky and who set us up Wednesday night and I'm suddenly swamped with aggravation. I had to track down Jane in the woods and find out if Chrissy Price went on a bender or was kidnapped. Then there was this craziness with Zeke Allen and the pseudo Stiletto he was supposedly working for. Now my mother and her friend were starting a rumble with the ladies auxiliary.

"Bubbles?" Roxanne was at the door holding the portable. "It's for you. That Mr. Salvo again."

I ungraciously snapped the phone from her hands. "I know, I know. I'm on for Sunday."

"You make those advance calls to the Catasauqua Republicans yet?" Mr. Salvo must have been calling from his home. The television was on in the background. Football.

"No," I said, curtly, "I've been too busy breaking page-one stories."

"Too bad I got such a short memory. I've promised Dix Notch you'll do a bang-up job on both Sunday stories, by the way."

I dead headed a purple mum by Roxanne's door. "Both stories?"

"Guess you didn't get the message. The Hellertown waste haulers are taking an early morning vote tomorrow on whether to strike. You should be there for that."

"Define early morning."

"Uhm. Five should do it. Tell you what. Since I'm such a nice editor, I'll fill out the photo assignment slip for you."

It was all I could do to keep myself from drop-kicking the phone into Roxanne's flowers.

"Oh, Bubbles? One other thing."

"Yes, Mr. Salvo?"

"You're fired. Don't forget that."

How could I? I was working harder than ever.

Chapter 21

The old brick Union Hall was near the end of Shale Street, a quiet side road framed by trees and juniper bushes, and it was deserted when I arrived in my Camaro. I had expected that at least a few people would be inside setting up for the big Hoagie Ho tonight. Thankfully, I was wrong. The joint was empty.

Except for Stinky, I hoped.

I parked a few blocks away and strolled around the building. There were two main entrances, a rear door and a front door, both padlocked shut. There was also one storm door to a basement. I tried it and it was locked, too. Though not always. I guessed Stinky used it to slip in and out undetected when folks weren't around.

I stood back and surveyed the setting. The Union Hall was one block east from the white and tidy St. Stanislaw's Church, where Mama was making hoagies, and one block west from that grungy bar called the Hole. I zeroed in on the pay phone by its back door. So that's where my fateful fax had been sent from. My would-be killer had stood on this very spot Wednesday night and dialed the Passion Peak. It sent a cold shiver down my arms.

I heard a car pull up and park on the other side of the hall. That was my cue. I had to get into the building and find Stinky now.

Access came in the form of a first-floor bathroom window that had been opened a crack for ventilation. It was wooden and had been painted so many times that it didn't need a lock. I zipped open my cosmetics case and found an old waxy lip pencil. I rubbed it along the casing and with some pushing and shoving, moved the jamb about a foot. Enough for me to scramble inside.

I landed on the dirty tile floor with a crack. Dang. I unzipped my right boot and frowned. Broken heel. Well, what can you expect for $15.99? I put the boot back on and *click, clumped* out of the bathroom into a long, dark hall.

"Hello?" I called, *click, clumping* toward the back. The wooden floorboards, dark with coal dust, dirt and wax, creaked as I made my way.

"Stinky? Are you here?"

I cupped my hands to my mouth. *"Hey! Stinky! It's me, Bubbles."*

Still nothing. Except for another creak that seemed to be coming from the main meeting room. I pressed my back against the wall and cautiously poked my head through the cased opening. Nada.

The dark green curtains that hung from the floor-to-ceiling windows were still drawn, but there was evidence that someone had been there earlier in the day. A wooden stage at the far end had been set up with chairs and music stands. A large white banner proclaimed the date and time of the Fifth Annual Hoagie Ho. The room smelled of spilled beer and stale cigarette smoke, spicy sausage and coffee.

I was about to leave when I noticed a series of intriguing black-and-white photos along the wall by the door. They were like ghosts peering out at me. Eyes bleached white by age and chemicals. Faces blackened by coal dust. Silent. Stunned. As though their souls had been lost and long forgotten.

Miners. Men mostly. But children, too. Haunting.

The first photo was of smudge-faced boys younger than G in caps and coats sitting hunched over bins sorting through coal to pick out the culm, or refuse, with their bare fingers while a stern man, a breaker boss, with a whipping stick stood nearby. The daily pay in the early 1900s, the caption below read, was seventy cents. One sweet-faced boy wore a wilted dandelion in his cap. He was dead by now.

The next photo was of the rickety breaker where coal used to be broken and sorted by the boys. Miners loaded the coal into a cable car that climbed to the top of the breaker. At the top of the breaker the car tipped and dumped the coal and slag into long chutes, breaking up the rocks in the process. The process also sent up clouds of deadly black dust that permeated everything, including lungs.

The three photos after that were of life inside the mines. Workers wearing nothing on their heads but wool caps, standing by buckling beams of timber that held up the shaft. Men and mules posing together in tunnels. A father and son, arms on each other's shoulders, their faces unrecognizable in their black soot masks.

"Heaven help me," I said out loud, suddenly realizing that I knew little, so very little, about my own father's family history here in coal country.

This is where the Yablonskys had first settled after the turn of the century to work for the English-speaking foremen like the Welsh and Irish. But as my father was dead, due to a safety glitch in the ingot mould of Lehigh Steel, there was no way for me to ask him what life had been like for his relatives here. I could only examine these faces and wonder. Which ones were my great uncles and distant cousins?

The next photographs were of mining disasters. Cave-ins. Explosions. A house that had fallen into the ground above a mine that had collapsed underneath. That was followed by a list of all the miners from Slagville who had been killed on the job. Many, if not all, of them had been related. Darrah, John and Joseph. Howland, Robert and John. O'Connell, Seamus and Sean. A son found dead in his father's arms during a flash flood. Brothers who had clung to each other after being trapped by a cave-in. All that for seventy cents a day. Sixteen tons and what do you get?

The last photo was of the Carbon County Prison where seven of the Molly Maguires had been tried and hanged for murdering coal mine bosses in the 1870s. An account of the Molly Maguires legend was pasted below. Granted, it was biased in favor of labor—this was a union hall, after all—but one wondered. Were the Maguires terrorists? Or had they been framed by the businessmen of their time?

Taken in the best light, the Molly Maguires had fought for better working conditions, often by resorting to violent means, the account said. They had relied on intimidation and physical threats to get results. They blew up coal cars, terrorized their supervisors and would willingly beat and cripple anyone who spoke against them. In short, they were a scary lot.

They were especially scary to those who owned the railroads and collieries. Industrialists like Franklin B. Gowen, owner of the Reading Railroad, and Asa Packer, founder of the Lehigh Valley Railroad, who left behind a $54 million estate when he died. Gowen and Packer suppressed all labor movements, including the Maguires. And so, bypassing the public legal system, they had used their own private police forces and judges to investigate, prosecute, try and execute the Molly Maguires.

I shook my head in amazement. That's not what they taught us in grade school. In grade school I'd been taught that Asa Packer was a hero philanthropist who had founded Lehigh University, donated millions to our town's hospital and started half a dozen charities that still bear his name.

No one ever told me that Asa Packer had framed the Molly Maguires, that he had squelched what some historians considered to be the birth of America's labor unions. On all those elementary school field trips to coal country, I'd have thought that some half-witted teacher might have mentioned that Asa Packer had been partially responsible for the deaths of seven labor activists who were hanged without legal trial and jury.

Seven men hanged in Carbon County.

Alexander Campbell. Michael Doyle. Edward Kelly. Thomas

P. Fisher. James McDonnell. Charles Sharpe and John Donohue. Yellow Jack, he was called. Yellow Jack Donohue.

"Donohue," I said out loud.

"Right behind you."

"Before we start," Chief Donohue said, throwing open the green curtains, "I think it's best that you don't try to lie to me."

"Oh, I—"

"Don't interrupt." Donohue moved to the next window. "I know everything in this town. That's my job. For example, I know that Zeke Allen's been on your tail, that McMullen met up with you in St. Ignatius and that Koolball stopped by your house yesterday in Lehigh."

Dust motes from the curtains caught the late morning light and made the stuffy air sparkle. I was sitting on the stage in the Union Hall and I prayed that Stinky wouldn't make the mistake of strolling past the window.

"I also know that Chrissy Price has gone missing, that her daughter ran to you, of all people, and that you are here." Finished with letting in the day's light, Donohue came over and sat beside me. "What you're doing here is what I don't know. So why don't you tell me so I don't have to bust you for trespassing, breaking and entering and," he waved his pudgy hand, "uh, misdemeanor property damage."

"What did I damage?" It was I who had the broken heel, thanks in part to landing on that hard tile floor.

"The bathroom window. The jamb's broken. That's how I figured out someone had broken in."

I crossed my legs and tried to act nonchalant. "I had a crazy idea that Stinky might be hiding out in the Union Hall. Obviously, I was wrong."

"How do you reason?"

"Look around." The place was terrifically silent. "The hall is locked tight. That bathroom window hadn't been opened in years and there are too many people here during the week for Stinky to hide out successfully."

"So when Stinky stopped by in Lehigh, he didn't say, 'Hey, Bubbles, why don't you meet me at the Union Hall?' "

"No. I can honestly say he did not ask me to meet him in the Union Hall." Okay. That was a bit of a fib, since Stinky had said the Hoagie Ho and the Hoagie Ho was at the Union Hall. "But I came here using my own stupid logic and it was wrong."

Donohue was old, I thought, seemingly older than when I first met him. His hair was snowy white and thinning. His skin was pink like a baby's and his irises had that weird clear blue rim old folks get when they're fading away. He should retire.

"Okay, Bubbles. I'll buy it this time. But I've got a piece of advice for you." He put a fat hand on my shoulder. "Go home. This afternoon we're holding a press conference, the coroner and me, to say that we believe Hugh McMullen shot Bud Price over some business dealings. They had conflicts over the Dead Zone, like your story pointed out. The show's over, in other words."

I had already whipped out my notebook and was writing this down. "That doesn't explain who sent me the fax and Stiletto the e-mail Wednesday night."

"You're right. That's why I need to talk to Koolball. So if you know where Stinky is, if you have been given any information about his whereabouts, you have a legal obligation to let me know."

I could feel Donohue's piercing gaze on me, but I just kept writing, afraid that if my eyes met his, I'd be forced to blab. "And what about Chrissy Price?" I continued, still focusing on my notes. "Who took her?"

"No one." Donohue stood and cracked his knuckles. "Chrissy Price is a case and a half by herself. From what I've learned about her personal history, she couldn't stay faithful if she was shackled to her wedding bed. The manager of Le Circe called me after he talked to Chrissy's daughter. Seems Chrissy left the restaurant last night with some guy in a blue sports car. Never returned to collect her own car or her family. I'll tell you, my heart goes out to her kid."

He pointed to my notebook. "Hey. Don't write that. That's off the record. Come on. I want you out of here."

"Sorry." I clicked off my pen and slid off the stage. "How did you find out Zeke Allen was tagging me?"

"From his mother, though she's more worried about you having a bad influence on her son than the other way around."

"She told you that?"

"No. That's what she told her pastor, Reverend Wyatt, on the phone last night." Donohue strode ahead of me, the handcuffs from his belt clinking as he went. "We got kind of an open communication policy in this town."

"Meaning?" I *click, clumped* faster in my broken heels to catch up with him.

"I listen to any call I want. It's perfectly legal, seeing as I have a tap warrant."

"Who gave you that?"

He unlocked the front door and we stepped out into the fresh sunshine. "I did. Hey, what's wrong with your foot?"

I showed him my boot.

"Jumping Jehovah. What the heck is going on?"

"Broken heel," I said.

"No, I mean over there." Donohue pointed toward the lawn in front of St. Stanislaw's Church where a dozen women in flowered dresses, wrinkled pantyhose, aprons and hairnets were gathered around what appeared to be a hulking referee and her biker sidekick. Vilnia was wagging her finger toward the odd pair, who pulled out rolling pins and started waving them about like French swords.

"That's my mother, her friend, Genevieve, and Vilnia," I said with a sigh. "Vilnia stole Nana Yablonsky's diary and Mama's seeking retribution."

"This a joke?" Donohue asked.

"It's no joke. It involves secret pierogi recipes and two Polish-Lithuanian housewives. What do you think?"

"I think that combination could be deadly," said Donohue, reaching for his walkie-talkie. "I gotta call backup. No way I'm handling them alone."

Chapter 22

"**O**kay, you two reprobates, out of the car," I ordered as Mama and Genevieve stepped sullenly from the Rambler. Genevieve had a black and blue mark on her shin where Vilnia had struck a low blow. Mama had a bruiser on her right eye.

Donohue must have been in a generous mood because he didn't charge them and he didn't charge me—on two provisions: that Mama and Genevieve go home right after the Hoagie Ho and that they not pick any more fights.

"We would've worked it out just fine if you hadn't gotten the fuzz involved, Bubbles." Mama trudged up the walk to Roxanne's. The cigarette behind her ear had snapped in two and her Righteous Red lipstick was smeared all over her upper lip.

"You need a steak for that eye," Genevieve added. "I'm glad I didn't get hit in the face. Pete asked me to the Hoagie Ho tonight and I want to primp up. I don't know what kind of action you can expect, LuLu, looking like that."

Mama opened the door to Roxanne's. "When you're as much a woman as I am, Genny, you don't go looking for action. It comes to you." They headed to the kitchen to rustle up some raw meat. I changed my shoes and then went into the salon to find out what had happened with Sasha and if Jane was back yet.

What I found was G with an orange silk ascot around his neck, using a purple pick to fluff up Mrs. Wychesko's hair.

"Wasn't Mrs. Wychesko here just a few days ago?" I ask Roxanne, who was taking a cigarette break by the cash register.

"I know. It's fantastic. Word's spread around town like wildfire." Roxanne sipped her cup of coffee. "I'm booked. Everyone's clamoring for a G Spot."

I tried not to gag. "A what?"

"A G Spot. That's his catch phrase. Like Marky Mark. I think it will go over well when he graduates to the New York salons." Roxanne exhaled and smiled at G like he was her new pet puppy. "Isn't he cute with that ascot? My Saturday at eleven bought it for him."

"Do you know that Chief Donohue listens to Slagville phone calls?"

Roxanne ground out her cigarette. "Sometimes. Tourists call this place Petticoat Junction and they're right."

"You have tourists?"

"Are you kidding? How can you resist a trip to the bottom of a mine in a coal car?"

That brought back memories of Wednesday night. I cringed. "I can resist. Some weirdo was going to kill me and Stiletto that way."

"All the more reason I'm in favor of Donohue listening in. It makes me feel a bit safer. And it should make you feel safer, too."

"How come?"

"Wasn't the fax to you sent from a pay phone outside the Hole? Maybe Donohue listened in to that conversation."

"I don't know how you can listen into a fax, Roxanne. I'm more upset by the possibility that Donohue's been tapping into my conversations with the *News-Times*," I said. "Why didn't you tell me?"

"Why didn't you tell me that Stinky told Jane to tell you that you should meet him at the Hoagie Ho tonight?" Roxanne folded her arms in triumph.

Busted. "Well . . . I asked you if you knew about the Hoagie Ho and you didn't."

Roxanne smiled thinly. She was ticked. "You asked me if there were any hoagie joints in town. A Hoagie Ho is not a hoagie joint."

"How was I to know?"

"I think you didn't want me to join in." Roxanne walked over to the sink where a client was waiting to have her color rinsed. "Lean back, Mrs. Frazier," Roxanne said, running her hand under the faucet to check the water temperature. She eyed me dubiously. "Isn't that right, Bubbles?"

"My assumption is that Stinky is in hiding for a good reason, i.e., your safety, Roxanne. What would happen if you met up with us and got caught in the crossfire?"

Mrs. Frazier stopped reading her *Cosmo* article to listen to us as Roxanne spritzed the water through her hair.

"I don't care if I get hurt, Bubbles. I love him and I need him. I want to see him and apologize and kiss him all over his naked, skinny body."

"My!" exclaimed Mrs. Frazier.

"All right, Roxanne. You can come with me to the Hoagie Ho," I said. "But you've got to play by my rules. Deal?"

"Deal," she said. "How about a royal blue dress with cubic zirconias?"

"Yeah. Blood looks good on blue."

I went off to talk to the G Spot.

"How's it going?" I asked.

G removed a pair of scissors from the deadly disinfectant. "Brilliant," he said, leaning down to cut an imperceptible stray from Mrs. Wychesko's flip.

"You need a license, you know. You can slip by cutting one head, maybe, but you'll need more schooling if you want to make a profession out of this."

"Not with my genius."

"I keep forgetting," I said. "G stands for God or genius, depending."

"And now it stands for G Spot," he said, wiggling his eyebrows.

"How was Sasha doing when you left her at the hotel?"

"I don't know." G put down the scissors and picked up the hairspray. "I didn't take her to the hotel."

Figures. G couldn't follow instructions to heat soup. "So, what did you do with her?"

"I didn't do anything with her. We drove about a mile from the salon and a cop pulled us over. He took her. I was back here in ten minutes."

Zeke Allen's caution about the nineteen ninety-nine Wal-Mart lights must have really made an impression because I was immediately suspicious. "What cop? What did he look like?"

G handed Mrs. Wychesko a mirror and unsnapped her plastic apron with a flourish. "He was an old guy. Older even than Stiletto. White hair, gut. Put Sasha in the back of the cruiser and said he was taking her to the police department."

Of course, Donohue. He must have found out about Chrissy's car at Le Circe and tracked down Sasha. "And Jane? Is she back yet?"

"What am I, your personal secretary?" G hissed as Mrs. Wychesko hobbled over to the cash register. "No, Jane hasn't called. She's still off with that professor of hers. And I could care less. I got a life to lead. I can't wait around . . . Hey, where are you going?"

Out the door, Tallow's press release in hand. It was two P.M. and my daughter wasn't home yet.

She was in trouble.

My Camaro was dangerously low on gas and I was dangerously low on cash. So I stopped at the Slagville Savings and Trust in search of an ATM. When I asked the old guy sitting on the bench by the bank's entrance where it might be, he put his hand to his ear and said, "Aunty Em?"

That's when I realized that of course Slagville did not provide automated banking. I entered the bank, prepared to put up a big stink about how the heck I was supposed to get cash in this time-warped town and was caught off-guard by a super friendly teller.

"Sure, no problem," she said, cheerfully accepting one of my Lehigh No Credit Union checks. "You look like the kind of woman who keeps her account in tip-top shape. Here's your fifty dollars." And she slid the money under the iron grate. "Have a great day!"

I felt like a bank robber.

Next, I drove to the Texaco, where the sprightly stepping, white-suited whistling Texaco man skipped over to my car and almost gleefully began filling her up. I paid for a full tank of gas— five bucks—bought some mints, a pack of gum, a Diet Pepsi and a street guide to Columbia County.

I had barely passed the Slagville softball field on my way to Limbo when two flashing blue lights appeared in my rearview. I predicted Donohue eager to wave me bon voyage after such a pleasant stay. Either that or it was one of those Wal-Mart pervs tagging me on a deserted country road. I mentally tossed a coin and decided I couldn't stop and take the chance. Didn't have time to get assaulted today.

I zoomed so fast the Camaro began to rattle (seventy-five miles per hour—it's old). Even so I couldn't keep ahead of the black vehicle with its better acceleration, which was soon by my side in the oncoming lane.

"What are you doing?" Stiletto asked, the wind whipping through his gorgeous brown hair.

I slammed on the brakes and headed onto the berm, forcing Stiletto to yank a U-turn and nearly roll his Jeep.

"Sorry," I said after he parked behind me and walked up. "I didn't know it was you. The Jeep has a top. Your Jeeps never have tops. Besides, I wasn't sure if you were a cop or not."

"So what? I bought a Jeep with an attachable top and I wanted to see what it's like with it on. Maybe I'm getting conservative in my old age. Not you, I take it. You thought I was a cop so you gave chase, is that what you're telling me?"

I told him about Zeke's warning and Stiletto leaned in the window. His eyes were blue. So very, very blue.

"Where'd you get those lights, anyway?" I asked.

"Wal-Mart, nineteen ninety-nine," he said. "Helps me zip through traffic when I'm on assignment. Mind if I get in?"

Without waiting for answer, Stiletto opened the passenger door and was beside me. "Hi, babe." He put his hand on my shoulder and pulled me toward him, kissing me tenderly. "We got a big problem," he said, after we broke apart.

"You and me both."

"Exactly." He pushed back the seat and turned toward me. "I got hold of Zeke in Colorado. Supposedly I sent him to look for Yablonskys in Colorado Springs, relatives you might be staying with."

"I have relatives in Colorado Springs?"

"I love it when you play dumb." Stiletto touched me on the nose. "No, you don't. Someone wanted Zeke out of the picture, fast, in case he met up with me in Slagville and we put two and two together."

I sat back and stared at the St. Christopher medal on my dash that Mama had stuck there after all my parking tickets. I had tried to explain that St. Christopher was for traveling, not for parking, but she said that as far as she knew there wasn't any parking saint.

"Who is pretending to be you?" I asked.

"How about who knows my itinerary, who knows every detail from my past and who knows my home phone number back in Lehigh?"

Come again. "Back in Lehigh?"

That sexy muscle in Stiletto's jaw twitched. "After I reached him in Colorado, Zeke contacted the telephone company which did a search an hour ago on all the calls he received at eleven o'clock over the past week, supposedly from me. They came from my house back in Saucon Valley. Not even from my apartment in New York."

"Ohmigod." I brought my hand to my mouth. Someone had broken into Stiletto's mansion. "Did you call the police?"

"Had to," he said. "Was the only way to get the bank to reveal who's been wiring money directly into Zeke's account. Police said they didn't find anything unusual at my house. And the bank's researching the money transfers. As we speak, Zeke's on a flight back to meet with state troopers. I'm going to pick him up at the Lehigh Airport in a few hours."

"You're leaving?" Why was this man incapable of staying in one place for more than a day?

"I have to check out my house, Bubbles. But this is why I tracked you down." He played with a strand of my hair. "I love you, Bubbles. If anything happened to you, especially because of me, I don't think I could take it." The Adam's apple in his throat rose and fell. "Come with me. If you're by my side, I can protect you."

Let me just say that the depth of emotion in this man's voice, this model of risk and passion, this gift to women everywhere, was breathtaking. Which is why it was so hard for me to say, "I can't. Jane's missing."

"Missing!" Stiletto dropped his hand. "Why didn't you say so?"

"Because I'm not exactly sure she's missing, missing. She's off with her professor who I've got some concerns about, but if I overreact and call in the Mounties she'll never, ever forgive me."

"I see," Stiletto said. "At least I think I see. You want me to help you find her?"

"Thanks, no," I said, recalling the spectacle Dan, Wendy and I had made at the dig. "I can do it on my own. But I'll make a compromise. If I don't find her by midnight, I might call you in."

"Just say the word and I'll be there." Stiletto leaned into me and I let go, tears creeping out the corners of my eyes. "Come here, you."

I put my head on Stiletto's shoulder and let it all out. It's the way of women, mothers especially, to keep it in until we find that one safe moment to be ourselves. Jane missing. A Stiletto impersonator sending Zeke to spy on me. It was a lot for a hairdresser to handle.

"You're not made of fluff, Bubbles," Stiletto said after awhile. "You've got inner resources—almost as intriguing as your outer ones." He smiled and kissed me first lightly and then more passionately. The Camaro seat creaked as I pushed myself against him and his arms enfolded me, our tongues exploring each other's, his hand sliding up the back of my shirt and over my skin, sending goose bumps up and down my spine.

He stopped and looked up at me. "God, you're great," was all he said before kissing me again. I slinked over until I was fully on top, straddling him. My fingers deftly unbuttoned his shirt and spread it apart. His bare chest was warm and inviting. And then I moved down, unbuckling his belt and daringly reaching in . . .

"Bubbles," he said, closing his eyes. "What about . . . Jane?"

"Shoot." I pulled out my hand and rolled over the stick shift. Jane. What was I doing making out with Stiletto when my daughter was missing?

"Ahem," he said, readjusting the seat and buttoning his shirt. "I thought I had to say something. We couldn't . . . you know . . . while your daughter was missing."

I glanced in the rearview and tucked back a few strands of hair. "Absolutely."

"Man," Stiletto said, a grin on his face. "That was nice. Very nice." He was all buttoned and belted now, ready to do battle. He put his hand on the door. "Good luck with Jane. I'm sure she's just fine. Remember, she's a very unusual kid. Extremely resourceful, like her mother." He pecked me on the cheek and stepped out.

Just then I was struck by a thought. I leaned my head out the window. "Stiletto. What if the creep who set us up was Hugh McMullen? He's dead now, so I'd be safe."

"I don't think so, Bubbles," Stiletto said, starting up the Jeep. "Apparently my impersonator called Zeke this morning to tell him to stick it out in Colorado for the rest of the day. Because after tonight, he said, it would all be over."

Chapter 23

Now more than ever I had to find Jane. So what that she'd grumble and groan when she saw me stomping through the woods after her. I had no compunction about snatching my precocious kid even if she was on the verge of finding the Celtic Rosetta stone. If there was a person out there who had sent a bogus fax to the Passion Peak and arranged for Stiletto and me to plunge to our deaths with a corpse in a coal mine, what was there to prevent him from harming Jane?

As I careened through the peaceful back roads of coal country, past the odd, abandoned, rusted breaker with its mounds of stone and slag piled about, I asked myself the question that any good reporter asks: Did I buy what the cops were selling?

Donohue claimed that McMullen, who clearly had been distraught and apparently had financial problems, shot Price with the same weapon he had used to kill himself. There could be any number of reasons why McMullen would have shot Price. Maybe Price, having discovered that McMullen's company had mined underneath his land, wanted to renege on the deal? Maybe he wanted McMullen to fill in the mine—a very expensive undertaking.

Or maybe they were fighting over what Stinky had to offer.

Fire extinguishers.

It was a preliminary theory of mine and a kind of wacky one, but when I learned there were a bunch of odd fire extinguishers in the basement—the same basement where Stinky had been holed up before he went missing—it sparked my imagination. As Pete Zidukis said, any coal company would kill to discover a way to put out the underground mine fire in Limbo. It wouldn't mean millions. It would mean billions.

Billions for McMullen, who was broke as well as broken. Billions for Price, who could then safely build a casino on his property without having to worry—or rather, without the state worrying—about a creeping mine fire next door. Billions for Stinky if his fire extinguisher worked and he managed to control the rights to it.

Stinky knew all about mining. He was a technical noodler and an ace cartographer for McMullen Coal. Was it so far-fetched to consider that he had invented a suitable method for extinguishing the Limbo fire? Maybe that's why he and Price were at the mine around the same time on Wednesday night?

But not only coal companies would have been interested in getting their hands on Stinky's formula. What about Donohue, the eavesdropping police chief? It seemed fathomable, given his access to all private communication in Slagville, that he would have discovered Stinky's secret and figured he could cash in. First, he had to get me out of town so he could find Stinky before anyone else did.

Then there was Chrissy Price. There was no underestimating the lengths to which a woman would go to free herself from a nightmare marriage. I didn't know much about Bud Price's personal life except that he was such a pig he wouldn't allow his wife's teenage daughter at the dinner table. That right there was cause for divorce, if not murder, in my mind.

What I did know was that Chrissy Price zoomed off on the same night Hugh McMullen shot himself, that she was alive and that she refused to tell her daughter where she was. Then there was Donohue's loaded statement about Chrissy's murky past. Seemed like a legitimate murder suspect to me.

I passed St. Ignatius Church standing like a sentinel in front of the gated cemetery, a white plume of smoke rising from the blackened earth around it. I headed down Troutwine Hill to what once had been the center of Limbo, cruising through the empty intersection where a boarded-up and dilapidated store, one of the last buildings remaining, stood on the corner.

At the top of the next hill was the fire department, all brand spanking new brick. A monument to irony. It overlooked the abandoned town with its grassy lots and sidewalks to nowhere. No place to run. No place to hide. Nothing to burn, if you asked me.

Following the directions to Tallow's retreat from the press release Jane had left for me the day before, I pushed my odometer and kept an eye out for Tallow Road as I snaked up a winding mountain highway. I spied a rusted sign on the right and hooked it. Suddenly I was off the pavement and on a dirt road, bouncing and bopping over rocks and through ditches and under trees. Camaros aren't meant to bounce and bop over rocks and through ditches. They're meant to drag at two A.M. on Stefko.

After miles the road ended abruptly at a low-roofed cabin in the woods. It was made out of logs and as soon as I saw it, the word "Appalachia" sprang to mind. I could picture a hardscrabble woman in dirty cotton and bare feet on the front porch churning butter, any untold number of children climbing around her skirts along with a few chickens here and there. Except that in this case there was a mint-condition royal blue TR6 parked out front.

Have courage, Bubbles. Motherhood is not for the weak of heart, I thought, getting out of the Camaro and taking my purse with me. The air smelled of wood smoke and pine. I knocked on the screen door.

"Hello?" I shouted. "It's me. Jane's mom." I gave the flimsy door a slight push.

"I'd say come in, but it appears you've already taken the liberty." Tallow, still wearing his beautifully worn green Barbour, was sitting at a weathered picnic table in the middle of the dark cabin, studying a large white map.

The room was furnished with worn antiques, a mahogany dresser by a single, unmade bed in one corner and a glass cabinet in the other. By the door was a black iron woodstove, the orange glow of a fire peeking through the glass. There was a gray soap-stone sink with a pump against the same wall where a dusty window opened toward the woods. It was really tranquil except for Tallow's presence in the room.

"I'm looking for Jane," I said, unsure if I should take another step. "Is she here?"

"No. She left a few hours ago. Insisted on walking back." He removed his glasses. "We've finished for the day. No one showed up at my press conference. Horribly disappointing." He replaced his glasses and returned to reading. "Ignorant reporters."

I had not seen Jane on my drive from Slagville to here. I had my doubts—and my worries.

"I hope she's okay. Do you think it's safe for her to walk all the way back by herself?"

"I do not run a daycare service, Mrs. Yablonsky."

"Miss. I'm not married, anymore."

"Miss Yablonsky." He twirled a black rock on the table and continued to focus on the map. "I teach college students. If your daughter is too young to be in my class, then I suggest you return her to high school."

I closed the door behind me and peered at the rock. "Where did you get that?"

"What?"

"That rock. It's identical to the one I saw in Chrissy Price's hotel room."

"If you recognize it, then I can only assume Mrs. Price purchased it from one of my collections." Tallow shoved the rock in his pocket, threw down his bifocals and slid from behind the table. He knelt down and opened the door to the woodstove to poke at the fire. "My rocks are very popular in Lehigh. The historical society sells them in their museum."

"They sell rocks? Rocks anyone could find for free?"

"They aren't just any rocks." He slammed the door, fastened it and wiped off his hands on a towel by the sink. "Tell me, have you heard of Stonehenge?"

"Seems like lately I've been hearing about it a lot."

"In case you don't know, Stonehenge is a collection of astronomically significant standing stones in Wiltshire, England, arranged thousands of year ago by Druids, otherwise known as Celtic philosophers. The inscriptions on the rocks around Stonehenge are ogam, the ancient alphabet used by Celts. For example," he removed the rock from his pocket and held it out for my inspection, "this particular rock shows the symbol for Wa, or mourning."

There was a big Y etched on it. Kindergartners could do better. "So?"

"So, I did not discover this rock in England." He dropped it back in his pocket. "I discovered it here, in Limbo."

He went over to a large, detailed wall map of the local area. "This unattractively named Dead Zone was once the site of an ancient Celtic colony. I believe it is because the topography, the undulation of the hills and the coal below them were familiar to the Welsh-born nomads who traveled up the Delaware and then the Lehigh river to Limbo around 55 B.C."

For a three-hour tour, my mind singsonged.

"As proof, I have unearthed numerous standing stones, a Druid throne and a winter solstice sunrise temple in that location." He pointed to grainy black and white photos tacked next to the map. "Which is where I held the press conference this morning. Of course, no one showed and so I expect all these Celtic treasures will be destroyed for . . . a casino." He punctuated casino with a tiny snort.

This was a perfect time to ready my trusty reporter's notebook and Bic pen.

"But what does that have to do with you and Chrissy Price ?" I said, flipping to a clean page. "Chrissy has been active in the historical society, which sells your famous rocks. Chief Donohue said she sped off from Le Circe with a man in a little blue sports car last night. Just like yours. Plus you arrived in town when she arrived. Coincidence?"

"What are coincidences, really?" Tallow asked rhetorically. "I, indeed, was at Le Circe, but I did not leave with Mrs. Price. We had a drink at the bar where I hoped to impress upon her the reasons why her late husband's casino should not be constructed. I'd had no luck convincing Bud Price, but after meeting up with you, Miss Yablonsky, at my dig in Emmaus, I was struck by an epiphany. Why not approach his widow? I knew her to be supportive of my excavations in the Lehigh Valley. I had even certified authenticity of the rock you'd snooped around and discovered in her hotel room. Therefore, I came here straight away to beg her ear."

"Couldn't you have waited until she'd buried her husband?"

"And risk his greedy car-dealing family brainwashing her to move forward on the project? In a word, no."

"Okay," I said, writing this all down. Brainwashing, car dealing, greedy family members. Loved it. "What did you do after meeting her at the bar?"

"Afterward I offered to walk her to her car, but she refused. As I drove out of the parking lot, I saw her climb into an antique pickup truck. I remember because I thought it very odd that a wealthy and cultured woman would be leaving in that kind of vehicle."

"He's lying."

Jane stood in the doorway, her hair electric blue in the sunlight filtering through the trees outside. In her hand she was holding yet another rock and some tools.

"About Chrissy Price?" I asked.

"What are you talking about? No, he's lying about these rocks."

"For Pete's sake." Tallow threw up his hands. "Enough with the rocks already."

Jane ignored him. "It saddens me to say this, Professor Tallow, but I have long been disturbed by your failure to implement the scientific method in uncovering archeological artifacts." Except for the ripped black T-shirt and mangled jeans, Jane had the air of a tenured professor on the university lecturing circuit.

"Therefore," she continued, "after our hike in the woods this morning, I poked around a bit and this is what I found in a smokehouse out back." She dropped the rock and metal tools on the table.

The rock resembled the other one he had shown me moments ago except that the Y was missing a line. "Your so-called Celtic treasures are no more authentic than the famous fraudulent 1885 Lenape Stone uncovered by a farmer in Bucks County."

"Blasphemy!" Tallow proclaimed. "I have been criticized, yes, but no one has dared compare my finding to the Lenape Stone."

"It's a risk I'm confident in taking," Jane said.

Lenape Stone? Sounded like a cubic zirconia competitor on the shopping channel.

"Hey, Mom," Jane said, as Tallow inspected the rock she had found, rolling it over in his hands. "What're you doing here? Oh no, you were checking up on me, weren't you?"

"No, no, no," I said, holding up my notebook as though that would prove I hadn't been.

"What about when I'm in college next year? Are you going to like follow me from class to class, spying on me from the bushes?" Jane had dropped the tenured professor shtick and was back to being an manic teenager. "That would be complete humiliation. I'd totally freak."

"You're going to college?" I slapped the notebook against my chest. "You changed your mind? What about grape picking? What about Mexico?"

"G and I talked about it and—."

"She's not going to college," Tallow said in a grave voice. There was an ear-piercing crash as he flung Jane's rock against the woodstove, smashing the stone into bits. "I'm her faculty advisor and I'll make sure that every university in the country learns that she is a plagiarist. She'll be blacklisted."

"I don't think so," I said. "It's you who'll be out in the cold when Jane's father threatens to sue his own university because you sexually harassed his daughter. Colleges are very sensitive about professors hitting on students these days. It's a far cry from the love-ins when you were a freshman."

"What? You have no evidence of that."

"See, that's the beauty of being an ambulance chaser like my ex-husband, Dan. He doesn't need evidence. Jane said you two stayed up all night after that Celtic service you performed Thursday. Dan could file a federal case on that alone."

"Mommm!" Jane moaned.

I dismissed her with a wave. "Think how that's going to look to the provost."

Tallow had gone paler than Keith Richards during a blood transfusion. Slimy sweat greased his forehead and his eyes darted back and forth searching for the right response.

"Oh, pooh," he exclaimed, staring wildly toward the road. "I've got to get out of here. I can't abide all three of you."

I craned my neck to get a view out the door. An apple red BMW roadster was riding slowly over each rock and ditch with earnest concern for its delicate bottom. It stopped and my ex-husband's new wife got out, giving the door a hearty slam. Wendy.

"Speak of the devil's mistress," I said.

"Where is that weasel?" she yelled, pushing up the sleeves of her Talbot's camel cashmere sweater set. "Tallow! Don't try to run from me." In her other hand she clutched a small black object. This was going to be good.

She threw open the screen door so hard that she ripped it off its hinges. Wendy entered ready for battle, her tight, surgically enhanced face straining against the cream headband that held back her brown bobbed hair.

"*You!*" she screamed.

"Eek!" squeaked Tallow, who was now cowering in the corner by his glass cabinet.

"You told me this was an ancient ogam grave marker. I showed it to Amanda Crowe of the Bucks County archaeological commission. Amanda Crowe has one just like it. She made it herself. As a Halloween hoax!"

"Calm down, Mrs. Ritter," Tallow whimpered. "I assure you that it is an authentic . . ." His hand slowly slid into his Barbour.

"I paid twenty thousand dollars. Twenty thousand dollars. Do you know how dumb I feel? I'm the laughing stock of my history group."

Tallow's hand gripped something under the waxed cloth of his coat.

"He's got a rock in his pocket, Wendy!" I shouted.

"Ha!" And with that the bogus ogam rock left Wendy's hand and went sailing in a perfect arc through the air.

I covered Jane. Tallow looked up pitifully as the rock hit his forehead with a crushing bull's-eye, bounced off and smashed into the glass cabinet, sending shards everywhere.

We froze. Paralyzed in fear and shock. Tallow slumped against the wall, a huge red gash oozing blood from his forehead down to his oat Ralph Lauren sweater underneath the Barbour. That was going to require serious dry cleaning. I stepped carefully over the crunching glass and felt for a pulse. There was one, but it was faint. Although that might have been a permanent condition for him.

"He's alive," I said. "He's unconscious, though."

"Oh, he's okay," Wendy said. "Just fainted like a girl."

"Nice arm," observed Jane. "You been lifting?"

"To head off osteoporosis, sure. And then there's tennis five times a week. Between the two, I got muscles that could take on the Yankee bullpen."

Another car pulled up. "That must be Mickey Sinkler," Wendy said. "I told him to meet me here and cuff the crook. I hope Tallow gets a helluva lawyer 'cause Dan's going to sue him to kingdom come for defrauding me like that."

"See?" I said to Jane. "I told you Daddy didn't need evidence."

"Thanks for tipping me off yesterday to the possibility that I'd been scammed, Jane," Wendy said, with uncharacteristic sweetness. "As soon as you called, I contacted Amanda. I couldn't stay put a minute longer after I realized it was a fake. Ogam, my ass."

"Aww geesh," Mickey said upon entering, shaking his head at the sight of Tallow. "Now what have you ladies done?"

We all told him at once and Mickey, sickened by the sound of female chatter, put both fingers in his ears. He felt for Tallow's pulse, came to the same conclusion I had and radioed for an ambulance. What excitement there must be at the Limbo Fire Department. Finally, finally someone had called.

"You know, I'm not a private security force, Wendy," Mickey said, while we waited for the paramedics. "You could have called the local police."

"Did I not purchase the stone in Lehigh?" Wendy lifted her chin defiantly. "Is not the jurisdiction of the crime dependent upon the location of the fraudulent transaction?"

"Did you ever think there might be more serious crimes than badly scratched rocks?" Mickey countered.

The Limbo ambulance arrived and took Tallow away. Mickey and Wendy followed. Jane and I stood by the Camaro watching them go.

"About that older man," I began.

"It's over." Jane opened the door and got in. "You were right about G. He's got his good points. Though I have to admit I was kind of taken aback when you started talking him up. I thought for sure this other guy was more your type."

Yeah, I thought, I'm a softie for psychopaths.

Chapter 24

"Where are we going?" Jane asked as I sped along Route 61 toward Slagville. "Back to Roxanne's, I hope. Justin Toritsky's parents are out of town and I don't want to miss his party. Given how slow G's car goes, if we don't leave by seven we won't get to Lehigh until the cops have cleared out all the kids."

"Plenty of time," I said, turning past a gate that advised us not to enter. "I just have to take care of business first."

We bounded over a wide gash in the road. The ground around us was dusty and spare of trees. A breaker loomed ahead, so large that it reminded me of a metal Godzilla. The rickety reddish wooden building next to it was identified by a sign as MCMULLEN COAL INC. I stopped the Camaro and started fishing through my purse.

"It's Saturday, Mom, I think they're closed." Jane stared out the window. "And didn't the guy who owns this kill himself yesterday?"

I pulled out a tube of lipstick. "Exactly. You going with me?"

Jane watched me as I applied a new thick coat of Fuchsia FooFoo to my lips.

"You're up to something. The brighter the lips, the darker the deed."

"The brighter the lips, the more of a distraction." I capped the lipstick and tossed it in my purse.

A stiff fall breeze blew us back as we made our way to the McMullen offices. The deserted colliery could have been out of the 1930s—the dust in our faces, the wind howling through the broken windows on the breaker and rattling the empty coal cars on the track, the way the broken storm door *whap, whap, whapped,* the yellow sulfuric clouds above us.

Funny how wealthy industrialists like Hugh McMullen or the late Henry Metzger from Lehigh Steel went to work in such dusty, weather-beaten places and then drove home to palatial surroundings. I'd never seen McMullen's home in Pittsburgh, but I imagined that if he sold a family mansion in Glen Ellen, it must be fairly nice.

"Hello, John Steinbeck," Jane said, when we arrived at the broken storm door.

"What made you think of pianos?" I asked, opening the door and letting her in first.

An equally forlorn security guard in a wrinkled blue uniform sat at the front desk watching a Pittsburgh Steelers game on a tiny television. He swung around in his swivel chair as soon as we entered the narrow hall that served as a lobby.

"We're closed," he said, putting the TV on mute. "No jobs anyway."

"That's good because I've got a job." I smiled my Fuchsia FooFoo mouth broadly to put him at ease.

"Then you should know we don't do tours no more, neither. Don't know if you've heard, but our president died suddenly last night. Mr. McMullen." He bent his head in a moment of respect. "All tours are off until further notice."

Cue for the business card. I handed him one and introduced myself as Bubbles Yablonsky, mortuary stylist.

"What's a mortuary stylist?" He flipped over the card to look at the back since the front didn't mention anything about mortuaries.

"I specialize in styling hair for funerals."

"Hair of the dead?"

"No. Of the living."

Jane, embarrassed beyond belief, wandered down the hallway, examining the brass plaques of coal mining merit or whatever it is coal companies get from the Rotary.

"Gee." He scratched the nearly bald head under his blue cap. "I've never heard of that before."

That's because you don't have any hair, I thought rudely. Instead, I said cheerfully, "Sure, funerals, why not? Hair style is often overlooked during moments of public grief. And yet, there you are, greeting Aunt Jessie and your dead husband's boss, and every other important person in your life, all the while looking like you'd stuck your head in the blender that morning."

"Hmmph." The security guard studied that business card again. "You must've seen the newspaper story about Mr. McMullen then."

"Yes." I placed my hand across my heart. "I'm so sorry. I'd really love to be of assistance at this time. Do you know who is planning the funeral service?"

"Memorial service," he said. "I can't say for sure, but I expect Mr. McMullen's secretary would know."

Secretary. The exact person I was looking for. "And her name is?" Out of the corner of my eye I caught Jane shielding her face with her hand.

"You can leave your card with me, if that's okay." He checked the Steelers. "I suppose that's why you've got them. For business."

"I usually make it my practice to leave with a name."

That put him over the edge. "Listen, you're lucky to get as far as you did." He pointed to a sign on the door. In big red lettering it said, NO SOLICITATIONS.

"Oh. I didn't see that." I picked my card out of his hands. No need to tip off the McMullen types that I'd been posing as myself. "Then you won't be needing this. Come on, Jane."

"Bye," Jane said on the way out.

"That was a complete waste," I said, stomping over the hard turf to the Camaro and yanking open the door. "All I wanted was a secretary's name. A last name and a first initial would have done it." I jammed the key in the ignition and started her up.

"What do you want a secretary for?"

I threw my arm over her seat to reverse. "Not just any old secretary. I wanted Hugh McMullen's secretary, especially if she was loyal and heartbroken." Done with the K turn, we steered straight down the McMullen Coal Road. "A loyal and heartbroken secretary would be pissed off when I told her that the cops were placing the blame on McMullen for Price's murder."

"I believe her name was Lamporini. Something like Lucy or Laura."

Screeech! I slammed on the brakes at the bottom of the drive. "Louise Lamporini?"

"That sounds more like it." Jane leaned over to turn on the radio.

"Louise Lamporini is Hugh McMullen's secretary? I did her makeup a couple of days ago, as a favor to Roxanne. Big woman."

"Then you shouldn't have any problem talking to her—unless you overdid her eyes and made her look like a raccoon. You do that sometimes, you know."

I knuckled her head. "You go, girl! How did you find out Hugh McMullen's secretary was Louise Lamporini? Wait. Let me guess. You read a memo upside down on the security guard's desk. No, that's not it." I snapped my fingers at the brilliance of my offspring. "You scanned the lobby photos and saw her in some company softball summer picnic."

"I read Professor Tallow's copy of the *Slagville Sentinel* this morning. Louise Lamporini was quoted as saying she couldn't imagine a nicer guy for a boss, yadda, yadda, yadda." Jane turned off the radio with disgust. "What's wrong with you? Why are you beating your head against the wheel, Mom?"

I lifted my head and shifted into first. "Don't ask. And don't tell Mr. Salvo, whatever you do."

According to a phone book outside of a 7-Eleven, a Gary and Louise Lamporini lived at 325 Main Street in Slagville, probably one of the row homes Stiletto and I had passed that first morning out of lockup. On the way over I searched my memory banks. Had I mentioned anything incriminating to Mr. Salvo while I was making up Louise's face? What had she heard? Had she stopped by Roxanne's that day with the sole purpose of cashing in her promotional makeover coupons so she could spy?

"Hey, Jane, you ever hitch a ride?" I asked as we drove past the school's well-worn recreation fields. Two boys were playing catch in the autumn twilight while a church bell called members to evening Mass. It was getting darker and darker, earlier and earlier these days.

"You caught me hitching Friday morning, remember? How come you waited this long for the lecture?"

"No lecture." I hooked a right from Terrace Street onto Main and checked the addresses. We were in the five hundreds and going lower. "I'm curious if you know about the old trick of the girl with her thumb out while the guy hides in some bushes?"

"Yeah. G and I do that. He says men would never stop if he was with me, so he makes me stand out by myself."

I pictured G taking a snooze behind a shrub while Jane did all the work. I sincerely hoped G would become one of those hairdressers who decided he loved men so he would stop messing up my daughter's life.

Three twenty-five Main was a simple brick row house surrounded by a wrought iron gate in the pattern of a grapevine. A light was on in the plate glass living room window and a green Saturn sedan was parked out front. A woman's car.

"You run up and knock on the door. Tell Louise you're related to Roxanne. Stall. Make up something. Ask her if she left her wallet at Roxanne's. Anything to get you inside and I'll come around the corner. Exactly like hitching with G."

"That sounds a little complicated, but okay." Jane got out of the car and ran up the steps. I parked on the side street, got out and turned the corner to see Jane and Louise smiling and chatting on the front porch. Brilliant.

They stopped when I appeared on the sidewalk.

"Don't I know you?" Louise said. She was in a white bathrobe with matching towel. Clearly, she'd just stepped out of the shower. "You're from the Main Mane."

"That's my mom," Jane said. "The one I was telling you about."

I joined them on the porch. Through the plate glass window I could see two children in their pajamas lying on the floor and laughing at cartoons on TV. "Bubbles Yablonsky. I did your makeup," I said, offering my hand. "You getting ready for the Hoagie Ho tonight?"

Louise shook my hand politely, if not warmly. "More like a girls' night out. But, listen, I can't talk to you about Mr. McMullen. I mean, his body's not even in the ground. It wouldn't be right."

I glared at Jane. "You told her?"

Jane threw up her hands. "What was I going to do? Hi, I'm Roxy's second cousin twice removed, uh, did you leave your wallet in my second cousin twice removed's salon two days ago? It was a stupid plan."

"She's right," Louise said. "I would have seen right through it. I can't tell you very much, anyway, except that the company will likely get sold since none of the other McMullen brothers wants to get in the business and their father is in poor health. That's it."

A man even larger than Louise came out of the house and onto the porch. He scared me a bit with his tattooed forearm and Hell's Angels T-shirt, his four-inch brown beard and nasty scowl.

"See ya, Louise," he said, pulling on a navy windbreaker and stamping down the front steps.

"Where the hell do you think you're going, Gary?"

Gary shoved his hands into his coat. "Out."

"What about the kids?" Louise slapped her hip. "Who's going to babysit? Tonight's my night with the girls."

"Ahhh." He waved her away with both hands. "That's your problem." He zipped up and trudged down the sidewalk.

Jane mouthed, "What a pig."

Louise folded her terry-cloth arms. "At least eat some dinner. I made it for you. Sausage and peppers in a skillet on the stove."

Gary stopped, wavering a bit in place. "With onions?"

"Fried."

He reversed, leaped up the steps, and threw open the front door without saying a word. There was the clatter of lids and pans on the stove and a plate being pulled out of the cupboard. Louise smiled knowingly.

"I'm sorry," she said sweetly. "Where were we?"

"The police are saying that Hugh McMullen shot Price over business dealings," I said. "If that's not true, you should speak up."

"I don't know if it's true." Louise sat down on an aluminum folding chair covered in green and gold plastic plaid. She leaned her elbow on the chair arm and thought for a bit. "Hugh McMullen was a mystery. If I had to describe him, I'd say he was a rich playboy who just wanted to spend the family money on cars and trips and fun."

I reached into my purse for my reporter's notebook, but Louise shook her head. "This isn't for publication. I'm telling you this so you'll understand that there's not much I could know."

Great. Essentially a long no comment. I folded my arms and leaned against the porch railing of iron grapes to stick it out. Jane sat in a matching folding chair next to Louise and glanced through the window at Gary, who was sitting on the couch with his children and enjoying a heaping plate of sausage.

"What do you mean about Hugh being a spoiled playboy? How does that matter?" I asked.

"Mr. McMullen could never live up to the reputation of his father, Donald," Louise said. "They called his father Senior McMullen in the company. When Senior McMullen came back from World War II, his own father gave him the colliery, which had essentially closed down after the Depression. Senior

McMullen built it up and made it a legitimate business again. When he had a stroke five years ago, he gave it to Hugh, who siphoned off its cash to pay for cars and trips and expensive clothes."

"Makes sense. Hugh told me he didn't care about coal," I said.

"He didn't care about much besides himself." Louise unwrapped the towel from her head and ran her fingers through her wet hair. "However, he did care about impressing his father. Even though his father was weak and partially paralyzed, he still called up Hugh every day and reamed him out. Until last year. That's when he hit bottom."

"Hugh or his father?" I asked.

"Both. Senior McMullen suffered another stroke and Hugh had to put his father in a nursing home. Since his father was out of the house in Glen Ellen, Hugh sold it and moved full-time to Pittsburgh." She folded the towel and laid it in her lap. "He'd only communicate with the office by phone. That's why I don't know about him and Price. Hugh McMullen rarely came to Slagville so I never took his calls or overheard his phone conversations."

"What did you do with your day?"

Louise laughed. "Not much. Checked the want ads because I was certain the company was going down the toilet."

"You ever hear of Carl Koolball?" I asked.

"Are you kidding? I must have typed his name two-hundred times on letters to other coal companies."

"Why?"

"Mr. McMullen said we had a legal obligation to warn them once we found out that Koolball was threatening our employees. He was worried that Koolball might get hired someplace else and become violent there and we'd be liable. You read so many newspaper stories about employees taking Uzis into work and such."

I'd heard from Roxanne that Stinky was threatening management if it didn't fess up to the state. But I'd never heard that he was threatening employees.

"Threatening employees, how?" I asked.

Louise glanced at her bare toes. "You know, now that you mention it, I'm not really sure. Mr. McMullen just told me that Stinky was a threat and that I needed to get those letters out fast. I guess I kinda took his word for it. I mean, he was my boss."

Smear campaign, I thought. "Before that incident did you know Stinky, I mean, Carl?"

"I never heard his name before, although I gather he was a cartographer in special projects."

I couldn't think of anything else to ask until Jane said, "Didn't Hugh ever come by the office, even on a lark?"

"Once a month he'd make a visit." She paused, weighing whether or not to go on.

I let her weigh. When I was starting out in reporting I used to jump in and offer suggestions to my interviewees, simply because I couldn't stand the awkward silences. Since then I've learned that awkward is good. Human nature can't abide silence.

"This is probably pretty tasteless of me to say, since he's dead now," Louise said eventually, "but I threw a fit last month when he called me into work on Labor Day."

"Labor Day?" I said encouragingly.

"Labor Day!" she said firmly, apparently hot at the thought of McMullen's inconsideration. "I mean, here this guy is never in the office. Then he decides to come to Slagville during Labor Day weekend, one of my few long weekends in the year, and he calls me in, too."

"What for?" Jane asked.

"I don't know. To type up those Koolball letters and order flowers for his girlfriend. He was so self-centered, he didn't care that I had a family and maybe wanted to spend a day with them."

"Girlfriend?" Jane said. "Hear that, Mom? Hugh McMullen had a girlfriend."

"Must have been 'none of your business,'" I said.

Louise leaned forward. "I think it was. I was supposed to go to a family reunion that weekend."

It took me a second to catch the misunderstanding. "No, that's not what I meant. When I ran into Hugh McMullen in Limbo, he said he didn't kill Price, that he had an alibi. Supposedly it was a friend he was with. When I asked him the friend's name, Hugh said, 'None of your business.'"

Louise sat back, a quizzical look on her face. "That was probably her, then. Twelve Tremont Road, Slagville. I know the address by heart. I sent flowers there all summer."

"And the name?" Jane asked.

Louise shook her head. "Have no idea. Sorry."

A lid dropped on the kitchen floor. Gary getting a second helping. It reminded Louise that she needed to get a move on. "I better go," she said, standing.

I thanked her and turned to leave, stopping myself as though a terribly insightful thought had just occurred to me. "Too bad you don't have the phone records of Hugh's calls when he was in the office. My editor swears by records. He likes to say more men have been saved by paper than by guns."

"He's probably right." Louise turned the knob on her front door. "Good night, then."

"Good night."

Jane lit into me as soon as we were safe in the Camaro. "More men have been saved by paper than by guns? Where did you get that one, Mom?"

"From a toilet paper ad." I was fixated on the list of Slagville streets on the Columbia County street map I had picked up at the Texaco. I may not read the articles in the newspaper, but I never miss a good TP ad.

Jane leaned over to inspect what I was doing. "Oh, goody. We're off to Twelve Tremont Road."

"Tremont. D-Five." I ran my finger down the D line and intersected it with the Five line. "What about that party you're so anxious to get to?"

"I can drink and smoke and dance anytime, but tracking down a murderer's girlfriend? How often does that happen?"

I kept my finger on Tremont Road and regarded my precious daughter. "You can drink and smoke anytime?"

She punched me in the arm. "Took you long enough to pick up on that. You're getting rusty."

Chapter 25

The sun had almost set by the time we found Tremont Road. It was at the edge of town and only three blocks long. Small Cape-style houses were set back from the street, their homey lights twinkling amidst the whish of falling leaves in the breeze. Unlike most neighborhoods in Slagville, this one was suburban, but the homes were as surgically immaculate as all the other homes in the anthracite region. People here had spent the Saturday raking up and pruning hedges.

Except for Twelve Tremont Road.

There were no lights on in the house and brown leaves littered the overgrown grass lawn. It was neglected.

"It's almost spooky," Jane said. "Slap a gargoyle on the roof and it'd be haunted."

"It's all the Halloween decorations around here," I said, getting out of the car. "You coming?"

"No thanks." Jane clutched her sweatshirt and slid deeper into the seat.

I rang the doorbell five times until a neighbor's light clicked on. I was being watched. Good. I strolled next door to Fourteen Tremont Road where the light had gone on and tried there. The welcome mat read THE FESTER'S.

A male Fester in a T-shirt, dirty jeans and work boots answered, smelling of mowed grass and barbecued ribs. In the background a mother Fester and two boy Festers were gathered around the table.

"I apologize for interrupting your dinner," I said. "I'm not soliciting."

"That's too bad. You look like you might have something that I'd want to solicit." He chuckled.

Mrs. Fester got up and joined her husband at the door. "What's wrong? You got a flat? Andy has a jack. He won't mind fixing it for you."

By now both boys were out of their seats. "I'll go get your jack, Dad!" announced one.

"No, it's not like that." I pointed to Twelve Tremont Road. "I'm trying to contact the woman who lives there. Do you know if she's at church and I should wait? Or out of town?"

All four Festers gaped at me as though I had asked if they could loan me the spare keys so I could break in and clean out their neighbor's silver. I reached in my purse and gave him the same House of Beauty business card I'd given to the McMullen Coal security guard. "I'm a hairdresser."

The mother frowned at the card over her husband's shoulder. "I don't think Mrs. Sullivan needs her hair done. What do you want her for?"

"It's kind of personal," I said, "and I'm leaving town later tonight, so if you know where she is, that would help."

Mr. Fester handed me my card. "I hate to be the bearer of bad news, but Mrs. Sullivan's dead. She passed on at St. Vincent's two weeks ago."

"Dead?"

"Oh, dear. You're not like a long lost baby Mrs. Sullivan gave up for adoption, are you?" mother Fester asked. "That would be so sad."

"That would be impossible," her husband scoffed. "This woman's barely forty."

Forty! Why didn't he say thirty? I had to start taking Vitamin E.

"No," I said, "it's that I . . . I thought she was alive. I just sent her flowers." Liar, liar pants on fire.

Mr. and Mrs. Fester exchanged uncomfortable looks. "So, you're the one," Mr. Fester said. "We've been trying to figure out who's been sending a ninety-year-old woman flowers all summer."

Ninety-years-old? Hugh McMullen was making it with a ninety-year-old woman?

"Would have been nice to think she had an admirer," Mrs. Fester said. "She was so alone."

"Except for that man who visited her occasionally," Mr. Fester said. "We assumed he was the one who was sending her flowers. Thought maybe he was her grandson."

"Grandson?" I said.

"I suppose he would be your long lost nephew," Mrs. Fester said. "That is, if you are Mrs. Sullivan's long lost baby daughter."

"I gotta get you off *Oprah*." Mr. Fester returned to the dinner table, his services as a tire changer obviously not required.

"Do you know how I can reach Mrs. Sullivan's grandson?"

"I don't. This other woman asked me that just the other day." Mrs. Fester folded her arms and leaned against the door. "Said she was a reporter from New York, though she grew up in Slagville. Had a real snazzy blue sports car."

"Snazzy blue sports car, eh?" I recalled my daredevil ride along Slagville's winding roads, missing trees by a millimeter in one mighty spiffy Mazda Miata.

"Is this woman tall?" I said. "Red-headed? Drives erratically?"

"I'll say. She nearly creamed my boys while they were playing field hockey in the street."

Roxanne's face fell, literally, as she peeled off my homemade gelatin mask. "You think Esmeralda Greene is investigating the same story?"

"I assumed I was the only one checking Hugh McMullen's alibi on the night of Bud Price's murder, but I was wrong." I fiddled with a tube of mascara on Roxanne's vanity. "I've been wrong about a lot of things."

"Not about this face mask." Roxanne pasted her face against

the mirror. "I can hardly see my pores." Roxanne was getting ready for her reunion with Stinky and she wasn't sparing a drop of makeup, nail polish or glitter.

"And it's a lot less expensive than those nose strips you buy in the drugstore for fifteen bucks," I said. "Maybe I should stick with beauty and drop this news business. Wouldn't have to work before dawn on Sunday mornings and I wouldn't have to compete."

"Or read the boring stuff in the newspaper," Roxanne added. She sipped from her Diet Pepsi and applied glue to a false eyelash. "Anyway, seems to me like you've been batting a thousand in this news business. You broke the story about the violations against McMullen Coal, right?"

"Thanks to you and that box of documents." I winced as Roxanne pulled off the sticky false eyelashes and tried for a more exact fit. "What are you going to say if Stinky asks if you still have the documents?"

"I'm going to hope he doesn't ask." She displayed a can of silver glitter. "Do you think all over body shimmer would be too much?"

"Go for it. Oh, shoot."

"What's wrong, baby?" Roxanne blinked. The eye with the false lashes looked abnormally enlarged.

"Those Catasauqua Republicans. I didn't make advance calls and now it's almost eight."

Roxanne deployed one last spritz of body shimmer into her cleavage. "Stop it. Saturday night and all you're talking about is work, work, work. It's the Hoagie Ho! Aunt LuLu's coming and I tried to talk Jane and G into going, but I couldn't convince them. They were eager to get home, I guess. Tired of this old coal town."

"Jane's got a party in Lehigh she's dying to go to."

"Yes, but . . ." Roxanne held up a finger. The nail was painted black and had a tiny rhinestone pasted in the center. "I reminded G that the Hoagie Ho is a great place to pick up clients."

"You think G is that talented, say?"

"I don't think. I know." She pinched a second lash from its container. "Mr. Salvo called, by the way."

"I'm not calling him back. He'll only tell me I'm fired again."

"Actually, it wasn't about work." She pressed the lash onto her lid and held it there until it set. "He was asking if you'd seen Steve Stiletto. The AP bureau's been trying to reach him and they can't find him anywhere."

All of a sudden my stomach felt very, very hollow. I could sense blood slipping out of my face. Visions of Wednesday night, Stiletto in the coal car, bloodied and unconscious, flashed in my mind.

Roxanne noticed right off. "Oh, I shouldn't have put it that way. I'm sure Steve's fine. When was the last time you ate, Bubbles?"

I thought about breakfast with Stiletto. "Not since around eight."

"Shame on you. You'll go all kinetic. Run downstairs and fix yourself something to eat." She let go of the lash and blinked.

"Maybe a sandwich," I said, heading downstairs.

"And don't forget to change," she yelled after me. "I don't want to be the only woman done up tonight."

I picked up the portable and dialed Mr. Salvo at the *News-Times*. Tucking the phone under my chin, I explored Roxanne's refrigerator for easy food. I was famished, I realized, but almost incapable of making myself a meal. Too darn nervous.

Where was Stiletto? Why hadn't he called? He'd promised that I could call him and he'd come. But now he was missing. He wouldn't go missing. Darn. I didn't know if he even had a new cell phone.

"Salvo. Speak." He was always grumpiest on Saturday nights, the end of his work week.

"It's me, Bubbles."

"You still in Slagville?"

I found some lettuce, a half a tomato and turkey. "Yup."

"You call the Catasauqua Republicans?"

"Nope."

"Christ. I wanted an advance story on that. Three to four inches saying they were meeting. Who? What? Where? and When? I'll have to take Eddy off obits to do it. Is Stiletto with you?"

"No." I cut the tomato with Roxanne's dull knife, sending seeds everywhere.

"Where the hell is he? The AP can't reach him in New York or the number he gave them in your area. There's no answer at his house in Saucon Valley and he doesn't have a new cell phone yet. They need him to cover the President tomorrow. He's doing a last-minute stumper in Jersey for statewide Republicans."

This isn't good, Bubbles, my mind was scolding. Stiletto would call. He would leave a message to see how you are. He wouldn't just drop off the face of the earth.

"You're not interrupting," Mr. Salvo said. "That means you know something. You always talk when you don't have anything to say and, ipso facto, the opposite is true. Tell me what's going on."

"Someone's been pretending to be Stiletto. The imposter has been making phone calls from Stiletto's house in Saucon Valley to a private detective in Slagville."

"Holy crow. What for?" Mr. Salvo was concerned. Almost like a real live human being. I unwrapped a loaf of rye bread.

"Whoever hired the detective wanted to keep tabs on me. It's a lot like Wednesday night when I got the fake fax from you and Stiletto got the e-mail message. Steve and I are pretty convinced it's the same person."

Mr. Salvo was silent. There was a pencil tapping in the background and then he said gruffly, "I'm gonna take this in Notch's office. Hold on." And he put me on hold.

I spread mayonnaise and lay down some lettuce and tomato to the digital music version of "Raindrops Keep Falling on My Head." Salvo got on right after the turkey.

"Why didn't you tell me about this before?" he demanded. "After what happened Wednesday night, Dix Notch wanted to be updated on any new developments with you. This would definitely count as a new development, Bubbles."

"I didn't know much until Stiletto told me this morning that the calls from the imposter had been made from his house. He knows the detective, Zeke Allen. He's a nice guy, religious. The fake Stiletto sent Zeke on a charter flight to Colorado yesterday, though he should be back by now."

"What's Stiletto doing about this?"

"He said he was going to meet Zeke at the Lehigh Airport. Then they were going to the state police and then back here. Zeke's flight was supposed to get in at four this afternoon."

I bit into the sandwich. It filled the void in my stomach, but not the pit. I was getting increasingly worried. My sixth sense was vibrating faster than a Dr. Scholl's battery-powered foot massager.

"I'm going to make some phone calls on this," Salvo said. "Spell that sham detective's name for me."

"He's not a sham. He's really nice."

"Don't get hoodwinked, Bubbles. You're a reporter. Keep an open mind. Now spell it."

I spelled it and took another bite.

"Allen. Like the Green Mountain Boys. You coming home now?" he asked.

"No, I, uh." I remembered that I hadn't confided in Mr. Salvo about Stinky's request that I meet him at the Hoagie Ho. I was afraid that if I had, I would have to reveal that Stinky stopped by my house Friday morning. Then Mr. Salvo would mumble all that legal mumbo jumbo about harboring a fugitive or obstructing justice and how modern reporters don't pull those tricks anymore. But I was one of those reporters who introduced herself as a mortuary stylist to get a secretary's name, so he and I shared a difference of opinion on what was technically ethical and what was technically not.

"I have to escort my mother to a dance. Her friend Genevieve has a date and she doesn't." That was a lie. Mama and Genevieve were at Pete Zidukis's house for a pre-Hoagie Ho get together.

"Christ. Then are you driving home?"

"Never fear, Mr. Salvo. I'll be at the five a.m. waste hauler's meeting."

"I don't care about that. I just want you home, safe and sound."

"You want to schedule some other reporter to cover the waste haulers?" I asked brightly.

"Hell, no. You can't use this as an excuse."

"Okay."

"And Bubbles?"

"Yes."

"For what it's worth, you're not fired."

I felt a lump in my throat. Though it might have been turkey.

"I know."

Bubbles's Peel-Off Face Mask

Gelatin is a mystery to me. Kids eat it for dessert. Adults mix it with vodka at parties. I use it to strengthen my nails and teenage girls wear it as a face mask. Hello? This recipe produces a firmly sticking mask that peels off like a Band-Aid. *Be careful* not to apply it to sensitive areas—e.g., upper lip. Think, Would I want a Band-Aid peeled off that part of my body? And don't use it everyday. It's really intense.

1 packet of Knox gelatin
1½ tablespoons of milk
2 drops of glycerin
(Optional: Substitute ½ tablespoon of straight aloe vera for ½ tablespoon of milk)

Mix in microwave-safe cup and heat on full power for ten seconds. Stir and test on inside of wrist. When it is cool enough, apply. Apply in covering coat across nose and face, careful not to spread into sensitive areas or to hairline. Let sit thirty minutes or until hardened and rubbery. Peel off. Moisturize.

Chapter 26

I opened the yellow Columbia County phone book and looked up Allen. Zeke lived on Railroad Avenue but no one answered his phone, so I left a message. Then I took a deep breath and dialed the other Allen I had circled. Earl.

"Hal-lo." Super. Zeke's mom.

"Mrs. Allen, it's Bubbles Yablonsky."

"Gracious. Champ's tootsie. How are you, Bubbles?"

I swallowed my pride and the rest of my turkey sandwich. "Mrs. Allen, I'm very concerned about Steve and Zeke. Are they back yet?"

"Well, Zeke is. He's taking a nap, poor boy. He was exhausted, all that flying around."

"Do you know if Champ met him at the airport?"

"I don't believe so, dear. It's why Zeke was late. He waited an hour for Champ to show. After that, Zeke assumed Steve must have been tied up. So Zeke drove home in his own truck that he had parked in the long-term lot, eight dollars a day. Though I have to say, I think your mother's friend should pay for the damage she did to my son's tailpipe. He walked in the door positively reeking of baked potatoes, not that baked potatoes are bad, mind you, only that—"

I held the phone away from my ear. Ay, yi, yi. If I had been Mr. Allen, I would have wood-paneled my wife into a soundproof booth.

"I don't mean to interrupt, Mrs. Allen—"

"Of course you don't *mean* to, dear. It's just your upbringing. Uncouth."

Ignore that, Bubbles, my brain instructed. "We're having a hard time finding Steve anywhere. I'm afraid something terrible has happened to him. May I speak to Zeke?"

"Have you tried his girlfriend?"

"Zeke has a girlfriend?"

"Mercy no, over my dead body. I'm talking about Steve. Steve's girlfriend Esmeralda. They've been working together for years, don't you know. We think it'd be wonderful if he'd propose to her. Just wonderful. Maybe Esme and Champ would settle in her hometown then. Slagville is such a nice place to raise children."

I fought hard, I really did, to keep the edge in my voice to a minimum. "Why do you think Steve is with Esmeralda?"

"Well, I ran into her in the Acme this afternoon. She said she couldn't stop to talk, that she was in a hurry and I said, 'Where to, dear?' And Esme mentioned something about going to Steve's house back in Saucon Valley. I couldn't catch it completely, what she was saying, because she was halfway out the door."

The phone cord twisted around my fingers, nearly cutting off the circulation. "If you wouldn't mind asking Zeke to call my cousin's salon when he wakes up, I'd certainly appreciate it. I'll check my messages after the Hoagie Ho before I return to Lehigh."

"I'll let him know," she said. But I doubted it.

I remained frozen with the portable in my hand for a good five minutes. Should I call him? Should I not? How many times have I and countless other women asked the same question? We women really should get rid of these phones. We'd be much better off.

Against my better judgment, I dialed the number for Stiletto's Saucon Valley mansion. 1-610—

"Hello?"

I froze. I froze like a fourth grader who had just called the gym teacher at home looking for a Jacque. Jacque Itch.

"Hell-oo? Who is this?" the sultry voice on the other end asked.

"Uh," I realized I was breathing heavily and clicked off the phone.

Esmeralda! She was there. In Stiletto's house.

Roxanne came down the stairs ready for the Atlantic City runway. Sapphire dress covered in rhinestones. Red hair piled up with matching clips and dangle cubic zirconia earrings (my contribution).

"How do I look? Do you think Stinky will take me back?"

"Definitely," I said, though I thought Stinky might take her to the insane asylum for showing up like that for a hoedown.

The phone rang in my hand. I could only stare at it. *Brrrring! Brrring!* Roxanne's caller ID system displayed Stiletto's number on the phone console. Esmeralda must have dialed *69.

"Aren't you going to answer it?" Roxanne asked.

"Nah." I clicked it on and then off, so the ringing would stop. "It's only Mr. Salvo. Let's go."

"You've got to get ready. You can't go in pants. I'll get a couple of wine coolers for us while you get dressed."

I waited until she passed through the swinging doors into the kitchen. That's when I disconnected the phone in the rear of the console.

Looking back, it was the worst move I could have made.

The Union Hall was hopping when we arrived. There was lots of whooping and cheering inside thanks to a lively boom-bass band and, I guessed, not an infrequent amount of bolio—coal country's potent whiskey cocktail.

"You're not coming?" Roxanne asked, fixing her lipstick in the rearview of my Camaro.

"I'm sticking around until Mama shows up with Genevieve."

"Listen, Bub, I know you're antsy because of this Stiletto imposter who hired Zeke to keep tabs on you. So, I took the liberty of buying you some self defense." She displayed a rounded oblong tube. It looked pornographic.

"Is that a—?"

"What?" She put it in my hand. "It's a battery-powered portable curling iron. To zing your stalker in the you-know-whats. Heats one minute after you pull it open, so plan accordingly."

"Thanks Roxanne." I said, stuffing it in my purse. "You're a great cousin. Gorgeous, too."

"That goes for both of us. Too bad Stiletto's not here."

Ouch. That hurt. Looking over my snakeskin bodysuit and taupe skirt, which I had purchased for a romantic night with Stiletto, all I could think of was Esmeralda letting her red hair fall against his bare chest. And here I was wearing an outfit that was snugger than cling wrap to a hoagie hoedown at the Union Hall.

Big drops started falling on the windshield. "My hair's gonna get ruined," Roxanne said, opening her compact umbrella. "What's our plan again?"

"You look for Stinky while I keep Chief Donohue occupied."

My pre-Hoagie Ho scope out of the Union Hall had been a failure, I decided. I hadn't found Stinky and I had tipped off Donohue to the possibility that Stinky was hiding somewhere in the building. I was only glad I hadn't told Mr. Salvo about my appointed rendezvous with the most wanted man in Slagville. Donohue would no doubt have listened in on our conversation and upended the Union Hall to find Stinky first.

"What happens when I find my husband?" Roxanne asked. "Then what are we going to do about Donohue?"

"I have a solution. All we need is a code word for when either of us finds Stinky."

Roxanne pointed to my purse. "How about the curling iron? That'll never register with Donohue."

"Excellent. Now go before the rain picks up."

She opened the umbrella and dashed across the road to the Union Hall. The golden oldies arrived fifteen minutes later in Pete's rust-colored Dodge Dart. Pete was dressed to the nines in a plaid shirt buttoned to the throat and brown blazer that didn't quite go with the shirt, but that was okay. It was the effort that counted.

He ran around the front of the car like a teenager and opened the passenger door. Mama got out first in her standard black leather and swaggered—as much as a Polish bowling ball can swagger—toward the door. Genevieve was next in a purple raincoat that made her look like a giant plum.

I cornered all three in the coatroom and gave them the skinny. Bless Pete and Genevieve for being such diehard conspiracy nuts. They ate it up.

"You think maybe it's FEMA that sicced Zeke Allen on you?" Genevieve asked.

Pete nodded in agreement. "I've thought for years that FEMA started the mine fire in Limbo, just so it could claim marshal law when the blaze got out of control. I bet Zeke's a secret agent for them. I bet he's involved in your Stiletto's disappearance."

I told them I still didn't know who had hired Zeke or if Stiletto had officially disappeared. I kept my private theory about him secretly cocooning with Esmeralda to myself. No point in coming off like a jealous girlfriend.

"But we do have to keep our eyes and ears open," I added.

"I'll turn up the cochlear," Pete said, giving his hearing aid a twist.

Mama was a harder sell. "What exactly are we supposed to look for, Bubbles?" she asked.

"I'm not exactly sure. But if you see someone out of place following me, that's not good."

"You suggesting that whoever this mysterious person is, he's going to bust in on your rendezvous with Stinky?"

"It's a distinct possibility." I put my hand on her tiny shoulder. "And that's where you come in."

"Me? I can't shoot as well as Genevieve."

"No shooting." I motioned them to the back of the closet. "Mama, I want you to occupy Chief Donohue while I meet with

Stinky. I don't care what you have to do, if you have to throw a fit about your arrest this morning, just keep him busy."

Pete cupped his hand to his ear. "We gotta arrest Donohue?" he hollered.

"Keep your voice down," Genevieve said with a poke. "I'll tell you later."

"No problem," Mama said, patting her gray permed hair. "Donohue and I have chemistry."

I gave her a doubtful look. "Since when is a demand that you get out of town by sunrise chemistry?"

"You don't know much about sexual tension, do you, Bubbles?" she said. "For your information, Donohue wanted me out of his sight so I'd quit being a temptation to him. We're star-crossed."

"They're running low on halupkies," complained Genevieve, who'd been peeking out of the coat closet. "Let's go."

We did a round of high (and in Mama's case, low) fives and emerged from the closet looking like the Odd Squad—me in my snakeskin bodysuit, Mama in her biker leather, Genevieve the purple plum and Pete the deaf Mr. Green Jeans.

It cost two bucks to be admitted to the Hoagie Ho and it was well worth it. White papered tables were piled high with noodle casseroles, stuffed cabbages, endless desserts and, oh yes, hoagies for sale from various organizations around town. Matrons in aprons dished out the food and pocketed the change, teasing their patrons mercilessly as they did so. A platform at one end supported a boom-bass band that was doing it up right with "Old Time Polka," including a fiddler who had dancers whirling their skirts and stomping their boots in a frenzy.

"Where's the rival gang?" I asked Mama, as I dumped a spoonful of macaroni salad on my plate. "I'd have expected this place to be swarming with Slagville Sirens."

"Maybe Genny and I scared them off. Either that or they're up to something like I've been saying." Mama sneered at a plate of pierogies. "The sirens must have dropped off this dish and run. Potato, onion and cardamom. A specialty from the Slagville Siren cookbook."

"They have a cookbook?"

"It's a necessity. A siren's always looking for new recipes, otherwise the Nag 'N Feed spell loses its effectiveness." Mama flipped open the switchblade from her back pocket and stabbed the pierogi, taking a tiny bite. "Hmmph. Not bad. Too much salt, though, for my blood pressure."

"Maybe that's why they stole the Nana diary," I suggested, helping myself to a cup of cider. "They just needed the new recipes."

"That's exactly what Vilnia told me after the fight at St. Stanislaw's. Guess Genevieve and I kind of jumped the gun."

"Yeah, kind of." I bit into a pierogi just as Donohue ambled through the door, his thumbs stuck in his black leather holster.

"What a pompous jerk," I whispered to Mama. "Do you know he listens in on everyone's calls in this town? He's sneaky."

"I think he's kind of dreamy, in a pig-like authoritarian way."

I squinted. Donohue dreamy? He strode around the hall puffed up and important. His black boots hit the floor with resounding thuds as he nodded to various citizens. But he was not here for a community festival or even to keep the peace.

He was here for Stinky.

"He's got the hots for me, oh yes. I could tell when he cuffed me, the way his hands lingered on my wrists." Mama put her plate on a table and removed a compact and lipstick that had bulged from her hip pocket, next to the switchblade. "I'll venture that he's never before seen a woman like your mother, so dangerous and feminine."

"You might want to get rid of this," I said, removing the cigarette from behind her ear.

Mama plucked it out of my fingers and replaced it. "Please, I got a bad girl image to maintain. Shut up, here he comes."

Donohue strolled over. "Well, well, well," he said, "if it isn't Belle Starr with the pastry pin."

Mama winked at me and mouthed, "Told you so."

"I figured you'd be on the road by now, LuLu," Donohue said. "Didn't I give you until sundown to get out of town?"

"You said I could stay until the Hoagie Ho." Mama fingered her dog collar, which was hidden among the folds of her neck. "Perhaps so we could meet again?"

Donohue looked confused and, may I add, rightly so. Before Mama humiliated herself further, I asked if Sasha was okay.

Again Donohue looked confused. "Pardon?"

"Chrissy Price's daughter. We were talking about her this morning in this very room. You said you pitied the kid."

Donohue blinked. "Why would I know what Chrissy Price's daughter was up to?"

I felt that same cold pit in my stomach, the one that ached when I learned Stiletto was AWOL. "Because my daughter's boyfriend said he was pulled over while driving Sasha back to the inn. A cop insisted that she get in the back of the cruiser and they supposedly returned to the station."

"Wasn't me. Maybe one of my men." Donohue yanked the walkie-talkie out of his belt buckle. "You have a description of the officer?"

"White hair. Older, G said."

Donohue frowned. "I'm the only one that'd meet that description. Unless, the officer was from another jurisdiction."

What other jurisdiction would take a seventeen-year-old girl? I wished G were here so he could clarify whether the cop was from Slagville or not. "My daughter's boyfriend is on his way back to Lehigh, otherwise I'd have him talk to you."

"Lehigh, huh?" Donohue was about to radio in when he caught sight of Roxanne. "Whaddya know," he said.

Roxanne was making her way across the room, her rhinestones glowing as much as her expression. Dangy. Now that questions had been raised about Sasha, I was eager to stick by Donohue until he sorted out what had happened to her. Never rains but it pours.

"Hello there, Chief," Roxanne cooed. "Beautiful evening, isn't it?"

"You awful dolled up there for a simple potluck, Roxanne," Donohue said. "You got a special evening planned?"

She brushed back a strand of hair. "Can't expect me to sit at home and mope because my old man up and ran off, now can you?"

"Did he run off, Roxanne?"

She stared at him dead-on straight. "He did, Chief. I've given up. On him at least. Not on men."

I found myself holding my breath as Donohue considered this. Finally he said, "Good for you. You're a decent woman, Roxanne. You deserve better."

"Thank you, Chief." Turning to me she said, "By the way, Bub, you didn't happen to bring a curling iron with you?"

Ohmigod. She'd found Stinky. I dipped into my purse. "Have one right here," I said, pulling out the travel iron.

"Great. I need to touch up a tendril. I hope you'll excuse me." Donohue tipped his hat.

"You want to come with, Bubbles?" Roxanne asked casually.

"Sure," I said. "You don't mind, Mama? You won't be lonely?"

"With this manly man?" She boldly reached up and linked her arm in his. "No way."

Donohue didn't say a word. He set his mouth and glowered, gripping his radio so hard it should have shattered.

"You think we convinced him?" Roxanne said as she steered me toward the ladies room.

"We won't know until this night's over. Where is Stinky?"

"I'll show you." Roxanne led me down the hall to a door with a padlock that wasn't really locked. She undid the padlock. The door opened to a hot stairway lined by cement blocks. A furnace rumbled below.

"The furnace room? He's been hiding out in the furnace room?"

Roxanne put her finger to her lips and led me down two flights of stairs. We landed on a cement floor next to three big boilers. A bare light bulb swung from the ceiling.

"Carl?" she called softly. "It's okay. It's me and Bubbles."

Stinky emerged from a door under the stairs. The first thing I noticed about him was how tidy he was for a man who'd been on the lam and hiding out in a boiler room. He wore a dark green cardigan over a spotless white shirt that was tucked neatly into his khakis. His thinning brown hair was combed without the flecks of dandruff scattered about like there used to be and he was wearing contacts. He was almost bearable.

And not a squirting corsage on him.

"I'm sorry you got involved in this," were the first words out of his mouth.

"What am I involved in?" I asked, opening my purse and pulling out my reporter's notebook.

Stinky shook his head. "Trust me. It started out as a good deed. What I designed was going to save my town, save everyone."

"Your eavesdropping device?" Roxy asked innocently.

"His fire extinguisher," I said. "To douse the fire under Limbo."

"What fire extinguisher?" Roxanne wanted to know.

Stinky was clearly shocked that I had discovered his invention. "How'd you find out?"

"Long story." I held up my reporter's notebook. "This okay?"

Stinky glanced at Roxanne. "Can you take notes now and then contact me when you're going to print the story? I'm not in hiding for nothing."

"Sure," I said, opening the notebook. "What I want to know is if the fire extinguisher works."

Stinky hitched up his pants in excitement. "Well, yeah. Of course it works. It worked when I presented it to Hugh McMullen months ago."

"Why didn't he use it? He could have made a mint."

"Really?" said Roxy, flummoxed by the revelation that her

husband had invented a mint-producing extinguisher. "How come you never told me about this, Stink?"

"It was supposed to be top secret until we had the patent," Stinky said. "But we were delayed because McMullen wanted me to make it fool-proof to avoid lawsuits. It worked perfectly on the tiny fires I was setting in the lab and spreading with the hairdryers. Nevertheless, McMullen demanded one-hundred percent assurance it would douse the mine fire in Limbo."

"That's what all that equipment was that I found in the basement—to put out the Limbo mine fire?" Roxanne said. "And there I went and ripped it all out. Oh, what an idiot I was."

"I had to move the equipment to the basement after I quit McMullen Coal. Too bad, because Mr. McMullen had provided me with my own lab and lots of cash. I miss that cash."

"Me, too," she added.

I jotted down notes. "Why did you quit McMullen Coal?"

Roxanne threw up her hands. "Because of the maps, remember? We've been over that, Bubbles. Let's get to Price's murder and why Stinky's Lexus was at the scene."

"Please, Stinky. From the beginning," I said.

Stinky nodded. "After I showed Mr. McMullen the prototype of my fire extinguisher, he treated me like royalty. Bought me two new cars, quadrupled my salary and took me out of the mapping division so I could devote all my energy to perfecting my invention."

"How did you find out about the maps?" I asked.

"One night this spring, after work was done for the day, I went into the Number Nine mine to test the extinguisher. That mine was perfect for what I wanted because it bordered the Dead Zone and was abandoned. Or so I thought. Once I got down there, though, I saw right away what had been going on. They must have been mining a good three hundred feet into that buffer area."

I wrote this as fast as I could. "Did you tell McMullen?"

"I called him in Pittsburgh, since he was never around, and

told him what had happened. He said he had had no idea and he'd get right on it. A few months later I went into the map room for some of my old supplies and decided to take a look at the maps of the Number Nine mine, out of curiosity."

"They were unchanged, right?" added Roxanne, eager to move the topic along.

Stinky kissed her quick. "Right, pumpkin. Not one map noted that the mine had been reactivated. I decided to check out the mine again. I thought maybe they had filled it in, though that's a very costly process. I waited until a day when the mines were closed and went down to the same spot in the Number Nine mine. Damned if they'd dug even further under the Dead Zone. That's when I got really mad."

"Because miners lives were at risk?" I asked, pausing from note taking.

"Not just the miners," Stinky exclaimed. "Everyone. Do you know what would have happened if they'd dug through to the mine fire? Kaboom!"

"Shhh," Roxanne scolded him. "People will hear."

"Did you call McMullen again?"

"I did. It was Labor Day, so I expected him to tell me it could wait until Tuesday. Instead, he rushed right up here and we met in his office."

"Labor Day, huh?" I thought of Louise Lamporini whose holiday had been ruined because McMullen had called her into work on Labor Day.

"And that's when I got really scared for my life." Stinky lowered his voice and glanced around the room, as though there might be spies hidden behind the boilers. "Mr. McMullen looked awful. His hair was on end and he was chain-smoking. He told me to snap my trap about the maps and get that fire extinguisher finished. He said he had a lot riding on it and he couldn't keep bankrolling me."

"I'm sort of amazed he could bankroll you to begin with," I said. "From what all my sources told me, he was strapped."

"That crossed my mind, too. I told him he could shove the project and I quit on the spot. I didn't want to be part of an organization that tinkered with human life. The next day, McMullen filed those restraining orders and sent letters to every mining company in the state saying that I was a dangerous individual. I started getting nervous that maybe I'd have no credibility left. That's why I pestered Sommerville at PMS—"

"PMS?" No. It was too coincidental to the bogus slug I'd tacked onto the mining story.

Stinky smiled. "Sorry. That's kind of industry shorthand. We call the Pennsylvania Bureau of Mine Safety, PMS."

Imagine.

"I didn't mean ill will against Hugh McMullen. I just don't think he understood the gravity of the situation. And he had so many personal problems."

"Then why did you go into hiding?" Roxanne asked. "Why did you leave me? Because I accused you of eavesdropping?"

"Because I hadn't been eavesdropping. Because someone was spreading that rumor to ruin your business, Roxanne. I didn't want you to get hurt, too, so I left and went into hiding. Figured it'd be safer for you if everyone thought we split."

"Awww," Roxanne said, blinking back tears.

But I was now really confused. If Stinky hadn't blackmailed Roxanne's clients, then who had?

People were talking upstairs. We listened for a bit, trying to determine whether or not they were coming down the stairs.

"I better go," Roxanne said. "Chief Donohue will search the building if one of us doesn't return to that hall soon." She planted a big smooch on Stinky's lips and then hightailed it up the stairs. "Don't go anywhere, hon."

When she was gone, Stinky's whole body language drooped. "How could I have done this to Roxanne? She's married to the Slagville boogieman now. A boogieman who lives in a hole and spends his life on the run."

"I think Donohue just wants to question you," I said. "He's already told the press that McMullen killed Price using a family pistol."

"I'm not talking about Donohue wanting me." Stinky bit his nail.

"Oh?"

"I know you're going to say I'm paranoid, just like Roxanne's always telling me, but honestly, Bubbles, I've had a lot of time to dissect this and I am convinced someone else was pushing Hugh McMullen. He was completely irrational during our last meeting."

"His father, maybe?" I thought of what Louise Lamporini had said about Senior McMullen calling up his son and reaming him out.

Stinky dismissed this. "Senior McMullen is almost comatose. But you're right in that it's probably someone wealthy and someone with authority over Hugh. You also hit it on the head when you said Hugh McMullen was strapped. He would never have been able to afford the cars and the high-tech lab on his own. The company was in the red. Almost bleeding."

"And then when you didn't produce the perfect fire extinguisher, the honcho controlling McMullen put the pressure on. That's why Hugh was so hysterical when you confronted him about the mine maps."

"That's why Hugh did what he did," Stinky said. "That's why he killed Price."

There was a clanging upstairs of the padlock on the door and footsteps running overhead. Then Roxanne's voice protesting frantically.

"I've got to get out of here," Stinky said, opening his door. "This leads to the outside, by the dugout in the Union Hall's softball field. I'll need a head start."

He started to crawl in. I called after him, "How do you know McMullen shot Price?"

"Bud Price and I drove to the mine together. He had contacted me Wednesday evening at the Hole, swearing accusations that I was in cahoots with McMullen. That's when I told him about the excavation under his Dead Zone and Price insisted I take him down that night and show him. So, a few hours later he arrived and we went down together through an access hole. Price was so pissed at the excavation, he wanted to get out right away and call McMullen." Stinky sighed and continued. "He ran ahead of me and that's when I saw McMullen shoot Bud Price. I think he saw me, too, because he took a couple of shots as I hurried back up the ladder."

Hence, the multiple shots in the mine. Hence, the reason why McMullen was so desperate to get hold of Stinky.

"I ran into the woods. I didn't even dare get into my car. McMullen knew my car. He'd bought it for me."

The door at the top of the stairs opened and Roxanne screamed, "Bubbles. It's Donohue."

"Wait," I hissed, crawling even deeper into the dark and grabbing Stinky's sweater. "Why did you send me the fax?"

"What fax?"

"The fax you sent to the Passion Peak Wednesday night telling me that a businessman had been shot in the Number Nine mine."

"I don't know what you're talking about, Bubbles. How would I know that you were at the Passion Peak?" He shook off my hand. "Now let me go."

Chapter 27

A s they say in the women's room at the Girls A-Go-Go strip club on Stefko Boulevard, when the going gets tough, the tender get naked. Unfortunately, this was the night I'd chosen a snakeskin bodysuit and getting naked was not a zip, slide and done deal like it usually is for me.

But I managed. I even tussled my hair.

"What the! . . ." Donohue's eyes popped out of their sockets as I crawled out of Stinky's den doing my Lady Godiva impersonation.

"Oh, Bubbles," clucked Mama. "Not again."

Roxanne winked. "See, Chief, I told you not to disturb her."

"Do you mind," I said, holding the little piece of bodysuit up to cover—barely—my strapless black Wonderbra and black thong. I had tossed the gored skirt onto the floor.

"Who do you got in there?" Donohue said, nodding to the door.

"What? Don't tell me it's a crime, Chief, to make a little hay at a hoedown." I lowered the bodysuit as if to step back into it.

"Hey, hey, hey," he said, cringing. "Don't do that."

"You don't want me to get dressed? I don't understand." I batted my eyes innocently. "You want me to stay naked?"

"No, uhm." Donohue turned his back. "I won't peek."

"You want me to stay naked and then you say you won't peek?" I protested. "I don't trust you. Go upstairs and come back."

"This is ridiculous. I know Koolball's in there."

"Jack Donohue," cried Mama in mock indignation. "This is my daughter here. What will people think when I tell them that the Chief of Police insisted on standing by while a naked woman got dressed?"

Donohue's neck reddened. "Five minutes," he said gruffly, stomping up the stairs. "Five minutes and then I'm looking in that door below the stairs."

"What are we going to do now?" Roxanne asked as soon as Donohue was out of earshot.

I shook out the bodysuit and stepped in. "Stinky says the tunnel lets out by the dugout in the softball field. Mama, find a man who's game to go down it. A man who won't ask why, just where."

"Gotcha." She scrambled up the stairs.

"And make him good-looking," I called after her. "I got a reputation to uphold."

"Will I ever see my Stinky again?" Roxanne asked, smearing away tears with her rhinestoned fingertips. "What will it take to get him back home?"

I snapped the crotch and picked up the skirt. "It'll take us finding whoever was behind Hugh McMullen. That's the guy Stinky fears most."

Bang! Bang! Bang! "You done yet?" Donohue hollered.

"I got a problem with the crotch!" I called back. "It's riding up my crack."

There was a stunned silence. "Disgusting," he replied.

Roxanne and I bit our cheeks to keep from giggling.

"How are we going to find the guy who was behind Hugh McMullen?" Roxanne whispered.

"Shouldn't be too hard." I got a brush out of my purse and attempted to fix my hair without a mirror. "He's the same guy who hired Zeke Allen to tail me. He sent me the fax and Stiletto the e-mail. And now I think he's intercepted Stiletto. All of which means he wants me to hunt him out."

"No way!" Roxanne's eyes were wide. "Sounds dangerous. I'll help you however I can if helping you means getting my Stinkster back."

"Move aside, Chief," Mama said. "I'll let you know if my daughter's decent."

She trundled down the stairs.

"What happened to all that chemistry?" I said.

"Might say it fizzled. Donohue's too much a square for this hot mama." She glanced at Stinky's door and then at me. "You decent?"

"Are you?"

"Decent as I'll ever be." She leaned around the railing. "Okay, Chief, you can come down now."

Donohue took the stairs slowly. "I know Koolball's in there, Bubbles."

I put my hand to my chest in shock. "Are you suggesting that I slept with my cousin's husband?"

"Don't give me that." He pulled out a ring of keys. "When I find him, I'm going to charge both of you with obstruction of justice."

"It's unlocked, Chief," I said. "No need for a key."

"Doesn't mean you're not hiding him." He pulled open the door and leaned in. "Carl? Carl Koolball? You in there?"

We waited a good ten minutes in silence. Roxanne was so dismayed that she rubbed her cheeks and got silver body spray all over her palms. I patted her back comfortingly. "Have no fear, Roxanne."

"Pete Zidukis is here!" exclaimed Donohue.

"Evening, Chief." Hunched over, crooked little Pete Zidukis crept out of the passageway. His knees were covered with dirt and there was a cobweb sticking to his plaid shirt. He put his hand behind his back and gave it a long crack.

Pete Zidukis? That was the best Mama could rustle up? That was my hoedown honey?

"Gosh, that felt good."

"I'll bet it did," said Donohue.

Pete narrowed his eyes. "I was talking about the stretch, Jack."

"I wasn't." Donohue bent down. "I hope you people have had fun with your joke. Now let me get in there." He huffed and groaned as he crawled on hands and knees into the dark passageway.

"That was a killer," Pete said to us, as Donohue inched his way through the tunnel. "I didn't have no light, neither. I was lucky I met Koolball on my way out. He loaned me this." He pulled the penlight out of his pocket and clicked it on.

"Thanks, Pete," I said, planting a kiss on his forehead. "You showed gumption."

"Gumption I got. Knees I don't." He bent over stiffly and massaged his kneecaps.

"You sure Stinky is out?" Roxanne peered into the passageway where Donohue's rump made a shadow against his flashlight.

"Free and clear," said Pete. "Told me to tell you not to worry. He said he was gonna get out of Dodge until this was resolved." He turned to me. "What did he mean by that?"

"He means that we have to tie up a lot of loose ends." I reflected on Stinky's use of the word "resolved" and all the pieces that needed to be put in the puzzle. There was one piece I hadn't asked about lately. Who were the men who had asked about me at Price Family Ford and then left their key chain on my kitchen counter? Who broke into Roxanne's dresser drawer?

Chief Donohue grunted as he backed out of the hole. "He's gone." He dusted off his uniform. "But not forgotten. Koolball's still in town and he needs to come forward, Roxanne. It's not right for him to be running from the law."

"Yes, sir," Roxanne said, barely able to disguise her relief that Stinky had escaped.

"Incidentally, Bubbles," Donohue said. "I'll be needing a phone number so I can contact that boyfriend of your daughter's." Donohue took out a notepad. "Dispatch radioed me back. No law enforcement officer in this county, including the state police and sheriffs, picked up a seventeen-year-old girl today. I don't know what's happened to Price's stepdaughter, but I can tell you she didn't go off with no cop."

"Now, what?" Roxanne said as we walked down the hallway toward the Hoagie Ho. "How are we going to get hold of Stinky?"

"Don't worry about Stinky," I said, my mind on other, more important matters. "Stinky's in the Hole."

"He is? But I thought Donohue couldn't find him there."

The boom-bass band launched into "I Don't Want Her. You Can Have Her. She's Too Fat for Me." Why don't they make a song, "I Don't Want Him. You Can Have Him. He Watches Too Much Football. Is A Lazy Slob For Me?"

"I'm talking about the Hole that's the bar next door," I said. "That's where Bud Price reached Stinky on Wednesday night. But don't go over there yet." I watched as Donohue helped himself to a huge slice of pie. "Stinky's safer there than anywhere else."

Genevieve approached us, her giant arm wrenched affectionately around the neck of her beloved Pete. "How did my man do? Not bad, eh?"

"Not bad," I said absently.

"You don't seem very appreciative, Bubbles," Genevieve said with disappointment. "Pete's got two metal hips after working fifty-odd years as a mechanic. He can't bend and scooch like a kid. You should say 'thank you.'"

"She did, Genevieve," Pete protested.

Mechanic? "Tell me, Pete," I said, getting an idea. "You ever hear of an F1 Ford?" It was an F1 Ford that brought the Slagville men to Price Family Ford and Tallow said Chrissy had driven off in an antique pickup. I was betting those were the same trucks.

"A beaut of a pickup," Pete said. "Made 'em in 1949."

"Know anyone around here who drives one?"

Pete pursed his lips and thought about this. "Nowadays you don't see them 'cept in parades. And we got a lot of parades in Slagville. Let me ask Norbert. He put together the Fourth of July event this year."

He hobbled over and spoke to Norbert, who thumbed his red suspenders and offered Pete a suggestion. Pete nodded and returned.

"There were two F1 pickups in the Fourth of July parade," he said. "One was owned by Geordie Hodgson, but he sold it to a yuppie couple from St. Louis. The other's still owned, as far as Norbert knows, by a Seamus O'Malley."

"Who is Seamus O'Malley? Does he live in Slagville?"

"Go on, Bubbles. You've met him yourself," Roxanne said. "He's Vilnia's husband."

Chapter **28**

"I knew they were up to something, those Sirens," Mama said, after returning from the ladies' room. "Come on, Genevieve, let's go get 'em. And this time we're not backing down. I got my pastry pin oiled and ready to roll."

Riled up like this, Mama reminded me of a Boston terrier who needed to lay off the dog chow. Fat, nasty and bug-eyed. Ready to nip the mailman on his heels.

"Hold on. How do you know the Sirens are involved?" I asked her. "Maybe Vilnia's husband took Chrissy Price on his own?"

"Get real. Vilnia's husband doesn't do anything on his own."

The Hoagie Ho was winding down and folks were going home. I checked my watch. After ten already. Chief Donohue was surveying the crowd, hoping perhaps for a quick glimpse of a disguised Stinky.

"Shouldn't you be headed to Lehigh?" Donohue asked Mama and Genevieve. "As I recall, that was the deal."

"Darn," said Genevieve. "Just when things were getting good."

Donohue cocked an eyebrow. "Oh? Is something going on that I don't know about?"

"They're going to Lehigh," I said, ignoring Mama's scowl. "Perhaps you'd like to escort them to the city limits. After all, the Hoagie Ho is over."

"Bubbles!" Mama stomped her boot. "But, I—"

"That would suit me fine," Donohue said, offering his arm. "Madame?"

Mama took it, although she stuck out her tongue at me when Donohue's head was turned.

"We'll let your friend enjoy her one last song," he said. "And then you're out of here."

Genevieve and Pete were in a slow dance. "Goodnight Irene" played on the accordion. Pete rested his head on Genevieve's bread loaf of a bosom as the two of them shuffled back and forth. In the spirit of reconciliation, Mama dragged Donohue onto the floor where they began an awkward box step.

"Let's go," I murmured to Roxanne.

"Now can we get Stinky?" Roxanne said when we were outside. "Donohue will be driving your mother and Genevieve out of town."

"Leave Stinky where he is," I said, unlocking the Camaro. "We've got to save Chrissy Price."

I unfolded my Columbia County street map, flicked on the interior light and tried to figure out the shortest way to Vilnia's using back roads, to reduce the chances of us being followed. Finally, I chose a meandering route that connected collieries.

"Why do you think the Slagville Sirens kidnapped Chrissy Price?" I asked Roxanne as we arrived in the patch.

"I don't know. My mother was a Slagville Siren, but I never was."

"How come?"

Roxanne opened a bottle of Diet Pepsi she'd bought at the Hoagie Ho. "Mostly because I never married a miner. That's one of the requirements to be a Slagville Siren."

"Oh."

I tried to conceive why a collection of miners' wives would kidnap the widow of a murdered car salesman. Was it that they were opposed to casino gambling? Were they hard up for money and hoped to hold her for ransom? I prayed that if they had kidnapped Chrissy they hadn't hurt her or Sasha.

Vilnia's house was lit up like a Christmas season shopping mall. Cars were parked on the sidewalk out front in an interesting arrangement suggesting that the rules of parallel parking did not apply. I thought it best to leave the Camaro at the end of the patch.

Roxanne, still in her sapphire blue with the rhinestones, and I in the snakeskin, walked down the opposite side of the street. I was freezing and wished I had brought a coat.

"How are we going to get in there?" Roxanne asked when we came into view of Vilnia's house. "You gonna knock on the door and say, open up, we know you have Chrissy Price?"

"No. We're going to start in the garden."

I decided that we needed to scope out the situation before we stormed the place. If there was a raucous party going on, then perhaps we could slip in undetected through the basement. Maybe Chrissy and Sasha were tied up down there. If all was quiet, then we'd have to create a disturbance outside, something to send the Sirens running into the street while one of us snuck inside and searched for the victims.

We pussyfooted down the alley and opened the squeaky gate to Vilnia's garden that was partially lit by her kitchen light. The tomato vines had been yanked, their stakes still in place for next season, and the ground had been mulched. It smelled of rotting leaves and damp earth. We stepped around carrots, spinach and a few pumpkins. Already a thick layer of frost was spreading across their orange flesh.

"What are they doing?" Roxanne crouched behind a rhododendron bush and peeked in the kitchen window. Vilnia was pacing, her hands behind her back, and dictating to a woman with her back to us who was working at a computer laptop, its screen blazing bright blue. Another woman was at the table, also typing on a laptop, except she was talking on the phone, too.

I tiptoed over to Roxanne for a closer look. It took me a few minutes to recognize them all.

"That's Tammy on the computer," I said. "And look, isn't that the client you were working on who wanted to know all about Stiletto? I nicknamed her in my mind the human prune." I pointed to a woman who was flipping through papers on a clipboard.

"Oh, you mean my Thursday at ten?"

"Who?"

Roxanne nodded to Mrs. Frazier, the woman who had been reading the *Cosmo* article and getting her hair washed earlier in the day. "Look. There's my Wednesday at six-thirty."

"And Mrs. Wychesko!" Mrs. Wychesko came barreling through with a tray full of cups filled with coffee.

"Over there is my Saturday at eight." Roxanne sighed. "Why, they're all my clients."

We watched them rush around, calling, faxing, typing, drinking coffee like they were air traffic controllers at O'Hare.

"This is quite an operation, Roxanne. What are they up to?"

"Maybe they've kidnapped Chrissy Price to sell her on the white slave market and they're negotiating with an Arab sheik for more money?" my sometimes odd cousin suggested. "Or maybe they're with the CIA. I've heard the CIA likes to set up shop in small towns."

"And you think your husband's paranoid."

"Whatever it is, they sure are organized. I've never seen women work together so well," she said. "You got six women there and they're not even stopping to gossip."

It was the word gossip that pulled my mental light switch. "Roxanne. These women, they are all the ones that Stinky blackmailed."

"You're right. Wow."

"Except, we now know that Stinky didn't blackmail anyone and that the equipment in the basement was for fire extinguishers."

"Uh-huh," Roxanne agreed slowly. "And your point is?"

"If he wasn't listening in on their conversations and using the gossip in the salon to blackmail them, then who was?"

Roxanne sat on her haunches and thought a bit. "The same guy who pressured Hugh McMullen to lean on Stinky to hurry up with that fire extinguisher?"

"No." I turned to her. "No one. No one blackmailed them."

"Huh?"

I saw my chance. One of the Sirens was walking to the kitchen door. I hurried over and hid in the shadow of the eaves. She opened the screen door and stepped out. From her pocket she removed a packet of cigarettes, shook one out and lit it. She exhaled and I leaped, grabbing her as Stiletto had grabbed me at the inn, by putting one arm around her waist and my other hand over her mouth.

She kicked and attempted to scream, but I clenched her tighter. Roxanne rushed from the bushes and froze when we moved into the light from the kitchen.

"Jesus, Bubbles. Do you know who that is? I recognize her from her picture in the paper."

The woman in my clutches was slender and wearing a deliciously smooth black silk blouse over her jeans. Her blonde hair was pulled back into a severe ponytail.

"Missy mice," mumbled my captive.

"She's *Chrissy Price!*"

"Let her go!" Vilnia said. The icy barrel of a gun pressed against my spine. I was in no need of further convincing. I let Chrissy go.

"Now put up your hands. You, too, Roxanne." Roxanne, her eyes the size of doughnuts, lifted her rhinestone fingertips.

"Run, Chrissy," I screeched. "Get the neighbors. Call the cops."

Chrissy, who was still holding her cigarette, took another drag and sneered as she exhaled. Her eyebrows were plucked to severe lines and those cheekbones were unreal. Implants. "Vilnia. Who is this tramp?"

"I came to save you, Chrissy," I said. "Why aren't you running?"

"Oh, I know." Chrissy wagged her finger. "She's that Bubbles Yablonsky. The hairdresser with the reporter complex."

"Bingo." Vilnia gripped the back of my neck and waved us in with her pistol. "Now let's go inside before the neighbors get interested. You, too, Roxanne."

"Are you going to kill us?" Roxanne said, stepping past me into the kitchen. "Like you shot Mr. Price?"

"I didn't shoot Price," Vilnia said, locking the kitchen door behind us and stuffing the pistol in her waistband. "McMullen did."

"He did?" Roxanne's hands were still raised. "For certain?"

"You missed that part. You were upstairs at the Hoagie Ho when Stinky told me he saw the whole thing." I dropped my hands and shook them. "I'm not doing that anymore. It hurts, like when we were in gym class."

"Have a seat." Roxanne and I sat. Vilnia addressed her crew. "Ladies, I doubt you need further introduction."

Roxanne's clients waved casually. The sparkling white kitchen was a far cry from what it had been on my first visit. Manila folders were stacked on the burners of the cold stove. The chopping board was littered with newspaper clippings. Gone were the pots of potato soup and the bubbling apple crisp. In were Rolodexes and whirring printers. Even Vilnia looked different. She was wearing a two-piece Adidas black nylon running suit and sneakers.

It wasn't only the apple crisp that was missing, though. The woman whose back had been turned to us was gone, too. And she'd taken the laptop with her.

Chrissy Price strolled across the kitchen, opened the refrigerator and took out a bottle of mineral water. Then she sauntered out to the living room with the air of a queen bee. Were these women working for her?

"Well, Bubbles," Vilnia said, crossing her arms, "I'm just glad we caught you before you really screwed up everything."

"What? What is this *thing* you've got going on?" I didn't know what to call it.

"We like to call it the Slagville Project," Vilnia said. "But first, cake." She went to the counter and sliced up two pieces of Entenmann's, the butt end of her gun sticking out beyond her Adidas jacket.

"Goody." Roxanne clapped her hands. "Cake."

I jabbed her in the ribs. "Be serious, Roxanne. Vilnia pointed a gun at us."

"Oh, yeah." She slouched. "Hope it's chocolate, though."

Vilnia handed us our cake. "It's chocolate, all right," she said. "The girls need the caffeine."

Roxanne dug in, but I put mine aside. "This has to do with being miners' wives, right?"

"Not completely." Vilnia addressed the group again. "Is it okay if I fill in Bubbles about the Slagville Project?"

The women unanimously said yes and went back to work.

Vilnia poured herself a cup of tea and sat down opposite us. "Thirty years ago, my son, a more loving boy you'd never meet, came home from Penn State for the first week of deer season. He went hunting in the woods with his friends not far from here and fell three hundred and fifty feet down an abandoned shaft owned—but not maintained, you see—by McMullen Coal."

I gasped. Poor Vilnia!

"I remember that," Roxanne said, swallowing a mouthful of cake. "That was awful, Vilnia."

Vilnia tossed her head. "It was years ago, but you never get over losing a child. All these women in this room have either lost a father or a brother or, in my situation, a son, because of mining. Most of their men died on the job because of cave-ins or black lung. Many are like me, we lost men because the coal companies took from the earth what they wanted and never fixed the damage. No matter, though, McMullen Coal was at fault."

"But the company was never held accountable," I said. "So McMullen Coal never paid for the harm it caused. Is that why you had Hugh McMullen shot?"

Vilnia sipped her tea and put her cup down slowly. "Women don't respond to violence with violence. We know that for every person who dies there is a mother who grieves." She put her fist to her chest. "We know that in our bones."

"It's so true." Roxanne was beginning to cry. Vilnia reached across the table and got her a tissue.

"Then the Nag 'N Feed spells are to control the men," I said. "To keep them around the house."

"To keep them alive," Vilnia said. "It's a short-term solution to a long-term issue."

The phone rang and a harried woman answered it with quick yesses and nos. She hung up, grabbed her wool coat off the back of her chair and took her purse. "I've got to go, Vilnia," she said. "That was my son. He's at a basketball game and needs to be picked up."

"Can't Arch get him?" Vilnia said.

"Are you for real? Arch is passed out in the wing chair by now." She waved good-bye and left.

"That's our problem," Vilnia said. "Almost all of these women work during the day. The only time they can get away is after dinner and even then family intrudes."

I still wasn't following. "What is it, exactly, that these women are doing? What do you want?"

"We want change. First we want the mining companies to fill up all the holes and gravel pits so that no more children die when they fall into them and drown," she said. "Do you know how cold that water is? And you can't get out once you're in because the rock face around the water is slippery smooth. It's impossible to get a grip, so you eventually develop cramps because of the freezing temperatures and that's the end."

"She's right," Roxanne said. "That happens a lot here in those old pits."

"Our final goal is more ambitious." Vilnia breathed in and out deeply. "We want the mining to stop, period. Forever. It is a dangerous, cruel, dirty and environmentally devastating industry. It widows women and orphans children. It has to end."

I sat back and picked at my uneaten cake. Vilnia was a toned-down Molly Maguire. Who would've thunk. "But how will people in Slagville earn a living?"

"We almost had the solution—until Bud Price was murdered. And that is what we're doing here." Vilnia swung around in her chair and surveyed the room of busy women. "Every night since Bud's death we've been researching the state and federal land use laws, putting together a comprehensive package for the state regulators on why they should permit this casino to be built. Our goal is to make sure that we have answers for every question. Let me tell you, it is not an easy task."

Canned laughter from the TV erupted in the other room. Chrissy Price giggled.

"Dim bulb, that one," Vilnia said, thumbing toward the living room. "That's our biggest obstacle to passage right there."

"So why did you kidnap her?" I said.

"Because we couldn't afford for her to get murdered, too. If there is, like I've been saying, a third party who is bound and determined to get hold of the land she inherited after Bud's death, the Dead Zone, then she needs protection."

Elaine handed Vilnia a computer printout. I mulled over what Vilnia had just said about there being a third party who wanted Bud Price's land. If that were true, then perhaps that third party was the same person who put pressure on Hugh McMullen to develop the fire extinguisher. It made sense considering that the Mammoth Basin, the largest deposit of anthracite in North America, extended under the Dead Zone. Only it couldn't be mined because of the fire. Until now.

Vilnia finished reading the fax and tossed it aside. "If we had stood idly by, there was also the chance that Chrissy would have sold the Dead Zone back to McMullen and pocketed the cash. And with Stinky's fire extinguisher—"

Roxanne practically leaped off the bench. "You knew about that? How come everybody in Slagville has heard of Stinky's fire extinguisher except me?"

"Chill, Imelda Marcos." Vilnia shook her head. "Those shoulder pads, Roxanne, they're hideous. You look like you're playing center tackle."

Roxanne sat down and touched her shoulder pads.

"But if you had Stinky's fire extinguisher, you could do with it what you wanted," I said. "You could keep it out of McMullen Coal's hands."

Vilnia held up a finger. "I wouldn't know what in the world to do with a fire extinguisher. That's why we told Bud Price about it. Bud contacted Stinky after he left McMullen and encouraged him to set up a lab in his basement. He offered himself as Stinky's backer. With that fire extinguisher, Bud's casino would have been assured of approval."

"I'm still perplexed as to how come everyone in my tiny town knew about this fire extinguisher except me." Roxanne pouted.

"I'm not perplexed." I recrossed my legs and leaned toward Vilnia. "Where's Louise? I need her."

Vilnia stood and carried her tea cup to the sink. "Who?"

"Louise Lamporini." I got up and joined Vilnia, who was suddenly inspired to wash dishes. "I know she's here. She was working on the laptop. I saw her through the window."

Vilnia squirted soap into the cup. "I don't even know a Louise Lamporini."

"She's a Slagville Siren. I witnessed her in action tonight when she tricked her husband into staying home so she could come here. She used sausage and onions."

The women behind us had stopped typing and faxing. They raised their heads and stared at us. Vilnia flipped on the water and rinsed the cup. I pressed further.

"Louise was Hugh McMullen's secretary. She typed up all those letters about Stinky being a threat. That's why you women made up those stories about being blackmailed, so you could stop coming to the salon without hurting Roxanne's feelings. You were afraid of Stinky because Louise told you he was dangerous."

Roxanne sighed. "Clients are always afraid of hurting a hairdresser's feelings. I once had a former client switch to another grocery store so she wouldn't have to run into me and explain why she wasn't coming to the Main Mane, anymore. It's so silly."

"Louise found out that Stinky was perfecting his fire extinguisher," I said. "She told you and you told Bud Price, your big white hope."

But Vilnia didn't budge. Just kept scrubbing, scrubbing, scrubbing that spotlessly clean cup.

"Louise is your connection to McMullen Coal. She's your underground mole, so to speak. I can understand why you'd want to keep her out of the limelight. She wants to keep her job. She doesn't want the company coming down on her, etcetera." I cranked off the faucet. "Forget that cup, already. There is someone besides Hugh McMullen and Bud Price who is interested in this extinguisher and getting hold of the Dead Zone, Vilnia. You said it yourself."

This caught Vilnia's attention. "Who is it?"

"I don't know why he doesn't just come forward and pay Stinky a tidy sum for the patent himself. I don't know why he's keeping his identity a secret, but he put incredible pressure on Hugh McMullen to produce that extinguisher. McMullen was a wreck, financially and otherwise. So much so that he shot himself."

"Too bad about Mr. McMullen." Vilnia shrugged. "But what's Louise supposed to do about it?"

I thought it wise not to comment on Vilnia's miraculous remembrance of Louise. "Louise has access to those phone records. Since McMullen conducted most of his business by phone, I am positive those phone records will lead us to the person who was putting pressure on him."

Vilnia blinked. Stubborn Polish mule is what she was.

"If you won't let me talk to Louise for that reason, let me talk to her because of Sasha, Chrissy's daughter. She's been kidnapped and I don't think she's in the other room watching TV with her mother. She got into a police car today, only the car didn't belong to Donohue and Donohue says no cop in Columbia County picked her up."

Vilnia let go of the cup. It smashed on the enameled sink.

"If he's got Sasha," she said, "then he's won." Looking up at me she said, "Tell me what you want and it's yours."

Louise Lamporini distributed computer printouts of McMullen Coal's phone records to the women in the kitchen. Louise had been secreted in the basement during our visit. Fortunately, she had had the good sense to stop by McMullen Coal on her way to Vilnia's and pick up the phone records, as I had suggested earlier. So they were ready for the inspecting.

"I wouldn't get your hopes up," Louise said as she scanned the August bill. "I did a cursory examination while I was in the basement and I didn't see anything out of the ordinary. Now, if we had access to Hugh McMullen's home phone records, that would be another story."

Chrissy Price, oblivious to the news that her daughter had likely been truly kidnapped, was fast asleep in the living room.

"I still don't want to tell her about Sasha just yet," a very worried Vilnia said. "Chrissy will lose her head and run out there, putting herself at risk for being kidnapped by him, too."

This was a point over which Vilnia and I had been arguing for a half hour. As a mother of a teenage girl, I'd have been livid if I were in Chrissy's position. But Vilnia said that whoever the third party was, he wanted Chrissy to react to Sasha's kidnapping like any other mother. To keep her in the dark was the only way to fight him.

"We have to give this all powerful, evil person a name," Roxanne said. "It'd be a lot easier."

We thought about this as the Slagville Sirens thumbed through the books of green and white records.

"Donald Trump," Vilnia said. "Why don't we call him Donald Trump? It's probably someone just like that."

"What if it is Donald Trump?" Roxanne said. "Wouldn't that be bizarre?"

"Donald Trump is into New York real estate," Vilnia said, "not commodities like coal and iron ore and steel."

Steel, I thought rather wryly. When you live in Pennsylvania it always comes back to steel. It was like a metal serpent reaching from the ground, gripping our ankles and not letting go.

As I studied September's bill, I considered the Donald Trump of steel I once knew. Henry Metzger. Where the iron serpent had kept its grip on workers from below, he had wielded his hammer from above. Metzger negotiated and threatened from the boardroom, getting his way for so many years that he transformed himself into an almost god-like figure. Even his many vice presidents considered him invincible.

The tough and fearless unions hadn't been able to rein in Henry Metzger, nor had the President of the United States when he asked Metzger during the eighth hole of golf to consider negotiating with the strikers. The environmentalists, with their nagging requests for controlled smokestack emissions, had been a pitiable threat. Henry Metzger's immortality was unquestioned.

Until his wife hit and killed Chester Zug, an elderly garbageman, in a park last summer and tried to get away with it. That stupid, thoughtless act, combined with the fortunate coincidence that Stiletto and I had practically seen it happen, is what did him in. Fleeing for his life, Henry Metzger and his lovely young bride had crashed and burned in Central America. An ignoble end to an ignoble man.

"Why are there so few calls on three days in a row?" I asked Louise.

Louise peered over my shoulder. "That was Labor Day weekend. Believe me, Labor Day was the first day I checked. I'm still pissed about being called into work."

My finger ran down the long distance numbers. There were only three, two of which were to New York. "What's this number?" I said, reading off one that began with a 345 area code. "It looks like it lasted only one minute."

Mrs. Wychesko typed it into the laptop, which was hooked

into the phone line. "I'll do a cross search on Yahoo!" she said. "Give it to me again."

I read it off.

She squinted over her bifocals. "Looks like it goes to a Sand Pointe Road in the Cayman Islands."

"Tax free," Vilnia said with a snort. "Probably one of McMullen's many getaways."

"Doesn't list the number as belonging to McMullen," Mrs. Wychesko said, pointing to the screen. "Says here it's a Zug, Chester Zug."

My fingers clenched September's phone records. My mouth could barely form the words. "Did you say Chester Zug?"

"That's what it says on Yahoo!"

Vilnia put her hand on my shoulder. "Bubbles. What's wrong? Do you know Chester Zug?"

"Do I know him?" I looked up at her. "I found his corpse."

Suddenly I knew who had sent me the fax, who had e-mailed Stiletto and hired Zeke Allen. He was someone who knew every detail of Steve Stiletto's past, who would have a key to his house, who would know about Stiletto's relationship to me.

Henry Metzger. Immortal as always.

Chapter 29

"Last summer," I began, "Stiletto and I came across a dead body in the park. It was the victim of a hit and run, and the body was later identified as having once been Chester Zug."

The women murmured to one another. Vilnia sat down.

"The person in the car that ran over Chester was a young woman named Merry Metzger. She was the wife of Henry Metzger, the former chairman of Lehigh Steel and undoubtedly the most powerful person Lehigh has ever known. Shortly after that accident, Henry Metzger fled the country. His plane crashed and burned on a Central American runway. He and his wife were presumed dead."

"I know of Henry Metzger," Vilnia said. "Of course, Lehigh Steel had working relationships with all the coal companies up here. Steel needs coal and coal needs steel."

"The Lehigh Valley Railroad connects the two," offered Roxanne.

"You're right. And I was thinking of that just the other day." Now I was the one who was pacing. "I should have put it together sooner. The fact that Steve Stiletto's imposter knew all about Stiletto and that he had access to his house. That's because Stiletto's imposter once owned his house." I paused, unable to verbalize the horrible truth that had held Stiletto back from freely committing himself to me, or any woman. "Henry Metzger was—is—Steve Stiletto's stepfather."

The women exchanged glances, confused.

"You guys," I said, resting my hands on the table, "the person who you fear will buy the Dead Zone from Chrissy Price, the person who hired Zeke Allen to stalk me and who put pressure on Hugh McMullen to get that fire extinguisher finished is Henry Metzger."

"But I thought he was dead," Vilnia said.

"My assumption is that he faked his death," I said. "And that doesn't surprise me. Henry Metzger can influence even the most responsible people to lie, steal and murder for him—especially a corrupt Central American coroner. I bet he's been pulling strings like a puppeteer from his home in the Cayman Islands."

"She's right. Henry Metzger is alive."

We all turned around to find Chrissy Price in the doorway, her hair rumpled from sleep and the oversized sweatshirt she was wearing wrinkled.

"Chrissy!" Vilnia hopped up. "Go back to bed."

Chrissy yawned. "I'm not tired. I just had a nap. So what's this about Henry Metzger, Bubbles?"

I stepped back and leaned against the sink. "Why don't you tell me?"

"Okay. Now that you've asked." She turned to the women. "Is it all right if I enter your precious inner sanctum or are you going to banish me to the living room to watch Bugs Bunny?"

Vilnia stood and offered her a seat. Chrissy sat while Vilnia brewed up another pot of coffee.

"Before I met Bud, I used to work as a hostess in a casino in Atlantic City. For the record," she held up her hand like she was volunteering in class, "I was the one who suggested putting a casino on the Dead Zone, thank you very much."

"Thank you," Roxanne said sincerely.

"Anyway, as hostess my job was to cater to the executives, often Lehigh Steel executives, when they came to our casino on junkets. For example, I found out what each man drank—and, yes, ladies, we're talking men only—so I had their brands in the minibar when they arrived in their rooms. If they wanted to play golf in the morning, I had the limo ready at eight to take them. If they wanted to gamble, I reserved a spot for them at the baccarat table."

"I'm sure that wasn't all they wanted, was it, Chrissy?" I said.

Her eyes glinted. "No, Bubbles, it wasn't. And I will personally come to your house and sock you in the mouth if you let this get out to Sasha, but I was Henry Metzger's favorite. I knew what he liked, I knew when he liked it, how often and where. I was an extremely attentive hostess."

"Bully for you," said Roxanne. "Hostessing is a lost art these days."

I lightly kicked her ankle.

"I also became extremely familiar with his voice. It was convenient, as you may imagine, for clients not to have to identify themselves to me when calling. Henry would telephone my office and reserve the following Friday and I'd know who it was." She smoothed the sleeves of her sweatshirt. "After I married Bud, I quit my job and moved to Lehigh. Sometimes Bud and I would be at the country club and I'd hear Henry talking in the hallway or out of sight and it was like being in Atlantic City all over again. It made me feel cheap and worthless, that voice of his."

Vilnia handed her a glass of water. Chrissy took a few sips and put it down. "I heard that voice again Wednesday evening."

She cleared her throat and Tammy gripped her hand. "Go on, Chrissy," Tammy said. "It'll help."

"We had just sat down for dinner, Bud and me because he didn't like Sasha to eat with us. But that's another story. Anyway, the phone rang. Wednesday evening is the maid's night off, so I got it. I can still hear him crystal clear. He said, 'Is Bud Price there, please?' I can't tell you how freaked I was. It was like hearing a ghost."

She began to cry and Roxanne passed her the box of tissues. Chrissy continued. "I said, 'Henry? Is it you?' And he said, 'I need to talk to Bud.' So I handed Bud the phone."

"Then what happened?" I asked.

She blew her nose. "I'm not sure, exactly. Bud took the phone into the library and shut the door. When he came out he was fuming. I mean about to explode. He said, 'I've got to go to

Slagville and talk to Koolball right now.' And he left. His Cornish game hens sat there on the plate, untouched. That was the last I saw of him. That's why I had to come here, to Slagville. To try and make sense of it all."

Chrissy was now in full weep. When she had recovered somewhat, I asked her if she had told the police that story.

"Partly. I told them that Bud had gone to meet Koolball, but I didn't tell them that the voice on the phone belonged to Henry Metzger. I mean, they would have thought I was a lunatic. Henry Metzger's dead." She let her hands fall on her thin little thighs. "Or so I thought."

"Or so we all thought." I studied my nails and tried to find the right words. "Chrissy, if Henry Metzger is alive, he may have been in Slagville today."

"Yeah?" She dabbed mascara off her cheeks.

"This afternoon a police car picked up Sasha."

Chrissy stopped dabbing. "Where?"

"She was in the car with my daughter's boyfriend. He was giving her a ride back to the inn."

Chrissy's whole body started to shake. "That kid. I told her to stay in the hotel until Donatello came on Sunday to take her to school."

"Listen to me, Chrissy." I put my hands on her shoulders. "Chief Donohue says that no cops in Columbia County picked up a seventeen-year-old girl today. My daughter's boyfriend described the bogus cop who took Sasha as white haired, older. I think he may have been Henry Metzger."

The look that passed over Chrissy's face is not one that I ever want to see again. It was pure, raw maternal horror. Horror turned to bewilderment and bewilderment turned to anger.

"I'll kill him," she said, leaping out of her seat. "Where is the bastard?"

"Grab her, girls," Vilnia ordered.

The women immediately pounced on Chrissy, their strong, coal-cracker bodies easily overtaking Chrissy's slender casino-hostess build. All I could see were her pretty painted red toes kicking in the air.

"Go, Bubbles!" Vilnia shouted. "We'll take care of it here. Go do what you have to do."

I dropped Roxanne off at the Main Mane where I changed into my black miniskirt, white T-shirt and orange cardigan. Carrying my suitcase down the stairs, I found Roxanne by the phone holding the cord.

"Look," she said, waving it in the air. "What if someone's broken into my house and disconnected all the phones? What if he's lying in wait until you leave to attack me?"

I slapped my forehead. "I am such a dufus. I'm sorry, Roxanne, I unplugged it."

She snapped the cord back in. "Why?"

"Nothing. It was stupid. Here, give me a hug good-bye." I dropped the suitcase and put out my arms.

Roxanne fell into them and hugged me tightly. "Thank you so much, Bubbles. You have saved Stinky and me and, who knows? Maybe you saved Slagville from being blown to smithereens, too."

"It'll all work out, Roxanne."

"I know. I pray the same for you, Bubbles." She let go. "I don't like you going to Stiletto's house by yourself. Why don't you call the police?"

"I will," I said. "First I'm going to wake up Zeke. He's got to help me. I don't want to do this alone."

"Smart idea."

She waved at me as I threw my suitcase in the back of the Camaro and got in. The streets of Slagville were wet, dead and silent after the evening's rain shower. The clock in my car said it was close to two A.M. Three more hours and I'd have to be at a waste hauler's meeting anyway. For a second, I thought I saw St. Christopher shake his head, as though he could not ensure protection if I decided to drive to Lehigh on rain-slicked roads while battling exhaustion.

I don't know why it took me so long to see his face in the rearview mirror, but it did. When our eyes met, he said, "Where are you going, Bubbles?"

I swerved to stay in my lane. "Oh, my God, Zeke. You just gave me a heart attack. I am so glad to see you. You've got to come with me to Stiletto's house in Saucon Valley. Something's happened to him, Zeke, and I think his stepfather, Henry Metzger, is behind it."

"You can't go home," Zeke said evenly. "I won't let you."

"What?" I pulled over, wrenched up the parking brake and turned around. "What's wrong with you?"

And that's when I noticed the gun in his hand.

"Let's go, Bubbles," he said. "Mother's waiting."

Chapter 30

It would be bad enough to be stuck in the wood-paneled rumpus room with Mrs. Allen if she weren't rocking in her chair and holding forth on blueberry pie tips while wearing a flannel nightgown and holding a shotgun in her lap at two A.M. But there I was and as far as I could see, there was no way out.

I scanned the room looking for a means of escape. Mrs. Allen sat by the door, right where Zeke had directed her. In the place of glass windows was wood. Tons of it. Wood and deer heads mounted on the wood walls. All of it highly shellacked. I don't know if Mr. Allen assumed people would be roller skating on his walls or if he just enjoyed the high of polyurethane. Whatever the reason, the golden room glistened.

"Course now, Aunt Martha, that's my namesake, Martha, used to make a blueberry pie without a top crust. Cooked it on the stove with a touch of brandy, that was her secret, and poured it into a prebaked pie shell." Mrs. Allen rocked at the memory of it. "I must have tried her recipe sixteen times and I never could get it to gel. Once I said, oh what the hey, and added a tablespoon of Knox. Still didn't work."

"Where's Zeke?" I cut in.

"Don't start up with that again, Bubbles," Mrs. Allen scolded. "Zeke's a man and he has the situation perfectly in hand. That's the trouble with today's women. They want to be the men in this world. They have to hold paying jobs and handle the finances. Why, when I was a young mother, Mr. Allen would come home on payday and hand me four crisp twenties. That was my allowance to pay for all the groceries and sundries and I lived within it. I didn't ask why eighty dollars or when he was going to give me a raise. You need to defer to men more, Bubbles. If you allowed men to decide what's right and wrong they wouldn't run off like your ex-husband did."

The only option was the door. It was slightly to the left of Mrs. Allen. To get there I would have to rise up and somehow smack Mrs. Allen unconscious, leap over her body and run out. But I simply could not bring myself to do it. I mean, Mrs. Allen was Mrs. Allen. To hit her would be like accosting Aunt Jemima. Though if she kept on talking about me not deferring to men and how that was responsible for the breakup of my marriage, she was a goner.

"Now Mr. Allen, he loves blueberry pie, though the tiny seeds do get stuck in the folds of his colon and give him gas."

Yup. I could do it. I reached into my purse and activated Roxanne's curling iron with one hand.

"Lately, I've been given to sieving out the seeds."

"Champ! Thank God you're here!" I screamed, pointing.

Mrs. Allen turned to look at the door. I pity people who don't watch *The Three Stooges*. They always fall for that moronic trick.

Whack! Roxanne's curling iron grazed the tip of her nose.

"Oww." She covered her face with both hands.

It was a momentary distraction, but enough for me to take two giant steps and grab the shotgun from her lap.

"Earl!" she screeched as I backed toward the door, the shotgun pointed at her belly. "Earl! Come quick. The tart got loose."

Upstairs I heard the creaking of bed springs. Mr. Allen coming to the rescue, as soon as he found his glasses. I dashed outside and remembered that Zeke had taken my keys. The windows and doors were locked. Damn.

Bless the Lord for Genevieve.

Genevieve was a firm believer in my personal mantra, Murphy's Law, that if a bad thing can happen, it will. I knelt down and slid my rear license plate a fraction of an inch. There was a spare key, right where Genevieve had left it. I was really beginning to like conspiracy theorists. They were growing on me.

Steve Stiletto's mansion was reached by traveling down a beautiful, shaded country lane lined by oak trees and rock fences. In the pitch dark of four A.M., however, the oaks overhung like preying monsters. There were no streetlights here and the overall effect was to create ominous dread in my stomach. I checked my speedometer. I was going fifteen miles per hour. I don't even go that slowly through cemeteries.

There were two lights on when I pulled into the large circular drive of his white stone home. Stiletto had gotten rid of all the caretakers when he inherited the mansion, keeping only a gardener who came in on weekends and a weekly cleaning maid. No one should have been in his house. No one except Stiletto. And I mean no one but Stiletto. Esmeralda was not a welcomed guest, in my mind.

However, there were no signs of Esmeralda. There were no other cars in the driveway and I was not in the adventurous spirit of checking the garage. So, I left the Camaro where it was, grabbed Mrs. Allen's shotgun and climbed the front steps.

The front door was open.

I stopped myself. Okay, I could get in the car, go back to Lehigh and call the cops, wake Mickey out of bed and tell him that Henry Metzger was back from the grave because Chrissy Price was convinced she'd heard his voice on the telephone. Then Mickey could call the men in white suits and they could cart me off.

No. I was doing this alone. I patted Mrs. Allen's shotgun as though it were a dog. I like dogs, I hate shotguns. If this shotgun were a dog, I'd call him Elvis.

"Good, Elvis," I said, pushing open the door. "Come on, Elvis."

Elvis and I entered the wide stone hall with its beautiful spiral staircase. No matter how many times I entered this house, it continued to amaze me. A Waterford crystal lamp was lit on a Queen Anne side table in the hallway. There was the sitting room with the cardinals on the curtains and the terrace out the back. Gorgeous.

There was also the moaning of someone engaged in erotic sexual pleasure above me.

I took two steps and cocked an ear.

"Oh, for heaven's sake," I said, leaning Elvis's butt against the floor. "Don't tell me."

Creak, creak. Moan. Moan. "Steve. Oh, Steve. Please, Steve."

That was it. I'd had it. I had hauled ass all the way down from Slagville, nearly killing myself on the wet roads because I had deduced Steve Stiletto might be in some sort of danger. And I got down there, exhausted mind you, chilled to the bone, hungry, stressed out and almost beside myself with worry, only to find out that he was spending the night on a down-filled antique four-poster bonking Esmeralda Greene.

"Let's go, Elvis," I said, taking the stairs two at a time. "Let's sic 'em."

We ran down the deep red oriental runner toward the moaning at the end of the hall. I didn't even wait to make sure they were through. I didn't even knock politely. I took my Payless pump and I kicked in that door.

Esmeralda lifted her head from the bed. "Bubbles!"

I froze in place. It was like flipping on HBO late at night and coming across "Real Sex."

"What the—?"

"Get me out of here." Esmeralda writhed to get free. "My arms are killing me."

Esmeralda was bare naked on the bed except for a pair—I am so happy to report—of rather worn gray all-cotton Fruit-of-the-Loom briefs and a white cotton bra. So much for the sophisticated underwear model. Her wrists and ankles had been handcuffed to the four posts of Stiletto's fantastic bed.

"I've never been in here," I said, gazing about the room with its hardwood floors, white walls, crown molding and twelve-foot high ceilings.

"Come on. This is no time to sightsee. Don't you have a hair pin or something?"

White gauzy curtains hung over mullioned windows. A brown leather couch was set beneath an old lamp around which were stacks of books. I imagined Stiletto—nearly naked, of course—reading in the night, filling that amazing mind of his with—

"Bubbles! Hurry! Steve's hurt."

Zwing! I reached in my purse and fished out a bobby pin. I started with Esmeralda's left wrist and stuck the pin in the tiny key hole. I wiggled it around, Esmeralda pulled and it snapped open. We worked like this wordlessly until she was free.

"Where's Steve?" I asked.

Esmeralda sat on the edge of the bed and rubbed her wrists. "I don't know. I haven't seen him. I heard a gunshot about an hour ago and I got worried, though."

"What were you two doing? What happened?"

She slipped into a pair of jeans that had been folded neatly and laid on a chair. "Nothing happened. I was in Slagville gathering the last information for this profile I was doing on Hugh McMullen—"

"Did you go up to Tremont Road?" I couldn't resist.

"Yeah. To see Wilma Sullivan. How did you know?"

I considered carefully how best to answer this question. Esmeralda may have been handcuffed on the bed and I may just have freed her, but we were still competition. "I got a tip and went over there myself. Mrs. Sullivan's neighbors said she was dead and that you'd been around asking questions. Why did you go there?"

"Because Hugh McMullen told the police he'd been with Mrs. Sullivan the night of Bud Price's murder. Mrs. Sullivan had been his nanny when he was a boy and she'd been ill lately. He sent her flowers all summer and assumed, I guess, that she'd cover for him if the police came around."

"Hard to cover when you're dead," I said.

Esmeralda smiled. "Gotta keep up with the obituaries. Anyway, I was leaving Slagville when I got a call on my cell phone to come down to Steve's house in Saucon Valley."

"Who called?"

Her auburn head poked through a black cashmere sweater. "He said he was Steve's dad. He said there was an emergency." She looked around for her shoes. "I didn't think twice that he'd be lying."

He wasn't lying, I thought. Henry Metzger was the only father Stiletto ever knew.

I bent down and found a pair of black Etienne Aigner flats under the bed. "Here."

"Thanks," she said, stepping into them. "I raced down to the house and this man answered the door. He introduced himself as Steve's father and invited me in."

"Tall," I said, standing. "White haired. Kind of looks like Paul Newman."

"Yeah. Wicked tan."

Nice living on the Cayman Islands. "Then what?"

She shivered and rubbed her arms. Post traumatic shock, dear girl. "Then he got me a drink and we talked about my work. We sat in the living room and he asked me how long I'd been with the AP and what did I think of the Republicans' chances to regain control of the Senate. The entire time I was thinking, what's this big emergency?"

Control. All Henry Metzger had ever wanted was control. More than steel, more than money. He craved control.

"I had two drinks, scotch and soda, and I was feeling kind of looped. The phone rang. He asked me to answer it. It was you, I think."

I dropped my eyes. Busted.

"After that, things started getting blurry. I can't believe the scotch went straight to my head." She massaged her temple. "The last thing I remember was him helping me up to this bedroom and laying me down. Then I woke up and I found myself cuffed and naked. That was about an hour ago and then you came in. Why?"

I picked up the phone. No dial tone. "I came because I had a hunch Stiletto was here and in trouble."

"No," she said. "I mean why me? Steve and I work together, but that's it. Why would his father have called me to Steve's house? Why would he have drugged me and cuffed me to a bed? What did I ever do?"

I hung up the dead phone. "You don't know Steve's stepfather."

"Except for tonight's cocktail hour, I don't."

"Then let me introduce you." I pointed to the doorway.

Henry Metzger grinned broadly. "Hello, Bubbles. It's been a while."

Henry Metzger was wearing a white turtleneck sweater over a pair of gray wool pants. The pistol he carried in his hands was like an afterthought.

"Put the shotgun down, Bubbles."

I clutched the gun. "It's not a gun. It's Elvis."

He smiled as though tolerating a child and motioned for me to put Elvis on the bed. I wasn't a very good sharpshooter, so I did as I was told. Henry took a few more steps into the room and held up the pistol. It was tiny with a pearl handle. Really spiffy. If it had been a dog it would have been a poodle. Elvis would have been a hound.

"Hands in the air, please."

I groaned and raised my hands. Not again.

"Hey. That's my gun," Esmeralda said.

"Found it in your glove compartment. Thanks ever so. I came prepared with my own, serial numbers sanded off, naturally. But this will work out so much better for the scenario I've devised."

"And that is?" Esmeralda was playing reporter.

"And that is," I interrupted, "that Henry is going to shoot both of us and position our bodies so it appears that we had a cat fight over Stiletto and shot each other."

"Oh." She snapped her lips tight.

"Bubbles knows that I am not a murderer," Henry said. "Isn't that right, Bubbles?"

"That depends on how you define murderer. If you mean that you never pull the trigger or drive in the knife, that's right, you're not a murderer."

He bowed slightly. "Thank you."

"But you've killed countless people. And I'm not talking only about the people you got Brouse, your henchman, to rub out. I'm talking about the average Joes who died on the job because you didn't want to spend the money on safety precautions. Their blood is on your hands."

Henry winced. "So dramatic. Blood on your hands. Don't tell me you're taking creative writing at the Two Guys now."

"Two Guys closed," I said.

"I see."

I saw, too. I saw that Henry meant he was not about to change his habits at this late date. The only reason he hadn't shot us yet was because the help hadn't arrived. We were killing time with this chitchat.

"So, seeing as we're waiting for your hit man, why don't you tell me how you survived the crash," I said, shifting my feet.

Henry's frosty blue eyes regarded me. "Central America is a very easy place to die when you have money."

"And you had plenty of it waiting in the Cayman Islands, I understand."

"I did. Steve received enough to keep him out of probate court asking for more. The lion's share was always under a number where I could access it, tax free."

"Can I drop my hands?" I said. "My shoulders hurt."

"No."

Brother. "Now, if I were you, I'd have sipped piña coladas by that clear turquoise water and counted my lucky stars. Why couldn't you leave well enough alone?"

"And forsake billions on the Mammoth Basin? Bubbles, I assume by now you realize just how much wealth is in there. If I had a front, Chrissy Price for example, I could wheel and deal like I used to. Hugh McMullen's mistake was in blabbing to me early this year that Koolball had the fire extinguisher."

"What fire extinguisher?" Esmeralda asked.

"One that could put out the fire in Limbo," I said. I bit my tongue to keep from adding, but I found out about it first, so hands off.

"That kind of extinguisher would be worth gazillions alone," Esmeralda said. "Why did McMullen tell you about it?"

Henry waved the gun. "Because McMullen owed me money. Correction. He owed his company money. Twenty million dollars. Before the accountants came in to audit the books, he contacted my old lawyer and friend, Max Factor, looking for help."

"But why did Hugh McMullen call your lawyer?" Esmeralda asked.

Gosh, I wish she weren't here. She was completely ruining my chances for an exclusive.

"Because Hugh's father, Senior McMullen, had come to me for money years ago. I gave him the cash and, in exchange, Senior made me a silent partner in McMullen Coal. After I quote-unquote died, Max handled my interests for me. I didn't give a damn about Steve getting this house, but I wanted that Mammoth Basin."

"And just like Senior McMullen owed you after you lent him money, Hugh McMullen owed you, too," I said. "You must have loved being in that position. Hugh McMullen sweating bullets. Big bucks to be made."

"I negotiated the entire process while fishing for barracuda off my yacht. My only concern was that Bud Price was in the way. He needed to be removed and McMullen agreed, though he was reluctant to pull the trigger." Metzger sighed deeply. "So I flew up to Pennsylvania to get the ball rolling."

"By calling Price at home and telling him that Stinky had signed over the fire extinguisher to Hugh."

"That's right. Price ran straight to Koolball for a confrontation at the bar. Which is where you came in."

I smiled.

"You?" asked Esmeralda. "You were reporting on a story in which you had a personal involvement? For shame, Bubbles."

I closed my eyes. I wish journalism schools would stop graduating these ethical tightwads. "I didn't *realize* I had a personal involvement. I didn't *realize* it was Henry Metzger who sent me a fax getting me to the Number Nine mine Wednesday night or that he paged Stiletto on his cell phone."

"It was a whim," Metzger said. "Actually, Max suggested it when he thought there was a possibility that Price was going to the mine that night. A good source who'd been keeping tabs on Koolball filled me in on his familial relationship to you, Bubbles. A mine explosion seemed like a perfect way to eliminate not only you, but also Steve."

"Your son?" Esmeralda said, incredulous.

"Stepson and a hindrance in many, many ways, as was Bubbles. She and Steve knew me too well and, like Price, stood in my way of assured success. I had to get rid of them."

"He's not what you'd call a warm and fuzzy father figure."

"Oh," Esmeralda said.

"McMullen cornered Price and shot him. Then McMullen escaped through the access hole and set off the explosion."

Except McMullen couldn't handle the guilt, I thought.

"The problem was Koolball," Metzger continued. "I couldn't have him killed because I needed the extinguisher. Yet I didn't know what he'd do about Price's murder, if he'd rat to the police, or if he knew about me. I was confident about one thing—that he'd try to reach you, Bubbles. You had been at the mine, had seen his car and were telling everybody in town about it."

"Which is why you pretended to be Stiletto and hired Zeke to keep tabs on me," I said.

"Yes." Metzger beamed like I was a star pupil.

"And you also put the pressure on Hugh to get hold of Stinky." I gestured with my hand. "Something like, find Koolball and I'll offer you protection. You won't have to go to jail for murder."

"Too bad you didn't give him Koolball, Bubbles," Metzger said. "Hugh would be alive today. Don't you feel guilty?"

"No," I said.

The front door downstairs opened and closed. "Hello?" said a deep voice.

"Up here," Henry said laconically.

"But why kill me?" Esmeralda said. "Is it because of my investigative reporting?"

"You're incidental," he said to Esmeralda. "But I knew Bubbles would figure out my plans. She's a better reporter. You, Esmeralda, are just a cover. A cover that must be blown—away, so to speak."

I tried not to be swayed by the better reporter part, although, I have to admit, I was rather flattered. "Where's Sasha?" I asked.

Steps came down the hall, slowly.

"Sasha is in a safe place, waiting for phase two. She is my insurance that Chrissy Price will make me her silent, seventy-five-percent partner in opening the Mammoth Basin. That way I'll have total control."

"And Steve?" I asked.

Metzger stepped back and let the visitor enter. "You're late," he said.

"Got held up," said Donohue.

Henry Metzger's so-called source. The one that had been filling him in about Stinky Koolball and his relationship to me.

Donohue tipped his hat. "Bubbles. Esmeralda. So, then." He rubbed his hands together. "How are we going to do this?"

Metzger looked at both of us. "Yablonsky first because I'm tired of her. Esmeralda's easier on the eyes. Do her next."

"Yeah?" said Donohue. "Okay."

"And what about you, Chief?" I said.

Donohue pulled out a pair of gloves from his pocket. "How's that?"

"May we drop our hands?"

The two men looked at each other and nodded. "Sure," said Donohue.

Esmeralda and I dropped our hands and shook our arms. "I mean, what about your soul?" I said.

"Soul, huh?" Donohue snapped on his glove. "What about my soul?"

"Your great-great something father was Yellow Jack Donohue, isn't that right?" I tried to recall in detail the photos at the Union Hall.

"That's right." Donohue snapped on the glove's mate and removed the gun from his holster.

"And didn't he go to the gallows as a Molly Maguire after he was framed by men like Franklin Gowen and Asa Packer?"

Henry Metzger handed him Esmeralda's gun. "Use this. She'll stop babbling soon."

They exchanged weapons. "Thanks," said Donohue, checking out the sight. "So what?"

"So, this man who is paying you off in a retirement house or whatever cash you're getting," I pointed to Metzger, "might just as well be the head of the Lehigh Valley Railroad in the 1870s. Henry Metzger, like Asa Packer and Franklin Gowen, did all he could to suppress the unions. He didn't give a damn about workers. It was because of him that I never had a father to run to when I had nightmares at night. He killed my father and, had he been living at the time, he would have shot Yellow Jack Donohue."

"Like this?"

Donohue raised Esmeralda's pistol and fired. It was one shot and it echoed through the house with a deafening sound.

Henry Metzger fell to the floor. Dead. Dead for sure.

"Holy shit," Esmeralda said, staring at the blood that seeped through the hole on Henry Metzger's forehead.

I was speechless. Simply speechless. Largely because I was worried about what would happen next.

"Sorry I had to do that in front of you, ladies." Donohue's knees creaked as he bent down and felt for Metzger's pulse. "We could have brought him to trial and all that crap, but I'm too old. I just wanted the S.O.B. dead."

I reached for Elvis.

"Stop. Bubbles, you can trust him."

Stiletto appeared at the door looking like death warmed over. Zeke was right behind him.

"Steve!" Esmeralda exclaimed, holding open her arms. "I'm so glad you've come for me."

Stiletto shoved aside Esmeralda and stumbled forward, taking me in his arms.

"Bubbles," he murmured, kissing me deeply.

And that's when I noticed he was bleeding. Profusely from the shoulder. His white shirt was a blackish red on one side, and damp. His face was ashen. Dark circles lined his eyes, which studied me with all the intensity they could muster.

"Are you okay?" He put a sweaty and cold hand against my cheek. "I love you so, so much."

His blue eyes began to roll. He leaned against me. I staggered and lay him down on the bed. Esmeralda pulled the gun out of the way.

"He's going into shock!" I said, grabbing a blanket from the foot of the bed. "We've got to get him to the emergency room."

"Darn it," Zeke said. "There's no working phone."

"I've got a cell," Esmeralda said, searching around the room. "If I could only find my purse."

"Hey, Allen," Donohue said from his position on the floor. "I distinctly remember telling you to get him to the hospital. Wasn't he passed out when you found him in the basement?"

Donohue took out his radio to call for an ambulance.

"He woke up halfway to the hospital and took the wheel." Zeke clutched Stiletto's wrist. "He insisted we come back for Bubbles."

I bent my head to Stiletto's chest and whispered a few heartfelt words. I have never prayed so hard or fervently in my life.

And then I felt Zeke's hand on my back. "It's too late, Bubbles. I think we lost him."

Epilogue

Needless to say, I did not make it to the Hellertown waste hauler's strike vote. That was okay because the strikers didn't want to get together at 5 A.M. on a Sunday, either, and they tabled the meeting. I did, however, manage to stop by the Catasauqua Republicans barbecue, which seemed to thrill Dix Notch more than the story I had about Henry Metzger's comeback and subsequent death.

Max Factor, of course, is in a heap of trouble. He had acquired all of Chester Zug's personal information and used it to compile a new identity for Henry Metzger. He also drafted a plan with Henry to execute troublesome parties—like yours truly—before moving forward.

Initially, Metzger's plan was implemented to perfection. McMullen shot Price. McMullen committed suicide. Metzger's plans to isolate Chrissy Price and pressure her to make him a silent partner in her company were foiled, however, by two entities—Professor Tallow and the Slagville Sirens.

Max Factor had called Chrissy at the inn Friday night and said he would provide her with secret information about Bud's murder if she met him at the Le Circe bar. Unfortunately for Factor, Tallow ambushed her at Le Circe first. He spent a half hour explaining how a gambling joint could destroy precious Celtic artifacts and why she shouldn't let it be built. He spent another twenty minutes trying to hit her up for funding. Disgusted, Chrissy left and was waiting for valet parking to bring her car around when the Sirens' husbands showed up in the F1 pickup. Max Factor tried to trail them in his Mercedes, unsuccessfully.

That left Metzger and Factor with no option but to kidnap Sasha, a move that skewered their, until then, very profitable relationship with Chief Donohue.

Max Factor had contacted Donohue as soon as he and his boss had learned from McMullen about Koolball's extinguisher at the beginning of the year. The history of coal mining had taught them that having law enforcement on the baron's side was not only beneficial, it was essential. Donohue provided them with daily updates, including my relationship to Stinky and my planned visit with Stiletto to the Passion Peak. In exchange, he was paid a handsome fee.

But Sasha's kidnapping changed all that. Donohue had tapped into the pay phone at Le Circe and listened to Metzger ream out his lawyer when Chrissy Price slipped away. After Metzger ordered Factor to pose as a police officer and kidnap Sasha, Chief Donohue had had enough. He decided it was time to switch sides, for he, too, knew his coal country history.

He called Metzger and offered to do the dirty work, should dirty work need to be done. With McMullen no longer available to play shooter, Henry took him up on his offer. The call came around one A.M., right after the Hoagie Ho.

Donohue immediately phoned Zeke for backup and the two of them drove to Saucon Valley. Zeke found Stiletto in the basement and got him out of the house. Then Donohue came to "kill" us, neatly turning the tables in the end.

Following standard procedure, Donohue has stepped down as Chief of Police while the state police conduct an investigation of Metzger's shooting. Donohue has claimed self defense in the shooting of Henry Metzger, and Esmeralda and I have decided that's good enough for us. Sasha, who had been sequestered in Max Factor's office, has declared the chief her hero. We hope the authorities will weigh these elements in deciding whether to charge Donohue further.

Max Factor, however, was arrested for kidnapping, assorted counts of fraud and attempted murder (after trapping me in the basement of St. Ignatius Church). His law license has been suspended, though he has been released on five hundred thousand dollar bail. Dan claims that since several of the charges are federal ones, Max will end up in Allendale, one of the cushier federal pens in Pennsylvania.

Chrissy, Stinky and the Slagville Sirens reached an agreement on the fire extinguisher. Stinky holds the patent and has licensed it to Chrissy's newly formed Buss Enterprises (Buss being a combination of Bud and Chris). Chrissy has pledged to use the fire extinguisher to put out the fire in Limbo and to make the underground safe for a casino. Buss Enterprises owns the mining rights under the Dead Zone and Chrissy has acquiesced to the Sirens' request that she not mine there.

Convincing the towns of Slagville and Limbo, once the fire is out, will be another matter since the mining rights could bring in tons of money. But Stinky's fire extinguisher has yet to be perfected and, as Vilnia says, why cross a bridge when you can stand under the bridge and taunt goats. I think she means she'll cross that bridge when she gets to it.

I asked Vilnia what was up with those old men following me, and she explained that she'd sent her husband and the husbands of other Slagville Sirens on an errand to Lehigh. Their purpose was to find out if I had any sinister angle regarding Bud Price or Stinky that they didn't know about. They were suspicious since I was at the scene of the murder and explosion that night. After the men asked around at Price Family Ford and then searched my house, they decided I had just happened upon the murder scene in the mine. So they cleaned me out of leftovers and went back to Slagville. They weren't sent on another "errand" until they picked up Chrissy Price in their F1 pickup.

Roxanne found Stinky in the Hole Saturday night and convinced him to come home. She tearfully confessed that the box of documents had been stolen while she slept downstairs and he confessed that he had been the one who took them. He had read the *News-Times* with my story about McMullen Coal digging beneath the Dead Zone early Friday morning. In his constant paranoid state, Stinky feared the documents would attract unwanted attention, so he slipped into the house shortly after dawn and took them. Then he drove down to Lehigh to meet with me.

By the way, he also snuck into Roxanne's house Friday night and cooked himself a burger, accidentally forgetting to turn off the stove when he heard a noise and fled. That caused the fire, which G so courageously extinguished.

Zeke Allen has become somewhat of a fixture in our lives and I don't think it's because he likes Mama's meat loaf or Genevieve's mashed potatoes. He seems to be taken with the wit and intelligence possessed by my daughter, Jane. They take long bike rides and discuss all sorts of deep religious issues. Reincarnation. Spiritual nihilism. Sex. Jane has turned him onto Buddhism and Zeke has given her a beautiful white leather-bound edition of the King James version of the Bible. All I can say is that it's better than G's nonstop *South Park*.

It took Zeke a while to get over the guilt of holding me at gunpoint. He was only doing what Stiletto had asked him. Unable to reach Roxanne's Saturday night—because I had brilliantly disconnected the Main Mane's phone—Stiletto had called Zeke and demanded that he do whatever it took to keep me from coming down to Saucon Valley. He said a trap had been set for me. Zeke waited in my car and forced me to his house with no explanation. His thinking was that if I knew a trap had been set, I'd have wanted to spring it. He was right.

Esmeralda and I ended up sharing a byline on a story that was carried coast to coast and even overseas by the wire services. Writing with her wasn't so bad, except she kept hogging the computer and correcting my grammar. Whom versus who, that sort of thing. And although she claims she has no interest in Stiletto, I suspect otherwise. I saw the way she gazed at him when he stumbled in the door that awful night and I suspect that for a moment there, she fantasized he was coming for her.

She is going to be a pain in my Sommersized backside.

That's because Steve Stiletto did survive, despite his near death experience. His injuries were so severe that the AP postponed by one month his transfer to England, where he is supposed to head a new bureau. But there's more.

The day after being released from the hospital, Stiletto declared that he was embarking on a spiritual quest to seek truth and purity and therefore he wouldn't be indulging in the delights of the flesh for a while.

That's right. Stiletto took a chastity vow.

"There's more to life than dodging bullets in Pakistan, you know?" he said as we were relaxing chastely in front of a toasty fire in his Saucon Valley mansion.

"I know that, Stiletto."

"Career. Danger. Travel. Those don't matter when you die."

"Oh?" We were on the floor, our backs against the couch warming our toes after a long hike in the woods. As part of his spiritual quest, Stiletto had been spending a lot of time becoming one—with nature, that is.

"Giving. Growing. Loving. Committing. Those are the important things, Bubbles." He put his arm around my shoulders and pulled me tight. "Don't you agree?"

I dared not to hope. "Yes."

"So what do you say? Why don't we give it a go?"

I turned my face to him. "Marriage?"

"The Peace Corps. Taking care of those who can't care for themselves. The monsoon-ravaged jungles of Asia. The drought-ridden plains of Africa. Two years, Bubbles. Two years in our lives committed to donating our skills so others may live. Let's do it!"

"Right." I sighed.

I didn't need the Peace Corps.

In Stiletto I'd already found the toughest job I'd ever love.

ABOUT THE AUTHOR

Sarah Strohmeyer is the author of *Bubbles Unbound* and *Bubbles in Trouble*, the first two mysteries in her award-winning series. A former journalist whose work has appeared in *The Boston Globe*, the *Cleveland Plain Dealer*, and on Salon.com. She lives with her family outside Montpelier, Vermont. She can be contacted through www.SarahStrohmeyer.com.